# NO ESCAPE

Romance is the last thing on reporter Skylar Shaw's mind when she covers a plane crash on a Florida beach. Her best source could be a mysterious Italian visitor, but he's strictly off the record—unless it involves indulging their electrifying attraction. Little does Skylar know, but that crash was only the beginning.

Luca Rossi is hiding a big secret: He's a journalist, too, and his anonymous exposé on the Mafia destroyed his world. Now, after a lonely year on the run, he will do anything to possess this vulnerable American beauty. But Skylar is as relentless as the Florida glare, and their world ignites with passion, obsession and murder. Soon erotic nights will bleed into dangerous days, and nowhere will be safe from the heat.

*Rebecca —*
*Happy Reading!*
*xoxo*
*Tamara*

# HOT SHADE

Tamara Lush

www.BOROUGHSPUBLISHINGGROUP.com

HOT SHADE
Copyright © 2015 Tamara Lush

ISBN 978-1-942886-77-8

*To Marco, my real-life Italian hero.* Ti amo.

# ACKNOWLEDGMENTS

I'd like to thank the following people for helping me with this book.

My husband, Marco Kornfeld. Without you, I would be nothing.

My parents, Peter and Nanci Lush. You believed in me even when I did not.

Heather Hanson, who read numerous versions of this story. I am forever indebted to you for so many reasons. I love you.

Susan Squires, who didn't laugh at me when I enrolled in her class and turned in the earliest version of this manuscript.

My agent, Amanda Leuck of Spencerhill Associates, for her support.

My editor, Christopher Keeslar, and Boroughs CEO Michelle Klayman, for taking a chance on a new author.

My critique partner Kat Faitour. You're the best friend I've never met in person. Soon.

My other critique partner, Tina Ellery. You're priceless. Thank you.

Leona Woolfolk of Literary Treasure Chest. You gave me the confidence to keep going.

Carol Druga, for the early edit.

Lyn Eckfeldt, for the other early edit, and for the endless, positive encouragement.

All of the early readers of this book: Marianna Rainolter, Angela Plumlee, Michelle Larson, Derna, Xariah, Nicole, Amanda, Rob Withrow, Lauren Runow. I'm forever grateful for your feedback.

And finally, a huge thanks to my colleagues in journalism, both at the AP and at all my previous newspapers.

# TABLE OF CONTENTS

# HOT SHADE

# CHAPTER ONE

Luca Rossi encrypted his email to the prosecutors of an Italian Mafia boss with the press of a button. Sighing, he glanced up from his laptop and was startled to see the nose of a plane overhead. It was a small two-seater, and it silently soared past the terrace where he sat.

It was too damned close. The wind from its wings cooled the sweat on his face as it sliced through the sun-washed Florida sky in rapid descent. It shaved a few fronds off a tall palm tree on the nearby beach.

Tensing his shoulders, Luca jumped from his chair and looked wide-eyed over the railing. His gaze zoomed in on a single beachcomber lazily shuffling across the sugary sand, his back to the plane. The man wore oversized headphones and waved a metal detector in front of his feet, completely oblivious to the impending disaster.

"HEY! HEY! MOVE! GET OUT OF THE WAY!" Luca hollered and waved his arms.

The man didn't hear.

Luca gripped the terrace railing with one hand and used his other arm to shield his face, unable to watch. The plane came down hard, hitting the sand with a thunderous smack. Uncovering his eyes, Luca saw it come to its final resting place in shallow water, about forty feet away on the other side of a gate that separated the public beach from the private enclave in which he was staying. Luca blinked several times, unable to process what he witnessed.

The man with the metal detector lay on the sand like a discarded doll. Was he twitching and squirming? Luca squinted in disbelief. How could the guy be alive?

His hands shook as he took the phone out of his pocket and pressed 9, then 1. He paused. Would he have to give his name? His address? Surely the call would be recorded. In Italy he would have to give detailed information, but he wasn't sure about America. He couldn't risk it, not in his situation. He slipped the phone into his pocket, feeling horrible. The man on the beach was suffering, and he had to help somehow.

Pulse pounding in his ears, Luca snatched a towel off a chair then grabbed his gun and his keys on the way out the door. He slipped the 9mm into the waistband holster tucked in between his hip and cargo shorts, then pulled his baggy T-shirt down to conceal the bulge. Would he ever get used to having a weapon nearby? He had traveled the world without one, but his uncle recently gave him the gun. Just to be safe.

It didn't take him long to sprint past the pool and out the gate leading to the public beach.

*Shit. Shit. Shit.*

The man writhed and screamed. Blood gushed from his left bicep. From the precision of the slash it appeared to have been made by the plane's propeller—or maybe even the tip of the wing. It was a miracle the guy wasn't decapitated.

Luca whipped his head around, looking for someone, anyone, to help. But he was alone on the beach with the bleeding man. The waves were feet away. Should he try to move the guy to drier ground? No, he'd read enough to know that he shouldn't move the injured, and he sent a silent plea into the universe, hoping the salt water wouldn't reach the man's wounds.

He wondered briefly about who was inside the plane, but the question dissolved as he caught a glimpse of visible muscle under the blood on the beach victim's arm, and Luca fought a violent wave of nausea. Dropping to his knees, he studied the wounded man's face and gently clasped his uninjured shoulder, wanting to provide comfort. Sand mixed into the guy's hair, and sweat covered the leathery skin of his narrow face.

"It hurts," the man yelled.

Kneeling and draping the towel he'd brought over the bleeding gash, Luca looked for other injuries. The man wasn't wearing a shirt, and his torso had no visible cuts or wounds, only a thick smear of blood, probably from the arm gash.

Luca cut a glance toward the plane. A balding man climbed from the cockpit, and Luca's heart sped up even more. In water up to his calves, the pilot turned. Slack-jawed, he waded a few steps forward and stood on the sand.

"I didn't mean to…I didn't mean to…"

Luca squinted up at him. "Are you okay? Are you hurt?"

"I…I think I'm okay. I might have hit my head on the windshield. The engine just cut out."

Luca wiped sweaty hands on his shorts then carefully wrapped his towel around the man's bleeding arm, ensuring it was snug. He called to the pilot, "Do you have a phone?"

The man gave a hesitant nod.

"Call 9-1-1. Now. Please."

Luca used a firm voice, and the pilot frantically shoved his hands in his pockets and pulled out a phone, tapping the screen with shaking fingers. The man under him continued writhing, and Luca pressed his towel down more firmly upon the gruesome limb. The guy's eyes were brown, wild and glassy. Luca swallowed hard to banish the growing lump in his throat.

"What the fuck happened?" the injured man panted. His arm twitched, and Luca grasped it tighter.

The wounded man still had yellow headphones over his ears. Clasping the towel and the mangled arm with one hand, Luca slipped the headphones off with the other, trying not to cause further discomfort.

"You were hit by a plane. Stay calm."

"I was hit by a—?"

The man groaned when Luca applied pressure. The thirsty towel turned red. When would the damned paramedics get here? The air smelled like rust and fear.

"Calm down. I'm going to try to slow the bleeding, okay?"

The man grunted again.

"It's okay. Be calm and don't move. You're going to be okay. The ambulance will be here soon. What's your name?"

"J-Jesse."

"Okay, Jesse. You're going to be fine. Breathe. Be still."

Jesse's moans turned into a long whimper, and Luca held firm to his arm. The seconds ticked by, becoming entire minutes, and soon it seemed they had been together for an eternity. Lines of sweat dripped down Luca's temples to his jaw.

The sound of feet slapping the sand mixed with the Gulf's gentle surf, and a group of men in crisp blue shirts and dark pants swarmed around the injured man and Luca.

"Sir, thank you, we'll take over from here."

Help had arrived. Finally.

A paramedic dropped next to Luca on the sand and scooped the injured man's arm into his hands. Taking a deep breath, Luca stood. Another medic clapped him on the back and said, "Good job. You definitely saved his arm—might have saved his life. It's a damn good thing this happened here where it's not crowded. Otherwise we'd have had a mass casualty on our hands."

Luca nodded, uncomfortable from the feeling of his T-shirt sticking to his back. He wanted to wipe the perspiration from his forehead but resisted the urge because Jesse's blood and sweat coated his hands. Grimacing, he saw three elderly people standing, gawking. But no one was taking video on their cell phones, thank God.

Paramedics strapped Jesse to a backboard, and Luca took the opportunity to slip away. Jogging up the beach and unlocking the gate to the private enclave, he made his way back toward the house, passing under an arched hedge made of jasmine vine. Looking down, he saw a streak of blood staining his hand and also his T-shirt. He stripped the shirt off and balled it up as he reached the pool then drew a huge breath and exhaled. Unlocking the back door, he walked inside.

The shirt went directly into the washer and Luca scrubbed his quaking hands in the kitchen sink. Craving something familiar, he made an espresso. He didn't care that it was hot liquid on an infernal August day; the coffee aroma might erase the lingering odor of jet fuel and blood. If only he had a cigarette. But he'd quit a year ago and wasn't about to drive to the store.

Taking the espresso upstairs, Luca passed through his bedroom on the way to his private terrace. Reaching down, he gingerly took the handgun out of its holster and laid it upon the patio table next to his laptop, which was still open to his manuscript. He remained standing and let out another long exhale.

He sipped the hot espresso and scanned the beach. The downed plane marred his normally calm view of the Gulf of Mexico, as did a growing crowd, and he wondered why the plane crashed. Squinting into the midday sun Luca memorized the N-number on the tail then pulled his smartphone from his pocket. He typed it into the FAA aircraft registry website and read the listing for the owner. He Googled the name and was relieved to discover the pilot was a retired manufacturing executive and a member of the Southwest Florida Flying Club. Online photos proved he was the same dazed guy who'd climbed from the cockpit.

Luca breathed a sigh of relief. The plane wasn't here for him. That much was clear. Had it been the Mafia, the pilot would have found a way to kill him right on the beach. His shoulders relaxed away from his ears, and Luca wiped itchy pinpricks of sweat off his brow. Maybe with the Mafia boss's arrest, he was truly safe. Maybe he really could stop being so paranoid, just like his uncle said.

The temperature hovered around ninety degrees, on the ugly edge of unbearable. Combined with the humidity it was like sitting in an oven inside of a steam room. Maybe he'd swim later in the pool. Or in the Gulf when the temperature dropped. He wished he was home in southern Italy with its dry heat and cool Mediterranean breeze—a frequent wish, but one he knew wouldn't come true anytime soon. He hadn't tasted those pleasures for more than a year.

Luca glanced at the blue expanse before him. Palmira Island was boring, but he did enjoy the water. It was bright blue, and gin-clear. He felt most free when he dove beneath its surface. When he glided through the salty sea he forgot about everything, including the fact that he was staying at his long-lost uncle's empty house on a tiny island in a strange American state.

Strange? Take this spooky, silent plane crash, for example. Just another weird Florida story. Crazy shit happened here all the time.

Luca stared at the wreck and the people gathered below. While his first instinct had been to help the injured, a second strong desire kicked in now. Luca imagined interviewing the pilot and taking notes. He could practically feel the pen and notebook in his hands. So many possible questions to ask.

Once a journalist, always a journalist.

Police unfurled yellow crime scene tape. More gawkers drifted over to check out the plane. Luca noticed a young reporter in a long white beach dress. She had a press credential around her neck. Why was she wearing such a ridiculous getup to cover a story? Luca scowled in her direction. *Amateur.*

She nodded while taking notes and interviewing the pilot, who wiped his cheeks with his palms. Luca remembered that part of journalism well, the quest to plumb the depths of broken, grieving people. These days, Luca had his own his own shattered world to deal with. It had been fifteen months since his parents were murdered, and the pain was still ever-present.

He watched the reporter move toward the gate separating the public beach from the private enclave and rattle the doorknob. Luca rolled his eyes. But *of course* she wanted to find more people to interview. Why did it annoy him so much when that was exactly what he used to do as a reporter?

Clearly she wasn't deterred by the sign that read PRIVATE PROPERTY. Somehow the young woman snaked her arm through the close-together iron bars to unlock the gate from the inside. As she opened the door and slipped in, however, the seam of her long dress caught on the rail's bottom spike, causing a huge tear.

Luca marched downstairs, out the door and toward the beach, intending to put a stop to the silly reporter's quest. Tensing again, this time with anger, he cursed silently at how the security gate of the beach enclave was so easy to breach. He'd have to tell his uncle to talk to someone about this. One unlocked door could lead to his death.

He approached the reporter with a sneer, watching her scan the homes. She gathered her long hair and arranged it over a bare shoulder.

"Can I help you?" he asked, biting back a displeasure that softened as his gaze swept down her body. Her ripped dress revealed a shapely and toned leg. The torn fabric of her dress, and what was underneath, proved impossible for him to ignore.

"Hi." She flipped her sunglasses to the top of her head. "I'm with *The Palmira Post.* I'm looking for people who saw the plane before it crashed on the beach. Do you live here? Did you see it? The plane?"

The reporter's press pass dangled in between her breasts and a red bikini flashed like a stop sign under her white dress. Luca rubbed his lips together. His hand went instinctively to his hip, and he realized with a pang of unease that he'd left his gun on the terrace. Exhaling, he hated himself for automatically being so paranoid. This woman wasn't a threat. She was just a young reporter. An amateur.

He shook his head and tried to ignore her pretty face. His eyes settled on a clump of sand clinging to her knee, and he was struck by an overwhelming desire to brush it off with his fingers and then run his entire hand up her smooth leg. "I don't want to be in the paper."

She flashed a little smile, and her gaze lingered on his chest. Oh. Right. He wasn't wearing a shirt. Her eyes shifted to the tattoo on his left bicep, her smile grew wider and her gaze skittered to the ground.

"My name's Skylar. You can call me Sky. I understand that you don't want to be quoted, but could you tell me anything off the record?"

When she raised her eyes he was struck by their pale blue hue, the color of the Gulf on a clear day, a startling and beautiful contrast with her chestnut-colored hair. Luca stepped back, shook his head again and smiled despite himself. "I don't do off the record. People should never talk to the media, you know."

She laughed. "Ohh, come on. I'm one of the good reporters. I won't misquote you."

"Really? Don't all reporters say that? Why should I trust you?"

She stopped laughing, which was too bad, because the sound was sweet as honey in Luca's ears. She blinked and stared at his hand, which was suspended in mid-air because he was trying to make a point while talking. He lowered his hand, suddenly self-conscious of the broad way he gestured.

"Trust me? Of course you can trust me. And, anyway, I'm really looking for the person who helped the man hit by the plane. One of the paramedics said he was young and maybe had a tattoo."

Luca shrugged when she pointed to his arm. She couldn't make him talk.

"You have an accent," she said, undeterred. "Where are you from?"

He swallowed, not prepared that she would try to get so personal so soon. "Europe," he muttered.

"Well, that narrows it down." She grinned and rummaged through her straw tote bag then handed him a business card. Plucking it from her fingers, Luca studied every inch of her face. Even the freckles on her nose were adorably sexy.

He glanced down and read her card aloud. "'Skylar Shaw. *The Palmira Post*.'"

She took a pen and notebook out of her bag. The pen's end was frayed with bite marks. Luca arched an eyebrow. He longed to flirt but knew he shouldn't, for all sorts of reasons.

"How long have you been a reporter, Skylar Shaw?"

"Three months, not counting my internship. I got this job at the newspaper right after graduating from journalism school."

He looked at her, then at her card and back. She tapped the end of the pen on her bottom lip and opened her mouth to chew on it. Her lips were plump, and Luca entertained a fantasy of rubbing his thumb over them. How he'd love to play with this girl. How bad of an idea was it to ask her inside for a glass of wine?

No, he couldn't do that. He could see she was in the throes of reporting a story, and although her grin was flirtatious, her eyes were intent. Serious. And he shouldn't be seducing reporters. Not in his situation.

He managed a tight smile and tried to focus on her forehead, but her blue eyes were like magnets that held his gaze for a few unblinking moments. He finally growled, "Congratulations on your graduation and on getting a job in a dying industry at the end of a global recession. Now, if you don't mind—?"

She laughed and pointed at the homes. "Well, congratulations to you, settling into a gated retirement community at such a young age. We all can't be so lucky."

He tilted his head, surprised.

She smiled sweetly. "Sorry. Couldn't resist. If you tell me anything off the record about the plane crash, I won't put your name in the paper. I can use you as an anonymous source. Do you know anything about the person who helped the injured man? Did you see anything?"

She was persistent, and he admired that—both in a journalist and a woman. Maybe she wasn't such an amateur. And yet, no way would Luca reveal that he'd aided the plane crash victim. He wanted publicity, and reporters, to stay as far away as possible.

Especially this gorgeous reporter.

He leaned forward and lowered his voice, acutely aware of his Italian accent. It was so different—seemed so…heavy—from her smooth American cadence that it made him feel again self-conscious. "Are you aware you are on private property? Reporters shouldn't break the law. Our community is called The Sanctuary, and it's gated for a reason, no? We like our privacy here."

The girl's face froze in an open-mouthed smile and a pink flush bloomed on her cheeks. She became even more beautiful than before.

"Oh." She pointed at the gate with her pen then grinned sheepishly. "I just came in over there. The gate was so easy to open, I... Well, I thought I'd find more people to talk to, more sources."

"Yes. I know," he said, trying to contain his attraction and fighting back a grin. Her tenaciousness, her eagerness to get the story, was endearing. Waltzing into a private enclave was exactly what he would have done when he worked for the newspaper in Italy. "I saw your elegant entrance as you broke in. Now I'll open the door out for you. I wouldn't want to rip more of your dress off."

Actually, ripping that gauzy dress off was exactly what he'd love to do.

He moved the few paces toward the gate. Turning the knob, he held the door open with an expectant look.

The young woman stared at him intently. She was short, and he couldn't help but imagine how he would have to bend slightly to kiss her. Her eyes went to his bicep, to his tattoo of an Italian saying, *Chi più sa, meno crede. The more one knows, the less one believes.* It was his motto, his truth. His quest to know the truth about everything made his world manageable. Especially since everything had fallen apart. In that moment under the Florida sun, all he knew, all he believed, was that he wanted to spend the rest of the day and all of the night with the woman standing in front of him, even though she was everything he should run from.

She was about a foot away, and her blue eyes, pale skin and pink lips were even more gorgeous up close. Less resistible. More deadly. His gaze drifted to the light sheen of perspiration that nestled in between the soft cleavage of her breasts as she said, "You have my cell number on my card...if you want to talk."

Luca grinned. Because talking was the last thing he wanted. "Talk?"

"Yeah. Talk. If you remember some details about the crash. Or if you suddenly decide you trust reporters."

Luca entertained the possibility of inviting her inside. If he did, he'd have to lie about so many things. Like his name and profession.

Not like he hadn't done that before with other women, but it was another thing to deceive a reporter. Those sorts of lies could come back to haunt him here in America, where his uncle was a well-known lawyer. And there was no way he could ask her inside without fully investigating her background, something he was sure to do at his laptop when she left the property.

Yet, if everything about her background checked out, what could it hurt to call her? Surely she'd be open to a one-night stand. American girls were easy. Her eyes were just shimmery and flirtatious enough to make him believe that she wouldn't say no to an offer of a drink, dinner or more.

"Have a good day, Skylar Shaw. *Buona fortuna* with your article. *Ciao.*"

As she swept past, she lowered her sunglasses over her gorgeous eyes and Luca caught the scent of her perfume. Orange blossoms.

Closing the gate, he smiled as she shuffled off through the sand toward the downed plane. *Luca Rossi, Italy's top investigative journalist, not answering another reporter's questions?* He laughed out loud at the rich irony.

# CHAPTER TWO

Skylar snapped her laptop shut. It had taken hours to interview everyone she could find and write about the crash. She'd sent a blog post and photos of the downed plane and the blood-soaked sand to the paper then followed up by emailing video clips taken with her cell phone and writing a longer article while sitting in her car.

Her phone buzzed with a text from her editor, Jill. *Great job on getting the pilot and witnesses. You rocked it today. You're free to go.*

Jill rarely praised her reporters.

Skylar grinned and gave herself a mental fist pump. This was just the story she needed. She'd been with the paper three months, and during her recent probationary review Jill told her that she was "doing well." Because she had always done better than well in school, Skylar needed Jill to tell her that she was doing excellent. Better than anyone else. She was starting her career in journalism on the bottom rung of the media ladder—a small, daily newspaper—and she wanted to be the biggest fish in this small pond. As that sexy, shirtless guy said, she'd gotten a job in a dying field at the end of the recession, and she was damned proud of it. Now all she had to do was prove herself to Jill...and eventually to editors at bigger papers.

This plane crash was her first big, breaking story since coming to Palmira. She was the only reporter to interview the pilot because she'd been the first reporter on the scene. By the time TV arrived, the pilot had left for the hospital. Because he'd revealed so many details and sobbed during the interview, she ended up with a kickass exclusive.

But—and there was always a *but* in journalism, a nugget of information that improved the story or a source that revealed hidden raw emotion—the article could have been even better. Skylar knew it in her core. Her ex-boyfriend had been right about one thing, maybe: She was a natural-born reporter, curious and greedy for information. Ironic, how James could give her such confidence professionally and yet personally destroy her.

The *but* with this plane crash surrounded the Good Samaritan. If she had only found the man who helped the victim it would have been a better story. More dramatic. More hopeful. She pawed through her tote bag for a pack of organic lavender-scented hand wipes as she considered. Where had he gone? It was as if he vanished into the misty surf of the Gulf, witnesses told her. Unless it really was that gorgeous guy…

Skylar wiped her hands with the cool cloth then dabbed her neck and arms. Glancing around to check if anyone was watching, she swiped her armpits. She'd spent a few hours in the Florida sun and probably smelled nasty. She flung the cloth on the floor of her car's passenger-side floor, which was cluttered with filled-up notebooks, granola bar wrappers and weeks-old copies of her newspaper, all the accumulated crap from long days of reporting on everything from government meetings to crime to feature stories.

Even though she was finished for the day, she wanted to peek at the crash site again because she anticipated writing a follow-up story the next day. The FAA had arrived and would probably be towing the plane away later.

Climbing out of her car, she strode down a wooden walkway and onto the beach. Trudging through the sand in her flip-flops, Skylar passed the yellow crime scene tape that cordoned off the plane. She wondered how long it would be until the beach was cleared of debris—this was where she did yoga on Saturdays. Hopefully the teacher would change locations because the place would have bad karma from the crash. Doing downward dog where a guy almost had his arm chopped off wasn't appealing at all.

She felt a pang of guilt at her thoughts. Her mother, who had been a yoga teacher, would be disappointed at her lack of compassion.

The salt air mixed with the smell of jet fuel and made her sneeze. A cop stood a few feet from the plane, texting.

He looked up. "Bless you. Hey, Sky. You outta here?"

It was Jimmy, a sergeant with the Palmira Police. He was Skylar's favorite officer. He always slipped her off-the-record information, probably because he was dating Emily MacLean, a sports reporter at the paper who was also Skylar's closest friend in the newsroom. He'd helped her earlier get past the crime scene tape.

"Soon. You haven't found the guy who helped the injured man, have you?"

Jimmy shrugged. "We're still looking. The pilot said the guy had dark hair. Another woman said he had blonde hair and a blue shirt. Another lady said he might have been elderly, but she was probably confusing the guy with the pilot."

Skylar opened her mouth to tell Jimmy about the shirtless guy with the tattoo, but Jimmy spoke first.

"Hey, me and a couple of guys on my squad are going for a beer later at the Sloppy Iguana. I know Emily's out of town, but you're free to join us. Wanna come? They're single."

Skylar wrinkled her nose. Jimmy and Emily were always trying to fix her up with one of his cop friends who were usually too old. Plus, she wasn't sure she wanted a man in her life, not after what happened with James. And it didn't feel right to date a cop, not when she covered crime.

"Meh, maybe," she said. "I'll text you. But you know I hate the Iguana. I'd rather go to Bacchus. It's slightly less tacky."

"Whatever." Jimmy rolled his eyes dramatically. "Aww, come on. How can you not love Iguana margaritas? Anyway, *I'm* outta here. Maybe I'll see you later." He pointed with his phone. "Talk to those FAA guys over there if you want any official quotes."

"Thanks, Sergeant." It was too bad there weren't any single guys on the force as cute and young as him, what with his easy smile and sleepy brown eyes. Then again, Jimmy wasn't as hot as the guy she'd tried to interview earlier.

Mmmm. That mysteriously sexy man.

Skylar swiveled her head to look at the cluster of homes beyond the gate. That attempted interview…? What a freaking disaster. She'd been so distracted by the guy's accent and model-like face that focusing was impossible. That level of interference had never happened during an interview before, not during her internship in Boston and definitely not during her short tenure at the paper. It wasn't like Palmira was a hotbed of handsome guys, though. The island was more like a senior citizens center.

But that guy? Unreal. His cheekbones and jaw were sculpted and angular, his top lip bow-shaped and his bottom lip full and sensual. Perfect for kissing.

*Whatever.* She'd made a fool of herself by breaking into his gated community and tearing her dress, and it wasn't like he'd given her information about the crash. Still, he could have been the Good Samaritan. Skylar chewed on her pen as she stood near the police tape, staring at the plane. Why would he be so evasive if he'd done a good deed? She considered again whether to tell Jimmy about the guy and then decided against it. She'd rather get the interview first, if possible. Break the story in the paper, be a step ahead of the cops. Jill would love that. If the cops hadn't found him, maybe they weren't looking hard enough. Maybe she could take another run at the whole thing tomorrow morning.

Skylar lowered her pen then yawned. The sun was about a half hour from setting over the water, casting a tangerine hue over the sand and the downed plane. That hot guy was somewhere inside The Sanctuary, probably with an equally stunning girlfriend. Or wife.

Skylar walked up the beach, parallel to the enclave's gate. Looking up and over the fence, she was surprised to find the sexy mystery guy standing on the second-floor terrace of the villa closest to the beach. He was looking down, seemingly at her. Smiling. To her delight, he still wasn't wearing a shirt.

She laughed out loud, stopped and waved.

Grinning, he waved back. Then he held up his index finger.

She tilted her head and lifted her hands, palms up, questioning. He held up his hand in a *stop* gesture; then he disappeared from the terrace.

Was he coming down to talk to her? Why would he do that? Maybe he'd give her the story!

With a rush of anticipation, Skylar ran a hand over her dress— and found the tear. She looked like crap. Tying the flapping, ripped seam into a knot and hoping she came off as fashionable and not homeless, she watched the guy appear and amble toward her.

"You're still here," he said. Grinning, he held the tall iron rail of the gate with one hand.

Skylar gazed without blinking into his eyes, captivated by their green-gray color that practically glowed next to his olive skin and dark hair. The setting sun softened the angles and hollows of his face and left behind only languid sensuality. When he stared at her, she thought she would turn to water and wash away into the Gulf of Mexico.

"I just finished. Do you have any news for me?"

He laughed. "What kind of news would you like?"

Skylar couldn't remember ever being made speechless by a man's looks, but this guy was different. Her eyes skimmed his chest then went lower. Dark hair trailed in a faint line down his six-pack abdomen, and Skylar quickly raised her gaze to his equally muscular arms. This man was pure peril. Or maybe she had been on Palmira long enough to forget what hot guys really looked like.

She gave the tattoo on his rock-hard bicep a sideways glance. It was one of many delicious details gracing his body, but what did it say? It was a line of words wrapped around the muscle in an old typewriter font. The words weren't in English. Maybe Spanish? Italian? Latin?

Recalling his question, she grinned, sensing that he was toying with her. "I'm still trying to find the man who helped the plane crash victim."

"You got some sun today. Your cheeks are pink."

Her cheeks were hot, but why did he ignore her question? As he reached an arm through the gate and motioned toward her face, she imagined playfully biting his finger.

"I burn easily," she said. "I think I might be a little dehydrated, too."

She knew she sounded too serious, but flirting didn't come easily. At least that's what James had repeatedly told her. She sobered at the thought, and her smile faded.

"Why don't you come inside for a glass of water?"

Skylar hesitated. She *was* thirsty. Maybe if she went, this mystery man might open up and tell her about helping the victim. Give her that exclusive. He didn't *seem* like an axe murderer or anyone she should be afraid of. And besides, people like that didn't exist on Palmira.

"Okay, I will. Thanks."

The man opened the gate and held it. "See, you don't have to rip your clothes off this time."

She paused and ignored his flirtation as best she could, but looking into his eyes sent little waves of excitement through her.

"What's your name, anyway? I generally don't go to people's homes unless I know their names."

He grinned lazily. "Luca."

"Luca. Italian?"

He nodded. "*Si.* Yes. Now come with me."

Luca. What a beautiful name. Skylar rolled it around in her mind as she followed. *Luca.*

He led her through a heady-smelling hedge of jasmine vines and through another iron gate. They emerged into a courtyard with a grotto-like pool surrounded by palm trees and bright green tropical plants. An enormous, Mediterranean-style home loomed behind the pool. She breathed in the scent, intoxicated by the fragrance and the obvious luxury.

"Gorgeous," she murmured.

"Make yourself comfortable. I'll get some water."

He gestured to one of four wide rattan chaise seats pointed toward the setting sun. Skylar sank into a white cushion. The diffuse orangey-red light and the sound of the gentle Gulf surf was soothing after covering such a depressing story.

Luca returned and handed her a tall glass with a lemon slice. She tried to be dainty but took two giant gulps. He sat on the edge of the lounger next to her and leaned in her direction, as if he was interested in watching her drink.

"Thank you," she said. "I guess I was thirsty."

His eyes unlocked from hers and traveled to her lips, then her breasts, then farther down to her hips and bare legs. Skylar's stomach fluttered as he so obviously checked her out. Such attention from such a good-looking guy was flattering and welcome after everything she had been through in the last year.

He hastily looked up at her face. "So. I read the paper's online story about the crash. Good job on getting all those witnesses so quickly. You also tweeted details throughout the day. Lots of sources. Impressive. You were busy."

He'd read her article? He'd looked at her Twitter feed? Luca's words might be the hottest thing any man had ever said to her.

*My words. In his brain.*

"No thanks to you," she said, unable to help smiling. "For all I know, you were the best source today."

"Maybe I was. But I owe you an apology. I'm afraid I wasn't polite to you earlier. I'm sorry."

Skylar shrugged. "It's okay. I'm a reporter. I need to get used to people saying mean things to me. Or weird things. Or nothing at all."

Truthfully, people had been mostly kind to her during interviews, although one man had slammed a door in her face the previous week when she tried to ask him about why he accidentally plowed into a post office with his car.

"I hope I wasn't mean," Luca said. "I'm glad you didn't put me in the paper. Thank you."

"You were fine. And it's not like you gave me any reason to put you in my article," she half complained, watching him drink his water. The way his Adam's apple bobbed made her want to lick the tan skin of his neck, and the fact that she entertained such an idea with a total stranger mystified yet thrilled her. She felt unusually alive and alert. "So, do you live here?"

He shook his head. "My uncle owns this house. I'm just visiting."

"From Italy?"

He nodded.

"Is your uncle or anyone else here?" She looked around, wondering if others would join them poolside. Like his girlfriend.

Luca shook his head. "I'm alone. My uncle's in Miami, working."

"Ah. And how long are you visiting for?"

"I'm not sure. Weeks? Months? I'm flexible."

He sipped from his glass but didn't take his eyes off her. Maybe he was single. Possibilities of future drinks, dinners, dates, unfolded in Skylar's mind. She asked, "What do you do in Italy?"

He laughed. "Americans are nosy, no?"

Was he flirting or reprimanding her for asking questions? She didn't like it when men chided her, because that reminded her of James. He'd never let a day pass without telling her how she did something wrong.

"Maybe we are," she allowed. "But I'm a reporter. *I'm* nosy."

"True," Luca said.

So, he didn't want to answer her question. Skylar would have been annoyed except he was smiling at her, all sexy-like. She stared into her water glass at the perfectly round lemon slice. When she looked up, he had a serious look in his eyes and rubbed his chin.

"How's the man who was injured by the plane? Any updates? Is he going to make it? Your article said he was in stable but serious condition."

Skylar shrugged. "I called the hospital about a half-hour ago and they said he would pull through. He was really lucky."

"*Certo che si.*" Luca paused and glanced at her. "Sorry. I think in Italian. Of course he was lucky."

She nodded. "Yeah, and I feel bad for the pilot as well. He was crying because he hurt the guy on the beach. He said everything happened so fast."

Luca's face screwed into a frown and he shook his head. "Weird story."

Skylar nodded again, and they both took a drink. She noticed Luca checking her out, opened her mouth to ask him whether he'd helped the victim, but he spoke first while tipping his glass toward her.

"Please forgive me for being forward, but is that a bathing suit under your dress?"

Skylar paused. "Yeah. I was at my condo pool when my editor called me to cover the crash. I was so flustered about getting out to the scene that I didn't go upstairs to change. I don't usually report in a bikini and a beach dress. It's pretty embarrassing. I didn't think people could see my suit."

"Maybe it's just something I noticed. I…notice details." Luca smiled and lowered his eyes to the ground, which was cute, then swept his glass toward the pool. "Um, you can swim now, if you'd like. It's still so hot, isn't it? I'm not used to this kind of weather. I can bring you a glass of chilled wine and we can get in the water, no?"

Strip to her bathing suit with a total stranger and float around in a gorgeous pool while drinking wine? Not something Skylar would normally do. But Emily was always telling her to stop being so serious. To think about something other than the newspaper and her career.

"That would be lovely."

She tried to sound like the kind of woman who spent sunsets near pools with handsome foreign men, but it was so far from the truth that Skylar almost laughed out loud.

Luca went inside. Skylar hesitated then pulled her dress over her head, tossed it onto the chaise and slipped into the pool. She dove down as far as she could, touching the bottom with her fingers then powering back up through the water. The movement gave her a sense of freedom, of weightlessness, that stopped when she did.

It would be awkward to reveal her body to the sculpted and muscular Luca. She was a little curvier than she liked, although the red bikini was flattering to her breasts. Standing on flat feet in the shallow end of the pool, she quickly tugged and pulled at the bikini cups, making sure she wasn't flashing a nipple or anything. She submerged herself again, enjoying the cool rush against her skin.

Her long hair floated around her in tangles as she held her breath underwater. She was already a sweaty mess, though, so what did she care? Looking pretty wasn't possible on this strange day. Not really. If this guy really wanted to know her better, he had to be satisfied with her true self, the one without mascara and heels and lipstick.

She came up for air with a splash, and when she opened her eyes, she spotted him. His lower half was submerged in the water as he sat on the middle stone step at the edge of the pool. She smoothed back her wet hair with both hands.

He didn't take his eyes off her as she slowly paddled toward him. Her heartbeat quickened.

"You turned on the lights," she said, parting the water with a breaststroke, sending ripples through the pool.

"*Si*. The water is now the same color as your eyes."

He handed her a wine glass, and she settled next to him on the step. She couldn't believe she was so naked, so exposed, near this tempting stranger. It was a struggle to pretend she wasn't affected by the closeness of his bare skin. What did he do for a living? Maybe nothing. He carried himself so languidly and his skin was so tan, as if leisure was his main occupation.

"*Cento anni*." He tipped his glass to hers.

"What does that mean?"

"It's a toast, like 'cheers.' It means 'one hundred years.'"

He was so sexy and so…adult. How old was he? From his unlined face and toned body she figured he was in his twenties, but she recognized a sadness in his eyes that made him look older. Did it mean anything to him that she was barely out of college?

She sipped the wine and realized it tasted like pears and smelled like flowers. It wasn't like her affordable boxed stuff, which was more like an alcoholic Gatorade.

"This is really good." God, she sounded stupid.

"It's Banfi Pinot Grigio San Angelo Toscana."

He spoke the words in a liquid Italian accent, and a surge of pure lust went through Skylar; she thought she might dissipate into the pool from the timbre of his voice. She was unaccustomed to this kind of instant sexual desire with a man she had just met, and she wondered if she should politely leave before things got out of control. There was no telling what she might do if he spoke to her solely in his native tongue.

No, she knew exactly what she would do: make some very poor choices that she would later regret.

"Where are you from, Skylar?"

She exhaled with relief. At least he had let up on the seductive-sounding Italian words. He was trying to make polite conversation, and there she'd been, assuming that he was trying to seduce her.

"Vermont. It's near Boston."

He regarded her with interest. "I'm familiar with Vermont. Do you have a boyfriend there? Or have you made a new boyfriend here on Palmira?"

She raised her eyebrows. "I thought Americans were the nosy ones."

He laughed. "Touché."

She pushed aside thoughts of James, her last boyfriend. Her only real boyfriend. He'd been an editor at the Boston paper during her junior-year internship, and when her job was finished he asked her out for a drink. They'd only made it through one cocktail before they kissed, and the majority of that first date was spent naked and tangled together. She'd been twenty-one at the time and he was thirty-six, a charming former war correspondent who told thrilling, funny stories about writing articles in hotspots all over the globe. Assuming he would be as passionate a boyfriend as giving reporting advice, she'd fallen for him. She'd been so damned wrong, though, about everything, and now she didn't trust herself one bit when it came to men.

But, she wasn't that college girl anymore, and she wasn't dwelling in the past. She also wasn't hopping into bed with any guy on the first night ever again.

She pasted on a smile. "Unlike you, Luca, I'll answer questions. I don't have a boyfriend. I broke up with him when I graduated from college."

A huge smile unfurled on Luca's face. "Right. I saw that online. The part about school, I mean. You graduated from Boston University at the top of your class."

She hesitated then grinned. "So, you checked me out online? Did a little Google-stalking?"

He glanced at her with a self-satisfied smile. "I didn't have to stalk. It was all there on your Twitter feed. Graduated in May at the top of your class. Majored in journalism. Minored in psychology. Nice photos of you on graduation day in your cap and gown, by the way. You looked cute."

So, maybe he was interested in her. A guy who did such a deep dive into her Twitter account had to be intrigued, at the very least. And he thought she was cute! She sipped her wine with a little smile.

"So, here's another question, Skylar. Why did you come to Palmira to work? Why didn't you stay in Boston? Or go to New York? Don't all reporters want to go to New York City?"

"Of course we do. But we all can't afford New York," she shot back.

Luca nodded. "What about Boston?"

Boston was out of the question because James was there. And because the paper had a hiring freeze. But she wasn't going to say that.

She shrugged. "I had an offer at a website in New York, but it was rewriting others' stories and aggregating content. It didn't pay much. At least here at the newspaper I'm able to do my own reporting and writing. *The Post* is actually a good paper. It has a reputation for training writers and we're gaining in circulation. Mostly because all the retirees here read it obsessively."

"Then it was a good decision, career-wise, no?"

"I hope so. I also came because I own property here." That felt funny to say, as if she were some trust-fund baby, which couldn't be further from the truth. She quickly added, "My grandmother died a year ago and I inherited her condo."

"I see. I'm sorry to hear about your grandmother."

"Thank you," she said, then steered the conversation back to Luca. "How do you know Vermont?"

"I went skiing there when I was at boarding school in Connecticut. Going to school here in America is why I can speak your language a little."

"Ahh. That makes sense. You speak English more than a little, though. Better than most native speakers."

"Thanks. Languages come easy to me. I also speak Portuguese, Spanish and French. And Italian, of course."

She didn't speak anything other than English and wondered if he knew that. "And do you use those language skills for your job?"

He grinned and moved his thumb and forefinger up and down the stem of his wine glass. She watched his hand, fascinated by the long, thick fingers and clean nails.

"You're persistent. To answer your question, I'm a graduate student at the University of Naples. I'm here on Palmira so I can write my, um, my master's thesis. I needed time to focus and a quiet place to think."

She wondered how rich his family must be if they owned this mansion, which sat behind a row of stately palm trees. Even though she was looking at the back of the house, she sensed it was a huge building and wondered about the interior. She nodded and lifted her eyebrows, as if she were interviewing someone. "Yeah, Palmira is perfect for peace and quiet. There's not much going on here, that's for sure. You won't have any distractions. What's your thesis about?"

Luca laughed, a short, brittle sound. "Ahh, it's about deconstructing the mythology of the Mafia hero in the media."

Her eyes widened, because she loved Mafia movies. "Oh. Oh! Wow. That's fascinating. Like *The Godfather* and *The Sopranos*?"

Luca smirked and looked up at the house as he took a sip of wine. Had he just rolled his eyes a little? Maybe she'd offended him. Undeterred, Skylar slipped into reporter mode, hungry for more details.

"Did you go to Sicily?"

He tilted his head and looked puzzled. "Uh, no. Why?"

"Isn't that where the Mafia is?"

Luca sounded troubled. As he talked, his English became slower and the pronunciation of his words became crisper. "The Mafia is all over my country. There are different crime syndicates in different regions. What you know as the Mafia is named different things all around Italy, kind of like different gangs here in the United States. It's *La Cosa Nostra* in Sicily. In Naples, there's the *Camorra*. In Reggio Calabria, there's the *'Ndrangheta*. There are organized groups in other parts of the country also."

"I had no idea." Skylar paused. "Are you looking at how organized crime is portrayed in Italian media or U.S. media, or what? Movies? TV? Books?"

"Both in Italy and in the U.S. Uh, and mostly movies and TV. Some books. A book. Another book. Yes, books."

He sounded humble and a little nervous about his work, which made Skylar like him more. "Do you know people in the Mafia, or in organized crime?"

Luca pressed his lips together and frowned. By his reaction, Skylar suspected it was a stupid question.

"Yes. Almost everyone in Italy knows someone who is doing something corrupt."

She was secretly thrilled. Intrigue was like catnip to journalists. "Oh. Kinda like Florida. Politicians, businesspeople, there's lots of corruption here." She tossed off the words like she was an old hand at Sunshine State corruption. Really, she knew she hadn't even begun to scratch the surface of this Wild West-like place.

He shifted his leg, and the lengths of their thighs pressed together underwater. Skin against skin. Luca's thigh was muscular against her softer, smaller curve, and she took a sharp breath as a jolt of sensual electricity sent shockwaves through her body.

He glanced at her sideways. "Aren't you a little young to be so jaded?"

"I'm twenty-two. I can't be much younger than you."

"I'm twenty-eight. How long have you been in Florida?"

"Three months."

Luca sipped his wine. "Not that long."

She fought back annoyance. "Corruption and weird shit happens here all the time. It's what my editor and all the reporters at the paper say. Right now I'm covering mostly boring stories—meetings and lame crime and some features. But everyone tells me I'll eventually witness the weird for myself or write about it if I stay in Florida long enough."

"Well, *that*'s something to look forward to."

They both laughed, and Skylar felt a little dizzy. Luca was funny and handsome. She worried that her voice was too excited, her laugh too eager, her eyes too interested in what he had to say. Her weakness had always been self-assured men who told good stories and made her laugh. She had even opined to her friends in college that it didn't matter if a man was handsome or not; if a guy could spin a good tale, he was worth a date or two. But Luca...well, he was gorgeous and spell-binding.

And probably only on the island for a while. Which made him instantly dangerous.

"I actually love it here," she said, trying to sound casual. "New England was boring. I love the strangeness of this place."

He nodded and laughed, and his leg pressed harder against hers. "Weird things do happen here, don't they? I watched a story the other night on TV about a strip club in Tampa offering free flu shots."

"Right?" Skylar said. "I saw that. And the face-eating zombie in Miami? Did you read about that?"

"Yeah. And, those...what do you call them? Potholes?"

"Potholes? No. *Sink*holes," she corrected with laugh. "Where the ground opens up and eats cars and houses and, that one time, a person!"

Luca's eyes met hers and he held up his wine glass. "To Florida."

They clinked glasses.

"To Florida. May we not get caught up in its insanity."

Why did Luca think that was so funny?

Skylar set her glass on the pool edge and slipped off the steps. "It's so stupid hot," she murmured, easing backward into the water, face up, idly wondering if she looked like a manatee. Luca followed, propelling himself forward with one broad stroke of his arms.

She'd reached the middle, so Skylar submerged her entire body and head. When she resurfaced and stood on flat feet, the water skimmed the tops of her breasts. Luca was nearby, and he seemed a lot taller.

"Your tattoo. Is it Italian?" she asked. "What does it say?"

He stepped closer, holding his arm above the water. She admired its sinewy bulk as she ran her finger about an inch from the skin of his bicep, not quite touching—although she wanted to touch him, very much. Why was her stomach clenching like that?

"*Si. E Italiano.* It says, '*Chi più sa, meno crede.*'"

She wanted him to repeat whatever he'd said, over and over, in her ear.

"What's that in English?"

He answered so quietly that the Gulf waves in the distance nearly drowned out his voice.

"'The more one knows, the less one believes,'" she repeated, nodding.

Here's what she did know: Luca was the most handsome man she'd ever been around, and she might regret it if she left now. Maybe out-of-control was something she needed. And yet James's words echoed in her mind.

*"You're cold. Unfeeling. So boring in bed."*

Bed. That was where this night could end, she was certain from the way Luca looked at her, all predator-like and hungry. It was more than flattering. It was hot. But Skylar didn't even know his last name, and no way would she give herself to a random stranger.

Or would she?

"Where did you get your tattoo?" she asked, trying to keep the conversation light.

"Milan. Three years ago."

Skylar blinked, unable to focus on his words when Luca stood so close. Was she finally having her own erotic adventure, one that didn't involve being demeaned and belittled? A small voice told her that she was all of those awful things James claimed, and that she should run from here before Luca discovered the truth. God, what she would give to allow herself to let go and forget about the past, to embrace this wild and wonderful present moment.

*No. Get it together and leave. Don't embarrass yourself.*

She had come here on business. To ask him about the plane crash. To be a journalist. She had promised herself that when she came to Palmira she would start fresh and respect herself more, at least where men were concerned. That's what her mother would have wanted, and God knew her mom would have been horrified if she'd been alive to see how Skylar allowed James to steamroll her confidence. Then again, Mom would probably also have been appalled by Skylar half-naked in a pool, lusting after a guy she'd just met.

"It's interesting. Like I said earlier, one of the paramedics told me that the man who saved the injured guy on the beach had a tattoo on his arm."

"Imagine that."

Luca's eyes met hers, and she couldn't read his expression. She tipped her head, and her wet hair spilled toward one shoulder. "Were *you* the one who helped the victim?"

Skylar's heart pounded when he smiled. He was so beautiful that it was unsettling, and the look on his face showed obvious confidence and desire. With previous dates—even the first time she was with James—she'd always had a running commentary in her mind: When will he kiss me? Now? Later? Ever? Tonight there was no guessing.

He reached through the water and wrapped his fingers around her wrist, gently guiding her hand to his shoulder. She automatically drifted toward him, clasping her other hand at his nape. She was so close that her breasts brushed his chest. His hands lightly cupped her jaw and neck, while her legs and arms and everywhere in between tingled from his touch.

His mouth hovered over hers, and Skylar was acutely aware of his smooth face, his searching eyes, his scorching fingertips on her skin. His soft mouth met her lips, tentative and gentle at first. He tasted like the wine, crisp and cool and new, and Skylar's lips instantly flared with heat. It was as if the shimmering blue light in the pool had entered her body and pulsed through her.

Luca pulled back and caught his breath, as if the kiss had taken him by surprise, then again pressed against her. The second assault, too, was shockingly sensual. It slammed into Skylar, defeated all her defenses. Almost.

She shifted her head away from his. Her gaze drifted downward, and she was fascinated by the hard surface of his chest muscles against the softness of the water that surrounded them. Trying to catch her breath, she licked her lips, and guilt over kissing a potential source stung her sensible journalist self. It was a stalling tactic to gather her thoughts, although her only desire was to kiss him again.

"You're not going to answer my question, are you?" she whispered.

With half-lidded eyes, he slowly shook his head and kissed her again.

### 

Luca pulled Skylar as close as possible. If his thundering heart was any indication, it had been far too long since he'd been with a woman.

She wrapped her smooth legs around his waist and her arms around his neck. He stood against the wall of the pool, and she was tight against him. Their tongues collided, the tips circling one another.

*"Che bella ragazza."*

"What does that mean?"

Her voice tickled his ear, teased his senses, and he translated, "What a beautiful girl."

And she was. Skylar Shaw was his perfect physical fantasy; curvy, with almond-shaped eyes and full, pouty lips. He had fully researched her after their meeting earlier in the day, and everything checked out. Public records revealed where she was born, where she'd gone to school, every dorm room and every apartment she'd ever lived. Her whole life was online, the scholarships she had won and the articles she had written in the Boston paper during her internship. Her Twitter feed detailed her stories here on Palmira, and her Pinterest page revealed that she loved green smoothies, true crime shows on TV, and smoosh-faced dogs.

She smelled like lavender, chlorine, and the sweetest of forbidden fruit. And the most captivating thing of all? She was a journalist—possibly the worst of all types of women he could hook up with.

Her clear blue eyes, her job, her curvy body…the combination was so seductive. His weakness. His kryptonite.

He didn't care.

After he'd checked her out online, he spent a couple of hours brooding. Considered calling her. Then he'd spotted her on the sand and knew he had to act. A one-night stand couldn't hurt, he'd rationalized, even if it *was* with a reporter.

No—he dragged his half-open mouth gently up her neck and felt her shiver in his arms—he probably shouldn't have told her his real first name, but how would she find out anything more about him? There wasn't anything to discover, not online anyway. He'd made sure of that. And he sure wasn't giving her his last name. Wouldn't, not when he took her upstairs to his bedroom, not when he kissed her goodbye later in the night.

His mind rioted. What the hell was he doing?

He'd hated lying to her about being a graduate student, actually. But concealing his true profession was a necessity. He wished he could tell her that he was also a journalist and a best-selling author. But since his anonymously-authored book came out, self-preservation trumped ego.

"*Tu sei bellissima,*" he whispered, dragging out each word. He kissed her again, hard, and took a handful of her wet hair and moved her head so that her ear was next to his mouth. "That's Italian and it means, 'You are gorgeous.'"

Her hands were suddenly in his hair, sliding down his neck, over his biceps. It had been too long since he'd had sex. The last time was three months ago, in Argentina at a backpackers hostel when he was lonely and a little drunk. Even before he kissed that waitress, he knew it was wrong because he felt nothing, only a release of energy when he climaxed. With Skylar, he knew it was wrong also, but in so many different ways and for so many different reasons.

"Your hair," he murmured. He skimmed his hands along her bare back under the water, and the blue shimmer of the pool danced on her skin. "Look at how beautiful it is floating in the water. You're a mermaid."

He gathered the ends of her floating tresses and captured her bottom lip in his mouth, but she squeezed his shoulders and slipped out of his kiss. "A mermaid. Yeah, right."

"Okay, how about a *sirena,* luring me to danger? Is that better? A siren?" Luca grinned wide and pressed his mouth to hers again. He hadn't wanted a woman this much in years. Maybe not ever. Their bodies made ripples in the water. His hands drifted low, down to her round ass, and he squeezed. God, her body felt incredible in his hands. And she *was* dangerous. His little siren. "Let's move to a drier spot."

She unwrapped her limbs from his body, and he led her out of the water. They stood there on the tiled pool deck for a moment, not kissing, just staring at each other while droplets of water ran down their legs. Luca played with Skylar's long hair, tugging it and running his hands carefully over the damp, chestnut waves.

"I can't wait to play with you all night long," he murmured. "Can't wait to watch that beautiful mouth of yours kissing and licking and sucking every part of me."

She opened her mouth in surprise. "Wow."

"What?"

"Nothing. You're just…very forward, that's all."

"Do you like that?" he murmured.

Her eyes drifted down and she stroked his bare chest with a hesitant touch. She explored the ridges of his muscles, her fingertips fluttering across his pectorals and pausing to circle his nipples, but she said nothing.

"You're stunning, Skylar Shaw," he said to draw her out of her shell.

"You're pretty stunning yourself, Luca-without-a-last-name."

Her big eyes, parted lips, and high cheekbones gave her a slightly astonished, sexy expression, as if everything he said or did took her breath away. He couldn't wait to make that breathlessness for real.

"Last names don't matter right now, do they?" he whispered. He was so captivated by her in that moment that he almost would have told her anything about himself.

Almost.

He grabbed her and drew her against him, gripping her hips and pressing her into his erection. She moaned a little bit, and he knew it was his night's mission to listen that sound over and over. He had hooked up with a few American girls when he was in boarding school and found them to be the easiest of all to get into bed. A few whispered words of Italian, and *pronto*, they were ready.

"*Vieni qui*," he said. "Sorry. Come here. Onto the chaise lounge. Or we can go upstairs to the bedroom if you'd like."

Her body tensed, and she moved back a half step. "Wait," she whispered, putting a palm in the middle his chest. "No. I can't. I'm sorry."

His hands cupped her face, and he stroked her bottom lip with his thumb like he had wanted to do earlier in the day. These were the steps of a dance he knew well. She wanted to let him know that she wasn't a slut. Fine. He'd play. "Why not?"

"I...I don't usually do this with guys I just met. I don't feel comfortable. I shouldn't tease you. This was a bad idea. I should go home."

"If you're sure..." His eyes narrowed as he trailed a finger down her throat and in between her breasts then circled the puckered nipple that strained against her wet bikini top.

She gasped and nodded. "Yes. I know my body's saying one thing, but my mind is telling me to slow down."

Her fingers clasped his hand on her breast then moved it to her shoulder. She stared at him, unblinking, defiant, and the message was clear: She really didn't want to sleep with him.

A twinge of annoyance and then a wave of relief washed over him. As much as he wanted her, this was probably for the best. Especially if he was going to be on this island for a while. He needed to lay low, not get laid by a local reporter. He'd known that all along.

Her face turned toward the ground, so he tilted her chin upwards. She closed her eyes. Something about how vulnerable she looked tugged at him, and he kissed her mouth tenderly then trailed his lips over her forehead. It was good that she was leaving. He couldn't afford to get attached to this alluring woman.

"It's okay. Don't apologize," he said, gathering himself and planting a chaste kiss on her lips. "Want me to walk you to your car?"

She inhaled, shivering, and nodded. Turning away, she went to the chaise where she had left her dress. He chewed on his lip while she pulled the garment over her head. Reaching into her bag, she pulled out an elastic, and he watched her scoop her long hair in both hands, twist it around and secure it. She missed a tendril that stuck to her neck, damp. He longed to move the wisp aside and bite her skin.

Luca opened his mouth, about to beg her to stay, but stopped himself. He wanted to respect her wishes. From what little he knew about her, he liked her too much to second-guess her decision to go home. And there were all his personal problems as well.

He accompanied her through the gate and up the public beach in the dark, sighing silently to himself while holding her hand. The downed plane was still there, illuminated by floodlights powered by loud mobile generators.

Skylar squinted in its direction. "I wonder when they'll take it away. I'd go over and ask the FAA right now, but I'm not really in any shape to do that."

Luca huffed out a laugh. He wasn't either.

They reached her car, and against his better instincts he cradled her head in his hands then put his lips to hers, touching her tongue with his and savoring every second of their kiss. Surprising him again, she pulled away.

"You have my card if you feel like talking."

"You said that earlier today," he murmured. His body ached because he knew this would be their final kiss. "I think you know that I want to do more than talk."

She did not answer. He watched her shut the door then give a sad wave as she drove off. While jogging back to the house, Luca felt regret punctuate every step. Skylar Shaw was the most intriguing and sexy woman he'd met in years, only at precisely the wrong time. Thank God she was saving them both by leaving.

# CHAPTER THREE

Bathed in an aqua glow, with pale wood and white leather seating, the lounge on the top floor of the Miami high-rise overlooked the city's glittering downtown from one bank of windows and the blue expanse of Biscayne Bay from another. It was the kind of place they would have gone on their honeymoon. Instead, Annalisa Martinelli was alone at the bar, searching for information on him. Luca Rossi. The man who should have been her husband.

She scanned the guys ordering craft beers and bourbon at the bar, sizing up which one might lead her to him. This was the obvious place to hunt for information about Luca. His only living relative, his uncle Federico Rossi, owned a law firm that took up three floors of the skyscraper. A woman working the newsstand downstairs said this was where the firm's lawyers drank after work. Surely someone here would know a little about the top attorney and his family—like where they lived and if Luca was indeed in Florida. If they didn't, Annalisa knew, she could entice them to find out.

As she sipped her mojito, she studied the people in the reflection of the mirror that hung behind the rows of liquor bottles. *Too old. Too fat. Too nervous-looking.* She appraised herself in the mirror and was pleased that her hair had stayed so straight and shiny, and that her low-cut silk blouse had long sleeves, to hide scars from the tiny cuts she had etched into her forearms.

She tapped her burgundy-painted fingernails on the glass of her mojito. Which one of these men looked most like a lawyer? With their expensive suits and carefully groomed facial hair, any of them were candidates. So she chose the most earnest-looking, a tall, younger man with close-cropped dark hair.

He was cute, which was a prerequisite. She would probably fuck him later.

Tossing her long hair, Annalisa fixed her eyes on the man. A beat after she caught his gaze, she smiled, closed-lipped, then lowered her eyes demurely, and within minutes he was next to her with two mojitos in hand.

"You have beautiful eyes," he said, setting the drink in front of her empty glass.

"Thank you," she purred. She took the mojito and raised it to his, and the glasses touched softly against one another.

"You work in the building?" the man asked.

Annalisa shook her head and launched into her prepared talking points. "Not yet. I'm interviewing at the accounting firm on the tenth floor. I think it went well. You?"

"I'm a lawyer with the Rossi firm. We're on floors twenty through twenty-three."

Perfect.

"Oh, the firm that advertises on television all the time?" Annalisa opened her eyes wider, but not too wide. She tended to look manic when her eyes were too big. *Act impressed when he talks. Laugh at the right moments.* Her mother had taught her how to respond to men, and those charms never failed.

"Yep. That one. What's your name?"

"Annie. Yours?"

"Carlos."

"Thank you for the mojito, Carlos. It's delicious."

"Annie. You're not Cuban like everyone else in Miami. I can tell. Where are you from? You have a different accent."

Annalisa grinned. She knew she couldn't hide her heritage but also suspected it would play to her advantage. "Italy. You?"

"Nice. An Italian girl. I'm like everyone else here. Cuban."

"Is it true what they say about Cuban men?"

He licked his bottom lip and grinned when she flashed her sexiest smile. "What's that?"

"That they're as good in bed as they are on the dance floor."

He laughed, hard. "Maybe you'll find out."

Yes, maybe. And later, if she had one more mojito and looked at Carlos the Cuban lawyer just right when he entered her, she would be able to imagine that he was Luca. She had done it so many times in the past, with so many different men.

Soon that would end.

# CHAPTER FOUR

Florida humidity was a bitch. Skylar's skin was sticky from her face to her feet. Combined with the sweaty sheen on her face, she was a wreck.

Wearing a suit to work was torture and she was glad the week was over. She wriggled out of her black jacket and tossed it onto the passenger seat, her arms finally free in her white silk tank top. At least she'd worn a black, knee-length pencil skirt that allowed for some circulation. Yanking out her ponytail, she shook her hair and swiped a slick of clear gloss over her mouth, rubbed her lips together, tried to gather her hair and tamp it down into a smooth column then tied it in a low, messy bun.

The week had been consumed by follow-up stories on the plane crash. The victim's wife had talked to her, thankfully, which was the one bright spot. She'd also gotten the scoop that the man definitely wouldn't lose his arm, which made Jill happy, but Skylar was emotionally strung out by the constant demands of deadlines and updating social media. She'd been forced to juggle several other stories from the crime beat as well, and to write a feature on an odd woman who collected rare orchids.

She wasn't often a features writer, but she routinely said yes to any assignment Jill tossed her way. Her editor had told her to push herself, and Skylar was doing exactly that. She'd also launched into a project on how the tiny local police department had spent hundreds of thousands on military surplus equipment. Failure wasn't an option, because she had no other options. She had no childhood home to return to, no mother or father or siblings to rely on. All she had was a tiny condo and a car, and student loans that cancelled out the value of both.

At twenty-two, she was alone in the world and it kind of sucked. Pushing herself was the only thing she knew how to do, since she'd been doing it so long, anyway. Maybe that was why, as she sat in her car soaking up the air-conditioning, she was still reeling from that kiss with Luca.

She was lonely.

Soon after their encounter she had searched on the Internet for a Luca who lived at that gated subdivision, but she didn't find anything. She'd perused online property records, but she only had his first name and wasn't exactly sure of the address of the house, since she had entered and left through the back. She also didn't have Luca's phone number, and even if she had, she sure as hell wouldn't have called or texted. Her New Age, yoga-teacher mother had raised her to be a feminist, to take charge of her relationships, but Skylar felt strongly that if a man was interested he should show it.

She sighed, thinking about how she wished she could talk to her mom about everything happening in her life since graduation day, but five years had gone by since her mom died, and a year since her grandma passed. Now Skylar was more alone than ever.

About to cry, she stopped herself and pointed her car's air conditioner vent at her face, blasting it to the max. The sweat on her face evaporated and she shut her eyes, reminding herself to cut the self-pity crap. She wasn't a victim. She wasn't special. She was just another unlucky person trying, against the odds, to succeed.

No mud, no lotus. Her mother had always liked to say that. It meant that only through suffering could real enlightenment and bliss unfold. Skylar was somewhat skeptical of this, as she was of all her mother's New Age sayings. When, exactly, did the mud end and the beautiful green grass of bliss begin?

She opened her eyes and grabbed her purse. There would be no further blissful kisses with Luca; that much was clear. He hadn't tried to reach her, which confirmed all of her fears about herself. He was probably annoyed with her and assumed she'd been teasing him. Or he hadn't been all that interested to begin with, if the speed at which he'd walked her to her car was any indication. He must've thought she was boring, just like James had.

So. She'd made the right choice to not have a one-night stand that would have surely ended in awkwardness. Or worse, shame and regret. It was better this way. She didn't need a man to distract her.

Her goal was to work hard at *The Post*, write excellent stories, and get hired somewhere bigger. To sell her grandmother's condo and be free of her student loans. Yet her mind kept returning to Luca, and not only because of the way he'd touched her so sensually.

Why hadn't he wanted to tell her that he was the Good Samaritan? She had put the question to Jill in the newsroom, conveniently omitting the part about how they'd made out in the pool, but her boss just shrugged and told her to move on. "It's Florida. People come here to lose themselves, not be featured in a page-one newspaper story."

Grabbing her car keys, Skylar hobbled into Greenway, Palmira's upscale health food store that smelled like fresh-cut flowers and strawberries. Her feet were swollen from the humidity, and she had turned down Emily's invite to a local bar, longing to be one with her pajamas, her sofa and Netflix. Plus she wanted to hit a yoga class early the next morning and didn't want a hangover. The yoga teacher hadn't moved the class from the site of the plane crash, and while Skylar didn't like the idea of practicing where a tragedy happened, it was titillating to think of being so close to Luca's house. She just might have to wear her most flattering yoga shorts.

Not very enlightened or yogi-like, she told herself sarcastically.

She scooped up a container of her favorite kale salad at the to-go counter and wandered over to the produce department. Shopping here was like a religious experience, because the vegetables and fruits always seemed to sparkle while gorgeous Baroque music wafted throughout the store.

Fresh guacamole and tortilla chips also sounded like good comfort food. She dropped a bulb of garlic in the basket. She was squeezing the Haas avocados for ripeness when she heard a familiar, accented voice.

"Skylar Shaw."

She froze, her hand on an avocado, then looked up. *Crap.* She was lost the moment she looked into his glittering eyes. It was glorious. Like someone had sent the best-looking man in the world to her health food store for her viewing pleasure.

He gave her a full, seductive grin. The produce misters blasted fine spray onto the nearby organic micro-greens, as if Luca was so hot that the sprinkler system came on to extinguish the invisible blaze. Skylar suppressed a giggle. It was maddening how he reduced her to such girlishness. Her mother hadn't brought her up to be coy around men.

He wore dark blue gym shorts and a white T-shirt with the word NAPOLI in black across the chest. Flip-flops adorned his feet, and unlike the other day he had stubble on his face, which made him look older—and sexier.

"Oh. Hi. I didn't recognize you with your shirt on," she said.

His eyes widened and he laughed, and when she recalled how he bit her bottom lip and moaned in her mouth as they kissed in the pool she wobbled a little and steadied herself. *Must be the tall heels.* Skylar squeezed the avocado harder so that she would have tactile contact with something.

*Don't fall for his many, obvious charms. Like his beautiful smile.*

He was probably a man-whore. She couldn't forget that.

"I've been reading you in the paper every day," he said in that sexy accent. "You're busy. I loved the story on the unusual orchid collector—how she grew that ghost orchid on hundred-year-old hickory wood."

He had picked out the most unusual detail in the story. It was as if he knew exactly how to flatter her.

"Thanks. But she wasn't just unusual. More like obsessed."

He tilted his head. "Aren't the best stories about obsession? About men and women who want only one thing, whether it's orchids or money or another person?"

She sucked in a breath and held it. What, exactly, was he implying? Her hand was still on the avocado, squeezing it in a death grip. His hands clasped his grocery basket, and she noticed his knuckles were white.

"Yes," she said. "I guess they are." She exhaled and straightened, not wanting to let on that his little monologue was making her insides quiver. "I'm just getting off work. The governor was on the island today for a news conference, and I had to cover that."

Like he was interested in the governor. Maybe she should shut up and leave.

"An interesting assignment, no?" He still had that delicious half-smile on his face. His eyes swept down her body, and it was as if fire licked her skin.

"Not really." She shook her head and wondered if she was coming off as too cold. How ironic. Was that a bead of sweat running down the back of her neck? She had a vision of his tongue in the same place.

He seemed so confident, with more than a touch of ultra-masculine edge in his voice. Even though he wore gym clothes, he commanded attention with those dramatic features and that amused grin.

*Say something! Stop being mute. He'll think you're stupid.*

He glanced in her basket. "And what are you making for dinner tonight, Skylar? Ah. Garlic. Well. You won't be going on any dates."

She snorted out a laugh.

Luca opened his mouth in a lazy smile, and his tongue slowly licked the corner of a lip. "I have a better idea. Why don't you come to my house sometime and I'll make you dinner. Surely you would like to enjoy a delicious Italian…meal."

Skylar stared at him in surprise then chortled, tossing her head back at the cheesiness of his words. He seemed to get her amusement and laughed, himself.

"That was a stupid line, wasn't it?"

"Oh yes. It was. At least you recognized it, though."

"But I'm serious. Why don't you let me make you dinner?"

She bit her lip and tried not to grin. Should she? It seemed he hadn't been put off completely by her refusal to sleep with him.

"I make a mean tiramisu."

Skylar smirked. The sexual tension between them *was* hot. And she loved tiramisu. And… "Hmm. When?"

"Let's see. The next few days, I've got family obligations." He paused and was obviously doing some sort of mental calculation before he grinned. Why was it so warm all of a sudden? Was that a dimple embedded in his cheek? All Skylar could think of was his mouth on her neck, and she swallowed hard.

Just then an older man approached. Probably a good thing. Skylar had visions of Luca kissing her atop the pile of avocadoes. What was happening to her? Where was all this lust coming from? She couldn't wait to escape.

"Luca, how quickly you've made friends on the island," said the man. He was in his sixties, handsome and shorter than Luca. She was startled by how similar his eyes were to Luca's. Identical, even. Was that why he seemed so familiar?

"Oh. Uncle, this is Skylar Shaw. She's a reporter for *The Palmira Post*. Skylar, this is my uncle."

"Hi. I'm Federico."

Skylar extended her hand. Now she remembered who he was. Federico Rossi was a personal injury lawyer who advertised on television and radio all over Florida. His commercials were notoriously cheesy, with the tag line, "We the People." The reporters in the newsroom chanted it in unison whenever the ads came on TV. She had heard the older Rossi owned a home on Palmira. His main law practice was four hours away in Miami, according to the commercials.

And Luca was his nephew.

He had mentioned an uncle the other night. Luca *Rossi?* Was that his name? She grinned. Now she'd be able to investigate him properly.

"Federico Rossi, right? The lawyer? It's nice to meet you, Mr. Rossi. I've seen your TV ads. Are you enjoying Palmira?"

"Yes, I am. Most of the time I'm in Miami, except when I want to spend time with my brother's son, my nephew here. Palmira is my second home, my vacation getaway." The older man winked.

"Oh yes. Luca told me all about how you've let him stay at your place while working on his master's thesis."

Federico smiled and his eyes widened. "Yes...that's right," he said slowly.

Skylar smiled back. How interesting, that Luca hadn't mentioned his uncle was a famous attorney. Now her curiosity was working overtime trying to figure out why.

"Well, we should be going," Luca said in a bright voice. "It was good seeing you. I'll call you."

His voice faded as she looked into his eyes. While she'd never seen such beauty or felt such intensity from a man, she was curious why he was now in such a hurry to leave. No way would she let Luca—or his uncle—slip away now. This random encounter was perfect. She wasn't going to pass up an opportunity to get to know Luca on her own terms or ignore a potential interview. Or to cultivate the elder Rossi as a source. A trifecta of awesome.

Turning to Federico, she beamed. "You know, Mr. Rossi, we have a weekly feature at the paper called People of Palmira. We profile a prominent resident and run a nice, big photo. Could I interview you? I'm sure you have some great stories."

"Of course, Ms. Shaw, I would be honored. I never turn down a conversation with a beautiful reporter. You could come to the house and we can talk. Right, Luca?"

Skylar shifted to regard Luca. His sexy eyes had turned steely.

"Um, sure, Uncle. Sure."

"Perfect," Federico said. "How about Wednesday morning at around eleven? I have to be in Miami later that night."

Skylar grinned, ignoring Luca. "Thank you. I'm free and I'm sure I can make a photographer available as well, Mr. Rossi."

"I live in The Sanctuary. The address is 100 Sea Grape Lane. Do you know where that is?"

Luca spoke in a flat tone. "She knows."

"I know," Skylar said at the same time. "See you both at eleven on Wednesday. Have a great weekend."

"You too, Ms. Shaw. It's a pleasure meeting you."

Luca still had the icy glare on his face. "*Ciao.*"

Skylar quickly made her way to the checkout stand, her cheeks blazing. She reminded herself that Luca wasn't James, that his flashing eyes weren't reprimanding her. He was sending some message to his uncle.

*Relax.*

Driving home, she chided herself for the millionth time about something else. James shouldn't have such a hold on her reactions to men. When would he stop looming large in her life? She'd been in two relationships—well, three, if you counted the guy she went to prom with her junior year of high school and lost her virginity to, but Skylar didn't count him as an actual boyfriend. He'd been a teenage prom-night hookup, and a lame one at that.

Devon had been her first actual "boyfriend," though in retrospect it too had been barely real. More like committed friends. Short and sandy-haired, Devon was from Boston and a communications major. He'd wanted to be a sportscaster. They'd met at a journalism department Christmas party their first year of college, and he'd made her laugh, a lot. Then he went abroad their sophomore year and the relationship fizzled. Skylar couldn't even remember who forgot whom first.

Throughout most of college, she'd been like Teflon to relationships: Sure, she'd attracted guys and even hooked up a few times during parties, but she never got attached because she preferred being alone and focusing on her studies. Until James. He'd been so captivating with his stories of Iraq and Afghanistan, of getting shot at by insurgents and living in a reporters' house in Baghdad. He'd used his expertise to help her, paragraph by paragraph, with her articles. Because of him she recognized what separated a powerful news story from a mediocre one. Because of him she knew when to ask questions during an interview and when to stay silent. And at first the sex had been wonderful, all caring and whispered sweet words.

He'd changed when he was laid off from the paper, though, as part of massive staff cuts, and began drinking two bottles of wine every day. Sex was less frequent, and it made her uncomfortable that he treated her a bit Svengali-like. She encouraged him to look for other jobs, but he claimed to have enough in savings and from a severance check to live on while he helped her with her career.

"You'll thank me when you win the Pulitzer someday," he'd said. "You're the future of journalism, with your stupid fucking Twitter and Instagram. I'm the past."

He'd eventually pulverized her self-esteem as a woman just as she felt like she was becoming one. Nothing—from how she sat sipping her drink at a bar, to how she moved her hips during sex—was ever good enough. A moment never passed with James without Skylar being left with the sense that something about her very existence needed correction.

It had left her wondering whether she could ever make a man happy.

### 

"What the hell did you do that for?"

Luca and his uncle were in the backseat of his uncle's Mercedes. An armed driver was behind the wheel.

Federico laughed. "My boy. For all of your talent, you're sometimes kind of dense. You were a journalist and bestselling author in Italy. You should know it's better to control the press than to have the press control you. Never turn down a chance for publicity. And I think the better question is, how are you already so acquainted with a local reporter?"

Shifting his body to face his uncle, Luca tried to tamp down his irritation. He didn't mind much that Skylar had met Federico, but he'd never imagined she'd want to write a story on the old man. It was a complication he didn't need.

"We met when that plane crashed the other day. She came over and had a glass of wine afterward, and…" Luca waved his right hand in the air in a circular motion.

Federico continued to chuckle. "Good for you."

"I just didn't think we'd run into her, or that she'd try to interview you. I really don't want her poking around and mentioning me in her article about you."

"Relax, Luca. I'll make sure she doesn't mention you. This is *The Palmira Post*, not *The New York Times*. I know the publisher, so I can always make a call if we think it's going to be a problem. And anyway, don't worry about Bruno Castiglione or the Mafia finding you because of a Florida newspaper article. If I were hiding you, would I go out of my way to be in the news? I'm in the papers all the time. Castiglione is awaiting trial. Your book did its job. Your days of worrying are over."

"I'm not so sure about that," Luca grumbled.

He didn't want to rail at his relative out of a sense of old-world respect, but sometimes he wondered if Federico took his concerns about safety seriously. It was difficult to tell. Even though Federico was his blood relative, Luca barely knew him. He was the older brother of Luca's father, and the two men had been estranged for the entirety of his life for reasons unknown to him. Federico had come to America before Luca was born, and had lived here long enough to assume the country's breezy, anything-goes facade. Which was why it was difficult for Luca to tell if Federico's concern for his situation matched its gravity. He'd feel safer when Castiglione—Naples's biggest Mafia boss and the subject of his first book—was convicted and in prison.

Which would hopefully be soon.

"And you didn't have to come to the store with me," his uncle chided.

Luca rolled his eyes. "I've been in the house for two weeks. I needed to get out. You're the one who said it was safe."

"Palmira *is* safe. And don't worry about the reporter. She won't put two and two together. She's young. Is she even old enough to drink? She won't find out anything. There's so little about you online. That was the benefit of writing your book anonymously, no?"

Luca snorted. "Yeah, only my agent and editor knew that I wrote the book. And my parents. And you." He made a fist and crushed it on the leather seat. "It still burns me that Castiglione found out I'm the author. I'd love to kill whoever told him. I'm doing my best to lay low until the court case is over. God knows enough people disappear in the months before a trial...."

"Then don't worry about my interview, Luca. Worry about yourself. Have you started on your second book?"

Luca grunted. He didn't want to tell his uncle that he had spent the last few days moping around, wondering if it was even worth it to write anymore. He didn't want any more complications, violence or death—three things that he abhorred. The inertia had lately morphed into a more sinister emotion: apathy. Usually he was outraged by the corruption that had seized his country in a death grip, and he wanted justice for his parents' murder. But, pfft. Justice. Hadn't done him or his prosecutor father any good. A desire for justice had gotten his parents killed and forced Luca to go on the run.

He constantly reminded himself that there were far worse places in the world to hide out. He had been in some of them in his attempt to disappear from Bruno Castiglione's scrutiny. Going on the run had worked, because he was still alive. But he longed to stop running. His uncle's summer home was as good a sanctuary as any, but sometimes Luca wondered if it was more like Alcatraz—a jail on an island, if one with 300-thread count sheets, a home gym and wine cellar. Worse, Luca felt added guilt for his life of luxury in the wake of his parents' murders, and guilt at his ingratitude. Guilt on top of guilt on top of guilt.

Maybe he wouldn't write the second book after all. It wasn't like he needed the money. Between his parents' inheritance and the profits from his first, best-selling exposé, he never had to work again. And his uber-wealthy uncle, who had never married or had children, made it clear that he would help Luca any way he could.

Still, Luca was itching for something different. His round-the-world trip hadn't quenched his restlessness or made him feel any safer. He was unsettled, unmoored, tense.

Was it the scorching kiss with Skylar that sparked this? What would it be like to really get to know her? Yet why would he want to, at this perfectly wrong time in his life? He'd always had short, meaningless flings, always made sure the women were aware that he didn't want attachments.

"*Zio*," Luca said, using the Italian word for uncle. "Why didn't you ever marry?"

It was an intimate question of a man he barely knew, but Luca had been without any meaningful encounters for so long that he hoped his uncle would forgive his curiosity.

Federico stared at him for several seconds. "I almost did. Once, back in Italy. No one since. You? Did you have a girlfriend before you left?"

Luca laughed. "Many."

"Ever been in love?"

Luca snorted. "No. I'm not even sure about 'love.' Not after what I saw my parents go through. I don't know if you were aware, but they were pretty nasty to each other while I was growing up. I never understood why they didn't divorce."

Federico stared out the window and cleared his throat. "Luca, here's what I can tell you about love. Love is when you feel regret decades later for making the wrong decisions. That's love."

What an odd statement.

Luca frowned, and there was silence in the Mercedes for several moments. Only when the car pulled into the gated community did his uncle turn to him and add, "I know you're anxious, and I know you miss your parents and Italy. Anyone would feel like that in your situation after what you've been through."

Federico continued, speaking in rapid-fire Italian. "You should relax while you're on Palmira. I invited you here so you could work on your second book and plan your next move. I'm trying to do everything I can to make you safe. Who's going to find you here? Who even wants to find you anymore? I got you the bulletproof Mercedes. I got you the gun. There's an excellent security system at the house. And I offered you bodyguards."

"No. No bodyguards." Luca raised his hand in a halting gesture. The idea of someone monitoring him around the clock made him queasy. He chided himself for earlier questioning whether Federico was taking his situation seriously. His uncle had actually done a lot for him. Much more than he'd ever expected. So maybe he should calm down. Palmira seemed sleepy and safe. Just what he needed, a quiet place so he could be alone with his mountain of guilt.

The car pulled into the driveway.

"Take it easy, Luca," his uncle said. "Rest. Here's what you should do. Find a girl on the island to fuck. Keep it light. You know how to do that. Don't get too involved. That's what I always do when I'm stressed about a big case. I find a cute girl to spend time with, take the edge off."

Luca's answer was a quick flick of his hand and a grimace. Hearing about his uncle's sex routine during personal injury trials wasn't what he wanted, and he didn't desire any random, easy American girl, not anymore at least. He wanted the not-so-simple Skylar.

Well, he didn't want a lecture from Federico about anything. He'd try to stop thinking about Skylar, and that was that. He didn't want any more complications. His life was already complicated enough, all because of his quest for the truth.

# CHAPTER FIVE

"You have a great condo." Annalisa rolled onto her side away from Carlos. She looked out the narrow, floor-to-ceiling window at the busy downtown Miami street.

He pressed against her and kissed her shoulder. She'd thrown on his button-down shirt before he woke up so he wouldn't see the scars on her arms. Went without underwear, though, knowing that would distract him.

The bed was too soft, and she sank into the pillowy mattress. She wanted to leave but still didn't have the information she needed. Hopefully this wouldn't require a weeks-long relationship. She didn't have time for that.

"Meh. It's only a studio. It's all I can afford now. I can't wait to be rich. Really rich. Like my boss. You should see the places Rossi has."

Annalisa rolled over and stroked Carlos's bare chest with her fingertips. "*Si?* How many homes does he have?"

"I know he's got the downtown penthouse. Not too far from here. He likes to walk to work. On the weekends he sometimes goes to this little place across the state. He took a bunch of his top-billing lawyers there for a Christmas party. It's a huge mansion on an island. Palmira. I think he also has a condo somewhere in the mountains. Asheville, I think."

As Carlos talked about how he loved the snow because it was so different than Miami's humidity, Annalisa tuned him out.

"What's this?" he abruptly asked, running a finger over three faint red marks on her inner thigh.

"Oh!" She wouldn't tell him that she'd carved the marks intentionally. With a razor blade. "Can you believe that's from waxing? This bitch at a place on South Beach really messed with my skin."

Carlos cooed and settled himself between her legs, kissing the marks softly before moving his lips to the junction of her thighs.

A couple of hours later, she kissed Carlos goodbye. She went to her hotel and changed into a casual sundress and a lightweight sweater, then sat at a café drinking espresso on the bottom floor of Federico's building. It would be worth scoping this out for a while, but she suspected Luca was on the island. He loved sun and sand. She remembered how he looked one morning, running along a beach near Naples, rivulets of sweat running down his tan chest and thick back muscles. Surely he would choose Palmira Island over Miami. It was smaller and safer. Calmer.

He was definitely somewhere in Florida. That's what her cousin had said. And God knew her cousin—Bruno Castiglione, Naples's most powerful Mafia boss—had informants throughout the government and Italy's banking system. Luca must have talked to someone in Italy, and that someone told someone, and that someone was on the payroll of Bruno. Or maybe Bruno's men had infiltrated Luca's computer. Who knew? It didn't matter now. All that mattered was that she was going to rescue him.

Luca was smart and handsome, but he wasn't infallible. He had never figured out that she and Bruno—the subject of his book—were second cousins. To be fair to his excellent reporting skills, she did have a huge family. It stretched back centuries and through neighborhoods in and around the sprawl of Naples, and even Annalisa hadn't met everyone. It wasn't like she and Bruno were close or had even grown up together; Bruno was older than her by twenty years. He was just one of dozens of relatives, some more criminal than others. It was only after Luca broke up with her that she hacked into his computer and stumbled on his notes about Bruno. While they were dating, she had no idea what his project was about, because he never shared it with her.

If Luca hadn't broken her heart, then she wouldn't have had the breakdown or snooped in his computer. If she hadn't had the breakdown, then she wouldn't have told Bruno that Luca was the author of the anonymous bestseller.

It was awful, though, how Bruno had Luca's parents killed. Signora Rossi was so kind. Made such delicious panettone at Christmastime.

In a way, Luca brought his troubles onto himself. But that was all in the past now.

"I'll always be grateful to your loyalty, Annalisa," Bruno had told her right after she revealed her discovery about Luca's book. He'd squeezed her bony hands with his big ones and she felt useful and needed. "That's why I'm paying for you to get better, so you'll stop hurting yourself."

She'd gone away to the hospital in a little town three hours south of Naples. One long year—that's what it took to get better, the professionals said. It didn't stop her from doing some of the things she loved, like fucking tall, dark-haired men. One of her conquests was even a doctor. And she'd managed to cut herself a few times in the hospital, once with a piece of broken glass she found on the grounds.

The psychiatrists tossed out all sorts of diagnoses. Probably genetic, they said, but her stepfather's advances when she was twelve hadn't helped either. After the long and tedious treatment, she'd convinced everyone that she wouldn't cut again and that she'd take her meds. Be a good girl and live a normal life.

After she was released, she had been trying, and somewhat succeeding, to forget about Luca. Then, a few weeks ago, Bruno called and asked her to visit while he was on house arrest. He told her that Luca was in Florida. The news triggered all of the old intrusive, obsessive feelings, and her need to see him flared up like lighter fluid on a bonfire.

Looking back, telling Bruno about Luca's book was the worst thing she could have done. How could she have been so horrible? But that was back when she hated him. Now she loved him again. Now she was certain about her feelings. Now that she was in the Sunshine State and off that stupid medication, her mind was calm. Purposeful. Invincible. She would make it all up to Luca by finding him and never letting go. She'd help him hide from her evil cousin. She would *die* for Luca.

"You need to stay away from him," her best friend told her before she flew here. "Get back on your pills and return to that hospital."

Closing her eyes, Annalisa allowed the morning sun to wash over her face. She wasn't crazy, no matter what her family and friends thought. She was in love. Luca would understand after she proved her loyalty to him. He would kiss her long and slow like he used to, and her pain would vanish.

The memory of their first meeting was still fresh and pure. The way he'd strode confidently into the newsroom at the paper in Naples, wearing a charcoal gray jacket over a white button-down, expensive jeans and dark leather shoes. How the corners of his mouth turned up and the way his eyes seemed to dilate when he saw her.

"I'm Luca. It's my first day. I'm covering crime. You?"

"I'm a features writer." Her heart had fluttered, something it never did with men. "Maybe we can get coffee soon."

By the end of the week, they were at the reporters' favorite bar down the street from the paper. She was two years older, but he had a calm confidence unlike most guys in their early twenties. Three drinks later, they moved to his car where he pulled her onto his lap. Where she gave him head for the first time. The love she'd felt for him even then seemed like it could engulf her.

It had engulfed her.

A car horn jolted her out of her memory. Annoyed, Annalisa swiped and tapped her phone, reading about Palmira. The island was filled with people and shells and wide, sugar-sand beaches. Four hours from Miami. She looked at a map and then shuddered at the name of the road she needed to take to get there.

Alligator Alley. She hated reptiles.

# CHAPTER SIX

Luca woke at dawn and for a brief moment didn't know where he was. The rooming house in Buenos Aires? The beach hut in Thailand? The yoga ashram in India? He had hadn't stayed long in any one place since leaving Italy. Now that he was on Palmira, his mind hadn't caught up with his body.

The pre-dawn light cast a gray glow through the windows in the bedroom, bathing the dark pine furniture and the white sheets with a magic hue. His eyes absorbed the light, trying to remember what he had been dreaming about. It was a sexy dream, and the reporter girl was in it. He was awake now, hard with longing.

Taking a deep breath and ignoring his cock, Luca climbed out of bed and went onto the terrace wearing only his boxers. The sun was starting to rise, frosting a few clouds with a pink tint against the pale blue sky. The water of the Gulf of Mexico reflected the colors, making everything look like a dreamy painting. It was his daily slice of happiness, the serenity and beauty of dawn. It gave him hope. Every day since he'd arrived on Palmira he stood on the terrace and soaked in the salty morning air.

Usually the beach was empty, save for a few lone shell-seekers in the morning mist. Today Luca noticed a group of people facing the water, away from him. It was some sort of exercise class. They were on the public beach near the gate that Skylar Shaw had slipped through after the plane crash. He had a good view of the group, and when Luca spotted mats and towels he realized it was a yoga class.

He yawned and stretched. Scratched his bare chest.

"Let's go into downward dog."

The small, blonde teacher's voice wafted up to the terrace. There were about a dozen people in the class, all bending in unison. He watched as the students twisted and turned as if in slow motion.

From his high vantage point, Luca could spy on the group with ease, but he guessed they weren't able to spot him from the ground.

He rubbed his eyes sleepily and admired the round ass and smooth legs of one student in the back row. She stood out because of her stunningly curvy body, and because she was the youngest one in the class by about twenty-five years. Her hair was the same color as Skylar's, he noticed. Her body was a similar shape, as well. She wore only a black sports bra and tiny black shorts while everyone else was in long spandex pants and baggy T-shirts.

"Okay, turn to the back of your mats and go into warrior two," the teacher said in a strong voice.

The students were facing Luca now, arms in the air. He zoned in on the half-naked girl with the nice ass.

*Oh.*

It was Skylar. Her long hair was pulled into a ponytail and her pretty face was flushed and shiny with perspiration. She seemed focused like a laser on the tip of her outstretched right hand.

Was he going to see her every day now? This island was way too small. Or maybe she was teasing him by doing yoga near his house, figuring that he'd see her. He hadn't noticed the class on previous days, but maybe it was a Saturday-only thing. Last weekend he'd slept in.

Skylar was in good shape. Not rail thin, but toned and womanly. Her sports bra stretched tight across her chest and accentuated her cleavage. She had a perfect hourglass figure; her tiny waist and flat stomach flowed into sexy, wide hips.

Fearing she could see him, he shifted to stand behind a tall potted palm where he could look at her and not be detected. His stomach clenched because he knew he was acting like a pervert and being reduced to spying on this sexy woman made him feel slightly ridiculous, like a teenager; yet it also sent a thrill through his body.

"Face the sea and put your feet in the sand on either side of your mat. Spread your legs wide," the teacher said.

The class and Skylar turned away from Luca. Her ponytail hung down her back, between her shoulder blades. Her legs were a wide, upside-down V as her feet burrowed into the sand, and Luca saw that there were no sharp angles anywhere on Skylar's body, only long, sensuous curves.

Visions of her naked invaded Luca's thoughts. He fantasized about gripping her ponytail in his hand as he kissed her with fury, imagined her plump mouth open, moaning with pleasure, and this made him adjust himself. He had become hard again as he recalled her sweet-smelling perfume and the way she'd looked at him as he was about to kiss her.

He should take his uncle's advice and find another woman. Skylar was much smarter and more rational than his usual hookups. Too smart and too rational, which could lead to so many problems. He shook his head and went to go inside, but he couldn't tear himself from looking at Skylar's beautiful, bendy body.

The yoga teacher called out more instructions. "Slowly fold over, keeping your back flat. Then move forward from the hips. Breathe."

Skylar did, folding in half and resting the crown of her head on her mat. Luca stared at her, unblinking, his breathing shallow. Erotic visions tumbled through his mind, one after the other. Christ, she was flexible. Her shorts barely covered her ass, which was high and tight. If only she were here with him, bent over. Was she wearing anything beneath those shorts? He imagined sliding the fabric over her hips and easing his hard length into her. Then there was her sexy mouth, and how she would eagerly suck on his thumb, his fingers, his cock...

A pair of all-too familiar feelings washed over him: loneliness and desire. Luca went into the bedroom, stripped off his shorts and closed the French doors.

# CHAPTER SEVEN

Annalisa lay naked on the bed in the hotel room. She had hoped to leave for Palmira that morning but instead drew the curtains and jabbed at the buttons of the air conditioner. The Florida heat sapped her strength, leaving her sweaty, puffy and lazy. She inhaled deeply and, as it often did when she was in bed, her mind went to Luca.

She recalled how his parents had been away one weekend. Back then, Luca still lived with his parents. He'd invited her over and made dinner. They made love in the living room afterward on the sofa. He took her from behind, just as he liked.

"I think I'll keep you," she'd said after they finished, pressing a kiss to his forehead.

A week later he'd sent her a text breaking it off. That night she broke into his house and pleaded with him not to end their relationship.

Annalisa rolled over and plucked a razor blade from the nightstand. Stretching the skin on her inner thigh taut with two fingers, she carved an inch-long shallow line with the razor. When the tiny blooms of blood came, they brought relief.

# CHAPTER EIGHT

"You look unusually dressed up today. You got a job interview or something?"

Skylar watched as Matt, one of the photographers at *The Palmira Post*, eyed her little black dress. If someone at the paper looked nicer than usual, it was assumed by everyone that they were searching for a job and their departure was imminent. But she only wanted to appear extra professional for today's interview with Federico.

Oh, and sure. She also wanted to look good for Luca. She had on a simple wrap dress, the one thing in her closet that made her always feel confident and beautiful. It showed off just enough cleavage. Too much, James had said when she bought it, but screw him.

Patent leather nude heels were on her feet and she hoped they looked serious and conservative while making her legs look long. Her thick hair was straight thanks to a marathon blow-dry session, and it hung down past her shoulders, although it was about to frizz due to the stupid humidity.

"Whatever, Matt. I'm glad you wore your finest cargo shorts and polo shirt to take photos of Florida's best-known attorney."

"Hey, he's a man of the people, right? He'll like me. I'm a man of the people, too," Matt joked in his rich North Carolina accent. He and Skylar were in Federico's driveway, about to walk up to the door. They had arrived in separate vehicles.

"Damn, this is a nice place," Matt said in a low voice as they stood on the doorstep. "I guess we should've become lawyers."

The home was a luxurious, two-story Florida beach mansion fit for a multimillionaire. The salmon-colored stucco and red barrel-tiled roof looked like lots of Mediterranean-inspired homes on Palmira. Squat palm trees lined a circular driveway, and a fountain with intertwined dolphin statues spurted water into a pool framed by a wide patch of tropical landscaping. It was the type of place everyone up north dreamed about.

Skylar rummaged around in her red leather handbag, making sure she had extra pens and paper. A nervous feeling invaded her stomach. She wasn't concerned about the interview, though. She was anxious over seeing Luca.

She rang the bell. The door opened, and Skylar beamed.

Luca.

"*Ciao*," he said. He was barefoot and wearing faded jeans and a slightly tight white T-shirt. Somehow he appeared rumpled yet put together, as if he had crawled out of bed and donned an expensive yet casual outfit for a fashion shoot. The look was both lazy and lusty, and she imagined unbuttoning his jeans and sinking to her knees.

She inhaled with a start, desire coursing through her. These surges of lust needed to stop.

"Hi," she managed to say. "This is Matt, the paper's photographer."

The two men shook hands, and Luca stepped aside to let them enter. Already Skylar noticed how he couldn't stop looking at her, how the corners of his eyes crinkled into a smile whenever their glances met. She reminded herself to be professional and concentrate on her article and the man she'd come to profile. Like she'd been taught during school and her internship.

Luca led her and Matt through an empty, high-ceilinged foyer. Skylar noticed a grand, curving staircase leading to the second floor, but they walked down a long hallway that flowed into the kitchen, a large and gleaming space with stainless steel appliances and black marble countertops. Skylar spotted an expensive-looking espresso machine and a blender that she coveted for smoothies but couldn't afford on a reporter's salary because it was four hundred fifty dollars.

Federico was sitting and reading *The Post* at a table nestled into a breakfast nook near a large picture window. He stood and extended his hand.

"Skylar, it's great to see you."

"You too, Mr. Rossi. This is Matt Reese, our photographer. Thank you for letting us profile you. I think Matt has another assignment, so if the two of you would like maybe you should get the photo out of the way first."

Matt nodded and turned to the older man. "Mr. Rossi, I'd like to shoot you in front of the tropical plants out front. I might need a light meter, though, and it's in my car. Want to come with me outside?"

"That's fine, Matt. Luca can take care of Skylar here in the kitchen."

*Take care of?* Skylar slid onto a seat in the breakfast nook and felt her face turning red. Had Luca mentioned their encounter to his uncle?

Luca leaned near the sink, not speaking. It made her uncomfortable. He wasn't smiling, just appraising her with those eyes. Today they looked more green than grey. Why was he staring at her? He was so seriously sexy that she almost couldn't stand to be around him. She babbled and flashed him a big smile.

"How's your week? Have you reconsidered whether you're going to give me the exclusive about being the savior at the plane crash?"

Luca laughed. "You are very persistent."

She grinned.

"Have you ever had an authentic Italian espresso?" He rolled the 'r', and its sound reverberated through Skylar's body.

"I've had lots of espresso. Every day. I usually have a shot of it in my iced coffee. The café near the paper makes a great iced red-eye."

Luca raised his eyebrows. "Iced espresso. Hmmm. That doesn't sound authentically Italian to me. I'm going to make you the best coffee you've ever had."

His playful smile looked boyish and cute and made Skylar's stomach flip-flop. She watched him move around the kitchen, taking out a small aluminum pot and a tin of java. It looked like he hadn't shaved in days, and black stubble covered his chin and the skin around his mouth. She normally didn't like men with facial hair, but somehow on Luca it looked primal and inspired an equally primitive desire in her. Would his stubble chafe her skin while kissing? He had been clean-shaven the first time they kissed, and she shivered when she recalled the feel of his skin on hers.

He put a small silver coffeemaker on the stove then slid in across from her at the breakfast nook. His expression was serious.

"Skylar, would you do me a favor?"

"Sure."

"Could you not mention me in your article about my uncle? Would you do that for me?"

She frowned. This was odd. Luca definitely had something to hide. "I wasn't planning on mentioning you. The article's not about you. But why are you so worried about being in the paper?"

"I'm a really private person," he said.

Private? That was all? Weird.

Skylar leaned forward. "Fine. I can do that."

Luca beamed and extended his hand to sweep a lock of hair away from her face, which made her heart pound. He twisted the strand of hair around his forefinger and said, "*Grazie*. Thank you. And your hair looks beautiful like that, all sleek. You also smell good."

Federico and Matt's voices made Skylar sit up straight, and Luca uncurled her hair from his finger, pausing to stroke her cheek for a half second. She shot him a warning glance as a flash of heat ripped through her body.

Matt appeared, standing awkwardly in the middle of the kitchen with several cameras hanging off his shoulders and neck while Federico took Luca's place at the table.

"So," the older man said. "About this interview. I'm doing it on one condition. That you don't put my address in the paper."

Skylar arched her eyebrows. Did both Luca and Federico have something to hide? What a strange family—but handsome. Eyeing Federico, Skylar wondered what Luca's parents looked like and if they, too, were genetically blessed.

"Okay," she agreed. "That won't be necessary for the article. We don't put addresses in the Palmira People profiles. But your address is public record under Florida's open records law. Anyone can find you. Of course you're aware of that."

"Of course, my dear. But, off the record…?"

"Yes?"

"This home isn't in my name. It's in the name of a corporate LLC. For tax and other business purposes."

Was that odd? Skylar didn't know. She needed to ask her editor later.

Federico gestured to Matt. "Please sit down. Surely you have time for an espresso. Luca makes coffee the old-fashioned way, in a

Bialetti coffeepot. We have that nice automated espresso maker, and he uses something that's sixty years old!"

Luca grinned and took the pot off the stove.

"He also doesn't use a microwave. Can you believe this guy?" joked Federico.

"Oh, I'm with Luca, I don't own a microwave," Skylar remarked. Luca nodded and grinned while pushing buttons on the stove.

"Sky's a hippie girl," interjected Matt. "She's always trying to get everyone in the newsroom to eat kale and go to yoga."

Skylar rolled her eyes. Just because she was the daughter of a yoga teacher didn't mean she was a hippie. Sure, she had been trying to eat healthier after gaining weight her senior year at school, but it was better than living off pizza like everyone else at the paper. Still, she wasn't skinny. James had never let her forget that she would soon be—as he put it—a whale.

Federico looked at her. "Where did you go to school, Skylar? Is this your first job?"

"I went to Boston University. This is my first reporting job, but I interned at a paper in Boston. I had hoped to stay on there, but the newspaper business isn't so great these days. I need to learn how to shoot better video and take photos. I've talked Matt into teaching me some multimedia skills."

Luca shot Matt a raised eyebrow and opened a cabinet.

"She's not a bad photographer," Matt said. "But I'm guessing she won't be on Palmira long enough to learn anything from me. She's too good of a writer."

Luca slammed the cabinet shut, making Skylar jump from the noise. "Sorry," he said, taking the coffeepot off the stove. He poured espresso in four small cups and brought them one by one to Federico, Matt and Skylar.

"Sugar?" Federico asked.

Skylar shook her head. Matt nodded, and Luca pulled a small silver bowl out of a cabinet. He handed Matt a small spoon and set it in front of him.

"Y'all must be European," Matt said, heaping sugar into his cup and stirring. "Only Europeans drink coffee this way, with tiny spoons and tiny cups. I'm partial to a 7-Eleven turbo brew in a big ol' Styrofoam thing."

Skylar saw Luca wince. Matt gulped the coffee down and didn't notice.

"I gotta go. I'm supposed to take photos of a hundred-and-three-year-old man at a nursing home. He's Palmira's oldest resident. It's been great meeting both of you. Sky, I'll see you back in the newsroom."

Federico eased his trim body to standing with a grunt. "God, my knees. Old running injury. Matt, I'll walk you to the door."

"Ciao," Luca called to Matt.

Skylar sipped her drink. "It's delicious. It does taste different than the iced espresso. Less bitter. Maybe I'll switch."

"You need to learn how to make it properly," Luca warned.

"Maybe you can teach me," Skylar said, grinning more at the speed of her comeback than at him.

Luca laughed. "Maybe I will. I'm impressed you're drinking it like a real Italian, without sugar. Your photographer has less refined taste, no?"

"That's Matt. He's funny. He's a good ol' boy from North Carolina."

"Well, he seems enamored with you, that's for sure."

She smirked. What was that supposed to mean? Matt wasn't interested in her. And what if he was?

Federico came back, and she shifted in her seat. "So, Mr. Rossi, let's start."

"Of course. Do you mind if Luca stays and listens? He can learn how a professional lawyer handles an interview." The older man winked at her.

"Absolutely, of course he can stay." But Skylar didn't look at Luca. She wasn't sure she wanted him around because he was too much of a distraction. He stood a few feet away, leaning against the counter and staring. She had to mentally erase images of them kissing in the pool, her legs wrapped around the low V of muscles that dipped below the waistband of his shorts.

She took her smartphone out of her bag so she could record her interview, and somehow, her pen had tangled in the pages of the notepad. When she pulled the pad out of her tote, the pen clattered to the floor. Luca bent to pick it up. He handed it to Skylar, and their eyes met. A zing of pure craving shot through her body.

Federico chuckled.

Skylar steadied her shaking hands with a deep breath and asked her first question. Federico responded at length, with a touch of superiority in his voice, and Skylar wondered if arrogance was a Rossi family trait. Five questions took an hour for him to answer, and her hand hurt from writing so much. Still, she was getting into the rhythm of the interview because Federico was detailed and interesting, with stories about big-money trials and his thoughts on the state's medical marijuana debate. She almost forgot that Luca hovered nearby.

She got to her next question and paused. The paper's feature editor wanted her to ask Federico his opinion of the best grouper sandwich on Palmira. It was a stupid question. She had something a little tougher in mind. In fact, she had an entire list of hard questions to ask. She didn't expect Luca's uncle to answer most of them, but she went on a fishing expedition anyway. Sometimes the best articles came from asking the most random questions, she had discovered during her internship.

"Mr. Rossi, do you think you'll ever run for governor?"

He laughed, a genuine belly laugh. "It's funny you ask that, Skylar. I never say never. But, governor? Not right now. All I've ever wanted is to be Florida's lawyer."

"Surely you have the money to launch a campaign. You have a net worth of one hundred million dollars by some estimates."

Federico looked amused. "I'm not hurting for money. But I'm not eager to throw cash away on politics, not yet. I don't have the time. Maybe next year. I'm about to file a big class-action lawsuit this week."

"Really? Care to tell me about the case?"

"Sure, why not. You'll have the exclusive." He leaned toward Skylar and, as she nodded, her heart sped up at the thought of being first on a good story.

"We're suing DogMunch, the dog food company, on behalf of hundreds of pet owners whose dogs died after eating their product. We've found that the company ignored complaints and evidence that the food had toxic substances probably slipped in from the factory in China. I can get you some Florida dog owners for interviews if you want. It's a federal lawsuit, so this is a good national story."

Skylar beamed. Jill would love this, especially if they found a person with a warm, fuzzy photo of their now-dead pet. Jill loved animal stories that tugged at readers' heartstrings because they got lots of website clicks.

"Thank you," she said. "And can you send me a copy of the lawsuit before it's filed?"

Federico slipped on a pair of reading glasses that hung around his neck and squinted at his phone. "What's your e-mail?"

Skylar told him, and he tapped. "Done."

"Yes, it's those lawsuits I enjoy. Where I can stand up for the little guy. The regular person."

She arched an eyebrow. Federico had slipped into one of his TV commercials, it seemed.

"That reminds me," she said. "I have a few more questions. I'm not sure how these will work into the story, but I did some research on you and was curious about some things."

"Of course. Fire away."

"Your advertising has been controversial. I've read where you spend $20 million on television ads alone each year. Is that true?"

"It's about right. More or less. What I put out in advertising I get back in clients and settlements."

Skylar nodded. "Is it true that you started your career by suing insurance companies that wouldn't pay sinkhole claims?"

"It's true. I then branched out to other kinds of defense litigation, including personal injury."

"You have lots of outside business interests, is that correct?"

Federico tilted his head and narrowed his eyes. Skylar's mouth turned dry, because she was building up to a bigger question.

"Sure. I'm a rich man. I invest in a lot of things. What are you getting at?"

"Through public records, I've discovered that you're the part owner of a chain of check-cashing stores throughout the southeast. I'm wondering why you would invest in such a business."

Federico smirked. "Skylar. QuickChex is a legitimate business that complies with all local and state laws."

"Some think those businesses practice predatory lending. There's often high fees and interest rates, and they take advantage of people who can't get bank accounts because their credit is awful. Isn't that the opposite of the image you portray as a lawyer of the people, of the working class?"

"QuickChex provides a service. It complies with all local and state laws."

Skylar saw Federico's jaw tense and the muscles near his ear bulge. She wasn't sure how much of this part of the interview would get in the paper, but it was satisfying to uncover some details about a powerful man and ask him lots of questions.

"Right. It's legal. But is it ethical? Would you divest yourself of that business if you did run for governor?"

"I would have to think about that. What time is it? I think I need to jump on a call. I really appreciate your interest in the class-action lawsuit."

Skylar glanced at Luca. He was holding his espresso cup in mid-air and looking at her as if she'd suddenly grown a horn in the middle of her head. Was he offended by the questions she was asking his uncle? There was no way he could understand how reporters did their jobs.

She smiled serenely at both men. "Thank you, Mr. Rossi. I appreciate it. I'm sure my editor will love the pet food scoop."

They shook hands, and Federico turned to his nephew. "Luca, can you see Skylar out?"

Luca put his coffee cup in the sink. He took Skylar's, and their fingers brushed against each other. Their eyes met, and the needy feeling surged through Skylar's body again.

"We can go this way," he said, pointing to the hallway and guiding her down it with his hand on the small of her back.

His touch. Finally. It was all she had thought about for days.

As they made their way down the hall, she glanced into a room that looked like a den, a space awash in tan and light blue hues. Skylar had grown up in a small rental cabin in Vermont decorated with funky batik throws, Buddha statues and stacks of books. Luca's family could buy a thousand of her childhood homes, and the cool order in Federico's house both excited her and made her feel lacking, somehow.

Skylar wondered what Luca thought about this showroom setting. Was this how he lived in Italy? His parents were probably filthy rich, like Federico. No student loans for him to worry about.

Luca was behind her in the hall, and as she passed another room he called out.

"Oh, come look at the study and the garden," he said, sounding awkward.

Luca definitely wanted to eke out a few more minutes with her. Who would give a stranger a tour of the study? Admittedly, it was a gorgeous space. Hundreds of books lined two walls. Skylar's eyes stopped on an imposing mahogany desk. A brief fantasy floated through her mind of Luca picking her up and sitting her on it, spreading her legs and entering her as she bit his neck and dug her nails into his back. She glanced at him and looked to the desk, feeling embarrassed. Those sorts of thoughts didn't usually enter her mind during work hours. Or any hours, for that matter.

Skylar paused at a large picture window overlooking a tropical garden. Giant leaves and colorful flowers erupted over a patch of trim lawn. She pointed to a grove of angry red flowers that slightly resembled pineapples. The blooms jutted out from spiny green leaves and the entire plant looked prehistoric.

"Do you know what those are?"

Luca shook his head and stood next to her. His eyes were as green as the tropical foliage outside, and Skylar stammered because the color was so arresting.

"They're...they're called hurricane bromeliads. I learned this while covering a garden club meeting. They bloom in August and September. People in Florida say the more they bloom, the bigger the chance a hurricane will hit that year."

Her mind wandered, remembering how Luca's mouth felt on hers. She licked her lips and tasted her gloss.

"Skylar, you have pen on your chin," Luca said matter-of-factly, jarring her from the kissing fantasy.

*Gah. That's why he's staring at me. I'm a babbling, ink-stained wretch.*

"Oh! Where?" she asked, her hand flying to her face.

"On the left side of your mouth."

Skylar rubbed with her fingers, trying to appear dainty but certain she looked stupid—or worse, coarse. Like a trucker scratching his beard.

"Um, no, the other left," Luca said, stepping forward and taking her chin in his hand. His thumb grazed her skin and set her cheeks ablaze.

Skylar's mouth was open because she was in mid-gasp from his touch. Luca's thumb shifted and brushed her bottom lip. One slow stroke to the right. Another to the left. She inhaled and looked into his eyes as his touch sent a million volts through her body.

"It's gone."

"Thanks," she whispered, and inhaled his scent. It reminded her of limes and cinnamon and clean laundry. She wanted to lick his skin and bathe in his essence.

"I can't be this close to you and not kiss you," he said in a hoarse voice.

He bent toward her and their lips met. It was a ravenous, hard kiss, and she suddenly couldn't control the rhythm of her heart. She knew this was wrong, making out with a source's nephew after an interview. If the story on Federico was already published, she'd feel a little less unethical. But she couldn't stop kissing Luca. Didn't want to. The intensity was too startling, especially in the blazing light of day. A kiss this hot should be confined to the dark corners of night.

She explored the tip of his tongue with hers and her palm grazed the dark stubble on his chin. It was soft, not bristly, and the discovery made her heart melt everywhere.

He threaded his fingers into her hair, and she resisted the urge to curve her leg up to his hip. She broke away from his lips and watched with satisfaction as he gulped in a few breaths. She was breathing fast, too. Their first kiss in the pool had been hot, but what had happened just now was scorching.

"You asked my uncle some interesting questions," he said unsteadily, looking up at the ceiling as if to regain composure.

Skylar ran her finger down the smooth skin of his neck and smiled. Was it wrong of her to enjoy teasing him? "And I still have a few questions for you. About the plane crash and where you were."

He took her hand off his throat and kissed her palm softly while looking into her eyes. "How about this? Have dinner with me and I'll tell you."

The story on Federico would be published by then. And even if Luca was the rescuer of the plane crash victim, she couldn't write about him at this point. Or *could* she write about a guy she kissed? She'd have to think on that more.

"Deal."

### 

One night. That's all he would need. One night of crazy, erotic sex. With a woman who could share an intelligent conversation in the moments between their carnal pleasure, no less. After everything he had been through, didn't he deserve at least that?

As they stood in the den, Luca stroked Skylar's cheekbones with his thumbs. Finally. She was giving in to him. The idea of spending the night with her made him hard with anticipation. Oh, who was he kidding? He was already aroused from watching her in that sexy dress, grilling his uncle with those questions. The way she'd worn that knowing little smile was too alluring.

"God, you're so sexy." He groaned out loud, and she giggled.

"Stop."

"So, dinner. My uncle's leaving tomorrow, and I'm alone."

"Alone is bad."

He brushed his thumb over her lips again. Her eyes fluttered shut. *So sensual, this girl.* "Thursday night at seven?"

She nodded and opened her eyes.

Luca grinned and slipped his thumb into her mouth. She swirled her tongue around the tip of his thumb and stared into his eyes, and his cock throbbed with a disconcerting need. It would be so easy to take her right here in the study. Shut the door and fuck her on the couch. Or bend her over the desk and shove her skirt over her hips. Or press her against the wall. But that wouldn't be right, not for the first time at least. If he was going to risk spending time with her, he wanted both of them to enjoy it. For hours.

He took his thumb out of her mouth and kissed her forehead. "Let's get you to your car before I do something we both regret."

She laughed. "You're going to make me have regrets? I don't like the sound of that."

If only she knew.

"No regrets," he whispered, then he quickly kissed her again.

Skylar followed him out of the study. They went outside and stood in the driveway, the sensation in his groin uncomfortably tight. Why couldn't he control his body around her?

"Do you like your little Italian *macchina*?" he asked, patting her Fiat 500's roof. He'd seen the car the night they first kissed, but was so stunned that she didn't want to spend the night that he hadn't commented on her choice in autos.

"I...I love it. I bought it when I graduated from college. It's sky blue, after, um, my name. Sky." She paused and looked up at him. "That's kind of precious and silly, right? That I bought a car the same color as my name?"

He smiled. "I think it's...it's...adorable." And he did think that. Nervousness washed over him, as if he were a teenager talking to a girl for the first time. Actually, he hadn't even been this nervous as a teenager. He'd always been confident around women.

"I drove it down from Boston."

"You and your little car, all that way." He paused and peered in the window. "It's kind of messy inside."

"Yeah, I work out of my car a lot." She bit her lip, and a look of embarrassment crossed her face.

Luca straightened his posture. "Are you interested in the photographer?"

She turned, snorting. "Where did that come from? No. I told you. I'm not dating anyone. And I'm trying not to date journalists."

Luca half laughed. "You're 'trying not to date journalists'?"

She shook her head. "My ex-boyfriend was a reporter. A former war correspondent. After we broke up, I figured I'd try to stay away from reporters, editors, photographers. They're too complicated."

Luca laughed, hard. Hopefully not too hard. "Probably a good idea."

She smiled in return. "Thanks again for the coffee. I'll see you Thursday. It's actually great for me. I don't have to go into the office Friday because I've worked overtime since the plane crash."

"*Perfetto*," he said. "Perfect. We can make it a late night. Or an early morning. Or something."

She laughed, so he leaned down and held her face in his hands, gave her a long kiss on one cheek and then the other. When she let out a little sigh-moan, it took herculean willpower not to kiss her mouth again.

"*Ciao*, Skylar Shaw."

After saying that, Luca went quickly inside. If he lingered, the urge would be too strong to push her up against the Fiat, grab a fistful of her hair and kiss her long and deep in the hot sunshine. The thought of their bodies, sweaty and naked, made him swallow hard.

Maybe they would make love on the terrace lounge chair in the middle of the day.

Yes. There. And several other places.

Luca padded into the kitchen. He washed the dishes to give his restless hands something to do, but Skylar's light pink lipstick stained the rim of an espresso cup and kept his mind on her. It had been amusing to watch how she asked questions of his uncle. Luca was once a young, green reporter like that, naïve and filled with ambition. Those days were over, though, had been for years. Now he felt old and jaded. Skylar was still the sort of reporter who thought she'd find truth in everything she wrote. She didn't know yet that the truth was subjective on every story. She'd learn soon enough.

His initial impression of her as an amateur was wrong, though. Dead wrong. All her articles he'd seen were top-notch, and she'd been comfortable while talking with Federico. It wasn't easy for a new reporter to speak with such authority to a powerful man. She'd paused, scrunched her forehead a little but looked at her notebook and asked the strong questions despite any reservation. She had done her homework and researched Federico's finances—which seemed ethically challenged, Luca had to admit. He hoped to God his uncle wasn't involved in anything criminal, because he was putting his full trust in the man. He didn't have much choice. Federico was the only family he had.

Luca paused in reflection. His mother had spoken cryptically about his uncle, saying that Federico was a good man but that she hoped he would stay out of Italy for the sake of the family. How he wished he could go back in time and ask his mother what she meant. Soon he would get to the bottom of the tangled relationship between his parents and uncle, though. He didn't see how he could avoid it while staying on Palmira.

Speaking of hard questions, he shouldn't have asked Skylar if she was interested in the photographer. But he'd felt an uncharacteristic jolt of jealousy when Matt looked at her. He'd recognized the attraction in the man's eyes.

*Of course that buffoon thinks she's beautiful. She is.*

Luca emptied the grounds from the espresso pot into the trash, slapping the funnel containing the packed coffee against the garbage can.

*So, she doesn't get involved with journalists.*

*We'll see about that.*

# CHAPTER NINE

Skylar woke to an ink-black bedroom. With scratchy, unfocused eyes, she rolled over and fumbled for her smartphone. It was three in the morning.

This had happened before. An invisible alarm went off inside her on the night a big story was published. She awoke at the exact time *The Post* was delivered to the newspaper boxes and the one convenience store on the island. Those copies were always delivered first, before the home edition.

The Rossi story. What if she had made a mistake? What if the copy editors had inserted an error? What if she accidentally misspelled a name? While it was true that if she made an error the online version could be tweaked, the paper had been lately publishing its longer stories exclusively in print to gain subscribers. There was no way a longer story could be changed. If there was a problem, she'd have a dreaded correction in the following day's edition.

Anxiety rose in her chest as the scenarios rolled in a loop through her mind. She knew her feelings were irrational, obsessive even, yet they consumed her. Already she had lost track of how many nights this happened since she came to work at the paper. The anxiety had also consumed her the night before exams. When the panic first appeared in high school, her mother's suggestion to meditate more had ended in failure; Skylar couldn't stop the waterfall of anxiety. Other than her mother, the only person she'd ever told about the panic was James…who'd scoffed, ordering her back to sleep because she had no idea what real panic entailed.

Waiting until 7 a.m. to read the delivered paper wasn't possible.

Climbing out of bed, Skylar slid a pair of pink cotton pajama bottoms on over her underwear. She added a white zip-top hoodie over her T-shirt, shuffled on some yellow flip-flops and grabbed her car keys. She didn't bother doing anything with her wild hair because she didn't give a damn. This was no time for fashion.

She opened her front door. A wave of nighttime humidity struck her face, and her skin was slick with sweat within seconds.

After looking up and down the long corridor, she pressed the button lock on the doorknob and stepped out. Her grandmother had bought the condo years ago, and the neighbors were either elderly, year-round residents, elderly snowbirds, or youngish restaurant workers. Everyone's front doors opened to a shared, outdoor hallway, like a cheap motel.

She tiptoed down the corridor, aware that her neighbors' bedroom windows were just feet away. It was a squat, two-story building, and her unit was on the second floor. There were just two good things about the place: her small balcony that overlooked the beach and the fact that she owned it free and clear.

Creeping down the stairs, she went to her car, parked in its assigned space. She paused there, pawing in her purse and hoping she hadn't locked herself out again. A surge of relief went through her when she found her keys. She'd been absentminded recently, her thoughts on her articles, and left them inside the house. Because of that, she'd taken to keeping her bedroom window cracked just in case. As a sometimes crime reporter she'd considered whether this was safe but eventually scoffed at the thought someone would break into her mostly retiree-populated building. According to state statistics, Palmira was one of the most crime-free places in all of Florida.

Her heart pounding with trepidation, Skylar drove the three miles to the other side of the island and its one 24-hour convenience store. *The Post* van was there, and she watched from her car as the deliveryman exited the building. In another parking space, a shirtless guy covered in blurry tattoos smoked a cigarette while draped over the tailgate of his truck. Skylar avoided eye contact, but his skeevy gaze oozed in her direction.

"Hey, girl, you look fine as silk," the guy said softly as she walked past.

Shuddering, Skylar ignored him and hurried inside. She grabbed a copy of the paper from a rack and held it in both hands, scanned it while standing there, the fluorescent lights harsh against the newsprint.

It was stupid and old-fashioned how much of a thrill she got by seeing her name in print, but Sky felt a swell of pride when she saw her name. The article was above the fold, the headline stretching across the page. Matt's portrait took up four columns. Skylar smiled a little. The story was exactly as she had written. Nothing was misspelled. It was perfect.

She glanced up to watch the shirtless guy's truck pull away and exhaled with relief. Picking up two copies, she beamed at the clerk and handed him a fistful of change.

"That's me," she said, pointing to her byline.

"Oh yeah?" asked the sleepy-eyed clerk. "I don't ever look at that rag."

Her nostrils flared and she stifled a frustrated sigh. Sometimes she wondered why she worked so hard when few seemed to read the paper or care what was in it.

### 

"*The Miami Herald. The Tampa Bay Times. The St. Augustine Record.*" Jill tossed printouts of stories from the state's big newspapers onto Skylar's desk, which was strewn with stacks of paper, pens with chewed caps and empty iced coffee cups. "*The Jacksonville Times-Union. The Palm Beach Post.* Even *El Nuevo Herald.* All credited *The Palmira Post* on the dog food lawsuit story from Rossi. Nice job."

Skylar grinned. Kind words weren't easy to come by in the news business, and neither were statewide scoops for a small-town reporter. "Thanks. It was nothing, I guess. He really opened up to me."

Matt the photographer strolled past her desk. "Yeah, Skylar did awesome on that story. I think Rossi's nephew was also *intrigued* by her."

He winked and walked toward the photo department. Skylar scowled at him and stifled a laugh. He jokingly stuck out his tongue, but only when he was behind Jill's back.

Since starting at *The Post*, Skylar had come to realize newsrooms were like adoption into a slightly crazy, profane family. Everyone cared—or at least pretended to care—what the others were doing each day. She had never known her dad, and her mom died when she was seventeen, so the newsroom camaraderie was welcome. It made her feel part of a team, part of something important.

"Rossi has a nephew?" Jill asked.

"Yeah, remember? He was the one I thought helped the victim at the plane crash. I think he's just visiting here from Italy." Sky shrugged, not wanting to appear too eager to find out more.

Jill tapped her ballet flat on the dingy newsroom linoleum. She was tall and wiry, with a dark bob flecked with grey strands. Her style was elegant and consistent: flowy black pants, a black tank top and a silver statement necklace. She looked more like a New York gallery owner than a hard-edged newspaper editor. Sky figured that Jill was in her mid-fifties and had been in newspapers forever. She had won a big prize for a wire service on a story about a corrupt southern governor, then had taken the job as editor of *The Post* a year before Skylar arrived. *The Post* was unusual for a community paper; because so many island retirees subscribed and so many businesses advertised, it enjoyed a larger staff than other publications its size. It won awards and was known in the industry as a training ground for good writers.

"Hmm. Okay. What are you doing today? You just sitting around the office? You're not gonna find a story here."

Sky blinked nervously. "I know. I'm leaving. Headed over to the police station to look at arrest reports and get some documents about that military surplus project. I also found out about a big vandalism case at the high school. The cops arrested some kids for smashing computers and spray-painting the gym."

Jill made a satisfied sound. As she walked off, she pointed at Emily, who was strolling into the newsroom. "Skylar, talk to Emily about that story. Maybe those kids involved in the vandalism are athletes and we can turn it into a bigger article."

"Hey, girl." Emily came over and gave Sky a hug. Em was her best friend in the newsroom. They were both from New England. Em was three years older, and her accent made Sky homesick.

Em shoved aside a stack of newspapers and pointed to a copy of *The Post*. "Great story on Rossi. He's hot for an older dude. If I wasn't dating Jimmy, I'd ask you to introduce me."

They both dissolved into laughter. Emily was tall and strawberry blonde, with a heart-shaped face and a tomboy's body. She wasn't drop-dead gorgeous, but she was sexy because she could make anyone laugh. She had dated guys of all ages, nationalities and persuasions, and she made no apologies for sleeping around. She thought Skylar should do the same. Jimmy was her latest conquest, but they seemed to be getting more serious now that they'd been together six months. Sky thought his big, boisterous personality matched Emily's Irish-Boston feistiness.

"God," Skylar said, "I haven't seen you in what seems like forever. How was your vacation on Cape Cod? How's your handsome cop boyfriend? Did he miss you? He helped me a lot on that plane crash. Took me behind the police tape so I could get close-up video of the plane with my phone."

"Vacation was good. I missed Jimmy, though." Emily leaned in to whisper, "We were reunited last night. And it 'felt soooo good.'" Emily crooned the words to the old song then leaned in to add, "Do you know what he did with the handcuff—?"

Matt interrupted by emerging from the photo department. Sky rolled her eyes in mock annoyance.

"Sky, did you tell Em about Rossi's nephew?"

"What?" Emily turned and pleaded for more information. "He has a nephew, Matt? Tell me, tell me, tell me."

Skylar let out a dramatic sigh. "Yes, he has a nephew. Luca."

Matt pinched Skylar's arm and teased, "Yes, Luca. Tall, dark and handsome Luca. He looks like one of those European soccer players. Excuse me, *futbol* players. And I think he's sweet on Skylar."

Emily's eyes widened and her mouth dropped open. "You did not tell me this, Skylar Shaw. Spill."

"There's nothing to tell. Rossi has a nephew from Italy. He makes great espresso. That's all I know."

Emily and Matt stood over her, nodding and smiling and clearly not believing they'd gotten all the gritty details.

She burst out laughing. "Okay, he's really hot," she said. "Like, insanely hot. With an accent."

*And his kisses are wicked and erotic and addictive. Not that I'm going to tell you that. Yet.*

Matt's cell rang and he wandered away, muttering something about how American guys never got any respect. When he did, Skylar leaned toward Emily and spoke in a stage whisper.

"Get this. I'm going out with Luca tonight."

Em grinned. "Sweet! Finally, you're going on a date. Where's he taking you? He must be loaded if his uncle's any indication."

Skylar shuffled some papers, trying to straighten her slovenly desk. Should she tell Em about the hot kiss in his pool? About the kiss after the interview? She wasn't positive she'd let this date go where Luca obviously wanted, and Emily would push hard for information.

"He invited me for dinner."

"Ooh. Romantic. Very serious for a first date. How's his English? Or will you be mostly using body language?"

No, she would definitely keep the kiss private. For now.

She smiled at her friend. "His English is perfect."

"And do you feel safe being alone with him? I know you're wary after Douchey McDoucherson from Boston."

Skylar frowned. She hadn't told Emily all *that* much about James, only that they'd had a bad breakup. And that he'd been rough with her once. Still, she was glad her friend was looking out for her.

"Yeah, I feel safe with Luca, but it's weird. I looked into his background and did a full Google search and didn't find anything. In fact, I checked him out twice. Once, right after I met him, and then again when I found out his last name and that he's Rossi's nephew."

*And not finding anything about him online bugs me even more because I know he has something to hide.*

"Nothing? No Facebook? No Twitter? No arrests?"

Skylar shook her head.

"Bankruptcies? Back child support orders? Photos of him posing with baby tigers?"

Skylar laughed. "Nope."

"Hmm. Let's see. You said he was from Italy, right?"

"Yeah. Naples. He's a grad student."

"Then you need to do a search in Italian. Make sure your language filters are set the right way and you'll only get Italian results. I'll bet you were searching only in English."

Skylar shook her head, annoyed at herself. "That's a good idea. Hopefully I'll have time after I go to the police station and before dinner. Thanks, Em. I should have thought of that."

Her friend squeezed her arm. "Sky? Text me when you leave tonight and when you get home, okay? I'll be at Jimmy's, so if you need us we're around. Or, text me to let me know you're having a hot time and are staying over at his house. I definitely want to hear all about *those* details. I've never been with an Italian man. Yet."

Skylar nodded and huffed out a little laugh, but anxiety gripped her stomach. Luca definitely planned to end their evening in bed, but she had other ideas. It was still too soon.

# CHAPTER TEN

Skylar paused at Luca's door. Looking down, she ran her hands over her hips and down her thighs, smoothing her long, light pink cotton dress. It had spaghetti straps, hugged her curves and didn't make her feel fat.

Taking a deep breath, she rang the bell. A half-minute later, Luca pulled open the door. He wore khaki cargo shorts and a white linen button-down that set off his olive skin. No shoes. He looked younger, probably because his shave was so precise and his skin looked so perfectly soft. She imagined pressing her nose and lips to it.

His green-gray eyes glittered as he smiled down at her. "Skylar. I'm glad you're here."

He reached for her hand, pulling her into his body and enveloping her into a hug after he shut the door. She closed her eyes as she inhaled his lime-spice scent. He touched his palm lightly to her cheek and planted a brief kiss on her lips. It was such a small gesture, but the feel of his mouth lingered on hers, tingling.

"Come." He drew away and led her by the hand into the kitchen, then out a door to the pool deck where they had shared their first kiss. He ushered her to a glass table under a navy blue umbrella where a candle flickered inside a hurricane lamp.

"Do you think it's too hot to eat outside?" he asked.

She shook her head, feeling unusually shy. "No. It'll be nice to see the sunset. Let's stay outdoors."

"Excellent. Why don't you sit and I'll bring you a glass of wine." He pulled a chair away from the table and motioned for her to sit. "Here."

She sank into the navy blue cushion and, as she slung her purse over the chair back, watched him walk off. Luca seemed nervous tonight also, maybe as nervous as she felt.

She hadn't paid much attention to it the night of the plane crash, but she looked around the deck and found it decorated in white rattan furniture with blue accents. The soft strains of chill, downtempo music floated from a speaker resting on a small table, and she became mesmerized by the rhythm and by the shimmer of the pool's blue water. Her index finger went to her lips and she touched them quickly, as if to confirm the heat on them was from Luca's mouth.

He returned with the wine and two glasses then uncorked the bottle. The cork made a small *pop* when he pulled, and he poured with an expert, fluid motion. His hands were strong, with long fingers. Skylar shivered when she imagined them entwined with her hair. Holding her wrists above her head, her body pressed into a bed with his weight.

"*Cento anni,*" he said, and they clinked glasses.

She took several small sips of the bubbly liquid. "Oh, it's not wine. Champagne?"

"It's prosecco. Like champagne, only Italian."

"It's delicious."

"When it's paired with peach nectar it's called a Bellini."

Would she ever stop swooning at the sound of his accent?

"I've never had a Bellini. It sounds yummy."

"They're perfect for breakfast. That's on the menu tomorrow morning."

So, he was indeed already planning a sleepover. An eternal optimist, apparently. She maintained her small smile as he grinned wider.

"I wanted to tell you again that I liked your articles. You're really busy. You did a good job on the story about my uncle. He seemed like a tough guy to interview."

"Why do you say that?" She tilted her head, her skin tingling at his praise.

"He's very…I don't know, commanding. Authoritative. But you showed a lot of confidence when you interviewed him. I was impressed."

Was she confident? People had told her that before. She guessed she projected confidence because of years of yoga classes and meditation at her mother's studio. Inside, she wasn't so sure.

"Thanks. All I've ever wanted was to be a reporter. I love to write. And I'm nosy. But you know that."

He laughed. "What's the weirdest story you've written here so far?"

"Hmm. That's tough. You mean, other than the orchid lady? And the one about your uncle, who talked about everything from dog food to smoking lawsuits to his torts class in law school?"

Luca grinned and rolled his eyes. "Federico's a trip."

"I'd have to say the weirdest story was about an alligator and a python getting into a death match at the Palmira Preserve on the north end of the island. Have you been there? It's an interesting place. It's a swamp. It's wild. A lot of Florida used to be like that before developers drained and filled and paved everything."

"Wait, what? An alligator? And a python? Got into a fight? No way."

She spun to rummage through her purse, extracting her phone. "Yep. I have photos. The fish and wildlife officer emailed them to me. This happened about a month ago."

When she leaned over to show him the photos, he wrapped his hand around hers that held the phone and tilted the screen toward him. His hand was so much bigger than hers.

"See? The python was thirteen feet long and the gator was six. Nobody won."

"That's not funny. But it is." Luca chuckled, and she guessed this wasn't typical date conversation for him. He leaned back and sipped his *prosecco*. "You said you grew up in New England. Why did you want to leave your family and come all the way down here?"

She gave him a look. "And you say that I ask a lot of questions. Sheesh."

He winked.

"My mom died when I was seventeen."

His mouth dropped open, and he reached down to squeeze her knee. "I'm sorry. I shouldn't have asked."

Lifting her shoulders in a shrug, she smiled. "It's okay."

He squeezed her knee harder.

"How did she die, Skylar? She must have been young."

Skylar was surprised by the tenderness in his voice as she launched into her stock answer, trying to sound breezy yet appropriately sad. The truth was, she was still devastated and rarely allowed anyone to know.

"She *was* young. Only thirty-eight. She died of melanoma."

"Wow. That's really awful. I'm sorry."

"Don't be. My mom was amazing. She raised me to be strong. So I'm strong." Skylar took a deep breath and mustered a grin. She always did that when she thought people pitied her because of her unlucky life. *Smile and fight on.* "And I don't mind answering questions, unlike some people."

It was her turn to wink at him.

"Okay, Skylar Shaw—your name is very sexy, do you know that?—I'll ask you all the questions I want."

Skylar said nothing, but God, was Luca adorable.

"How about your dad?"

"I never knew him. He left my mom when she was pregnant with me."

Luca nodded silently and looked into his glass.

Skylar swallowed, annoyed at herself. God, she was a downer. She wasn't going to get into the whole story about how her parents met at a music festival, fell in love, blah blah blah. How her dad ran out on her mom shortly after she was born. No. This wasn't first date material at all. But if it no longer bothered her, it wasn't worth talking about. She believed in forgetting about the past and moving on whenever she could, because if she didn't, the panic and sadness would catch up to her.

"Brothers or sisters?" Luca asked.

Skylar shook her head.

"So, no brothers and sisters, no mother and father. How can you afford to live on such a wealthy island on a reporter's salary? Are you an heiress?"

She looked at him, not sure if she was surprised or amused. "Wow. You really are asking a lot of questions. You should be a reporter."

He grinned and licked the side of his mouth.

She shrugged. "Because of my grandmother's condo, which I think I told you. I'm living rent-free, which is pretty awesome. I love it here. I used to come here as a little girl on winter break, so Palmira already feels like home to me." She sipped her prosecco, trying to stay casual. "You know, Luca, I feel like I'm being interviewed. I'm usually the one who asks the questions. I think you know my life story now. And what about you? I don't know anything about you."

He leaned over and brushed a quick kiss on her lips. "I think it's time for dinner."

### 

"*Mia cara, siediti sulla sdraio per favore.* That phrase in Italian means, 'my dear, please sit on the chaise.'"

Skylar was a little tipsy from the prosecco and the bottle of white wine they had shared over dinner. The pasta, little tube shapes bathed in simple red tomato sauce, had been out-of-this-world tasty. And the flow of Luca's Italian made her full with desire. He had peppered their dinner conversation with words and phrases.

As they talked, her words tumbled out of her mouth and her voice notched up a half-octave. She laughed a lot, and everything he said seemed fascinating. When he launched into a long explanation of how he made the pasta sauce, she nodded, rapt, then realized she had never before been so interested in the topic of tomatoes.

"Are you speaking Italian just to sound sexy and exotic?" she teased him at one point, giggling.

"Am I that obvious?" He grinned.

"Yeah. You are. I think you're trying to seduce me with food and your language."

That made him laugh, hard.

He didn't, however, seem eager to talk about his family or his work. She did find out some details about him, things that were interesting and curious and so very sexy: He loved old Superman comic books, he disliked peanut butter, he'd run the Boston Marathon when he was in boarding school.

Skylar quickly texted Emily, telling her everything was going well, then moved over to the wide chaise lounge as Luca picked up their plates to bring them inside. She kicked off her wedge sandals.

Luca paused at the foot of the chaise as she wriggled around, trying to get comfortable. "I saw that you post a lot on Twitter, and not just about news stories."

"Stalking me on social media again?" she teased.

"Maybe."

"The paper wants me to tweet stories and news tidbits. We're told to 'build our brand' as journalists."

He nodded. "Right. 'Your brand.' Um, I don't do social media at all, and I'd like to ask you not to post anything about me. Okay?"

*Weird,* she thought as he laughed and walked away. What was that supposed to mean?

She finished her wine, enjoying her buzz, mulling many questions. Luca was so private, but he seemed interested in her life, which was a welcome change from James. Never had a guy been so curious about her. She wondered about Luca's motives, but that thought instantly made her sad. Maybe this was how relationships were supposed to be. With James, he was always the star, sucking up all the attention, never caring about the details of her life.

Luca returned with a bowl of strawberries in his hand and sat next to her on the chaise. It was dark now, and he had lit several candles in different hurricane lamps around the deck. She studied his face, captivated. His dark brows, his strong nose, the distinct angle of his jaw under his ear—everything about Luca was so masculine.

"Why don't you want me to post about you on social—?"

With his thumb and forefinger, he plucked a strawberry out of the bowl and interrupted her question. "Can I feed you?"

She nodded and opened her mouth. He rested the berry on her tongue. She chewed, a tiny smile on her lips. He stroked her cheek with the backs of his fingers then fed her another strawberry.

"You're so sensual when you eat," he murmured. "I like watching you."

She didn't know what to say. Her cheeks flared and she lowered her eyes. She lay back, looking up at the summer night sky. He turned and put the bowl on a nearby table then sprawled on his side, looking at her.

Her eyes traveled to his linen shirt, and she gave in to temptation, tugging at his collar with her thumb and forefinger. "It's funny, I was under the impression that Italian men wore expensive suits and stuff. You're always casual."

"I'm in vacation mode. I do have a suit. And a collared shirt and real pants." His voice was smooth, like a caress.

"I'd like to see you dressed up someday," she ventured.

"I'll make that happen." He leaned in and planted a soft kiss on her cheek, then backed away.

"Great music. I love downtempo stuff," she murmured. She turned her body so that she faced him, propping her ear on her forearm and mirroring his posture. "Have you heard this album from Thievery Corporation?" she asked. "It's my new favorite."

"Which one is this? Is this *Saudade*? I love the songs on that."

"Yes. What's that word mean, anyway? Is it Italian?"

He shook his head. "Portuguese."

"What does it mean?"

"Hmm, it's difficult to explain in English…"

Luca inched closer to her. She wasn't wearing a bra because her dress had built-in support, but when her nipples hardened they still showed through the fabric. The downward flicker of his eyes meant that he noticed.

"*Saudade*." He drew the word out. "*Saudade* is an emotion. It's kind of the love that remains after someone is gone. How do you say in English, 'longing'? But it's more than that. It also refers to the love left behind after someone dies. Or a feeling for a person in your life right now who is going to disappear in the future. It's a little complicated."

He blinked slowly as he spoke, and she wondered if he was thinking of someone specific. Skylar was well acquainted with the feelings he described.

Luca's bare feet found hers, and his toe trailed across her arch. A current shot up her leg, and she grew even more nervous. They stared into each other's eyes. Skylar thought her heart would burst, it was beating so fast.

A new song played, sung by a woman with a sexy, ethereal voice. Luca studied Sky's face, his eyes resting on her lips as he spoke. "This one is my favorite. '*Sola in Citta.*' It's the only song in Italian on the album. The lyrics are beautiful."

"Translate for me," Skylar said.

Luca trailed his fingers up and down her bare arm, and goose bumps spread across her skin. "It's about a person in a new place looking for someone."

He spoke in a quiet, velvety tone. Sky closed her eyes, hoping to steady the slight dizzy feeling in her head. Was it the wine or him?

She inhaled, taking in the aroma of the ocean and his skin. He smelled so good. Spicy and warm and edible.

Luca's hand shifted to slide deeply into her hair, his palm caressing her neck and his thumb stroking her jaw. Her entire body ached with desire, but she wasn't sure exactly what she wanted. A kiss? A touch? Sex? She opened her eyes to look at him as he translated the lyrics.

"The first line goes, 'Where are you?'"

He spoke in a near-whisper, and she melted.

"Then it goes, 'I need to meet you.'"

Skylar realized she was holding her breath.

"'I want to feel you close.'"

She heard her heartbeat in waves inside her ears and shut her eyes.

"'I want to hold you close to me.'"

The song ended, and Luca's hand was still in her hair. He said, "Skylar."

"Luca," she whispered.

"You know what I've thought about all week?"

He didn't wait for an answer, just put his lips to hers, kissing her with force. She pulled back, breathless, and shook her head.

"This," he said. "I wanted to feel your lips."

She lay on her back and he was suddenly above her. He stroked the front of her neck with his thumb and her whole body trembled. Sliding her hands onto his arms, Skylar could feel the softness of his linen shirt under her fingertips and his hard muscles underneath the fabric.

"And kiss your face," he said, grazing her cheek. "And kiss your eyes."

Luca brushed his mouth against her closed eyelids, one after the other. Skylar was swimming in desire. Never had anyone kissed her so sensually.

"*Bellissima*," he whispered.

He kissed her again and grasped a handful of her hair and moved her head so that her ear was next to his mouth. Skylar loved how he moved her around, positioning her exactly the way he wanted. She wanted to let him do whatever he desired, and her willingness to give in scared her.

*Too soon. Too soon.* And into her lusty fog, James's unwanted voice intruded. *Your skin is too warm,* he'd criticized. *What's wrong with you?*

Luca pressed his lips behind her earlobe and trailed them down her neck. A bit of perspiration clung to her hairline. She wondered if he liked the way she felt, if she was the right temperature for him, if she was right for him in any meaningful way or if he was just sating a passing urge. Already Skylar could see herself falling hard for him, and she didn't need that right now. He'd surely been with lots of women. He was too gorgeous. Too worldly. Too confident.

*He will break my heart.*

But her thoughts dissolved as his tongue collided with hers and she caressed his chest.

He moaned a little as he kissed her and nibbled on her lower lip. One of his hands was on her thigh, inching the fabric of her long skirt upward. His touch was slow and teasing, and by the time he had worked the hem up to her knee Skylar's skin sparkled underneath his fingertips.

Her skirt slid up and he pressed himself against her as they stretched out. Their bodies were crushed together from chest to hip, and their legs tangled. His erection pressed into her, and she opened her legs wider and wondered if she would be able to resist him.

Luca propped himself up on his forearms and gazed at her. His lips were red and kiss-stung. She opened her mouth to speak.

"Do you have a question for me?" he asked, amused, kissing her nose.

She giggled. "Were you the—?"

With a mock roll of his eyes, he interrupted. "Guy who helped the plane crash victim?"

Their eyes locked, and they both laughed.

"You're kind of a pest, Skylar Shaw. But you're a sexy pest."

"I'm going to take that as a compliment."

"You should."

She ran her hands up the sides of his torso and could feel the wonderful muscles there. Slipping her hands under his shirt would be perilous, and yet, she wanted to touch his bare skin.

"You did help the guy after the crash, didn't you?" she pressed. "You're the Good Samaritan."

"Oh, I am good. Very good."

With a slow thrust, he pressed his hips harder against hers. She sucked in a breath and said, "I have no doubt about that."

"But I want you to find out just *how* good."

He kissed her, and Skylar tried to will away the throbbing need between her legs. Luca paused and gazed at her breasts. With the lightest brush of his thumb, he stroked a nipple poking through fabric, and her mouth opened in a tiny gasp.

"For argument's sake, Skylar," he said, "let's pretend I am the person who helped the plane crash victim."

His voice was raspy, and she nodded, trying not to whimper with desire as his thumb continued stroking. "Okay. And?"

He lowered his head and softly closed his lips around her pointed nipple through the fabric, tugged just enough to send a ripple of fresh heat through her body. Now she was unable to contain herself, and a small noise came from the back of Skylar's throat. Luca replaced his mouth with his hand, and he stared at her as he cupped her breast.

"Would you be able to write an article about me now that we've kissed? Now that I've run my hands through your hair? Now that you've felt how much I want you? Would that be ethical? Can you write an impartial article under these conditions about someone who can't stop thinking about you?"

She studied his face and released a breathy laugh. "Why are you giving me an ethics lecture?"

She couldn't take it anymore. With her hand on the back of his head, she eased him toward her, kissing her way up his neck until she found his ear, and then she put her lips to that soft lobe and nibbled until he groaned.

"Why are you driving me crazy, Skylar?" he said.

She ran her hands under his shirt and over the smooth skin of his lower back. The sensation was divine. Then she panicked a little. Sucking in a breath, she noticed that her skirt was hiked to her upper thighs and her underwear was showing. He was grinding into her. It was time to slow this down—*way* down—because she didn't want a repeat of James. She didn't trust herself to be able to read Luca's true motivations or character. She didn't want a one-night stand, no matter how much she lusted after him, and she sure didn't want to get involved with another man who would just put her down and make her feel like crap. Not that Luca had given her any inkling that he would do such a thing.

Luca's breath caught, and he gazed again at her breasts. His thumb stroked the edge of her dress as he inched the fabric downward, threatening to expose more skin.

"I want you," he whispered. "Will you stay tonight? I want you in my bed so I can play with you for hours and hours. Let's go inside. Please? I can beg if you want me to. It'll turn me on to beg you."

Skylar wriggled out from underneath him, sat up, and tucked her legs underneath her. She tugged her skirt down. Her dress was wrinkled and stuck to her hot skin. She tried, and failed, to catch her breath, instead shuddering out a big, sloppy inhale. Being around Luca was overwhelming, and she didn't want to tease him. It wasn't as though she was physically afraid of him. Quite the opposite, in fact. There was an underlying kindness, a gentle undercurrent about him, that made her trust him. But...

"I'm sorry. We need to tone this down." Her voice was firm, but inside she was scattered.

He sat up and smoothed her tangled hair with a gentle hand. "Don't worry. I have condoms. And I've been tested recently. I went to the doctor when I first arrived on Palmira and I haven't been with anyone in a while."

She had to admire his honesty, but shook her head. "It's not that. It's... I'm not ready to sleep with you. Please don't be angry."

"Hey, hey. *Mia cara*." He took her face in his hands. "I'm not angry. At all. But can I ask why?" He paused. "Are you a virgin?"

"No," she said.

He brushed his lips over hers very quickly. "Okay. Are you religious?"

She shook her head.

"So you're not attracted to me? You seem like you're attracted to me."

She rolled her eyes. "I am crazy attracted to you. I think that's why I'm not ready. You kind of scare me."

"You're attracted to me but you're not ready to be with me? I don't understand. And I'm not trying to scare you."

"I know you're not. But I don't want just a one-night stand."

"Okay," he said with a foxy smile. "How about if you stay all weekend? It's only Thursday, so we have until…what? Monday morning?"

She swatted him on the thigh. "You know what I mean."

"I guess." He stroked her cheek with the back of his fingers. "I've found American women were more, I don't know, open about sex."

She shot him a skeptical smirk. "Yeah, and?"

"American women are feminists who like casual sex. So…what happened to you?"

Skylar raised her eyebrows. "What happened to me?"

"I assumed you'd be like that."

"Like what?" Her voice was icy. "Easy?"

He smiled and nodded.

She sighed. Men could be so obtuse. "Being a feminist isn't about casual sex or no sex. It's about making the best choices for me and my body. That changes from day to day, situation to situation. Right now, in this moment, I'm bit guarded because of something, someone, in my past. And because I don't know you. And because you have stupid assumptions about American women."

"Fair enough, I guess." He ran his hand up her bare calf, leaving sparks in its wake, and Skylar shivered. Why couldn't she just be like any other twenty-two year old and have a casual hookup?

"And anyway," she managed to say, "I get the impression that you've had lots of sex—and good for you. That's totally cool. But you're a bit judgmental about American women taking control of their bodies and their sex lives."

He shrugged. She put her hands on the tops of his thighs and rubbed. He sure was sexy, but it seemed he had some caveman-like beliefs. She'd have to prove to him otherwise, if he'd let her.

"If an American woman wants to sleep around," she asked, "how is that any different than you, an Italian man, sleeping around and never committing to one woman?"

Luca lifted his shoulders again.

"I think that's probably what you want from me anyway. Just sex."

"How do you know what I want?" he growled.

She pulled at the hem of her dress. "I don't even know if you have a girlfriend. Or a wife."

He laughed. "No girlfriend. No wife. Promise."

"Good to know," she said. "But I take it you're not looking for one, either. And that's okay, because I don't want to get married or anything. I just don't want to be used."

Luca's expression grew troubled. "I'll admit I can't promise you anything long-term, but not for the reasons you think. I don't want to use you. I don't know how long I'll be on Palmira. I'm hoping for a few months. But...I like being with you. I want to make love to you. Let's just see where this goes, no?"

"I'd like to take it slow," Skylar replied. "You're fun. As far as the sex, you'll have to wait. I'll understand if you don't want to, though." She glanced at him. Maybe he would be honest enough about wanting no-strings-attached sex, say goodbye, and she could move on with a bit of dignity.

He was silent as he chewed on his bottom lip. She knew this would be their first and last date, because he would never agree to what she was asking.

"You're not used to waiting, are you?" she said.

He shook his head. She re-buttoned part of his shirt because his chest was distracting.

"Guys like you don't wait, do they?"

He cocked his head. Then he answered. "But I will. For you."

She was shocked into speechlessness, and she narrowed her eyes in disbelief. "Really?"

He nodded. "I know you don't believe me. But I'll wait. I think you're worth waiting for. But answer one question. What are *you* waiting for, Skylar? Why deny yourself pleasure? And weren't you going to use me to get to a good story?"

"That's three questions," she said.

He growled and kissed her.

"My last relationship was pretty toxic," she said when he pulled back. Her mouth was still tingling. "I want to make sure I'm fucking someone for the right reasons and not because I'm being manipulated or used."

Luca put his finger to her lips. "Hold on. I'm not going to fuck you. That's not what I want. I'm going to make love to you. *Fare l'amore.*"

"Hmm." She was skeptical. Wouldn't this be what he'd say if he *was* a player?

"Say it in Italian. *Fare l'amore.*" He kissed her nose.

*"Fare l'amore,"* she repeated.

"Very nice."

She shook her head, trying steel herself against his flirtation. "I don't know. I also want to make sure that you don't think I'm boring, or fat, or lame in bed. And I want to make sure you're not...like my ex-boyfriend."

Luca scowled. "Did your ex tell you that? That you were boring, fat, and lame in bed?"

She nodded.

"He's not here on this island, right?"

She shook her head.

"Good. Because I'd have to have a word with him, and it probably wouldn't be a pleasant one. In fact, I'd probably want to kill him. And I hate violence. But hearing that makes me angry." He leaned over to take her in his arms. "You're none of those things, you know that, right? You're the opposite. You're gorgeous. Your body is perfect. I want to devour you."

"Whatever." She rolled her eyes, but it felt good to hear. "Do you think I'm a tease?"

"Maybe a little. But teasing isn't a bad thing. It makes me want you more. If you want to tease me, go ahead. I'm looking forward to teasing you, too. This will just make it so much sweeter when we do end up together." He kissed her deeply, then paused and placed his forehead to hers. "You're going to be the one to decide when we should have sex. *If* we should. It's all up to you. I'll feel better if you're comfortable and really want to be with me."

"So"—she stared deep into his eyes—"if I go home now because I feel like things are getting out of control, you'll want to see me again?"

"Yes."

"You're not going to pressure me to fuck...uh, have sex every time we're together?"

He smiled. "Nope. No pressure. But don't mistake that for me not wanting you. Because, when you're ready, I'll be ready. I want you very badly."

She didn't ask the obvious question, but it loomed in her mind. Would he still be around by the time she was ready for him?

She didn't ask because she didn't want to know the answer.

### ###

Luca sat alone at the edge of the pool, his feet and calves dangling in the water. He sipped from a full glass of wine, swallowed and then grimaced. A humid breeze barely cooled his hot skin, which still blazed from kissing Skylar goodbye.

"You're dangerous," she'd whispered to him right before she left.

"You don't know how dangerous, *mia cara*," he'd responded. *If not wholly intentionally so.*

Swirling his feet in circles underwater, Luca wondered why he was so captivated by Skylar. The American girl was frustratingly bewitching. She could turn into a bit of an obsession if the frequency of his thoughts about her were any indication. And all because she kept putting him off.

Or was there more to his interest?

He couldn't get her orange blossom scent off his skin. He could practically feel her breath on his neck and her warm lips on his. And how she talked, animatedly, about writing and books.

Her intelligence was a turn-on. And her eyes, big and ocean-colored, made his heart crash around his chest. He wanted something he'd never desired before: to get to know a woman perfectly. What made Skylar tick? What motivated her? How had she become so strong after her mother died?

No matter how many times he pleasured himself to the thought of her, the end result was the same. He wanted her. Desired her more each time he saw her. It defied explanation and reason. When Skylar eventually said yes to him, the erotic rush would be so worth the wait. Almost like getting a tough source to agree to an interview then listening in fascination as the person bared their secrets. That's what being with Skylar would be like. She would let him in, drop that eggshell-thin yet impossibly tough exterior and reveal her innermost desires. Once she gave herself to him they would be explosive together.

Wanting her, and the buildup to their sex, would eclipse all of his other worries in the coming weeks. Skylar's surrender, her vulnerability and her secrets had the potential to turn him on more than a thousand models. Although…something about her little lecture about feminism and sleeping around unsettled him. Did she really think of him as promiscuous? *Was* he? It had never occurred to him that he had a double standard about promiscuity. How odd, that with a few words Skylar could make him look at something differently.

Although he wanted her, he'd have to soon tell her that he definitely couldn't have anything serious. The thought of having that conversation made him feel guilty, because he hadn't been totally upfront like he normally prided himself on being. He was a hypocrite because of his circumstances. He wished his life wasn't so screwed up, otherwise he'd just let the relationship unfold normally. Like a normal person.

Frowning, he opened his eyes and glanced down at his phone, wondering if she would actually text him like he asked to confirm she had arrived back at her condo safely. He sighed at the phone's blank screen and swiped at an app, making sure that his incoming and outgoing text messages were encrypted. Her safety was a priority to him, even though she wasn't aware of it. Plus, her confession about her parents and her ex-boyfriend had touched something soft and protective inside of him. She was alone, with no one to look out for her.

Skylar was like him in more ways than one. Broken. Hurt. Maybe not as broken and hurt as he was, but he detected a melancholy in her. He could make her joyful for a while, if only she'd let him. God knows she'd already lifted his mood.

So, he would wait. It was early August. Skylar was his summer fling. Autumn was still weeks away in Florida.

His phone buzzed with a text. It was her, and she was home safe.

He caught himself smiling, and that made him frown. In the short time that he'd known her, she'd affected him like no other woman. So, maybe he should walk away. That would be the safer route. Safer for both him and for her. After what happened to Annalisa in Italy... His mood instantly soured when he thought of the woman he'd slept with a couple of years ago while working at the newspaper. They'd been colleagues and he'd told her he wasn't interested in anything serious, which was his usual speech. She'd taken it hard, but they'd eventually parted friends. She was a good woman, a talented writer. Then his book came out and his parents were murdered. A week later came an ominous, anonymous letter saying that Annalisa had disappeared. That's when he'd left Italy.

That's when he'd realized that he couldn't be a normal person anymore.

It made sense for him to be concerned about Skylar's safety, but his uncle kept reminding him he was secure here. Things seemed calm. Bruno Castiglione was under house arrest and awaiting trial. Surely Skylar wasn't in danger. Right?

He tapped out a text to her.

*Sweet dreams, mia bella ragazza.*

# CHAPTER ELEVEN

When she drove over the bridge to Palmira Island in her rented Toyota, Annalisa felt like a caged panther, trapped. It was a surprisingly small place. But she wouldn't be here long. Luca would surely want to take her somewhere even nicer.

Methodically she drove the road that circled the island, noting all of the quaint stores and bars and restaurants. Where could Luca be? The area was so small that she could practically go door to door looking for him—and she would, if it came to that. Americans were so friendly, surely someone had seen him and would tell her. He would stand out here like a sparkly vampire in a teen movie, she thought with a laugh, passing older retirees on three-wheeled bikes and golf carts. He was probably going crazy on Palmira, bored out of his mind.

She found the Sand Castle Hotel, which looked both run-down and like a 1960s beach movie set. Online it had looked quaint and clean. Now she wasn't so sure, and that sent her into a snit.

Pouting, she flounced into the office. An older man smiled.

"I have a reservation. The last name is De Rossi." Of course she would register under a fake name. Why not one similar to Luca's?

"Yes, miss. You're in room 110. Great view of the water and the sunsets."

Annalisa filled out the paperwork quickly, thankful that she had taken time to practice her English while in the hospital. Her stepfather's words came back to her. *"You're beautiful and brilliant, but you're just not right in the head."*

"You from Italy?" the hotel desk clerk asked, sucking his teeth.

She nodded and shot him a tight-lipped smile. "How did you guess?"

"Your name. Your look. My father was in World War II and he brought home photos of all the pretty Italian girls. Like you."

She laughed.

The man slid a key attached to an aqua-colored piece of plastic toward her, then a few tourist brochures and pointed with his pen to a number imprinted on the plastic. "Here's your room. We have breakfast every day from seven to ten. Coffee, pastries, juice. And here's some things to do around Palmira. Of course you'll go to the beach." He patted a folded map. "And there's a nice shell museum."

Annalisa forced a tight smile. When would he stop talking?

The man unfolded another brochure. "This is pretty neat. Palmira Preserve. Hardly anyone goes there anymore. There's boardwalks over the swamp. Lots of birds, turtles, big alligators. Might want to check it out if you're looking for something different."

No fucking way would she go there. Annalisa shuddered.

"Tell me," she said, scooping up the key and pamphlets. "I heard that a well-known Italian-American lawyer has a home here on Palmira. Maybe you know him? Federico Rossi?"

The man's mouth dropped open and he pointed at her. "That's so funny you ask. I was just reading about him." He turned and rifled through a stack of newspapers on a shelf, then handed her one. "Here. That's the local rag. *The Palmira Post.* He's got a big case coming up. They did an article."

Annalisa looked at the front page. There, in full color, was Federico Rossi. He was striking, and his eyes were so similar to Luca's that she almost gasped. Shooting her sexiest smile at the clerk, she lowered her eyes to scan the headline: **PART TIME PALMIRA RESIDENT FILES CLASS-ACTION LAWSUIT ON BEHALF OF PET OWNERS.**

"Oh, miss? I almost forgot. I need a driver's license. Or a passport. For my records."

"Of course."

Extracting her Gucci wallet out of her matching purse, Annalisa took out the fake license she'd bought on Miami Beach a week before and handed it to the man, who studied it.

"Sabrina De Rossi. Any relation to the lawyer?"

She shook her head. *Not yet.* "He's Rossi. I'm De Rossi. They're variations on a common name in our country."

As he scribbled down the pertinent information she scanned at the byline on the newspaper article. *Skylar Shaw.* Annalisa frowned, wondering if that was a man or a woman's name. Sometimes it was difficult to determine the gender of English names. *Skylar.* It sounded like a little boy's name. And Skylar was another possible way into finding Rossi, and maybe even Luca.

"How do I get in touch with this reporter?" she asked the clerk, tapping on the newspaper. "Do you know Skylar?" She wasn't even sure she was pronouncing the name correctly.

The clerk shook his head. "The paper's downtown, on Main Street. Near the Bacchus wine bar. I'm sure you could just stop in and ask."

Annalisa carefully tucked the newspaper under her arm and went to her car. She flung the brochures on the dashboard and grabbed her bag. From there she went to her dank, shabby hotel room, and she sank into a hard chair straight out of a mid-century museum exhibit and pored over the newspaper article. The story was all about a pet food lawsuit, Rossi's political ambitions and his background as a young lawyer.

*Useless.*

Scowling, she took out her phone and pecked out the name "Skylar Shaw" and the words "Palmira Post" into a search engine.

*Check out the latest tweets from Skylar Shaw.*

Annalisa tapped on the link. She tapped again to see the profile picture.

*Fuck.* Skylar Shaw was a woman. A young, gorgeous woman. A little on the plump side, but definitely pretty. She had big, innocent blue eyes, and Annalisa would have liked to be her friend.

In another lifetime.

Annalisa wished she hadn't seen Skylar's photo. Now she'd obsess all night, maybe all week, that Luca had met this reporter. She would think and think and think until the pressure grew too great, and then she would have to slice her skin until she felt calm again.

# CHAPTER TWELVE

"Skylar, let me get this straight. You went to hot guy's house for dinner. The two of you had good conversation, lots of laughs and a hot kiss. Then he was okay when you said you wanted to take things slow and not fuck on the first date. He said he'd call you. I'm not exactly seeing the problem here."

Emily and Skylar were each on their first beer while sitting poolside at Skylar's condo, dissecting Luca's words and the previous evening. It was Friday afternoon, and Skylar had the day off because she had worked so much overtime. It felt decadent, almost like she was on vacation, to be lounging with her best friend on what was normally a workday. Normally she didn't like beer and never drank in the middle of the day, but the rarity of a day off seemed like a good time to loosen up.

Sitting on a chair beneath an umbrella, Skylar wore a floppy straw hat, while Emily sat in the sun. Although she loved being outside in Florida, Skylar was wary of the UV rays because of her mother's lethal skin cancer. She was also skeptical of Emily's assessment. The farther she got from his good looks and charm, the more she questioned exactly who he was.

"Doesn't it seem weird? Why wouldn't he talk about his family or his past? And why would a guy *that* good-looking want me?"

Emily rolled her eyes. "Are you fucking kidding me? Don't start. You don't need me to remind you that you're hot."

"I'm fat."

"You're curvy and men love that. Jimmy said all the cops talk about your ass."

"Whatever." Sky grunted at the thought of cops discussing her body and took a long sip of beer.

Emily sighed. "Skylar. Calm down. Who knows? Luca sounds a little old-fashioned, but honestly he also sounds kind of sweet. At least he's definitely not just some bro dude who demands to fuck and run. Maybe he *is* just private. You should be happy. This sounds promising and fun. Damn, I'd screw his brains out the next time I saw him. What's the big deal? As long as you know what you're getting going in."

Emily drained her Corona, and Skylar just stared at her. She wished she could be so practical about sex herself.

"You're always looking for the bad," her friend continued. "Remember when you were trying out OKCupid last month and you got a perfectly nice message from that marketing guy in Tampa? You texted something to me like, 'Just got a well thought-out, kind message from a cute guy. He must be a serial killer.'"

Skylar sighed. Emily was right. She was too hard on men. And on herself.

"Yeah," she muttered. "Damn James."

The mention of her ex's name elicited a wary stare from Emily. "Christ. How many times do I need to say it? You need to forget about that asshole."

Skylar mumbled an agreement. "Did I ever tell you the final straw?"

"No," Emily said, "but I can't hate him any more than I already do. After you told me that he pushed you off the bed I didn't want to know more. Really, Skylar. You're so strong and tough. You put yourself through college. You're an orphan. How could you let a man do that to you?"

Skylar winced at the word *orphan*. "I sound like a cliché, but the emotional abuse just kind of happened subtly, over time. He waited to ask me out until after my internship was over, and I thought that was chivalrous. He was funny and cute and…I dunno, I thought we had a good connection. And I was ashamed to even admit to myself that things had gotten to such a shitty point."

"It was more than just emotional abuse from the sounds of it. So, what made you break it off?"

"It was my graduation day. He didn't come to the actual ceremony but said he had a surprise for me later. Wanted to celebrate my graduation and my job offer at *The Post*. I went to his house and…surprise! He had invited another woman over. He wanted us to fuck while he watched."

Emily grimaced. "Shut up."

"Yep. I mean, I don't have anything against people who have threesomes or whatever. But not for me. He told me that this woman—some redhead from South Boston—was my graduation present. Can you believe that? Out of the blue like that? He said it was so I could indulge my fantasies. I think he really thought I'd like it."

"Asshole. Indulging his fantasies and pretending they're yours. What did you do? I would have kicked him in the balls."

"I told him to fuck off and left. Haven't seen him since."

"Listen," Emily said. She reached out and put a hand on Skylar's arm. "I think Luca's just what you need right now to forget about all that. Just enjoy something casual. You don't have to marry him, no matter who he ends up being. The important thing is it sounds like he'll be great in the sack."

Skylar sighed and opened the little blue cooler sitting near her feet. She popped open two more Coronas with an opener and handed one to Emily, who asked, "Did you look him up in Italian like I suggested?"

"No, I didn't have time between working my story and going to his house. And this morning…well, I got busy trying to outline my new reporting project."

Emily tossed a disgusted look her way. "You need to cut that shit with the unpaid overtime. Get out your iPad."

Skylar always had her iPad with her. She extracted it from her tote and swiped the screen, and as Emily drank and texted Jimmy, Skylar figured out how to search websites only in Italian. There were thousands of hits because Luca Rossi was apparently a common Italian name.

"Okay, here we go, maybe," she finally said, after scrolling through several pages of results. Emily set her phone aside and slid in next to her on the chaise lounge. "It's an article from *Il Mattino*, a newspaper out of Naples, Italy."

"Luca said he was from Naples, right?"

Skylar nodded as she copied the website address and found a site to translate the web page into English. Both she and Emily could see from the photo that the article was about a house fire. The huge home looked like it was bombed. Luca's name was in the story, but was it the same Luca?

*"Due persona muoiono in un incendio domestico,"* the headline read. *Two people die in house fire.*

The translation of the web page wasn't grammatically correct, but they gleaned the details. A man and woman named Cristiano and Sofia Rossi died in a fire in Naples. Cristiano was a prosecutor in the region of Campania. The cause of the fire was unknown, but investigators were looking into whether it was intentionally set. The Rossis left behind two surviving family members: a son, 26-year-old Luca, and Cristiano's estranged brother, Federico Rossi, a lawyer in Miami, Florida. Luca was out of the city at the time and was not considered a suspect, the article concluded.

"Damn," sighed Emily.

"Wow," Skylar said, feeling her stomach clench as she thought how awful it must have been for Luca after his parents were killed. The incident also explained why he was so hot and cold. She knew firsthand that trusting anyone, getting close to anyone, was difficult after surviving the death of a parent.

"He must feel so much guilt for not being there when they died. No wonder he's a little different," she said softly.

This would also explain why he was so guarded. Of course he wouldn't want to get close to anyone after something like that.

And why did the article say that Federico was estranged from the family? It was an odd word. Skylar scowled. Maybe the online translator wasn't all that reliable. She studied the article more.

She typed Luca's name into the box near the little search symbol at the top of the Italian newspaper's home page. Nothing else came up other than that one story, and she scowled at the screen. How much of the paper's archive was available? A few keystrokes and website translations later, she discovered the answer was only two years of past articles; anything before that required a subscription in Euros, and she wasn't about to plunk down her credit card to snoop into Luca's life. That seemed to cross the line into obsession.

She entered his parents' names into the search tool. One other small article ran two weeks after the fire. Skylar plugged it into the translation website, and she learned it said the Camorra likely set the blaze.

"Camorra," Emily said. "What's that?"

A chill went through Skylar despite the oppressive humidity. Hadn't Luca mentioned the Camorra the first night they met? She couldn't remember. Luca had said so many things in Italian. She navigated to Wikipedia and read aloud, "'The Camorra is an Italian Mafia-type crime syndicate.'"

She and Emily looked at each other with huge eyes.

"Whoa," Emily whispered.

Skylar didn't say anything.

They found nothing else online about Luca or the fire.

None of this made sense, Skylar decided. Why hadn't he mentioned this about his parents? Why hadn't his uncle said anything? Sky tried to categorize the information in her mind and was beginning to realize there was a lot she didn't know about the Rossi family. Too much.

She said, "Luca said his master's thesis was about the Mafia."

Emily sent her a knowing look. "Maybe the fire had something to do with Luca's father being a prosecutor. Or, what if Luca's in the Mafia? What if his master's thesis is bullshit and he's really a criminal and his parents were killed for retribution? What if he's like Furio, the sexy guy with the ponytail in *The Sopranos* who came over to be a Mafia enforcer for Tony? What if he's starting a branch of the Mafia right here on Palmira?"

Skylar burst out laughing. "Thank God you cover sports and not crime. The Mafia's not like a fast-food franchise."

But, maybe Emily had a point. Could Luca be a criminal? It would explain why he was so evasive with details about his past. And Federico seemed a bit shady himself, what with that business about not listing his house under his name for tax purposes.

"Do you think I should see him again?" she murmured. "If he calls, that is. He might not after last night." She tapped her beer bottle with her nails: index finger, middle finger, ring finger, pinky. Rinse, repeat.

"Do you really think he's a criminal?"

Skylar's intuition told her Luca wasn't, although clearly her gut had been wrong before. And she had read too many true-crime books to know that some men were excellent liars. Sociopaths, even. But Luca didn't seem like he was lying. He just evaded lots of her questions.

Skylar shivered in the hot Florida sun, as if someone had run an ice cube down her spine, then shook her head.

Emily shrugged. "Dunno, then. Sure. Why not? It's not like you've got anyone better knocking on your door. And *he's really hot.* If you want to screw him, do it and don't get emotionally involved."

Skylar nodded. Avoiding any emotional involvement with Luca was probably a good plan regardless of who he turned out to be. She didn't need a complicated guy like this to divert attention away from her career. She needed to get out of Palmira and to a bigger paper. When she'd taken the job she'd given herself two years, max, to get enough clips to move up and out. When her mother was dying, Skylar made her a promise: to not ever languish in a dead-end job in a small-town.

Her friend interrupted her thoughts. "At least we know why he didn't want you to put him in the paper when you first met him. Because of this Camorra thing."

Skylar nodded and sipped more beer. Emily was likely right. But now she was even more curious about Luca's past, and the only way to find out was to get to know him better.

# CHAPTER THIRTEEN

"I do not understand. I thought that all property listings were public record here in Florida. That is what I read on your state website. Why wouldn't Federico Rossi's address be public? I know he has a house on Palmira. It said so right in the newspaper."

Annalisa tried not to let her annoyance show to the bureaucrat sitting across the counter. She had searched online in public records databases for Federico's address and yet found nothing. After a confusing volley of phone calls to government offices, she'd been forced to drive off-island to the county's property appraiser in Fort Myers.

The bureaucrat shrugged. "Sometimes people list their properties under a corporation or a business name."

Annalisa sighed. She needed to locate Federico's house. It was the only way to find out if Luca was there. She opened her oversized Gucci bag and took out that day's *Palmira Post*. She also extracted three, crisp $100 bills from her wallet. This was the way things were done in Italy and worth a try in Florida.

The clerk watched her set the money on the newspaper then fold the paper in half.

"Surely everyone must know where Federico Rossi's island mansion is," Annalisa said, her voice softening and taking on a greater Italian lilt. She slid the paper toward the bureaucrat, who took the paper wordlessly.

He rose from his seat, and Annalisa wondered if this little scheme would backfire on her. But, what was the worst they could do? Try to arrest her on bribery charges? She could get out of anything with tears.

After a moment, the clerk returned with an orange sticky note. He handed it to her. It said, *The Sanctuary, 100 Royal Palm Drive, Palmira, Florida.*

"Thank you, sir." Annalisa strode out of the office, feeling triumphant.

On her way back over the long bridge to the island, her phone rang. Annalisa recognized the Italian number and answered with, "Mama?"

Her mother spoke in a long string of Italian sentences without pausing to take a breath. "I know you're in Florida. Please come home. You don't need to be there. I spoke with your cousin and he's going to help you again. He wants you to know that everything is taken care of with, with…"

"I'm fine, Mama. Just taking a little rest on the beach. I'm not doing what you think I am."

Her mother sighed. "Bruno wants me to tell you that he's on top of the situation in Florida and there's no need to interfere. He didn't want me to say anything to you, but I can't help it. Please come home."

"Mama, I'm not interfering in anything."

"Bruno says he's sending someone."

*What the fuck?* Annalisa's voice dropped to a whisper. "Here? To Florida?"

"Yes. Now come home."

"No. I'm enjoying myself on the beach. Please. Trust me. Remember, the doctor said I'm fine as long as I take my medicine, and I'm taking it. How's the kitty?"

Her mother chattered on in a nervous voice. Annalisa didn't care about the family cat and she refused to ask about her stepfather. In fact, fuck her mother and the entire family. Her mother hadn't protected her from her stepfather, so why should Annalisa tell her the truth about anything?

As she came close to The Sanctuary and Federico Rossi's house, she hurried her mother off the phone with more lies. "I have to go, Mama, my spa appointment is coming up. I love you, Mama. I'll send you a postcard."

Annalisa hung up then slowed the car. But, dammit, there was a guard at the gate. One more obstacle.

She pulled into the nearest public beach parking lot and climbed out. Walking down a wooden path between the dunes, she spotted a long gate and the mansions of The Sanctuary behind it. Which one was Rossi's house? It was difficult to tell the addresses from outside the complex. She considered talking to the guard at the gate, maybe bribing him. That would have to be a last resort, in case Luca's uncle was with him, or if there were others in the house. Somehow, she had to get Luca alone. And soon.

What did her mother mean when she'd said that Bruno was on top of the situation? He wouldn't send someone here to kill the man she loved, would he? Annalisa's heart dropped to her stomach. Yes. Her cousin would. So Annalisa needed to find Luca and protect him. To take him away. To make him understand that she was his only hope for safety.

She leaned on the wooden rail of the walkway, and a hot breeze made her short sundress flap against her thighs. She slipped into a daydream, the sun lulling her into a fantasy world. This was a beautiful beach, and she knew Luca would want to kiss her here at sunset.

Also, if Bruno was sending someone to Florida, she didn't have much time left.

# CHAPTER FOURTEEN

Later that night, after Skylar napped, read *The New Yorker* cover to cover and researched more about the Camorra in Naples, she met up with her coworkers at the Sloppy Iguana. Every Friday was '80s night, which meant it was packed with those who had actually lived through the 1980s and the handful of younger people on the island who wanted to dance to cheesy music.

The Iguana was the newsroom's bar of choice for celebration, usually when someone at the paper had a birthday or was leaving. That evening's party was for a copy editor who'd been hired on at *The Tampa Bay Times*, and everyone at *The Post* harbored a mixture of jealousy and happiness at his departure.

Skylar walked in to the strains of an old Madonna song. She didn't much like '80s music because it made her think of her mother, who'd played the decade's songs all during Sky's childhood. She remembered riding in the family Subaru, signing all the synth-pop hits in unison with her mom on their way to and from school. That was one of her favorite childhood memories. Favorite, but painful.

Tonight she had agreed to be the designated driver for Emily, who wanted to drink but didn't want to get stopped by her boyfriend's cop buddies. It would be a long night, therefore, and Sky wished she was home. Usually she liked hanging out with everyone from the newsroom, but tonight she wanted to be alone in bed so she could think about Luca. She couldn't shake the image of his parents dying in a horrible, suspicious fire, leaving him all alone. Who'd even told him that his parents died? Had he seen their bodies in the morgue? Had the case been solved?

She wondered how he'd coped with the funeral. It reminded her of her own mother's slow death from melanoma. Sitting alone in the funeral home she had silently and miserably realized she was supposed to be picking out a prom dress and not a casket. Then she'd felt guilty for even thinking that way. A big part of her wanted to hold Luca tight and talk about their parallel, painful lives. Another very small part wanted to entice him to tell her his story because she was so damned curious.

Somehow, in the years after her mother died, she had developed an ability to read, listen and talk about tragedy without getting too emotional. She occasionally wondered if her mother's death had shocked her feelings into stasis, which in turn had made her an even-tempered, balanced journalist. She figured her balance also had something to do with her upbringing at her mother's yoga studio. Yin/yang. Inner peace. Equilibrium. To James, that inability to get *too* passionate had made her a cold bitch.

"Why don't you call your Italian stallion?" Emily shouted in her ear.

Skylar rolled her eyes, smirked and shook her head. That would be too awkward. No way would she call him first.

"The people-watching is good tonight," her friend called out. She gestured around them at the bar.

Sky sipped her iced tea and laughed. "I was just thinking that. It's the best thing about being a journalist. You just learn to kick back and watch people. Humans are so funny."

They both looked around and enjoyed the show, giggling.

To Skylar's left, a fifty-something guy in a black Ed Hardy T-shirt tried to chat up the bartender, who was wearing a tight white T-shirt and black nylon shorts. In front of them, a group of women about their age, tourists probably, drank shots.

"Five more blowjobs!" yelped a tiara-wearing woman, and her friends all laughed.

"I'm never having a bachelorette party," Emily vowed, downing a fireball shot. She grinned. "But you can hire a male stripper for me anytime."

"Fuck that. I'm never getting married," Skylar responded with a laugh.

Her phone vibrated in her purse. She pawed around and checked the text message.

*Ciao, cara bella. How are you?*

Skylar grinned despite herself. Her pulse quickened whenever he used those little Italian pet names.

*Bored. I'm at the Iguana. Want to join me?*

"Em." She waved her phone in the air. "It's him."

*Nope. I don't do bars. Are you safe to drive? How much have you had to drink? Who are you with?*

Hmm. Was he actually jealous?

*I'm the designated driver. Not drinking tonight. I'm bringing my friend from sports home later.*

Skylar wondered whether she should explain that Emily was a woman, then decided not to. She didn't owe Luca anything. He hadn't exactly been forthcoming with *his* life.

*Text me later, when you get home*, he wrote. *Please be careful.*

Her heart stirred from his little show of concern and she responded, *Ok. TTYL.*

He probably thought the sports reporter was a guy. She wasn't going to explain the truth right then, though. And toying with Luca and his Italian male sensibilities might not be a terrible idea.

Emily elbowed her arm. "Is he coming here? I wanna meet him."

Sky shook her head. As much as she wanted Em to see how hot Luca was, she wasn't ready to introduce him to her newsroom friends. Not in any personal setting. She wanted to make sure it wouldn't be awkward or weird.

After dancing with Emily and enduring a couple more hours of bad music, she drove her drunk friend home. Finally back at her condo, Skylar showered to get the nasty smell of cigarette smoke out of her hair and off her skin, slipped into a camisole and underwear and nestled into bed with the lights off. There was nothing better than cranking down the air-conditioner and getting under her puffy comforter. At last, phone in hand, she scrolled to Luca's number and sent him a text.

*Hey. I'm home.*

He replied immediately. *Skylar. It's been three hours. Are you okay?*

*I'm fine. It took us a while to leave and I had to shower.*

*How's your friend? What sports does he write about?*

Oh, Luca was definitely jealous.

*SHE is fine, and SHE covers high school sports. HER name is Emily. You thought it was a guy, didn't you?* ;)

Skylar's phone rang a few seconds later. She grinned despite herself.

"Uh, I did think it was a guy."

Luca sounded embarrassed. Hearing his voice was so much better than texting, and she laughed. "Jealous?"

"Hmm. Maybe a little. How could I not be when lots of guys are probably after you?"

Ignoring his remark, Skylar changed the subject. "What are you doing?"

"I'm in bed."

"Oh. Me too."

"So, I wanted to see if you'd like to come over tomorrow. Watch a movie with me. Have dinner."

"Will your uncle be back?" Federico had emailed a quick note saying he liked the article, and Skylar wondered how much he knew about her and Luca. And how much time he spent in Palmira.

"No. He's still in Miami."

"Okay. Yeah. I would like to come over."

"Excellent. I've been thinking a lot about you. And thinking more about what you said. I think it makes sense to take things slow. I'm kind of a complicated man, Skylar."

"It's okay. I don't mind," she said. For a moment she was reminded what she'd discovered about his parents and considered raising the subject, but that didn't feel right, not over the phone. "I mean, I don't want you to think that I'm not..."

"Not what?"

"Not attracted to you. Because I am. Obviously."

He laughed, a low, sexy sound. "Well, I'm obviously attracted to you, too. If I could, I'd teleport you here and have my way with you."

"Oh really? Can you elaborate?" she teased.

"I could, but I'd prefer you tell me what you want. What do you desire?"

Skylar paused. She hadn't ever had phone sex before. She hadn't even sent sexy pictures to James because she was too worried that they would be leaked somewhere and her life would be ruined. But indulging in erotic chat with Luca seemed fun. Casual. Hot. And very safe, since at least two miles separated them.

Better yet, this was different and unexpected. She had been so used to James orchestrating their sex life that she rarely took the reins. When she'd tried to be on top, or talk sexy, or tell him what she wanted, James laughed at her for being inept and inexperienced. Now, with Luca on the other end of the phone, it seemed like an interesting way to explore her fantasies. Or embarrass herself. She wasn't sure which.

She took a breath. What did she desire, anyway?

"Hmm. I need some information first. This is a cliché, but here goes. What are you wearing?"

Luca chuckled. It was a genuine sound, and it put her at ease. "Nothing."

"Oh." Her heart skipped a beat at the thought. "Where are your hands?"

"Where do you want them to be?"

She laughed but stopped when an image of his strong hand resting on the hard planes of his stomach came into her mind. She pictured his hand shifting lower, between his legs. Wrapping around his erection.

"I'll do whatever you ask." His voice was playful, low.

"Can you describe your, your...how do you say it in Italian?"

"My what, Skylar?"

She hesitated, grinning into the phone and feeling bold. "Your cock."

He growled a little. "Let's see. Cock. *Il Cazzo*. That also has other meanings, like—"

"I don't need a thesaurus," she interrupted.

"You're getting stern. And I'm getting harder."

She gasped then laughed more. "Describe your cock."

"Well, let's see. It's, um. Do you want me to measure it? I don't think I have a ruler handy."

Skylar cooed playfully, and he continued.

"Okay. It's longer than my hand. And I can just get my thumb and middle finger around the thickest part."

In the glow of the cell phone light, she held up her hand, circling her thumb and middle finger together. Wow. And that was her hand. His was much bigger.

"Okay. How hard are you, on a scale of one to ten?"

"Umm, about a nine."

"Really? Why? I haven't said anything particularly sexy."

He hummed. "Your voice turns me on. I like American accents."

"I like your voice, too. So, are you, like, stroking yourself? That's what I want you to do."

"I am."

"Slow? Or fast?"

"Slow. Very slow. I'm kind of teasing myself the way you're teasing me."

Her breath hitched at the thought of him moving his hand lazily up and down his shaft. "Luca?"

"*Si, mia cara?*"

Every time he spoke Italian in his languid accent she melted.

"Have you stroked—um, jerked off—thinking of me before tonight?"

He laughed, a low, slow and wicked sound. "What do you think?"

"I...I don't know." She held her breath, because she suspected the answer. "Yes. You have."

"More times than I want to admit," he said. "Does that bother you?"

"No...definitely not. Are you imagining it's my hand on you right now?"

"I am. And your mouth. I think about that a lot, you on your knees. Your mouth. Your tongue. Coming in your mouth..." His voice trailed off.

"Harder. I want you to stroke harder," she said, her voice firm and low. She felt a surge of power. Where had this demanding, sexual woman been hiding? Never before had she been so insistent with a guy. James had always wanted her to talk dirty, but she'd never been comfortable. Something about Luca made her feel safe.

He inhaled sharply. "Oh, Skylar. You have no idea what you're doing to me."

"Tell me what you think about when you jerk off," she said, her voice dropping to a near-whisper. She kicked off the comforter because it was suddenly too warm. She imagined Luca's hand grasping her hair as she took him in her mouth.

He growled. "I think about kissing you hard and soft and any way I want. For hours. Then taking off your clothes slowly but leaving your panties on. Running my fingers over your body, tracing your nipples... I saw how they got hard last night."

"More. I want to hear more."

"I fantasize about spreading your legs wide. I know you'll be wet for me."

Her breath came out in a long sigh. She was already wet—had been for days, it seemed.

"Are you wearing panties right now?"

She swallowed. "Yes."

"Color?"

"Pale blue. Lace."

"*Bellissima.* And they are wet, no?"

Her entire body throbbed, thinking about how his fingers would feel inside of her. How they would open her and explore every nerve-covered peak and valley. She responded in a whisper. "Um…they are…soaked."

"*Che bella ragazza.* I want to run my fingers over your panties and tease you for a long time. Then take them off and slide two fingers into you. Lick you very slow, until you cry out a little bit. Then make you ask—no, *beg*—for an orgasm." His voice was thick with pleasure.

Toying with the elastic edge of her panties, Skylar slipped her hand down the front of her underwear and touched herself, unable to wait until she got off the phone. "What if I want *you* to beg?"

He groaned, and she had never heard such a masculine sound, never felt such a primitive need for a man. "How close are you?" she asked in a whisper.

"Really close. Are you touching yourself?"

"Mmmhmm," she whispered.

He didn't respond, and she made little needy noises while running her finger through her wetness. She heard his breath, fast and forceful. The words slipped out of her mouth, from where, she had no idea, because she normally wasn't so demanding. "You can't come until after I do. Stop."

He released his breath in a long expulsion. "Maybe you have a dominant side you weren't aware of, *mia cara.* You seem to enjoy teasing me."

"You said I could. So stop touching yourself and tell me more of what you want to do to me."

"I'd lick you until you were right on the edge of coming, then I'd kiss you. So you could taste yourself on my lips. I'd keep kissing you until you begged for my cock. Before I entered you, I'd rub the head slow over your clit. Skylar, touch yourself now and imagine it's my cock."

"Oh, I'm imagining." Her fingers glided through her swollen, separated folds.

"Sky, can I stroke myself? Can I come? Please?"

"Not yet." She wasn't sure what turned her on more, Luca's voice or her command over him. Her fingers turned their attention to her clitoris, and the backs of her knees perspired. She longed to feel his naked body, his heavy weight on top of her.

Luca moaned and said something in Italian.

"God, it's so sexy when you talk in your language." She would definitely come soon if he continued talking in phrases like that. The ache in between her legs grew to an all-consuming need. "Ahh, Luca? Translation please?"

"I'm saying that we'll be incredible together, Skylar. I can tell. I want you. I want to consume you. *Ti voglio consumare.*"

Her orgasm burst through her body when she heard his words, and she gasped louder than she intended, crying out and filling her little bedroom with the sound. "Now. Luca. Come now."

She heard Luca gasp and shudder a helpless moan as her own entire body vibrated. Not knowing what to say afterward, she murmured a long *Mmmm* noise. She could hear her heart beating, felt it in her lips and on her fingertips.

Luca exhaled. "Sky?"

"Yes?"

His voice was gravelly. "I want you to do exactly that when we're together."

"What? Make myself come?"

He laughed and sounded tired. "Yes, I'd love that. But, no. I want you to tell me exactly what you want. Don't ever be shy about it. The more you tell me what you want, the more it'll turn me on. Can you do that for me?"

"I think I can."

Yet, despite the heat that her body threw off after her orgasm, Skylar shivered. She wasn't sure if she would reveal anything more of herself to this beautiful, complicated and secretive man, because once she did she knew she'd be in trouble.

# CHAPTER FIFTEEN

They had been kissing for hours. It started when Skylar arrived and he gave her a long and lazy kiss, pressing her into the door as he locked it. They smooched throughout dinner, in between bites of the pizza he made. Then he led her upstairs to the TV room attached to his big bedroom, and they made out on the sofa for a long time, pausing to talk and laugh as their bodies molded together.

Luca hadn't spent so much time kissing without having sex since he was a teenager. Skylar's lips, now practically bruised from his nips and nibbles and bites, made him feel young again. Innocent. He had promised that sex wasn't an option for them until she gave the go-ahead, and he found himself delighted by the teasing, wanting, aching feeling inside him. Neither had mentioned the hot phone sex, yet that coupled with her in-person shyness drove him wild.

"Are we really going to watch a movie?" She tickled his side. "Or are you going to kiss me all night?"

"I'm going to kiss you while we're watching a movie. It's really old, from the seventies. In English it's called *The Passenger*, but in Italian it's *Professione: Reporter*. It's about a reporter who takes on a different identity and then falls in love with a woman and they run from criminals. There's subtitles."

Skylar grinned. "Sounds good to me."

Luca chuckled softly. They reclined on a wide, tufted brown leather sofa, and she snuggled her back to his chest as he pressed play on one remote and turned down the lights with the tap of another. He put his arm around her, wishing she wore a shirt and not a dress so he could easily caress the skin of her stomach.

The movie started. As he stroked the curve of her hip and pressed his lips to her shoulder, he was slammed with an overwhelming, unusual feeling. Normalcy. He had never really been intimate with a woman like this. High school, college, post-college—all were spent on quick hookups. He hadn't ever taken a relationship slow because he never really attempted to have one. He'd bounced from boarding school to university to internship to his first newspaper. In his early twenties, his career had come first. But somehow, here on Palmira, when he was supposed to be writing a second book, he was spooning a sweet woman and watching a movie. Acting like a man whose parents hadn't been killed as retribution for his first book. Pretending that he hadn't spent a year on the run. Appearing as though he wasn't waiting with dread for a Mafia boss to go on trial.

To an outsider, it would look like he cared about the girl in his arms. And he was starting to care about her. But why her? Why Skylar and not any of the dozen or so other beautiful women he had hooked up with over the years?

It was more than the physical attraction, obviously. Was it because she made him laugh, or was it her quick mind and how she read voraciously? Her favorite book as a child was *Harriet the Spy*, and now she read true crime. None of the women he'd screwed in recent years read much, and if they did, he hadn't spent enough time with them to find out their preferences.

He swept Skylar's hair away from her neck, and she pressed her body closer to his. The coral hue of her little dress made her skin look more velvety and pale, and he longed to lick her from head to toe. They lay tight together, watching the slow movie. He became absorbed in the plot.

After an hour or so, she rolled over and pressed her nose into his chest, puffing out a little snort. He almost laughed aloud at the thought of putting a woman to sleep *before* sex, but he didn't want to wake her. So he hugged her close, ignoring his erection. Every so often he'd gaze down at her face and brush his thumb over her cheek. She looked young yet regal. Her mouth turned up at the corners, and her dark eyelashes grazed the tops of her cheekbones.

When the movie was almost over, thunder rumbled in the distance. Skylar nuzzled deeper into his arms and sighed.

"I should go," she whispered. Her eyes opened, revealing a hazy blue color, then fluttered closed again.

Poor thing, she was exhausted. She had talked about working overtime on a reporting project and he wondered if she was pushing herself too hard.

"Sorry for falling asleep," she murmured.

"Why don't you stay? You had a lot of wine and you're sleepy. And it sounds like it's about to rain. You shouldn't drive."

"Mmmm." She kissed his neck.

"You can sleep in my bed and I'll take the guest room. Or the sofa."

She let out a cute growl of dissatisfaction and pressed her forehead into his chest.

"Or we can sleep in the same bed. I promise I won't try anything."

She opened her eyes slowly and looked at him. "Okay."

He climbed over her body and then pulled her to standing. She followed him through a door and into his bedroom, which was decorated in the home's formal, tropical-colonial furniture. Luca was ambivalent about his uncle's home and its luxuries. After backpacking and staying in grungy hostels in third-world countries, the Palmira house and its formal decor seemed cold, like living in a showroom. The four-poster bed with a canopy top in his room was probably the most ostentatious piece, but it would be rude to ask his uncle to redecorate. At some point Luca wanted to remove the gauzy, faux malaria curtains tied to the canopy rails that made him roll his eyes whenever he looked at them.

"Ohh, pretty," Skylar said dreamily as she touched the curtains hanging around the bed. "Romantic."

Okay, maybe they weren't so bad.

He led her to the master bathroom and found a towel.

"Toothpaste?" she asked drowsily, and he set a tube on the wide counter. She shut the door after he left. Like he did every night, he locked the door leading to the hallway and made sure his gun was in the nightstand drawer.

### 

Skylar brushed her teeth with her finger and took off her bra and stuffed it in between the folds of the towel, not wanting to fling it casually in a corner like at home. Thank God she had worn one of her many cotton tank-top dresses. It would double as a sleep shirt, because there was no way she would trust herself if she slept naked next to Luca.

The bathroom was huge, as big as her bedroom. It was all blonde marble and porcelain. There was a ginormous Jacuzzi tub, a separate shower, a toilet, a bidet and two sinks. She closed the door and sat on the edge of the tub, trying to gather the thoughts in her sleepy mind.

By spending the night, she would be at his mercy. At the mercy of her own desires. Would he sleep naked? She suspected he would put on boxers if she asked. He had been so polite all evening, doing nothing but kissing her. He hadn't mentioned their phone sex from the previous night, and neither had she, but between that and the nonstop kissing she had been wet between her legs for hours. Her stomach tightened with desire when she recalled how he'd pressed his erection into her when they were on the sofa.

It was embarrassing how she'd fallen asleep, but she'd felt so relaxed lying there with him. Hopefully he wasn't offended.

She smiled weakly to herself in the mirror. Maybe Luca wasn't the most forthcoming guy about his past. But really, what did it matter? Hanging out with him was awesome.

Emerging from the bathroom she went to the gorgeous bed, parting the sheer curtains and climbing inside. Luca was at his bureau, taking off his shirt, revealing taut muscles. He wore black boxer-briefs and she noticed that his ass looked really firm. Tonight would take all of her willpower to avoid sex. And yet, what exactly was she waiting for? Why was she holding herself back from pleasure?

He used the bathroom then shut out the light, joining her in bed. When he leaned over for a kiss, she tugged him on top of her. She ran her hands down his back, then lower. Yep. His ass was indeed as tight as it looked.

They kissed for a long time, and a fierce Florida summer storm raced ashore. The room was dark save for flashes of lightning. When a loud crack of thunder exploded overhead, Luca protectively squeezed her closer.

"You're sure you're okay with not having sex?" she whispered.

"I'm totally okay. This makes me happy."

He kissed her neck, wrapping a fistful of her hair in his hand and pulling slightly, tilting her head. When he bit her, Skylar traveled to a different dimension. She opened her mouth, gasping at how his lips sent waves of heat throughout her body.

Luca sat up, kneeling, and pulled her to him, her back to his chest. Her hands squeezed his muscular thighs and she lightly raked her nails over his skin. With his strong arms wrapped around her she felt small and safe. Luca's hands caressed her thighs under her dress, alternating between gentle strokes and possessive squeezes. Her breasts were heavy with longing in a way they'd never been.

She was also kneeling, and he pulled her arms back and threaded his own through the crooks of her elbows so she couldn't touch him or move, while his hand raked her front. Her dress and panties were still on, and his underwear did nothing to obscure the erection pressing near her ass.

"I want you to touch me," she whispered in a tentative voice. "Will you take off my clothes?"

"Of course," he said.

Slowly he removed her dress, pausing to reach around and stroke her breasts. Then he eased her panties over her hips, but only partway, so the fabric strained around her thighs. He took a fistful of her hair and turned her head so that his lips were near his ear.

"Tell me if you like this," he whispered. From behind, his hand cupped her ass then stroked her lower. She felt one of his fingers inside of her.

She gasped. "I like that. A lot."

"Good," he murmured, taking his other hand out of her hair. "And how about if I do this?"

He gently folded her forward so she was on all fours and then reached around and slid his finger into her wetness, over and around her clit. The sensation of his fingers working her with a slow rhythm in both places made her cry out softly from the intensity. She urged her hips back into his hands and rocked.

"Oh, Luca," she whispered.

The thunderstorm was everywhere now, loud and insistent. She wasn't sure if the electricity in the air was from the atmosphere or them. Luca whispered something in Italian then switched languages.

"You're so wet."

His voice was hoarse, and she arched her back, wanting more. She felt damp and creamy everywhere. For a chilling second she thought of James and how he'd once told her that she was too slippery.

"Am I *too* wet?" she asked, feeling self-conscious.

Luca stopped and pulled her up. Spun her around to face him and planted a long kiss on her lips. "Sky. *No.* Don't ever ask that again. You will never be too wet for me."

"Will you keep touching me?"

"I think the better question is, will I be able to *stop* touching you?"

She slid her panties off her legs and lay down, opening her legs. A low growl emerged from Luca's throat and he lay atop her, his skin hot and demanding. He ground his hips into hers and the only thing separating them was the fabric of his underwear. She fed on his lips, sucked on his tongue. And yet, she wanted to wait, wanted to prolong penetration.

"Lie next to me and touch me again," she whispered.

He did, trailing his nose down her cheek and pressing his open mouth into her jaw as his hand went in between her legs. His fingers glided through her slick heat and sweat bloomed at her hairline. Two of his fingers entered her, and she whimpered with pleasure at the delicious, straining feeling. She spread her legs even wider in response, and he shuddered a breath in her ear.

Lightning crackled, illuminating the room and their bodies with brief white flashes. The rain came, pounding loud and insistent against the roof of the mansion.

"This is…this is perfect," she said, feeling like she was telling him a deep secret. She almost wanted to cry from the intensity because she felt so close to him and knew this moment was fleeting and impossible to repeat. Thank heavens it was dark, because her eyes welled up a little and she shuddered. This was different, special.

And might never happen again.

Luca's breath caught, and he spoke in a low whisper into her ear as he slid his fingers over her swollen clitoris, causing her stomach muscles to twitch in response. "It is. It is perfect. You're right. We're perfect together."

She hoped he wasn't lying.

He teased and touched her, circling her clit with his fingers. She was so close to coming. So close. Her insides coiled. Tightened. Her body was ready for the release.

"Please, Luca. Please. Please," she whimpered, and he responded in Italian.

"Sorry," he said after a breathless moment. "I'm loving you in my language."

Skylar's heart skipped a beat. She shuddered with violent need when he slowed his circles around her clit, breathing hard in her ear and occasionally whispering words she didn't understand. Dimly, she realized they were words of passion and beauty, but she couldn't think, couldn't speak.

His finger's circles around her clit grew smaller, firmer, more insistent. An orgasm tore through her, over and over, and she cried out louder than she ever had, turning into him and crushing her body against his. She reached the apex of pleasure, not wanting it to end. Through her daze she knew that no man had ever made her feel this way. The only time she had come this strong was when she pleasured herself, and she was shocked to find that another person's touch was as good as her own.

Better, even.

Luca held her as she trembled. Then a thought came to her. How could she be so selfish as to not please him in return? This must be torture. She put her hand on his chest and gently pushed him onto his back. Sliding atop his body, she kissed him, teasing his lips with her tongue. She sat and straddled his hips, running her hands over his chest, pausing to roll his nipples in between her thumb and forefinger. He gasped, and his chest twitched in response. She pressed her lips to his neck then slowly trailed her tongue down his body, her hair sweeping his flesh.

"You don't have to—"

He gasped when she removed his underwear, freeing his straining cock. She looked up and said, "But I want to. I want to feel you."

She knelt and wrapped her hand around his erection. He was far bigger than any man she'd been with, and she grasped his fever-hot skin, stroking him slowly from base to head. A flash of lightning illuminated the room and she caught sight of his gorgeous face. Luca's brow furrowed slightly, and his lips were parted.

"Is this okay?" she asked. God, how she hated being so self-conscious. But she couldn't help it.

"It's incredible. Please don't stop."

She stroked for a few more moments and he groaned.

"I'm not... I can't... I won't last long, Sky."

With a steady rhythm, she pumped her hand up and down his cock. Then she paused. She teased. She went faster, running her other hand down his thigh, lightly scratching with her nails. He let out a low moan and came, and she had never heard such an erotic sound.

Skylar slid down next to him and kissed his cheek. Feeling him pant and tremble was so satisfying. She knew he was much more experienced than she was, but his kisses afterward seemed worshipful and grateful. As if the night meant something to him.

After they each used the bathroom, he took her into his arms again. They dissolved into sleep, exhausted from desire. Skylar had one last thought before drifting off.

*This is too perfect to last.*

# CHAPTER SIXTEEN

Luca woke to Skylar's screams.

His heart hammered in his chest, jolting him awake. He jumped out of bed and followed her voice, panic spreading through his body like a wildfire. *They've found us. The Mafia. They're going to kill her. Kill me.*

Her screams echoed from inside the bathroom. Luca practically broke the door down to get to her. Fuck. The gun! He'd forgotten the gun.

She was wearing one of his big T-shirts and stood atop the edge of the Jacuzzi tub. "Luca! Oh God! Right there," she cried, pointing at the wall behind him.

Luca spun around, sweat forming on his face. "Skylar, what? What?"

"The cockroach on the wall. I hate them. Please make it go away," she squealed. "Do you see it? It's right above the toilet. I can't deal with it. It's the worst thing about living in Florida."

Luca took a deep breath and slumped against the bathroom counter. She had almost sent him into cardiac arrest over a two-inch bug. He walked into the bedroom to grab her flip-flop.

She was still standing on the edge of the tub when Luca returned and calmly thwacked the shoe against the wall, killing the insect. His heart finally resumed its normal cadence, and he grinned at Skylar while washing his hands. She remained on the tub and muttered something about how every building in Florida had cockroaches.

Luca wrapped his arm around her legs and gently lowered her down, then picked her up and carried her back to bed. "Don't do that, Skylar. I thought something really bad was happening to you. It scared me. Next time you see a bug, wake me up without the screaming, okay?"

### ###

The sound of steady rain against the bedroom windows roused Skylar from sleep. A delicious thrill went through her. Snuggling into the duvet, she stretched and allowed the covers to swallow her. An ache had settled in her body, like after doing hours of yoga at a retreat.

Luca, who was lying on his back, worked his arm under her and pulled her close. Her hand lay flat on his hard stomach, and she felt the sheet shift from the twitching of his erection. Gently she pulled the sheet back to look at his cock in the gray, stormy morning light. He had remained naked all night, while she had put on her underwear and slipped on his T-shirt, which smelled of his spicy aftershave.

She glanced up at his face. His eyes were closed but his lips turned up in a lusty smile as she curled her hand around his shaft.

"I think you're harder this morning than you were last night," she whispered.

Still grinning, he opened one eye and looked down. "I don't know how that's possible."

He put his hand around hers, and together they stroked, slowly, which made Skylar ache and throb between her legs. Luca then removed his hand and clutched the sheet near his hip, sucking in a breath. "If I'm harder this morning, it's thanks to you."

His eyes were on her hand as she pumped for several tantalizing minutes. Licking her lips in fascination, she stopped moving and touched the tip of her index finger to the head of his cock, swirling a drop of clear fluid around the sensitive skin. He gasped then came.

So far, taking things slow and not having sex was proving to be extremely hot.

A while later, while she lolled in bed half-asleep, Luca emerged from the bathroom in a T-shirt and shorts, his hair wet. He sat on the edge of the bed and caressed her hair.

"Sky, I need my espresso in the morning. Do you want to come down to the kitchen with me? Or should I bring you breakfast in bed?"

Skylar didn't know if he was serious. No guy had ever offered to make her breakfast in bed. Since she didn't know if he was joking, she shook her head. "I'll meet you downstairs."

In the bathroom, she marveled for several minutes inside the shower stall, which was tiled in a deep blue and had a wide nozzle, allowing the water to fall in a column. A teak bench in the shower made her wish Luca was there with her, and she imagined someday sitting on his lap, making love to him on that bench.

*Soon.*

Running soap over her skin, she thought about how Luca was so respectful of her wish to wait. Maybe he was truly old-fashioned, a gentleman.

She found him in the kitchen. The rain was coming down hard, pelting the roof in staccato beats. He had tuned a wireless speaker to a jazz station. The song was old and sensual, something about a valentine. Standing at the kitchen island in his big shirt and baggy boxer shorts, Skylar watched with a mix of fascination and desire as he ground the coffee beans. He flashed her a little-boy happy smile and she walked over to kiss him.

*It's like we're married.*

The thought popped into her head, and just as quickly, a feeling of shock. Skylar had never, ever dreamed of marriage. Not with James, and they'd dated for nine months. Not with any other guy, either. She hadn't ever considered what marriage would be like. It wasn't something even presented as an option to her as a girl.

*"You're not put on this earth to serve a man or get married,"* her mother would tell her. She wasn't raised with bride fantasies or Disney princesses. She and James had never talked about marriage, because she'd thought she was too young, and he'd always asserted it was a stupid, outdated institution. So dreams of a wedding cake or a man who would sweep her off her feet were about as foreign to her as living on Mars.

Until now.

Her chest tightened with anxiety. This was just a fun fling. She had to keep reminding herself of that. He was probably hiding something. Maybe he had a criminal past. Luca was so far from a prince or knight or whatever in shining armor, it wasn't even funny. And yet, the element of danger behind his silence added a layer of intrigue to his seductive charms.

"Ok, so here's what you need to do," Luca said, interrupting her thoughts. He was at the counter and holding the coffeepot. He positioned her body close to the counter and kissed her neck. "This is the Bialetti. Come. I need you to see this so you can learn to make me espresso. Oh, and I have some chocolate biscotti."

"How did you know I love chocolate?"

He softly bit her neck. "I guessed. You probably haven't had the good stuff, though. I'll have to find you some real Italian chocolates."

Her heart fluttered. She would make him espresso and eat chocolate with him anywhere. He spun Skylar around and they swayed a little.

"Do you like this music? It's jazz. Chet Baker." He kissed her on the forehead.

Sky nodded. The music, the coffee, him. It all made her so happy.

After a few minutes, the Bialetti percolated. Opening its lid a half-inch, Sky noticed the thick coffee bubbling up into the top chamber.

Luca chuckled. "It can explode if you're not careful."

She shot him an alarmed look.

"A Bialetti once exploded on my mother when I was ten," Luca said, continuing to laugh. "I remember the whole unit just went POOM and coffee splashed up to the ceiling. Come to think of it, I believe every Italian family has coffee on their ceiling because of an espresso explosion."

"Uh, thanks. When I'm not with you I'll stick to my iced coffee," she said, kissing him.

Did it make him sad to think about his mother? They sipped coffee, and Sky decided to ask about Luca's past. She could ask him about his parents, or she could try to ease into her probe with a softball question.

"I can't believe you're single. You seem too good to be true. You're handsome, you're smart, you make great food." She tried to say this with a playful grin.

Luca sighed and shifted away from her. He took the pot off the stove and poured more into their cups. His shoulders rose with tension, and Skylar cringed, worried she had said the wrong thing and wondering if he would explode like a Bialetti.

His voice was serious. "I'm single, I've told you that. My longest relationship was with a woman for a month or so in Italy, but I broke up with her. We just didn't...I dunno. I didn't feel a spark for her. I haven't had anyone serious in my life, ever. I'm not really a good... Let's just say I'm not really the relationship type."

"What was her name?" Skylar didn't even know why she was torturing herself by asking.

Luca frowned. "Annalisa."

A stab went through her gut. Was it jealousy for this Annalisa woman, who'd been lucky enough to spend a month with him? Or disappointment? Both? A competitive feeling welled inside of her, similar to when she was working on a news story. She wanted not only to be the best, but the only. And yet, no man had ever loved her enough to make her actually feel special. She had felt this weird competitiveness when James talked about his ex. She wanted to be better than any woman that had come before her, and Annalisa was no different.

"What was wrong with Annalisa?"

"She...she..." Luca's voice trailed off and he waved a hand in the air in a circle, as if trying to find the right words.

Trying to stay casual, Skylar sipped her coffee and wondered what Annalisa looked like. She had a beautiful, feminine name, and in Skylar's mind she must be petite and fashionable. European. That word conjured up a slightly aloof nature, a practical breeziness, an effortless thinness—all of which Skylar didn't possess.

Luca stammered, and she didn't respond. It was a reporter's trick to stay silent and hope the other person continued talking.

Luca rotated the little white cup on the granite counter with his fingertips and didn't look at her. He sighed then said, "Sky, I think it's best if we set some ground rules about this. I won't ask you any questions about your past if you don't ask any questions about mine."

She frowned. "But I don't mind if you ask me questions. I don't have anything to hide. I have no problem telling you about my ex-boyf—"

Luca interrupted and put a finger over her mouth. "I don't want to know. I don't want to imagine another man touching you. That's one of the many reasons why I don't want to talk about our pasts. I have a jealous streak."

Skylar recalled their conversation after her night at the Iguana. "Okay, I get that. But why do you have a problem with talking about your past?"

Luca chewed on his bottom lip. "It's really complicated, *amore*. I don't want to involve you in it. That's all I'll say."

She sent him a skeptical, cynical look and then remembered how his parents died and softened. "Complicated how?"

"I'm not going to talk about it with you," he said in a flat voice. "My past, your past isn't important anyway. What's important is right now, this moment. Live in the present, that's all I'm trying to do. That's all I can do, no? It will make *us* a lot easier."

Skylar noticed his emphasis.

"What is going on with us?" she asked, pointing her finger at him then herself.

There was a long pause. "I don't know. Let's just not label it."

"And the future? Is talking about that off-limits, too?"

"Yes," he replied.

"Why?"

He shook his head, a mournful look on his face. His eyes drifted away from her, to the corner of the room. "I...I don't know how long I'll be here in Florida. I can't promise anything. I don't want to make a promise I can't keep."

Feeling a sharp pain in her chest, Skylar resolved to maintain distance. This was only casual fooling around, friends with benefits. Her first impressions of Luca had been correct. He was a complex man, a player. Not boyfriend material at all.

And yet, she didn't want this to end. Not yet. She wasn't willing to walk away. No, she had to create some boundaries of her own, some parameters so she could continue to spend time with him and keep her dignity intact.

"Okay, well...I have a rule, too, Luca."

His gaze dropped to her face. "What is it?"

"As long as we're doing this"—she waved her hand between them—"you don't screw anyone else."

"I'm not screwing anyone else."

"Or 'make love.' Or *fare l'amore*, or whatever."

"Very good on the pronunciation." He cracked a smile.

"Don't turn your Italian charm on me," she said, trying to make her voice steely but laughing a bit inside. "If we're going to continue to be together, you need to be exclusive with me. It's only fair. I don't ask you about your past, you don't screw other women."

A little smile crept onto his lips. "Okay. Agreed. I can do that."

She nodded slowly. "I'm glad."

He kissed her then suggested they take the coffee and some biscotti up to the second floor terrace, off his bedroom. As they carried everything upstairs, she considered informing Luca he didn't need to worry about her falling in love with him, she wasn't ready for a relationship. She didn't want a boyfriend, not really.

Of course, if she did want one, he'd be exactly like Luca.

# CHAPTER SEVENTEEN

Ugh. The water looked pretty and blue but it was as warm as a bath. Wearing an ugly pink one-piece swimsuit that she'd bought to blend in with the rest of the Americans, a floppy hat and big sunglasses, Annalisa waded out until the Gulf was hip-deep.

Using the address the bureaucrat gave her, she had located Federico's house. She wasn't ready to bribe the guard for information, not yet. Since the house was so close to the public beach, she didn't want to attract attention by lingering at the gate, so she went out just far enough in the water so she could spy from a distance through a tiny pair of binoculars. Surely if Luca stood on the terrace of that big house he couldn't see her.

Her foot touched something underwater and she kicked frantically, nearly dropping the binoculars in the water. The hotel desk clerk had warned her about stingrays hidden in the sand, and the very thought of touching one with her toe turned her stomach. It was just a rock or a shell, though.

She slowly turned to face the beach and raised the binoculars. Thank God there weren't many people out, and they all seemed too absorbed in sunbathing or reading to notice her odd behavior. Then again, this was America, where everyone let their freak flag fly. Who cared if she was spying on houses? People probably thought she was looking at those ugly white birds with the skinny legs.

Through the binoculars she spotted a familiar, black-haired head and almost started to cry. It was him. Her Luca. Then another figure came into view. A woman. Annalisa adjusted the focus on the binoculars and sucked in a breath when she saw Luca wrap his arms around the person.

She had dark hair, wore a sloppy-T-shirt, and from the shape of the nose and the plump lips, she looked like Skylar Shaw, the local reporter. Swaying palm tree fronds blocked Annalisa's view and she lowered the binoculars, her mouth drooping along with her mood.

Fuck. How much time was he spending with Skylar? Surely she was just one of his many conquests. It would be trouble if the American became involved.

Annalisa shuffled through the water. She didn't want to hurt anyone, much less a reporter. She liked reporters, because she had been one. But she'd come all this way and wasn't above eliminating a woman if it meant getting to Luca.

# CHAPTER EIGHTEEN

Setting her coffee on a table, Skylar stood at the terrace railing and looked out at the view of sand and water. She nodded appreciatively. "You must have had a great view of the plane crash."

Luca leaned on the rail, his back to the Gulf. The corners of his eyes crinkled into a smile.

"You did see the crash from here. And you didn't tell me. You're so bad," Skylar teased, then pointed. "That's where I do yoga."

Glancing at him again, his head was bowed and he was biting his bottom lip, grinning.

"Have you seen me do yoga?" she asked, astonished.

He nodded. "Confession time. Yes."

Laughing, she stood in front of him and squeezed his forearm. "You have? Why didn't you come join me? Or say hello? Or did you just enjoy watching me bend over?"

Still grinning, he scratched the back of his head then went to sit on a chaise and sat his coffee on a nearby table. "It was the Saturday after we saw each other at that store. You were right there, practically in my backyard. And you were really flexible. Sexy. I did enjoy watching you bend over, if you want to know."

She leaned into his ear. "Sometime soon I'm going to let you watch me do something else. Something we talked about on the phone."

She kissed him. When she turned away, he swatted her ass and she yelped, giddy. He grabbed her wrist then pulled her into his lap. Sliding his arms around her waist, he pressed his mouth to hers.

"How did you get so good at yoga?"

"My mom taught it. I practically grew up in her studio, but then I took lots of classes and even taught little kids during summers in high school."

Her mom also worked at a health food store until six weeks before her death to make ends meet, but Skylar didn't reveal that. She didn't want Luca to know that if it wasn't for her mom's job at the health food store, they wouldn't have had money to eat. Or that one January when Sky was twelve, her mom didn't make enough to pay for heating oil and they wore coats inside all winter long.

"Did you learn to meditate and everything?"

"I grew up a New Age Buddhist kid."

"What does a New Age Buddhist kid do? Were you on a commune?"

Skylar grinned. "No. But I had friends who were. They had a house rule that they couldn't smoke pot until they were thirteen."

Luca shook his head, incredulous. "But…is New Age Buddhism even a thing?"

She rolled her eyes and chuckled. "Who knows. My mom was into a lot of fake spirituality. Lots of talking about peace and love and respecting the inherent worth and dignity of all human beings."

"It sounds kind of nice, actually."

She shrugged, not wanting to get into how all that inner peace didn't help her mom die in a calm way. Something about telling Luca the story of her mom made her sad. Chemotherapy and radiation had made for lots of suffering, and enlightenment be damned.

"Yeah, it was good, mostly. I learned to meditate when I was a toddler, that's what my mom said. I don't do it as much as I should now, though."

"That must be why you seem so calm on the outside. Strong."

She tilted her head. Was this his way of saying that she was cold and passionless? She wriggled out of his arms. "And on the inside, what? Emotionless? Vacant? Stupid?"

"God, no. Not even close. What?" he asked, looking surprised. "I was paying you a compliment. You seem really mature for twenty-two. Balanced. I love how calm you are. I grew up around Italians. We're excited and crazy all the time. Loud."

She shrugged and ran a few fingers through his short hair. "My, um, calmness, whatever you want to call it, is a sore point. My ex-boyfriend used to tell me I was cold and frigid. Oh. Sorry. We're not supposed to talk about our pasts."

"No. Actually, I want to hear about this *stronzo*. That means asshole. *Stronzo*. I want to know exactly what he did to you so I can figure out how to undo the damage. Who was he?"

Skylar let out a snort and slipped off Luca's lap, settling next to him on the chaise. "James was an editor at the newspaper where I interned. We started dating after my internship was over. He was a lot older than me, but I liked him. He was interesting. Told good stories. He was a former war correspondent. At first we got along really well."

"And what happened?" She noticed that Luca looked at the sky as she spoke.

"It's difficult to say. He just became gradually more...I don't know, demeaning. Abusive. He got laid off from the paper. He'd tell me that I was boring in bed. He told me I was getting fat. It was like a slow erosion of my confidence. Then he got a little physical with me. Once, when he didn't like something I was doing, um, sexually, he pushed me off the bed. Like, *pushed* me. Hard."

Luca said something in Italian. "Sorry. I use the nastiest words in my native language. Skylar, why did you stay?"

"I don't know. I thought that somehow he would become nicer, that he was just under pressure. It sounds so stupid and lame now. And I guess my self-esteem took a hit and I was too ashamed to say anything to anyone."

"But you broke up with him?"

"Yeah. I worked up the courage after he invited another woman to his house to fuck me. On my graduation night."

Laughter exploded from Luca's mouth, and Skylar's heart sank. He must have seen the troubled look on her face, though, because he sobered and reached for her hand. "Skylar. I'm not laughing at you. I'm just shocked. I can't believe anyone would do that to you. It's so absurd."

She shrugged. "I dunno. I think all men want threesomes. He was just upfront about it. And an asshole."

Luca groaned. "No. All men don't."

"Please. I'm sure you've had threesomes. You probably have women throwing themselves at you."

"Skylar, I can't deny I've had a past. But I'd never share you with anyone, man or woman. It would make me crazy to see anyone else touch you."

The sound of the soft waves of the Gulf filled the silence.

"And yet, you don't want a relationship, so what does it matter?"

Luca licked his lips, and Skylar wondered if she'd been too caustic, self-sabotaging this fledgling relationship before it had a chance to hatch. Suddenly she didn't feel like hanging out with him, was embarrassed about spending so much time wrapped up in him when he probably would never reciprocate her feelings.

"I think I'm gonna go. I have lots to do today. I had a really good time with you."

God, this was awkward.

His green-gray eyes clouded and flickered downward for a brief second. Was he disappointed? No, he was probably glad to get rid of her.

"Okay. I'll call you, or text. But you can, too. You know that, right?"

She smiled, but a sad feeling washed over her. "Yeah. I do." But she wouldn't. She would make him come to her. If he wanted.

### 

Why the hell did she have to leave? Why hadn't he tried harder to make her stay? More importantly, why did he care so much?

Sitting before a blank screen of his computer, Luca sighed. Maybe he should drive to the store for cigarettes. Writing was easier while smoking; it made him think more fluidly. All the reporting notes for the second book on another Mafia family were transcribed and he had an outline. But tonight he didn't feel like creating sentences or paragraphs or chapters. Grabbing two pens, he tapped them on the desk like drumsticks, and the sound matched his quick-beating heart.

He wanted to lounge more on the sofa with Skylar. That little taste of normalcy, of watching a movie, of sleeping next to her and waking to her kisses, was oddly seductive. The intimacy and the cozy cuddling was just part of it though, and a gnawing need still raged inside of him. Skylar's touch, how she brought him to orgasm with only her soft hands, had stirred an intensity inside him that he had never experienced before. So much so, that concentration on anything else was impossible. The memory of how she slowly rubbed her finger over the tip of his cock made him hard, and he thought about jerking off.

He considered her request. Her rule. Of course he wouldn't seek out anyone else. Why would he want to? The way the pain fogged her eyes when she talked about her ex-boyfriend made his heart pound uncomfortably against his chest, and hearing about how the guy pushed her had nearly taken his breath away in anger. Luca now realized why, as he thumped the pens harder against the desktop. He'd covered some nasty domestic violence stories while at the paper in Italy, and he'd never forgotten interviewing one woman in particular. Her husband had beat her severely, and her tears and pain had imprinted on his 22-year-old brain. He'd felt helpless, knowing that his article was probably meaningless. The story, like so many others he'd written as a young reporter, was an unbylined brief. Five paragraphs to sum up a tragedy.

The idea of a man putting his hands on a woman in that way sickened him. He tossed the pens on the desk.

It was irrational, but Luca wished he'd been able to protect Skylar from James's abuse. The only thing he could do now, though, for her future, was to not hurt her in any way.

# CHAPTER NINETEEN

Skylar walked into the newsroom on Tuesday morning to find a box on her chair. What had she bought? Why had the package slipped her mind? She had been forgetful lately because of Luca and work. It wouldn't be surprising if she'd ordered something and totally spaced out.

Slicing open the tape on the box edges with a pair of scissors, she discovered another box nestled inside, wrapped in gold paper and tied with a gold ribbon. She carefully unfolded the attached note card and tilted her head in curiosity.

*Più baci per te.*

*—Luca*

Sky laughed out loud. She'd look the Italian words up on the Internet as soon as she opened the gift.

Sliding her finger under the thick wrapping paper, she extracted a midnight blue box. *Baci*, it said in light blue cursive letters on the front. Grinning, she lifted the lid to find twenty-eight chocolates wrapped in sparkling silver foil.

He'd remembered.

She looked around, anticipating her coworkers would cluster around to tease her—or, more likely, to beg for candy. No one was nearby, thankfully. This was a moment to enjoy alone. She plucked a chocolate from the box and unwrapped it, biting into the sweet and closing her eyes. It was dark and delicious. As the chocolate melted on her tongue, she sank into the chair and went to an online translator to type in the words of Luca's message.

Her heart soared when she read the translation. *More kisses for you.*

###

Luca tugged at his shirt collar as he settled back into the tan leather seat of his uncle's private jet. Federico had invited him to Miami, suggesting a change of scenery for a couple of nights. After pacing the mansion for two days, thinking only of Skylar, Luca couldn't argue with his uncle's logic.

Of course, he had first sent Skylar chocolates, and she'd sounded so happy when she called to thank him that he wanted to stay on the island and invite her over. But he needed to slow down with her. Not be so eager. That's why he didn't tell her where he was going. It also still felt odd to reveal his plans to anyone. So he'd put on a real button-down shirt and pants and a jacket. He carried a smart-looking, black leather overnight bag, as if he were any young professional on a business trip, then left the house. He felt like an impostor, since he'd gotten so used to the beach-bum attire of shorts and a T-shirt. He'd parked his uncle's Mercedes at the island's executive airport, tipping the security guard an extra few hundred to keep it safe.

After a quick flight across the state, a limo whisked Luca to his uncle's downtown Miami penthouse. He grinned when he walked in, because as tropically ostentatious as the beach house was, the penthouse was something out of a sleek Miami dream. Like stepping into a cliché. Floor-to-ceiling windows overlooking the ocean. Everything—the furniture, the walls, the floors—was decorated in white. What wasn't white was clear glass, as shiny and tranquil as the ocean just beyond the windows.

"I didn't take you for a minimalist," Luca laughed, clapping his uncle on the back as they hugged.

Federico shrugged. "It helps me think. Let's have a drink." He led Luca over to a chair—white, of course—and then stood at a bar. "Scotch?"

"Absolutely," Luca said. His uncle had great taste in booze.

Federico handed Luca his drink and then sank into a matching white sofa. They made small talk, and Luca was surprised how comfortable he felt. This was good, getting to know his only living family member.

He rattled the ice in his glass. "*Zio*, I meant to tell you. The workers came to fix the fence. Thanks for calling about that. If Skylar opened it so easily that day, who knows who else could come in?"

"Excellent. And, speaking of that, how is the reporter girl? She did a pretty decent story on me, actually."

Luca grinned. "She's good."

"So you've seen her again?"

Luca nodded.

Federico leaned back into the sofa and took a sip. "Does she know about the book?"

Luca shook his head. "No. I've thought about telling her, though."

"Might not be a bad idea. Because you're not in too much danger anymore. And whatever danger you're in, you've got it under control with my help. You seem to like this girl. A lot."

"Who says I like her?" Luca said, shrugging.

"I know the look of a man who is totally captivated. Trust me. I've been in your shoes, and I've regretted making some wrong decisions."

Luca let that sink in, and it reminded him of something else that had been on his mind since coming to Florida. "You know, *Zio*," he said, "I've been wanting to ask you. What happened between you and my father? And why did you never get married?"

His uncle sighed and looked down at his feet. "Changing the subject. Okay. Well, I knew you'd ask that eventually. And the answer to both of those questions have to do with the same reason. It's why I asked you here."

Luca jiggled his leg nervously. Something about his uncle's tense face was unsettling.

"I hesitated on whether to tell you this, but I think it's time," Federico continued in a quiet voice.

"Time? For what?"

Federico sat back and sprawled an arm over the back of the sofa. "I knew your mother before your father did. We were in love. I don't know if your parents ever told you, but we all grew up in the same neighborhood."

Luca's eyes went big and he cocked his head. He remained silent. What the hell? He knew that his mom and dad were from the same area of Naples, but it never occurred to him that Federico also grew up with his mother.

"Your mother and I talked about marriage. I came to the U.S. for law school and she stayed behind in Italy. When I returned, she was dating Cristiano, your father. It was…awkward." Federico sighed big.

Luca reminded himself to take a breath. He had never considered that his mother might be with anyone but his father, much less dated his uncle. "I had no idea."

Federico shook his head. "Of course you wouldn't. Cristiano and I stopped talking to each other. You and I never got to know each other."

"Well, it was thirty years ago, right? I guess things like that weren't uncommon." Luca smiled tightly.

"No. Not uncommon. For many years, I beat myself up for losing her. I loved your mother, Luca. Never stopped loving her. Still love her."

Luca bent his head and tears pricked at his eyes. Federico's connection to his mother made him feel a bit closer to the older man, and he was grateful for it. "I miss her."

"I know. I miss her too—or miss who she was all those years ago."

"Her death was my fault."

His uncle took a deep breath. "You say that, but Cristiano played a part, Luca. Don't kid yourself. He was a prosecutor. You know he tried lots of criminals and Mafia bosses. And he encouraged you to write your book, you said so yourself. So did your mother. They were both hardheaded about doing the right thing and never backing down."

Luca nodded and drained his Scotch. Federico was right. "Pigheaded" was what the papers called his father when he'd tried a famous Camorra boss when Luca was only seven. Luca remembered that summer as the one where he and his mother went to live on his grandfather's citrus farm and he didn't see his father for months.

"Cristiano sought justice. Always. Almost to a fault. Everything was black and white with him."

Luca nodded again. "When was the last time you saw my mother?"

Federico stood and paced the room, standing at the window, gazing at the fading daylight. Luca's mouth went dry as the minutes silently ticked past.

Federico turned. "A month before your parents were married. And nine months before you were born."

The words hit Luca like a swift kick to the stomach. Did he just hear his uncle correctly? He reminded himself to breathe. "What are you trying to say?"

Federico came to the sofa next to Luca's chair and sat facing him. "I flew to Italy before her wedding to Cristiano. I wanted to try one last time to convince her to marry me. She was confused, and one night, we…we were intimate. She told me that she hadn't yet been with your father, that he thought she was a virgin…"

Luca winced. Oh God. He stared at the gleaming white floor.

"Then she went ahead and married your father. But I got her pregnant. She later sent me a letter telling me that that she was having morning sickness the day of the wedding and knew the baby was mine."

"So. You're my…father?" Luca whispered. "That's insane. Why…why didn't anyone tell me? Why wouldn't my mother have said something?"

Federico exploded. "She didn't want to leave her family behind to come to America, which is what I wanted. And she thought she wanted your father. Maybe she saw him as a better prospect, someone more noble. I was going to be an ambulance chaser, a personal injury lawyer in Miami. But I wasn't going to destroy my brother and tell him that his son—the apple of his eye, the love of his life—wasn't really his."

Luca froze, unable to move. *No. No. No.* This couldn't be happening. Not after everything he had been through.

"And I knew your father loved you more than anything and would take care of you. Probably better than I would. Hell, I screwed up with your mom. I left her behind. I was stubborn and refused to return to Italy. I didn't think I'd be a better father. But that's why I was so happy when you called me when you were in Argentina. I could finally help you. My son."

"I don't believe you." Luca's voice was hoarse. When his eyes met Federico's, though, he knew that the older man wasn't lying. Federico's eyes were the same color as his own.

"I'm sorry, Luca."

Luca sank back in his chair, winded. He gaped at Federico warily. After a few minutes, the man tipped a pour of liquor into his glass.

Luca spoke, but his voice sounded like it was coming from someone else. Detached. Confused. How could this be happening?

"Is this why my parents fought all the time?"

Federico, standing at the window, turned. "Maybe. I'm not sure. Your mother sent me an email about three years ago. Apologizing. She told me about you, and how proud she was that you were a reporter. She said that she and Cristiano had a loveless marriage and that she wished she'd made different decisions."

Luca exhaled long, pushing out his lips. The whole conversation had left him reeling. Exhausted. He stood up, unable to look at his uncle, and he shook his head vigorously as if to remove the memory of Federico's words from his brain. "Where am I sleeping?"

With a sigh, Federico rose and walked down an all-white hall. Luca followed, and Federico pointed.

Opening the door to a guest bedroom, Luca turned. "I don't know what to say. What to call you. What to think."

Federico put his hand on Luca's shoulder and squeezed. "Let's just take things as they come, okay?"

Luca nodded and stumbled into the bedroom, flopping down onto the white modern platform bed. He took his phone out of his pocket and brought up Skylar's contact. His finger hovered over the screen. He wanted to call her, to hear her voice. To tell her about what he'd just learned. But he knew that if he did that, he'd have to explain everything else about his life.

He wasn't ready to do that.

# CHAPTER TWENTY

At least the American reporter girl drove an Italian car. She had that going for her. Otherwise, Annalisa was growing more annoyed with the American by the moment.

She watched Skylar walk out of the newspaper and into a cafe down the street. The girl's style was all wrong. First of all, the high heels. Black was for nighttime, not hot summer days. The dress was too plain and she needed better jewelry. Annalisa sniffed with distaste as she saw Skylar emerge from the café with a big plastic cup.

When Skylar pulled out of her parking space in front of the newsroom, Annalisa followed in her rental Toyota at a safe distance behind. Skylar drove into a parking lot, and Annalisa hung back and watched her get out of her car and walk toward the adjacent building, pausing near a giant plant to take a call. She watched Skylar grin and laugh flirtatiously while chatting, and Annalisa wondered if it was Luca on the other end. Probably, since Skylar twirled her hair with her finger and looked upwards, coyly.

Making matters worse, Skylar had great hair. Annalisa had to admit that.

Her stomach flipped as she watched the woman practically glow from the conversation. This was not good.

# CHAPTER TWENTY-ONE

Skylar's phone rang just as she was about to walk inside the building, and her mood soared. It was Luca. She hadn't heard from him in a couple of days, and the edges of panic were setting in, which was silly since he'd sent her the chocolates. Still. Why hadn't he called or texted in two days?

"*Buona sera*, what are you doing tonight?"

"Luca. It's good to finally hear from you." She didn't want to seem clingy, but she did want him to know that she was a little annoyed that he'd disappeared on her. Her job was making her restless, too. This assignment was a meeting at the island's community center, and it promised to be a snooze. She'd already written two articles today. One was about an unusual migration of horseshoe crabs on Palmira's north beach; the other was on a rash of thefts at several of the island's upscale clothing stores. Basically, this was a long day of unpaid overtime and frustration.

"*Tesoro.* I apologize for not calling. I was in Miami, visiting my...uncle."

She was about to ask whether Miami had phone and text service but then thought better of it. Something in his tone made her not want to get too scrappy with him. And it wasn't like he owed her a phone call every day. They weren't officially dating.

Her eyes went to a large tropical plant with foliage almost as big as her, and she reached out with her free hand and ran her finger over the veins of a giant green leaf. She then twisted a strand of her hair around her finger, recalling how Luca liked to do that. "I have an exciting night planned. I'm writing a story on bridge tolls. You couldn't understand how boring this is."

Luca chuckled. "Well, I can't stop thinking about you. What are you doing later tonight? The rest of the week?"

She turned toward the giant leaf and beamed. "Umm, tonight around nine I'm joining some people from the newsroom at a wine bar on Main Street...."

"Oh? Which bar?" Luca didn't sound jealous, just curious.

"It's called Bacchus. It's right near the newsroom. Just down the street."

"Hmm. And Thursday? On Friday, you're mine for the weekend, no?"

His words made Skylar unsteady with desire. "I'm yours for the weekend. On Thursday I have yoga. There's a new studio I'd like to check out. Do you wanna come with me?"

There was a pause. She totally didn't expect him to go to yoga. Most guys didn't do yoga.

"Yeah. Yoga. I'd love to. What time and where?"

Skylar all but did a little dance. She couldn't wait to tell Emily.

After they hung up, it was a lot easier for her to concentrate on her assignment. The bridge toll meeting wasn't awful. Or maybe it didn't seem boring because Skylar spent most of it thinking about Luca. As a department of transportation official turned down the lights for a PowerPoint presentation, she zoned out and remembered of all of the places on her body where Luca had kissed her the previous weekend. Her neck. The inside of her wrists. Just above her bellybutton. When the lights in the community center came up, she was uncomfortably wet between her legs, and Skylar pulled the hem of her black sheath dress toward her knees.

An hour later, after filing her article for the paper, Skylar bounced into Bacchus to meet her friends. A giant glass of sangria called her name as a reward for a long day.

It was crowded for midweek in Florida in August, and Skylar realized it was due to a seashell collectors' convention on the island. Weaving through the crowded bar, she found her newsroom friends sitting at a table in the middle of the room. Kira, the editorial assistant, Rebecca, an advertising salesperson, and Megan, who was a news reporter like Sky, were all there. Emily said she'd try to join them later after covering a high school football game.

With a faux fresco mural of the Parthenon on one wall and paintings of nude people frolicking amongst vineyards, the place had a slightly tacky yet pleasant ambiance. Usually a bad Jimmy Buffet cover singer crooned in the corner, but Skylar noted with relief that there was no live music that evening. In her three months in Florida, she had gotten so sick of that "Margaritaville" song.

Bacchus also wasn't outrageously overpriced, which the cash-poor newspaper employees appreciated. The bar drew a mix of locals and tourists, and the women from the paper liked to scope out the potential single vacationers on the island. Although she had never actually met a tourist that she wanted to hang out with, Skylar liked doing that, too, just for the hilarity of joking with her friends.

Now that she'd met Luca, the charm of ogling random men was gone.

She greeted the girls and considered telling them about Luca but decided against it. It was one thing to tell Emily, but it was another to tell every woman in the newsroom who lived on the same tiny island. Maybe if she and Luca were still together in a month. Then she'd tell them.

She ordered her sangria and focused on the conversation. Megan was a little drunk and railed against the paper's new edict for shorter, tighter articles, tossing her shoulder-length curly hair as she spoke.

"I am, like, never going to get anywhere if I can't write more than six hundred words per story. What the hell is that? It's bad enough I had to write a feature about the rainfall totals for July and then about a billiards tournament at the senior center. I should be covering New York Fashion Week."

Everyone laughed. Being a twenty-something journalist on a Florida island filled with mostly retirees definitely had its challenges. This was not the glamorous profession they had anticipated while in journalism school.

"O-M-G. Oh my God." Megan's eyes moved from left to right as she leaned in to whisper to the group. "Right behind Skylar. Gorgeous guy. Holy shit. Sky, you're the only one who can't see him, but don't turn around, it will be too obvious. Especially since Kira is drooling in her wine."

Kira snorted. "Whatever, bitch."

"Megan, I thought you were dating Daniel from advertising?" Sky said, amused. She sipped her drink. Previously, this conversation about a hot guy walking into the bar would have interested her.

Megan sat back, her eyes focused behind Skylar the entire time. "I am, but I can still admire and look for someone for the rest of you ladies. Sky, just get up and go to the bathroom. He's at the bar. He's got on jeans—oh wow, what an ass! And a black T-shirt. A slightly tight, black T-shirt skimming his broad, strapping chest. Short dark hair, smoldering eyes… Shit, I need to stop reading those romance novels. Oh God, he just turned around and looked at us."

Megan averted her gaze and buried her face in a menu. Skylar chortled.

"Sky, go check him out. He's super hot," Rebecca said.

Okay, Skylar would play along. Just for laughs. After Luca, she didn't think Brad Pitt, George Clooney or Ryan Gosling would impress her if they were standing at the bar.

Sending a snarky eye-roll to her friends, Skylar rose and turned.

*Oh my God.* It was Luca.

Skylar caught her breath and tried not to look surprised. Tried not to gasp out loud.

His lips held a secret smile as their eyes met for a quick second. Sky was wearing her tall black heels and wobbled a little. Her fingers found the back of her chair and squeezed, seeking some stability so she wouldn't fall over. Luca glanced again at her then scanned the bar, still smiling in that mysterious way.

"See, I told you. He's so hot you can't even stand up," Megan hissed from behind the menu. "Jesus, was he looking at you?"

What was he doing here? Teasing her? Checking up on her?

She turned to the group and attempted a smirk. "No. He was not looking at me. But I have to go to the bathroom anyway. I'll scope him out."

Skylar walked slowly by a few tables then past Luca. He looked like a model tonight, something out of the pages of Italian *Vogue*. Dark and dangerous, and so fucking sexy. She noticed several women staring at him.

But why was he even there, with a beer in front of him? He'd said he didn't feel comfortable in bars.

From where he was situated, she knew he could see her walk down the long hall to the bathroom at the side of the restaurant. Skylar went inside and locked the door.

# CHAPTER TWENTY-TWO

"Miss. *Miss.* The bathroom's down the hall. This is the kitchen."

Annalisa peeked between the crack of the double swinging doors and ignored the cook. She had followed Skylar to Bacchus, where the American met her gaggle of poorly-dressed American girlfriends. What she hadn't anticipated was Luca walking in looking like a Roman warrior, primal and commanding. She'd barely escaped being seen by him. Thankfully the place was crowded and she had taken a seat near the kitchen so she could scramble in there when he walked toward the bar.

Then again, he would have never noticed her, because he hadn't taken his eyes off that awful woman.

"I'm sorry, you can't be in here."

The cook touched her arm, and Annalisa flicked it off with an impatient grunt. She asked, "Is there a door to the parking lot from the kitchen?"

"Yes, it's right this way."

She couldn't tear her eyes away from Luca's gorgeous face. With rising anger she saw his gaze follow Skylar walking past, and then she watched him leave his seat at the bar.

Never had he looked at her the way he stared at Skylar. His eyes were wide and hungry. Filled with desire—and something so very obvious that made hot tears come to her eyes. He looked at Skylar with pure adoration. Luca looked like a desperate man, drunk with love. If Annalisa were watching them in a movie, she would have sighed and swooned.

She was not watching them in a movie.

# CHAPTER TWENTY-THREE

There was a knock at the bathroom door. "Sky," a voice said softly.

She flung the door open, her heart racing, and Luca slipped inside and locked it behind him. His lips were slanted in a sexy smirk. Before she could speak, Luca pressed her against a wall painted with a mural of green parrots flying over a vineyard. His body was heavy, insistent, and his heat seeped into her every pore. His lips were fierce and urgent, and he gripped the side of her neck with his hand tighter than ever, and he kissed her violently. Tonight he smelled different, faintly of spice and wood.

"Sky, I can't get you out of my head," he whispered into her ear. "I thought about you nonstop while I was in Miami."

He plundered her mouth, and she greedily accepted it, wanting more of his sweet taste.

Luca's other hand wound its way up her dress, and his fingers raked over the thin fabric of her black cotton panties. Sky turned her head so he could claim her neck with his mouth, trying not to gasp out loud as he stroked the outline of her labia with a delicate and tantalizing touch. Her clit throbbed and she wanted him to rub it, but when she tried to move his hand into her panties he resisted.

"Please," Sky whispered. "Please?"

Luca shook his head and kept teasing her, brushing his fingers over her with a feather-light touch as he inhaled her neck with ferocity. She pressed her face into his shoulder, and biting him was the only way she could keep from crying out loud from pleasure.

Why was he doing this to her here? Did she even care why? Skylar grabbed his head and pulled his lips close, wanting to consume him.

She rubbed the heel of her hand over his jeans, feeling his hard length under the rough denim. When she folded her arms around his neck, he took his hand from between her legs. He simultaneously hoisted her up as she gracefully jumped, wrapping her legs around his waist. Grinding his hips into hers, she felt only white-hot need as they rocked their bodies together.

"Luca…" She gasped, barely able to form words through her thin breaths. "Oh, fuck, Luca."

His lips grazed her neck and rested just underneath her earlobe. It was a good thing he had pinned her to the wall, otherwise she would have crumpled to the floor when he again whispered in her ear with that accent, "I have actually, physically craved you. It's as if I need you to live, like air or water or food. *Ti desidero.*"

Abruptly, he stopped. Eased her down. Backed up about a foot.

He was grinning. He licked the corner of his mouth and leaned in for a soft kiss. Skylar panted and was about to ask him what he was doing when he kissed her again.

"See you tomorrow night at yoga," he whispered in her ear. Then he walked out of the bathroom. As the door closed, she watched him enter the men's room across the hall.

Skylar was flushed and flustered. Her hair was wild. Her entire body trembled, and between her legs she was a wet, slippery mess. Leaning back on the wall, she tried to catch her breath. Being this intensely, obviously sexual was so foreign to her. Never had she felt this with James, or with anyone. Luca made her want to unleash every sexual fantasy she had, and lately, she had lots of them. This all-consuming need pushed Skylar to the edge of her comfort zone, yet she would be lying if she said she wasn't enjoying it wholly. She was.

Maybe too much.

She slicked her hair back into a ponytail and put on some red lipstick, hoping to hide the freshly kissed look. Soaping her hands, she ran her wrists under cool water for a long time, hoping the scorching feeling inside of her would go away. Would her friends suspect what happened? What did just happen?

Her heart beating double-time, she walked out past the bar and Luca. He tipped his beer to his mouth and caught her eye as she did, but Skylar only allowed that for a second. She didn't want to stare at him because her face would flush even more.

What kind of game was he playing? The fact that she was so turned on almost terrified her. Since James, her only real relationship, she aimed for order and predictability, not frenzied groping in bathrooms. Yet, wasn't this exactly what she was looking for? Wasn't this what Emily had suggested, and wasn't it the exact reason she'd demanded Luca be with her exclusively?

When she returned to the table, Sky's coworkers were immersed in an absurd conversation and barely noticed as she sat.

"I am not covering a feature story about the nudist trailer park in Fort Myers. I don't care how much Jill wants me to. I'm not wasting my time on that," said Megan.

"All of the people you don't want to see naked are at the nudist resorts," Kira agreed, her tone matter-of-fact.

"So gross," Megan said then looked at Sky. "Hey, did you run into Mr. Fuckable on your way to the bathroom? We saw him go down that hall right after you."

"Oh, no. I didn't." Sky shook her head and hoped the red in her cheeks had receded. She picked up the wine list and pretended to read. Touching her chin with her index finger, she wondered if Luca's stubble had left a mark, because her skin there felt raw. Her lips felt raw, too. In fact, her entire soul felt hypersensitive, rubbed bare.

"Suuure," said Kira. "It was probably like that scene at the coffee shop in the movie *Unfaithful*."

Skylar shot her a confused look over the top of the menu. Kira was always talking about movies. She wrote unpaid film reviews for the paper in hopes of someday becoming a critic.

"Did you see that movie? Diane What's-her-name and that handsome French actor? He slips into the coffee shop and screws her senseless as her friends are sitting there unaware. It was so hot."

Skylar shrugged and took a gulp of sangria. Out the corner of her eye she watched Luca toss a few bills on the bar then stride away without giving her a glance.

"Nope. Must have missed that one, Kira."

# CHAPTER TWENTY-FOUR

Annalisa stood before the glass case in the dive shop, carefully considering her choices. Should she pick the Survival Series Ultimate Knife or the one called the Halcyon, which was a fine name for a blade? The knives lined the case, each with their own special charms. She almost wanted the camouflage-handled one. It seemed so American.

"That one." She pointed to the corner of the shelf. "That's the one I'd like to get my boyfriend for his birthday. He dives a lot and needs a new scuba knife. He mentioned this to me the other week."

The clerk extracted a shiny silver knife and droned on about the features. Scalloped edges that made it easier to hold. Something called a skeletonized handle, which meant it had five holes in case she wanted to slip her fingers into them for a firmer grip. A stainless-steel blade, a spear-point, a serrated edge and a plain edge.

Turning it over in her hands, Annalisa smiled as she wondered what it would feel like to cut skin with the gleaming weapon.

"I'll take it."

# CHAPTER TWENTY-FIVE

He was used to risk. Traveling alone, he took plenty of calculated risks. Since his parents were killed, Luca hadn't taken a risk for a woman. Hell, he hadn't risked anything for a woman *before* the mess with the book. Hadn't ever wanted to. The decision had been simple. Black-and-white. Relationships weren't worth the trouble.

Until here, on Palmira. Skylar was a living, breathing gray area. A sexy risk. Spending time in her presence was a risk. Going to the Bacchus bar to see her was a risk. And now he was at a yoga class, bending and twisting his body so he could be near her. His gun was in the glove box of the car. Another risk.

Palmira seemed so safe, though. Maybe none of this was risky. Maybe all of it was. Maybe the biggest risk was to his heart, because he was willing to go out of his comfort zone for Skylar. For the first time in forever, he was allowing himself to feel something for another person.

He'd been edgy since kissing and touching Skylar at the bar the previous night. God, he'd wanted to ravish her in the bathroom. But he didn't want to risk being in public for longer than necessary. He'd only gone to the bar to see who Skylar was with, and his stomach finally settled when he realized she was there with female coworkers and not a date—or with someone even more sinister. It was almost shameful to admit, but he'd needed to see with his own eyes that she wasn't betraying him to the Mafia—or betraying him with another man.

Something about finding out that his uncle was really his father had made him even more paranoid about the people in his life. Who could he trust? His own mother had lied to him, and that was the most troubling fact of all.

*The more one knows, the less one believes.* His tattoo was truly his personal, ironic motto, mocking him every time he looked in the mirror.

After spending two emotional days talking to his uncle in Miami, he'd concluded that he might never have any real answers about his mother, about why she'd never revealed who his real father was.

"Just remember that she loved you," Federico said several times.

Now that he was back on Palmira, Luca was still troubled. He looked over at Skylar, who had lifted her hands above her head. Her eyes were closed, her mouth was turned up in a smile, and she looked blissful. She always looked blissful, and that soothed some of his angst. He felt guilty for being so distrustful of her, yet discovering her truthfulness had endeared her even more to him. Add to that her sharp mind, her sexy laugh, her sweet lips, and he was totally distracted.

So here he was. At yoga. Trying to forget about everything in his life except Skylar.

Their mats were side by side in the crowded class and they stole glances at each other. Grinned like fools. The teacher lit sandalwood incense and candles flickered in the dark. The class was called Zen Flow, and the poses were languid, sensual. Slow chant music played, and he tried to concentrate upon being mindful and not on Skylar's body. To stay in the moment, to not think about his problems. Or his imminent hard-on.

Luca hadn't told Skylar that he'd spent three months at a yoga ashram in India. That was the first place he went after leaving Italy. He was pondering how to explain his yoga knowledge when he caught a glimpse of her in a pose. She was on her back and holding her feet with her hands, knees bent deep toward her armpits in what the teacher called happy baby pose. It was more like happy Luca pose. Maybe she would recreate that contortion for him naked.

"Okay, class, partner up," the teacher said.

Luca turned to Skylar, grinning.

He felt the eyes of several women, but he grabbed Skylar's wrist and pulled her toward him. "You're my partner, no?" he asked.

She giggled softly.

The teacher had them stand close, back-to-chest. Luca was in back of Skylar, and following the teacher's instruction he placed his hand in the middle of her spine to feel her breath. He slightly tilted his hips toward her ass so she could feel the stirrings of his erection. It was a good thing his shorts were super baggy.

"I can feel you breathing. Can you feel me?" he whispered in her ear.

He watched her in the mirror as she grew wide-eyed. They switched positions so Skylar was behind him, and she scratched his back softly through his shirt. He entertained a brief fantasy of leaving class and making love to her in the car. If only she would let him. It both surprised and mystified him that they still hadn't had sex, and that he was even more interested in her now than when he first met her.

The teacher had them sit on the floor cross-legged and facing each other.

"Now, raise your hands to shoulder level, palms facing your partners, and press your hands into your partner's hands. Look each other in the eyes and breathe. Try to coordinate your breath with your partner. In Sanskrit, yoga means yoke, or union. The most important thing we can do is be in a union, be one with someone else. We're all in this life together. Let's be together and live in the present."

A twinge of anxiety rose in Luca's chest. This was too intimate—more intimate than sex. Skylar's bottom lip trembled, so maybe she was nervous, too. And yet, he didn't separate from her gaze or her hands. She didn't break from his, either. Her mouth parted and softened in the candlelight.

The teacher spoke again in a quiet voice. "I'm going to read some lines by the thirteenth-century Sufi poet, Rumi, then we'll gaze at each other's auras in silence."

Luca tried to breathe as he listened to the words. As he stared into Skylar's blue eyes, for long quiet seconds his heart felt like it was going to burst out of his chest it was pounding so hard.

Mercifully, the teacher asked them to lie down in final relaxation on their mats. Luca and Sky sprawled next to each other, and he reached for her hand. The teacher told them to empty their minds of thoughts, but Luca was filled with them. He tried to breathe his way through the anxiety and remind himself to focus on the moment. Not the past. Or the future.

When class ended, Skylar was in a bubbly mood. She was so tempting in her ponytail, little black shorts and matching tank top. With a breathy voice, she leaned in close to his ear.

"Want to come back to my place?"

Of course he did.

### 

From the parking lot of her building, Skylar ran up the stairs to her condo. At the top, Luca grabbed her around the waist and pressed her into the wall.

"I don't think I can go to yoga with you again. You were too sexy. You don't know what it's like to do a downward dog with a hard-on," he groaned.

They were near the door of her elderly neighbor, and Skylar laughed, hoping no one would poke a head out and see Luca biting her neck. "That's not very mindful," she laughed.

And yet, she felt the same way. It had been difficult to concentrate during class because he looked so masculine and strong when in a handstand, his triceps hard and sculpted. But she was trying to approach tonight with a cool, even head and not through the prism of lust. It had been so intense practicing with him, but she reined in her emotions now that they were at her condo.

They kissed as they walked down the interior corridor, tumbling inside her apartment. She flicked on a light.

"Where did you learn yoga? You were really good," she said while locking the door. Her question stopped him from nibbling on her neck.

"I've traveled a lot. I...I spent three months in India at an ashram about nine months ago."

Interesting. So, he'd done that after his parents died? When was he going to tell her? Sky wondered if now was the time to ask him about the tragedy of his family. She opened her mouth, but he spoke first.

"I'm kind of sweaty. Let's shower together."

He pressed her against the door and gave her a long, sensual kiss. He undid her ponytail and threaded his fingers through her hair.

"Wait—," she said, wriggling her head from his lips. "I want to ask you something else."

He *mmm-hmmed* in response and kissed the palm of her hand, then dotted her arm with kisses, which tickled.

"I thought you didn't like bars. Didn't feel comfortable in them. Why did you show up at Bacchus last night?"

Flashing a sly smile, Luca shrugged. "To kiss you."

"You wanted to kiss me, or you wanted to see who I was with?" Sky asked.

He backed up and held his hand out, pushing the air with his palm. "Relax, Skylar. Maybe a little of both."

She wasn't sure what to make of his answer. She also wasn't sure if she liked his possessiveness. Or maybe she did, and that didn't sit well with her, either.

"Why would you care who I was with if you made it clear that you weren't interested in a relationship?" Sky asked.

Luca stepped back about a foot, biting his lip. "Skylar, I do care who you're with. You wanted me to be with just you, right? I just don't want to talk about our situation, about us. It's easier this way."

"Easier for you, maybe."

"It's not easy for me," Luca said, his eyes downcast.

"Why are you doing this to me?"

"Doing what?" Luca asked, shaking his head.

"This…these…sexy things. Like last night at the bar. No one's ever treated me that way," Skylar said. She wasn't sure if she was complaining.

They stared at each other. She couldn't read his expression.

"A physical relationship is all I'm capable of, Sky. I can't give you anything more right now because it's so complicated. I can't give you a future."

*Well, that hurts.* Even if he'd said as much before, a lump of sadness welled up in her chest. She didn't like it underlined. Though, she supposed she was pushing. But she couldn't help herself. Pushing, questioning, was second nature.

"Complicated how? You seem pretty perfect to me."

Luca shook his head and looked at her with anguish. "Skylar, please. No questions. Please."

"What if I want a future? What if I need one?"

Luca reached out with his hand, and his index finger slowly brushed a wisp of hair out of her face. His previous words and that one tender move broke her resolve to demand more answers. Hadn't she already agreed to his terms?

She pulled him into the bathroom and shut the door, reminding herself for the millionth time that this was a casual fling and it would lead to nothing, no matter how much she wanted it to. And, hadn't she said yes to that? Wasn't she mature enough to take this for what it was, assuming they were both straightforward with each other? Maybe she was only good for sex and nothing else. At least James was wrong and she was good for that.

Turning on the shower and testing the water for warmth, her mood was melancholy. When was she going to take control of her own pleasure? When would she stop allowing a man to dictate when, where and how she enjoyed herself sexually? Maybe now was that time. Maybe Emily was right. Maybe Luca did have a purpose in her life: to show her that she could enjoy sex without strings, without emotions. That's what he wanted, so why couldn't she as well?

She roughly pulled his shirt over his head and yanked his shorts and briefs down. Pure carnal contact and nothing more—that's what she wanted. The encounter in the bar the previous night and his sensual yoga moves had left her craving his body. Enough with feelings.

No. She couldn't convince herself. She wouldn't have sex tonight. That was still out of her comfort zone. She felt weak and powerless, almost as much as when she'd been with James. That was silly, perhaps, because Luca had been nothing but respectful, so maybe she should allow herself to go a little further with him, explore other things that she had been afraid of doing. Just to see if she could without an explosion of emotion.

Luca tried to kiss her, but Skylar shook her head and led him into the shower. He tried kissing her again, but she shifted away.

"No. Let me do what I want with you," she said, pouring jasmine-scented bath soap into her hand. She ran sudsy hands over Luca's chest, caressing his arms, the ridges of his stomach and finally his stunning erection.

He tilted his head back and let the water run over his forehead and dark hair while she knelt down. Her eyes turned upward, and the look of surprise and sheer pleasure on Luca's face was so satisfying that she vowed to enjoy him and his body as long as she could.

She licked and teased and sucked. Luca gasped and steadied himself with one hand on the tiled wall and the other on the shower door. It made Skylar feel powerful to turn him on so much. James had always been lukewarm when she tried to take charge in this way, and he'd said she had bad technique when she went down on him. From the sound of Luca's moans, he obviously didn't think her technique was bad.

Gently touching her wet head, Luca looked down at her. "My God, you're amazing."

She opened her throat wide to take him in, and squeezed his thighs with her hands. She wanted to give him an orgasm that sliced into his heart the way her own had the other night in his apartment. He let out a long, exhaled groan, cupping the back of her head with his hand. Then he came in long pulses, and Skylar swallowed everything.

She slid up his body and kissed him, hard. He leaned against the tile of the shower and reached for her, his hands shaking before they touched her face.

"You're going to destroy me, *amore mio*."

### 

Skylar woke up looking like a sleepy kitten, and Luca turned to brush her messy hair from her face so he could kiss her skin.

"Mmm, how long have you been up?" she asked, burrowing into the covers and pillow. Her voice sounded gravelly and tired. They had been up late talking about everything from the new Dr. Who series to debating whether Wikileaks or Woodward and Bernstein had more of an impact on American history. He had also given her two orgasms with his fingers, but she'd stopped him from tasting her, which drove him wild with pent-up need.

"For about an hour. Since the sun came up."

It was seven in the morning. He was sitting in Skylar's bed reading one of her books. *In Cold Blood* by Truman Capote. Something he'd always wanted to read.

She peeled back the sheet and duvet and made her way to the bathroom. "Great book. Wanna borrow it?"

"I'd love to, thanks," Luca said, calling after her, captivated by her naked ass.

When she came back into the bedroom they kissed. She tasted like mint and smelled like the orange blossom perfume that he loved. Luca shut the book, setting it on the nightstand, then kissed her more. He was hard again. What he really wanted was to make love to her, but he didn't want to pressure her. She was close, so close, to letting her guard down. He wondered if he would be in love with her by the time she did.

The thought stunned him. Could he be falling in love? Did love happen just like that—when one least expected it, at the worst possible moment?

"Hey," he whispered. "You didn't let me reciprocate last night."

She smiled. "You did. I love when you touch me."

"But I want to taste you. Please?"

She bit her bottom lip and nodded. "Wait. Let me take this off," she said, wriggling out of her tank top. He practically dove for her breasts, sucking on one nipple until it tightened in his mouth then turning his attention to the other as she made little moaning noises.

"My panties. Off."

He sat up and grinned, tugging her underwear down and tossing them aside when they were free from her legs. "I love it when you tell me what to do."

She opened her legs wide. Her skin was the color of cream, the hue of the sensual women he had seen on Renaissance frescoes in churches back home. When he scanned her body, his gaze stopped in between her legs.

"*Bella, bella, bella,*" he whispered, looking at her with adoration and stroking her inner thighs. "You have such a beautiful pussy."

Skylar gasped. "Oh my God. Did you just say that? No one has ever said that to me."

"I said it, and I meant it." Leaning forward, he pressed his mouth into the smooth skin above her bellybutton and she shuddered with pleasure as he gently bit her. As he touched and kissed down her body, a trail of goose bumps sprang up. Her orange blossom scent was both intoxicating and familiar, and Luca realized why he loved the way she smelled. It made him remember springtime at his grandparents' citrus grove back in Italy when he was a child.

Skylar smelled like home.

He closed his eyes and nuzzled her flesh, awash in pleasures past and present. He slipped a finger inside of her tight wetness then knelt to look at her beautiful body.

"You feel so good, *amore mio*," he said, his mind faintly registering that he had started calling her such an intimate name. "So fucking incredible."

He withdrew his finger and parted her folds, bowing his head to her. She moaned and put her hand on his head. She still seemed a little hesitant when his tongue touched the pink nub of her clitoris.

"Do I taste okay?" she whispered.

Circling her with his tongue, he teased the entrance to her core with his fingertip then licked in the same place. He lifted his head and grinned. "More than okay, *mia bella ragazza. Delizioso.* Delicious."

She inhaled loudly and grabbed his hair by the fistful. Bit by bit, he slid his finger deep inside of her, tantalizing her, moving slowly. The tip curved slightly upward as her hips tilted and bucked. She pressed against his mouth, getting wetter by the second.

"Another, Luca. Put another finger inside."

He pressed his forehead to her thigh and stopped licking her for a few seconds to steel himself, for his need was so great. He wanted something other than his fingers inside of her. And yet, he had promised her that she would be the one to decide when they would finally have sex. He had to keep his promise, even if it killed him.

Never had his cock been so hard and never had he wanted any woman this much. He slipped another finger in, and the erotic connection between them slowed, expanded, exploded. His thumb rubbed her clit slowly, forcefully. He moved his fingers inside of her, his chest tightening, aching, from his need. Watching her flutter her eyes shut, her mouth in a perfect 'O' shape, was enough to make him beg her in desperation. Beg for sex, for love, for her soul.

"Is this okay? You're tight, *amore mio*."

"I love it," she whispered. "And I love it when you call me *amore mio*."

He lowered his mouth again to her wetness. With several forceful flicks of his tongue, Sky cried out, loud. It didn't take much to make her come, and the release was so beautiful to feel and watch. Her flesh contracted and pulsed.

She tugged him up by his hair and put her arms around him. "Never… I've never come that way…"

Her voice trailed off, and he felt her heartbeat, or maybe it was his. Pressing his moist lips to her forehead, he fantasized about them staying in bed all day, in their own sex bubble.

"*Tu sei un angelo perfetto.*"

Skylar opened her eyes and looked at him, dazed.

"Sorry, *amore mio*. You are a perfect angel."

After several drowsy moments of hugging, she sighed. "I need to get to work."

She showered, and Luca put on his shirt and shorts from the previous night's yoga class. He'd shower when he got home. In her small kitchen, he made a pot of weak American coffee and then sat on the sofa reading *In Cold Blood*.

Skylar came out wearing a silk, long-sleeved cream-colored blouse and a camel-colored skirt. Her flats matched her skirt and her hair was pulled back into a casual ponytail, her lips pink with gloss.

He didn't deserve such a sweet, innocent woman.

# CHAPTER TWENTY-SIX

"Skylar. *Skylar.* Did you bring a story to critique? Hello? Skylar?"

Skylar snapped to attention.

"Um, Jill. I'm sorry. Let me look. I think I have one at my desk."

She jumped up and ran back to her cubicle. She couldn't concentrate on anything, and all because of Luca. Usually she liked the paper's weekly writing critique session, but today it had slipped her mind. Jill did this every Friday at lunch in an attempt to make them better writers. The reporters would read the first five paragraphs of their stories aloud and critique each other's work, and then Jill would talk about what worked and what didn't.

Sky grabbed a recent story and went back to the meeting.

"Sorry," she whispered, slipping into a chair next to Emily, who kicked her under the table and gave her a side-eye and a grin. Sky ignored her and doodled in her notebook while Jill talked about crafting a good newspaper intro.

After the meeting, Jill asked her to say behind.

*Shit.*

"Skylar, you did an excellent job with the Rossi story, but lately you've been a little distant. Disengaged. Anything wrong?"

Jill's green eyes were searching, and Skylar shook her head and wondered if her boss would understand if she admitted she was lovesick over a beautiful, secretive Italian man. No, that definitely wasn't a conversation she should have with her editor. She needed to get her shit together.

"Sorry. Nothing's wrong. I've got some good stories in the works."

Jill nodded. "Good. I really want to see you succeed, Sky."

"Thank you," Skylar said softly. "I'll step it up."

She walked back into the newsroom, dread settling in her stomach as she sat at her desk. Luca had worked his way into every fiber of her body, and he'd admitted that their relationship couldn't go anywhere. She needed to unravel him from her life. Being a journalist was all she had ever wanted, and she'd be damned if she would let a man screw it up for her. She was stronger than that.

Emily leaned against her desk. "Sky, wanna come with us to the Iguana tonight?"

She shook her head. "Luca and I—"

Emily interrupted and held up her hand. "Say no more. I saw you spacing out during the meeting and doodling in your notebook."

"Oh God, was I that obvious?"

Emily nodded and cackled.

Sky groaned and steeled her resolve. "I've gotta get a handle on myself. I think tonight I'm going to tell him that I need some space. I have to focus on my job."

Emily rolled her eyes and put her hands in a yoga prayer gesture. "Skylar. Balance. No one's telling you that you can't have hot sex and a good job."

"We haven't had sex."

"What? Why not?" Emily whispered loudly. "But...you spent the night at his place. I thought you had decided to just be friends with bene—"

Skylar stood and took her friend by the arm. She pulled Emily into a corridor near the bathrooms where no one could overhear their conversation and said, "Shh. I've decided to wait."

"For what? Is he a shitty kisser? Does he have a small dick?"

"No." *Far from it.* Skylar grinned.

"Then why wait? God, Skylar, you're wound so tight. Just fuck him."

For a moment Skylar thought she was in high school, what with the peer pressure. She rolled her eyes. "I just want to feel good about it. Like I'm doing it for myself, not because he wants it."

Emily shrugged. "Okay. But don't be a cock-tease, either."

"Whatever. He seems fine with teasing." Luca seemed to love their ever-heightening erotic encounters. "But I'm worried he'll be the best sex I've ever had. He has to be. We've just fooled around, and it's better than anything I've experienced with any other guy."

Emily stared skeptically. "And you're worried about...what?"

Skylar didn't expect her friend to understand, and she sighed. "I know it'll be amazing with him. I just know it. And then it'll be emotionally impossible for me to move on when we break up. When he says goodbye. He's already said he won't be in Florida for that long, and I'm not sure I can deal with the emotional aftermath of breaking up with my sexual soul-mate."

"You haven't fucked him and you're worried about the emotional aftermath of when you break up? Sexual soul-mate? What kind of crap is that? Maybe he's awful in bed."

Skylar could see that Emily was losing patience. "No. He won't be awful. That's the thing. I can feel that we're totally, completely perfect for each other sexually. I've never felt like this before. All my past boyfriends have been…just a waste of time. I see that now."

"Okay, this is getting way too complex. Just fuck him and enjoy it."

Skylar rolled her eyes and forced a laugh. "Fine. I'll keep you posted. I'm going for coffee now. Want to come?"

Emily shook her head. "Nope. Gotta make calls."

Skylar nodded and decided it was best. She needed some space, anyway. Time to think.

As she walked the few blocks to the café, she became lost in thought. For the first time that day her mind wasn't on Luca. It burned her that Jill thought she was distracted. I mean, she *was*, but Skylar hated being reprimanded, even a little, for anything. Her inability to take criticism was a shortcoming, she knew. As an only child, she strove to please authority figures. She'd always loved her teachers, got perfect grades and did everything her mother asked of her. Hell, she was still trying to please her mother five years after her death.

So, what was she doing? Living on Palmira, hanging out with Luca, working at a small island newspaper—Skylar didn't think any of this was what her mother had wanted. A guilty feeling settled over her as she walked into the building and ordered her iced coffee, and her thoughts spiraled out of control. She was a terrible reporter. She would be fired. She'd have to take a waitressing job to pay her student loans, probably have to work at the Sloppy Iguana wearing a tight T-shirt that said "Is Eight Inches Enough?" in reference to the bar's hot dogs. She'd break the promise she'd made to her dying mom to be successful and change the world with her words.

Probably she'd make more at the Iguana than at the newspaper. That thought depressed her even more.

As she left the cafe, Skylar looked down at her feet, dejected. Then she felt herself bump into something—or someone.

"Oh! I'm so sorry!" she gasped, feeling iced coffee dripping onto her hand. The lid clattered to the ground, and a few ice cubes skittered along the tile near Skylar's ballet flat. She had indeed run into someone, a birdlike young woman who was wearing white pants that now had a golf ball–sized brown coffee stain on the thigh.

"Crap, I'm sorry. God, I am a klutz," Skylar said as looked at the woman, whose light brown eyes were narrow slits. "I wasn't paying attention. It's totally my fault. I am incredibly sorry." Somehow her own clothes were unscathed by the liquid.

"Look at my pants," the woman said in a harsh voice, then added something in a foreign language.

Skylar paused for a beat, tilting her head. The words sounded Italian. And the woman looked classically Mediterranean, with long, dark hair and olive skin. She was gorgeous, actually, with perfectly made-up red lips, high-heeled strappy sandals and long, dark lashes.

The woman stared at Skylar, and their eyes met. The woman's gaze traveled slowly down Skylar's body, and Skylar felt a mixture of self-consciousness and fear. Something in the way the woman clenched her jaw and thinned her lips seemed unnaturally incensed. Unhinged-looking, even. Skylar knew that she should have been paying better attention as she walked, but it wasn't *that* big of a coffee stain. Nothing that water and soap, or dry cleaning at the most, couldn't fix.

"You should pay attention to where you're going," the woman hissed. The shade of her nails matched her lips perfectly, and Skylar briefly wondered if she herself could ever look that organized, that put-together.

"Really, I'm sorry." The way this tiny woman stared at her made her feel like she was outdoors during a New England blizzard. Cold. Uncomfortable. In danger.

"Forget it." The woman shot her a disgusted look and then turned toward the bathroom, tossing her hair.

Embarrassed and creeped-out, Skylar whispered another apology to the woman's back then fled the café. She shivered, grateful for the blinding Florida sun and the heavy humidity. It took several moments for her body to warm up.

# CHAPTER TWENTY-SEVEN

Annalisa scrubbed at her white jeans in the bathroom, swearing softly in Italian. Skylar was not only fucking Luca, she wore terrible clothes and was clumsy. How would she punish the little bitch?

Skylar didn't deserve to be killed, not really. Even Annalisa wasn't that crazy. Or was she? A smile spread across her face. Maybe the American girl could at least be scared into staying away from Luca.

She scrubbed harder at her thigh, leaving balled-up residue of brown paper towel behind. The stain had nearly disappeared, but an ugly wet patch remained. Annalisa tossed the frayed paper towels on the floor and swept out of the bathroom.

While she waited to get her order, a short, bald man approached. "I wondered if I'd run into you here," he said in Italian. "It's the only place where you can get a decent espresso on this island."

*Oh, fuck.* Annalisa looked into the man's dark brown eyes and tried to hide her fear. Gianni Palo. One of her cousin's men.

"What are you doing here?" she hissed, continuing the conversation in Italian.

"Same thing you are." He ran a thick hand over his bald head. Annalisa had always thought Gianni sexy in a raw way. There was something about his compact, powerful body, the way his upper lip curled into a slight sneer, and, of course, his bald head, that was attractive.

The barista put her espresso on the counter, and Gianni put his hand on Annalisa's back. "Let's go chat in my car."

Annalisa nodded then paused. She needed to bide her time with him. A lot of people chatted with Gianni and many didn't end the conversation alive. He was known around Naples for being a little stupid and a lot lethal. A thousand thoughts ran through her mind. Was he here to kill her? Kill Luca? Kill them both?

"Wait," she said. "Can we go to mine? Some bitch just spilled coffee on me and I have some wipes there."

Gianni shrugged. "Sure."

Annalisa swallowed hard as he guided her outside, then she pointed to her burgundy Toyota. Trembling as she slid into the driver's seat, she fired up the car and blasted the air. She pawed around in her purse and found a stain-removal packet.

"Calm down, Annalisa. I'm not here to kill you."

She pressed her lips together and exhaled. Stared at the steering wheel. "So, you're here to kill Luca?"

"Not exactly." Gianni sipped his coffee. "Your cousin sent me here for two reasons. To find you, because you know where Luca is. Or you'd be with him. I'm surprised you're not in his bed yet."

So was she. So was she. But since he never left his gated fortress, it was impossible to get inside. She'd even seen security, or some workers, doing something with the gate and fence near the beach, so it was challenging to get him alone, when he definitely wasn't with his uncle or that horrible girl.

She offered Gianni a smile. "I'm close."

"I'm sure you are," the man said softly. His eyes traveled to her cleavage and then to the wet stain on her leg that Skylar Shaw had caused. Annalisa unwrapped a wipe and scrubbed hard at her leg.

"Bruno wants me to put you on a plane home. He doesn't want you here, interfering. He wants you to get help. I'm supposed to tell you that he'll pay for whatever you need. Now, don't get upset. Bruno's grateful that you led us to Luca."

Annalisa nodded slowly. "Have you been following me since Miami?"

"Of course. We've been tracking your cell calls, too."

Annalisa's heart sank. How stupid could she be? "Wait. Is that why he told me that Luca was in Florida? Because he knew I'd find him?"

Gianni laughed. "Bruno knows you're a better researcher than any of us. And your English is excellent. He figured that finding Luca quickly would be easier for you. My English sucks, and I have no patience. And Bruno doesn't have access to as many of us as he used to, not when he's under house arrest."

Annalisa grimaced. She should have known that her family would interfere. They always did. They never trusted her or her feelings. She swallowed a lump of rage and told herself, *Think. Think.* How was she going to get out of this?

"What are you going to do with Luca?"

"Bruno wants me to bring him back to Italy to testify, say the book was all a lie."

Annalisa shifted in her seat and shot Gianni a skeptical glance. "Like the judge will buy that? Bruno will need a lot more than Luca's testimony to get acquitted. I've read that there's a lot of evidence against him."

Gianni sighed. "Yeah. Bruno's working on other witnesses and alibis on the murder charges. He figures he'll serve time for a few counts of racketeering, but hopefully he'll get off on some of the murder charges. But the judge in the case was a sailing buddy of Luca's father. So Luca's testimony could go a long way. It's worth a shot."

"How are you going to get Luca back to Italy? That won't be easy."

Gianni curled his fingers and inspected his nails. "I'm going to tell him that I'll kill his uncle if he doesn't go. He won't want his only living family member to die. We were going to use you as collateral, had you started sleeping with him again. Now we won't need to go through that charade."

Annalisa exhaled. Her cousin was even more heartless than she was. "And I suppose you want me to tell you where he is."

"Exactly." Gianni watched two police officers walk toward the café. They each checked Annalisa out as they passed, and one even smiled lasciviously and winked. "But let's go somewhere a little more private to have this conversation, no? I don't like being so exposed here, especially with you. You attract too much attention. You're too pretty, Annalisa."

Annalisa nodded and tried to think. Should she take him back to her hotel room? No, that wouldn't do.

Gianni reached onto the dash and grabbed the brochure for the swampy preserve that the hotel clerk had given her a few days earlier. "Oh, hey. Let's go here. This looks private. I heard about this park."

Annalisa winced. It was the place with the fucking alligators.

### ###

The long wooden boardwalk into the swamp seemed to stretch for miles. Dense green foliage pressed up against both sides of the waist-high wooden rail, and Annalisa fought back a wave of revulsion.

"You never imagine Florida being like this," Gianni remarked. "You think of the sand and water, of Disney, of clubs on South Beach. This is actually pretty cool."

Annalisa stopped to read from a wooden sign. "Says here it's an eighth of a mile to the river."

"Let's do it. You okay in those heels? I just didn't want to go to either of our hotel rooms. Didn't want to attract unnecessary attention."

Annalisa smiled. "I'm fine."

Of course, she was far from fine. She hated this place. Nature made her feel claustrophobic. Out of control. It was so quiet in the swamp that Annalisa jumped every time she heard the buzz of a mosquito. They were seemingly the only visitors in the park. Which made sense, because it was two in the afternoon and hotter than fuck. No sane person would be out at midday in a Florida swamp in August.

Gianni peered over the side of the railing, and Annalisa wondered why he didn't mind that his blue soccer jersey was touching splintery wood.

"Look, it's water under here. Hey, check out that big white bird!"

He pointed, mouth agape, and Annalisa sneered. The hit man was a bird-lover. Wonderful. She wanted to roll her eyes but didn't dare. Birds creeped her out. Gianni creeped her out.

She scratched the back of her neck nervously as they walked. It felt like a thousand bugs were crawling across her skin, ready to suck her blood. Stifling a sigh, she hitched her purse a little higher on her shoulder, stopped at the edge and pretended to look over but groped in her bag for a tissue. Something in this awful place was making her nose run. Maybe she was allergic to nature.

"How did Bruno track Luca to Florida, anyway?" she asked. Her voice seemed especially quiet against the ambient noise of the swamp. A dragonfly the size of a bird buzzed her face.

"It took us a while, but we figured out how to hack into his Skype. When he called his uncle, we kind of figured he was headed here. I guess Luca needs his long-lost uncle after all, eh? Probably because Federico's rich as fuck."

Annalisa laughed, angry at herself. "And then Bruno made a point of telling his crazy, obsessive cousin that Luca might be in Miami, and boom! Problem solved."

Gianni laughed too. "I'm sorry. I know that you loved Luca at one time. I'm sorry that we're going to have to kill him after he testifies. But you were going to do that anyway, weren't you? Once you found him and fucked him, no?"

No. She wasn't going to kill him. She was going to love him. But she couldn't tell Gianni that.

"Of course. I want him dead for what he did to me. Breaking my heart. *Stronzo*."

They walked in silence for a while, the sound of her heels clacking against the wood.

Gianni's steps were silent, but he inhaled loudly. "This is nice. Thank you. I needed a little bit of peace and quiet to take the edge off. It was a stressful flight. Bruno made me fly coach, and the drive here from Miami was brutal."

They reached the end of the boardwalk. It was a wide, wooden platform overlooking a tea-colored river. It smelled earthy and a bit like rotten eggs. The river didn't seem to be moving much, and bugs buzzed the surface. Annalisa pressed her hand to her mouth and swallowed a gag. How was she going to stop Gianni from taking Luca away from her?

Without touching the wood, Annalisa peered over the edge of the rail and grimaced when she spotted a swimming turtle. Gianni walked to the other side of the platform, near an opening in the railing where a ladder led down and into to the murky brown river. She glanced at him, and at the sign, which said, LADDER FOR RESEARCH PURPOSES ONLY. DO NOT CLIMB.

What kind of idiot would climb into that water?

"Holy shit, Annalisa! It's a huge alligator. I gotta get a photo of this. Those bastards back home won't believe it."

By the time he pulled out his phone, swiped it with his finger and knelt on his knees over the ladder, she had slipped her feet out of her strappy sandals. She swiveled her head, looking for other people.

Her hearing seemed attuned to every rustle of every leaf, and she could only hear the horror of nature.

When he lifted his phone to snap a picture, Annalisa already had her hand on what she needed. She crept toward him as he turned his phone horizontal and vertical, shooting at different angles. He was in an all-fours position, stretching his neck out over the water, except one of his hands grasped the phone, pointing it downward.

"It's so big I can't get all of it in the frame."

Bending over him as if she were looking into the water, she reached down. Noticed that his bald head was shiny with sweat. Touched the knife to his throat. Pressed hard. Sliced. It was like cutting into a giant steak, difficult at first and then gristly and squishy. He dropped the phone in the water and protested briefly with a few stammered words. Flailing, his hands at his throat, he tried to clutch at the wound, but his skin was so split open that he gasped and crumpled onto his belly.

Annalisa stepped back. Stopped breathing. At least until she knew he had taken his final breath.

She had never seen so much blood. Never knew that it could spurt and gush with such force. Like a man's orgasm.

Mesmerized, she watched the blood seep into the wood of the walkway, through the cracks of the boards, onto his shirt. She watched him the whole time. He gurgled and flailed, and after a while his eyes fluttered.

Dropping to her knees, she grunted as she pushed Bruno toward the edge of the boardwalk. Wow, was he heavy. She managed to push, tug and push some more, and finally she sent his thick body tumbling into the murky river with a splash. She peered after it, watching his blood swirl into the disgusting, tannin-colored water. Nearby, the alligator floated ominously, its bulging eyes watching her.

Annalisa picked up her sandals and stuffed them in her purse. She looked down. And she'd thought Skylar's coffee had ruined her pants! Gianni's blood was so red, so bright, against her white jeans. Almost like a candy cane at Christmas.

A plan formed in her mind. If she could make it out of this awful park, she'd strip to her black lingerie in the car and wrap a towel around her waist as if she'd just been to the beach.

She ran and ran, her feet slapping the wooden boardwalk. The green thicket of jungle on either side threatened to crush her.

# CHAPTER TWENTY-EIGHT

Her plan to back away from Luca had fallen to the wayside the hour she walked into his house, the minute he kissed her mouth, the second he put his arms around her in a long embrace. No man had ever treated Skylar this tenderly, this carefully. On Friday night, Luca cooked for her. He gave her a foot massage. He tried to teach her how to play Scopa, a card game from Naples, but they ended up laughing too hard as he explained the rules so they abandoned the effort.

Saturday, they lounged in bed and he read Italian news on his laptop while Skylar scrolled through the *New York Times* on her iPad. They read passages of articles to each other, or began conversations with, "Did you know?" and "Wow, listen to this!" They spent at least an hour reading aloud from the Twitter feed of Florida Man, an account that posted funny, crazy stories about weird Florida stories. Skylar had followed the feed earlier in the week and showed it to Luca. She'd known he'd love it even though he wasn't on Twitter.

"Oh God, listen to this one. 'Florida Man goes to police to report stolen drugs,'" Luca read, practically crying he was laughing so hard.

"No, no, how about this one?" she cackled. "'Florida Man surprised to learn mannequin he brought to dump is actually real dead body.'"

She was so comfortable around Luca. Despite all her recent concerns, it was like they had known each other forever. He didn't stop touching her as they lazed about. His leg was always on top of hers, or he would lean over while reading and nuzzle her shoulder, or play with her hair. Every now and then he would give her a devastating deep kiss that sparked her skin then turn back to his laptop.

It was interesting how much attention Luca gave to the news. He devoured several different newspaper websites from around Italy, and Skylar tried to sneak glances at his screen. He spent a long time on an article with a headline that had the word "Camorra" in it. She wondered about his parents, and probed gently at various points in their conversation. Had she been interviewing him, she wouldn't have hesitated to pepper him with questions, but because she was becoming attached and knew he was hiding something—pain or something darker—she treaded lightly.

"What's Italy like?" she asked, interrupting his reading. "I've always wanted to go. Everyone always talks about Tuscany and the food. My mom used to love that movie, *Under the Tuscan Sun.*"

Luca shut his laptop and held it in his hands. He didn't look at her. They were both sitting upright, propped up on pillows.

"I wish Italy was that appealing in real life," he said. "I wish it had that magic on my people. That's not the Italy for the Italians."

Skylar scowled. "What do you mean? I thought Italy was like a paradise."

"The country is a disaster, *amore*. There's been decades of political corruption. Incompetent politicians. Fraud. And the organized crime is completely out of control. The violence, the fear that the Camorra and the other groups bring to the country…it's something you cannot imagine."

Luca inhaled, and she watched him clutch his laptop, the veins in his hands straining from his grip.

"What's happened to my country makes me angry. I spent many years in a rage because of it. Everyone stays quiet, and the whole corrupt situation just continues while things get worse for the average Italian—the average Italian who is apathetic and just worried about surviving day-to-day. If you don't watch out in America, things could become like that here, too."

Skylar shook her head. "What do you mean? That sounds nothing like the United States."

"*Amore.* You're still young and…what is the word in English? Naïve? Yes. You're naïve. You haven't noticed how most people in your country are apathetic, just like in my country. Apathetic people don't vote, and this means the worst leaders get into office. It's ripe for corruption here, whether you want to admit it or not."

She wasn't sure what to say. His usual honey-toned voice was cold and jarring. This flash of emotion was tied to Luca's past, Skylar knew. How could it not be, given that his parents had died in that fire, maybe tied to a Mafia syndicate? But his assessment of the U.S. seemed wrong to her, and she was somewhat annoyed he hadn't come clean about his past.

"That's a cynical view of America," she said. "And of your own country."

Luca stared at her for a moment then relaxed his grip on his laptop. He leaned over and kissed her on the forehead, and his expression was wistful. "I'm sure someday you'll get to Italy, *amore*, and you'll see only what's good and right. As an American— as a tourist—you'll only see *la grande bellezza*. The great beauty."

He opened his laptop again and continued to read.

Skylar went back to her iPad and tried to read an article in *The Miami Herald*, but Luca's words distracted her. She put her tablet on the nightstand, about to say something, but he scooted down and folded her in the crook of his arm.

Skylar reached over his chest to run a finger over the tattoo on his bicep.

*Chi più sa, meno crede.*

### 

Luca mulled Skylar's questions about Italy as he held her close. She napped in his arms, her head resting against his chest. A part of him wanted to tell her about his past, and about what he'd just discovered from Federico. He longed to say that he was just like her, a curious journalist, one who had bought great success with a slice of hell. He wanted to tell her his memories of the two people who raised him.

It was difficult for him to think of them as his parents anymore. And yet, he still loved them both fiercely. The man whom he had called *papa*, the brave prosecutor. His mother, the primary school teacher. The summers they'd spent in San Mauro la Bruca at the country house, picking oranges, and the smell of the olive trees near his grandparents' villa. How his mother taught him to cook. How he and his father had hiked the hills in comfortable silence. Now, those memories were confused. Polluted. After years of explaining others' lives as a journalist, he was no longer certain how to explain his own.

He longed to tell Skylar about his book, *Uomo di Sangue*—in English it translated to *Man of Blood*—about Naples's most powerful Mafia boss. It had been a bestseller for eighteen months in Italy. He was certain Sky would love to hear stories about covering Mafia murders, about his off-the-record sources in the Italian government and going from an intern at *Il Mattino* to a popular political blogger then an author. He wanted her admiration and desired her approval of his work.

It would take years to share everything, though, years that he and Sky didn't have. Could never have. Or maybe, once Bruno Castiglione was convicted in court, he could begin life anew. With Skylar.

Was that a possibility?

As Luca kissed the top of her head, she stirred and opened her eyes. Smiling, she rolled over onto her back. He took this as an invitation to slide on top of her and enjoy her little noises of pleasure as he kissed and ran his tongue over her breasts and lower. She now trusted him enough to sleep nearly-naked.

Luca dragged his half-open mouth over the velvety skin of her stomach. The tiny freckle near her bellybutton drove him crazy. He kissed it, and she made a soft *mmmmmm* noise. Which also drove him crazy.

"Open your legs, *mia cara*," he said, positioning himself between her thighs.

She still had her underwear on, simple white cotton bikinis. Luca stroked her over the damp fabric then hooked his finger into the panties and raked the cloth gently against her clit, teasing her. Wanting to see all of her up close, he sat up and slid the underwear off, then spread her legs again. It was impossible for him to describe how she looked down there, because it was perfection. Flicking his tongue into her cleft, he grew harder by the second.

"Do you have any idea how much I want you?" he said in a gruff voice. It was the first time he'd alluded to his need to have sex with her, and she responded with a foggy, lust-filled smile. Why had he encouraged her to tease him? This was all his idea.

Skylar was so wet, and she whimpered while running her hands through his hair. She tasted warm and sweet, and he couldn't get enough. She was so deliciously tight that he had a difficult time believing that he wouldn't hurt her when he finally put his cock into her, however gently.

"Why are you stopping? I don't want you to stop." Skylar tried to catch her breath as Luca kissed her thigh, and she gave his hair a petulant tug. He moved up her body so he could whisper in her ear.

"Show me."

Breathless, she responded. "Show you what?"

"I want you to touch yourself. Like you did when we were on the phone."

She bit her lower lip and smiled lustily.

He knelt between her spread legs, and Skylar caressed her breasts and stared at him with a wicked smile on her face. Her hands pinched and twisted her nipples, and she feathered her fingers across her stomach, inch by inch. His breath hitched when she spread herself even wider for him with two fingers. With her other hand, she ran her index finger around her folds.

He started to stroke himself.

"No," she whispered. "You have to wait."

He groaned and squeezed her legs, watching a flush bloom on her chest. He was ready to explode.

"I love giving you orders."

"Tell me what else you want me to do?" His voice cracked with lust.

"Your fingers. I want them in me."

She opened her legs even wider then, and he plunged two fingers into her while grazing with her clit with his other hand. Skylar cried out, arching her back, unable to hold on any longer. He became even more engorged while watching her, feeling her come on his hand. Every moment he sensed he was falling deeper under her spell.

"Now," she murmured. Her voice was soft, but the way she looked him straight in the eye was insistent—demanding, even. "You can come now. *Here.*"

She cupped her breasts and tapped her cleavage with her forefingers. Without hesitation, Luca straddled her just above her waist. He grabbed her hands and tore them off her chest; then, stroking fast, violently even, he positioned his cock above her breasts and rubbed the tip slowly on her nipple, which made her whimper. Unable to control his body any longer, the sensation of her breast on his sensitive skin plunged him into a deep orgasm that started in his thighs and moved upward. He pumped himself hard a few more times, then released into her cleavage, hot spurts accompanied by a long, guttural moan and a body-quaking spasm.

He gave her a hesitant glance. "Sky, I'm sorry, is that what you wanted? I just…I couldn't control myself while I watched you."

"That," she said, grinning, "was so hot."

Dropping onto all fours, he dipped down to kiss her deep. "I've never wanted a woman as much as I want you," he whispered.

She rolled her eyes and quirked the corner of her mouth.

"What?" he asked.

She shrugged.

"You don't believe me." He planted a quick kiss on her forehead. "Why?"

"You won't tell me anything about your past, and you don't share many details about your present. And you don't want anything long-term with me. It's tough to see how far wanting me goes."

Luca sat up and sighed. "Skylar, have you ever thought it might be dangerous for you to know about my past? That it might be dangerous for you to be part of my future?"

She stared. "Why? Tell me why that would be."

He stared back at her, his previous gentle mood evaporated. "Stop asking questions, Skylar."

She flashed him a defiant look and muttered something about how that wasn't possible.

Holding a hand above her wet breasts, she climbed out of bed and went into the bathroom. Relieved to be rid of her insistent regard, Luca rolled onto his back and shut his eyes. His heart was racing, and not just because he kept having mind-blowing orgasms with her. The truth was, his plans for casual, no-strings sex were deteriorating. He had to stop himself before either he or Skylar became too attached.

Hell, who was he kidding? He was *already* too attached. Her words danced in his mind: *"This is perfect."* He had agreed, while adoring every one of her kisses.

*We are perfect together.*

Yet what did that mean? Maybe in another life they could have been perfect together. Now, after all the pain he had caused, he could never be perfect with anyone. Not until Castiglione was put away, if even then.

And if he did tell her everything, she wouldn't want him anymore. Who would want a damaged man with no home, no roots, no compass? A man whose mother lied about his parentage? A man whose work got his family killed? Skylar needed a man with stability, and he wasn't a stable man.

No, Skylar Shaw needed to remain exactly what she was: a summer fling.

### 

The next morning, Skylar awoke when Luca slipped out of bed to use the bathroom. To her surprise, he didn't go downstairs to make coffee afterward. Instead he climbed through the gauzy curtains hanging from the canopy rails and got back in bed, kissing her. He smelled like mint.

Still sleepy, she used the bathroom too. When she returned, she paused after parting the curtain. He was asleep, and the sheet only barely covered his hips. Wow. His mouth, full and sensual, was relaxed and supple. She imagined it around her nipple. Reaching her hand in the air, she only just stopped herself from touching his lips.

Would she ever tire of this insatiable attraction? No. He was breathtaking, that bronzed skin against the white covers. Like a Roman god in repose. Her eyes went to his muscular chest, then to the tantalizing trail of hair below his bellybutton. Just thinking about what was beneath the sheet set her body aflame, aflame and desperate to feel that body part's true purpose.

It was time, she realized. She had denied herself for too long.

Stripping off her T-shirt and panties, she slid under the sheet next to him, wrapping her bare skin around his body. He shifted, encircling her with his arms. Trailing his hand down her back made her shiver. His hand went lower, over her cheeks. His fingers stopped in that sweet, wet triangle where her ass met her thighs.

*There. Right. There.*

A little moan escaped her mouth, and he pressed his erection into her.

"This is a nice surprise, waking up to you naked and wet," he whispered.

Every muscle in her tightened as he kept the heel of his hand on the bottom of her ass, also slipping a finger inside of her. She could feel herself becoming swollen, needy, and she kissed him fiercely.

Keeping two of his fingers inside of her, he rolled her atop him. She spread her legs and writhed on his fingers, feeling his hard cock against her pubic bone.

"Your boxers are going to have to come off," she whispered.

"But. Do you want…?" He took his fingers out of her, and she sat up, straddling him.

"Yes. I want you inside of me."

They stared at each other, the morning sunshine filtering through the gauzy bed curtains. Every nerve in her body lit up, and her need was almost unbearable. Taking his hand, she guided his thumb in between her legs, between her folds, to her throbbing core.

He sucked in a breath as his thumb made contact with her clit. "You want me?"

She made an unintelligible noise that she hoped translated to *yes*. His touch brought her close to the edge, and she didn't want to concentrate on words or thoughts.

"Can I make you come first? Please? I love watching you come," he whispered. "Then I'll fill you up with my cock. Is that what you want?"

Nodding, whimpering, she thrust herself toward his hand. Rocked and rubbed on him and shut her eyes. She was close, so close.

And then her phone rang.

### 

Luca watched Skylar's face go from hazy and sensual to panicked and wide-eyed. The sensual mood shattered.

"Fuck!" she exclaimed.

It was a good thing she didn't understand Italian, because he couldn't control himself, either. He said something really vulgar out of frustration.

"Do you have to get that?" he bit out as she lunged for the nightstand, fighting with the gauzy curtain. He tried to help her find the opening, and it was almost comical how they were tangled together, their hands madly pawing at the fabric. Comical, if it wasn't for his raging hard-on.

"Yes. I do. It's the paper. I have a special ringtone for my editor."

He groaned and shifted in the bed. This was the problem with dating a reporter.

She put the phone to her ear. "Jill!" she said, breathless.

As Skylar talked, Luca's hand slipped below the waistband of his boxers and he adjusted himself. He longed for release and took his hand away from his cock. Shifting to Skylar, he spooned her and cradled her breast as she spoke. Her nipple was still hard, and the first thing he'd do when she got off the phone was to put it in his mouth. She had such round, beautiful breasts, and he pressed his erection into her backside, just thinking about how her nipples puckered like raspberries when she was excited.

Fuck. This woman would kill him.

He rubbed against her body. She lightly swatted his leg, which he'd slung over her hip.

"An escape? No way. That's crazy. Of course I'll come in to cover it. I'll be there in a half hour, tops."

Rolling onto his back, Luca shut his eyes and groaned silently. He heard her tap her phone forcefully and set it on the nightstand. She flipped over and gave him a quick kiss on the mouth.

"Luca, I'm sorry. I have to go to work. There's been an escape at the primate sanctuary."

He opened his eyes. "Don't apologi— Wait, what? A what?"

She giggled. "Did you know there was a primate sanctuary on the other end of the island? Near the bridge?"

"I didn't."

"Well, apparently one of the monkeys escaped. A macaque who was a retired movie actor."

Laughter exploded from his mouth. "You're kidding, right?"

"No. I'm not. This is big news. Neighbors are worried about Ebola. I have to write a story. Jill says I'm the best reporter to cover this because I love weird news."

Still laughing, Luca grabbed her and wrapped his arms around her body, hugging tight. Despite his sexual frustration, her decision just endeared her to him even more; he would have done exactly the same thing once. "Just come back after you're done, okay? I'll make you dinner and we can finish what we started."

She kissed him. "I will. And thank you."

"For what, *amore mio*?" he asked.

"For being so understanding. Most guys would be upset about this—interrupting what we were doing to cover a story about a monkey. It's not easy dating a reporter."

He grinned. She was so cute. And she was his. And she was ready to give herself to him.

Studying her pretty face, he knew that he wanted to come clean about his secret soon. She deserved to know. Maybe when she came back.

Her mouth dropped open. "Oh, I didn't mean to use the word 'dating.' It just slipped out."

"But that's what we're doing, no?" He kissed her again, and his heart softened even more. "You need to get out of bed now, before I keep you here," he growled, spanking her lightly on the butt. "You have a monkey to find."

# CHAPTER TWENTY-NINE

"So, they found the monkey at some guy's house. It was trying to break into the lanai. There was a bowl of fruit on the patio table."

Skylar was sitting in Luca's kitchen, telling him about her day. He couldn't stop laughing, and she couldn't stop swooning, thinking about how their bodies had looked so erotic together that morning before her editor's phone call. About how sensual they'd be later, after dinner, when they would finally have sex for the first time.

"No way. Come on. Monkeys don't really eat fruit."

She giggled. "It's true, Luca. They do. They found the monkey trying to rip through the screen door. They used a tranquilizer gun to immobilize him. Oh, and the monkey's name was Cheetah."

God, she loved making Luca laugh. She sipped her wine and watched him stand at the open fridge, trying to decide whether to make chicken or fish.

Her mind shifted vaguely to her fledgling herb garden back at her condo on the balcony. The plants might be dead by now. Maybe she could bring them over here. Surely Luca would take good care of them. Skylar envisioned them gardening together. I mean, he'd admitted they were dating. So why couldn't she dream of a future?

Luca took out a package of chicken breasts, a package of cherry tomatoes and a head of garlic. "*Pollo alla parmigiana,*" he said. Jazz wafted softly through the air, and Skylar allowed visions of her life with Luca to unfold in her mind. Speaking Italian. Cooking together. Ski vacations. Making love on beaches and in front of fireplaces in the mountains. The fantasies were limitless and sparkling, urbane and classy.

He rinsed a few of the small tomatoes and held one between his thumb and forefinger, then walked over to her. He kissed her softly and nibbled on her bottom lip.

"Your mouth is so fucking sexy," he murmured. "Open for me."

With slippery lips, she did, and he set the small red tomato on her tongue. Their eyes met as she chewed, and her stomach clutched with nervous anticipation. Tonight would be their night.

He kissed her forehead and went back to the other side of the kitchen island, to the cutting board. Skylar took another sip— Luca had opened a bottle of chilled pinot grigio—and pondered whether she should enroll in an online Italian class.

"Where did you learn to cook?" she asked.

He chopped a clove of garlic. "My mother. I watched her in the kitchen from when I was a little boy. We even cooked together the night before she…"

Luca went silent.

"Before she died in the fire," Skylar prompted, absentmindedly finishing his sentence. Then immediately regretting it.

Luca stopped chopping and cocked his head. The good mood, the laughter, dissolved into the ether. He didn't say anything. Skylar sat on a barstool at the kitchen island, and he faced her on the opposite side. Skylar noticed his hand gripping the large knife, and her pulse quickened as she recalled a true-crime book that centered around a woman who was stabbed to death.

"Tell me, Skylar," he said, resuming work in a methodical, precise way. *Chop. Chop. Chop.* "How do you know my mother died in a fire?"

He wasn't looking at her. Instead, he glared at the knife and the garlic.

She swallowed hard. It seemed she didn't truly know if Luca was a dangerous person or not. Why did he seem so angry? Was there any good reason he should be furious that she'd done some background research?

Skylar opened her mouth and closed it. Unsure of what to say, she went with the truth. She didn't expect him to understand, exactly; he wasn't a woman, and he wasn't a journalist. Still, this shouldn't be *that* big of a deal. "After I met you, I looked you up."

"You backgrounded me." *Chop. Chop. Chop.* Luca's eyes bored into hers, and he sounded disgusted. "And…? Tell me what you found. Tell me the results of your research."

Skylar inhaled sharply. "Um. Luca, you're scaring me with that knife."

He looked down, and with precision he set the knife aside. His voice was soft yet still icy when he spoke. "I'm sorry."

She was grateful to defuse the situation, even momentarily. "I found a couple of articles in *Il Mattino*. One about your parents dying in a fire. Another that said…"

Her voice trailed off because she was a little scared to say it.

"Another that said what, Skylar?" Luca gripped the side of the island counter, arms extended.

"One that said the fire was probably set by the…the Mafia. The Camorra."

Luca smiled, a wry, sad expression. "The Camorra," he repeated, drawing out the word and rolling the 'r'-sound. The menacing way he pronounced it made Skylar uneasy.

"Yes."

"And what else did you find?"

She shook her head. "Actually, I thought it was weird. I didn't find anything else about you. I looked everywhere. Facebook. Twitter. Public records. Google. I couldn't find any other details about you. I guess I just figured that you're a private person."

Luca laughed, a mean sound. "Yes, Skylar, like I told you, I am a really private person." He paced the kitchen and didn't speak. "So, let me get this straight. We met. We shared…I don't know, a connection. An attraction. Yes?"

"Obviously."

"So the first thing you do is run a background check on me like I am, I don't know, a criminal?"

His voice was slightly louder. He was clearly angry now, and Skylar tried to keep her own voice steady. "Luca, I'm sorry, but I need to explain this in context. You've only been in Florida a few weeks. As a single woman here, it's crazy. Every third guy has been arrested, served time in prison or gone bankrupt. It's dangerous for women like me to not check someone out. All of us do it." She paused to breathe in and out. "Well, all of us female reporters do it, anyway."

Luca was stone-faced. "And so, since you could only find those two articles on my family, what conclusions did you draw about me? Come on. I want to hear them."

"Nothing," she lied. Unconvincingly. "I just thought about what a tragedy it was that you lost your family. It must have been devastating."

"Bullshit." His nostrils flared a little bit. Skylar wondered if she could get to the front door quicker than him. Probably not.

Suddenly, she was angry. There was no salvaging tonight. This was his fault, anyway, for not being forthcoming. She decided to tell him everything.

"Look. I'll be honest. After I read that, I wondered if you were in the Mafia—the Camorra, or whatever it is. I figured you might be lying about your master's thesis, too. You never talk about it. I thought the fire might have been set as some kind of retribution or something. I don't know, though. I know nothing about the Mafia."

"You. Thought. I. Was. In. The. Mafia." Luca enunciated every word perfectly and began to pace the kitchen, slowly running his hands through his hair. At least he wasn't holding the knife.

"Well, are you?" she asked. "If you didn't have this stupid rule that we can't talk about each other's pasts, this whole conversation wouldn't be happening. Normal people, normal men and women who meet and hook up, they share details of their lives with each other. You didn't even want to tell me your name when we first met. What was I supposed to think?"

He glared at her. "'Normal people.' You think I am a normal person? You have no idea who I am. And what do you think this is, you and me? It's been 'hooking up' to you?"

Sky didn't reply. He was being irrational. What did he want her to say?

"That's the trouble with you Americans," Luca continued. "You see Italians and immediately think of *The Sopranos* or Vito Corleone. I didn't say anything the first time you mentioned that, the night we met. But it's offensive. You think we're all Latin lovers with no conscience. We just eat pasta and pizza and screw our way through life. And the Mafia. Jesus. You have no idea what the real Italian crime families are like, what they do or how they affect my country. You're so sheltered here on your stupid little island, covering your bullshit news."

This was out-of-bounds. There was no need to criticize her newspaper and her career. "Maybe if YOU didn't come off as so sketchy, I wouldn't think you were in the Mafia. YOU won't talk about your past. YOU won't talk about the future. YOU were nasty when we first met during the plane crash and I asked you questions. YOU said that we shouldn't define this. *Us.* What am I supposed to think?"

Her words hung in the air. They glared at each other and several tense seconds passed.

"I'm going home. Where are my car keys?" Skylar demanded.

Luca walked out of the kitchen then returned and put the keys on the island counter. Raising his hands so they were in an X, he sliced them through the air. "*Basta,*" he said.

Skylar didn't know the word, but she understood the meaning. *Enough.*

She plucked the keys off the counter and went upstairs to the bedroom, where she grabbed her purse. She didn't even bother trying to find any of her other clothes that she had brought, or her small overnight bag. She slammed the front door behind her and ran to her car in the rain, barefoot. The road blurred out of focus from the downpour and her tears, and she couldn't make it home without pulling over and sobbing. She hadn't cried this hard in years, and the feeling made her body heave and roil and gag.

She stopped in the parking lot of a pharmacy and pulled into a space at the end of the lot. She intended to buy tissues, but when she opened the door a large puddle was almost up to her small car's floor and she slammed it again. Crying harder beneath the yellow glow of a streetlight, she battled back guilt over their fight. What else could she have done? Should she have tried to lie more convincingly to Luca about knowing the details of his past? No, that wouldn't have worked because she was incapable of lying. And why should she have to?

She inhaled deeply and forced herself to stop crying. Why was she sobbing, exactly? She had nothing to be ashamed of. Maybe she should have told Luca earlier that she had pried into his life, but still, he had no reason to be so angry. No, she was the one who should be mad. She had let someone new into her heart, and once again she had made the wrong choice.

Fresh tears rolled down her cheeks.

####

A full blown panic-attack gripped Luca's chest as he listened to Skylar drive off. He tried to catch his breath and steady his mind. She knew about his family and hadn't said anything? How long had she known? Since the beginning?

Something had snapped in him when she mentioned his parents. He'd wanted to be the one to tell her if he had chosen to tell her, which he hadn't. But he'd been about to. Still, this felt like a betrayal, especially since he was still nursing the rawness of his uncle's revelation. Skylar had researched him as if he were a common criminal. As if she didn't trust him.

He snorted. Like he hadn't done the exact same thing to her. Although, he probably wouldn't have backgrounded her if the Mafia wasn't after him. No, he would have trusted her, probably, because she was a reporter and he assumed that journalists were more honest than regular people. And yet, he'd assumed that he could look into her past for whatever reason but she didn't have the right to inspect his. God, he felt like such a hypocritical asshole. He shouldn't have yelled at her, shouldn't have uttered those brutal words.

Not okay.

*Why can't I just be a normal person with a normal life?*

Luca held his head in his hands and slumped onto the kitchen counter. Why hadn't he just told her the truth? Why didn't he tell her that he was a journalist? An author? That he wasn't in the Mafia?

He wasn't thinking straight. Walking into the study, he sat and poured himself a big glass of his uncle's expensive Irish whiskey. He downed the glass and poured another. Maybe it was time to move on from Palmira.

But was he ready to say goodbye to Skylar?

# CHAPTER THIRTY

Stupid, she knew, but Skylar hoped Luca was reading her Twitter feed as she snapped a selfie of herself, Matt and some guy from advertising as they sat at a table at the Iguana. Her cleavage looked awesome in the low, U-neck cotton dress, one of many she had bought on sale in anticipation of a hot Florida summer.

She posted the photo on all of her social media accounts. The previous weekend, when she and Luca were getting along, she'd persuaded him to sign up for Twitter under a fake, anonymous account name _Italy-Man111_ and he'd followed her. So maybe he'd see her post.

*"After deadline. #VodkaRedBull. #80snight #Partylikeajournalist."*

She slammed back her first drink quickly then sipped her second because her stomach was approaching Queasytown. Her stomach had been like this for days, ever since she and Luca had their fight. Now it was Friday night, five days later, and she was at the Iguana listening to stupid '80s music. She should have tried to join in the conversation with her newsroom friends about that day's selection of front-page stories, or about the massive layoffs at several Florida papers, but talking about journalism held no appeal. Instead, a memory of Luca drifted into her mind. They had been on the beach one afternoon the previous weekend and he had kissed her ferociously, as if it was the final kiss of his life. She got sweaty behind her knees just thinking of it.

When she snapped out of her reverie, her friends were still talking. The thought of never kissing or touching Luca again made her stomach hurt more. Scooping up her phone, she checked her messages, voicemail and email for the thousandth time.

Like he'd ever messaged her or emailed her. Really, he had only ever called a few times and never left voicemail. He had left no trace of himself in her life, and it almost made her sob when she realized that he probably wanted it that way.

Thank God she hadn't had sex with him. At least she was getting out of this relationship with a gossamer-thin thread of dignity. At least, until she got drunk enough to call him. Annoyingly, she had left some clothes and her favorite lipstick at his house and she thought about drunk-dialing him when she got home. She imagined teasing him on the phone, enticing him into coming to her house…

No. She was still angry at him for acting like an ass.

The DJ said something about how that evening was called The Flashback Café, and he said he was going to play some classic, slow-dance '80s songs. Skylar rolled her eyes at Matt, who chuckled.

*Matt.* He was single. He was cute. Maybe she should hook up with him to forget Luca. He had driven her to the Iguana tonight, so maybe he'd been thinking along the same lines.

No. Screwing Matt was a shitty idea if she'd ever had one. Imagine if she did and they had to face each other in the newsroom or go on another assignment together? She shuddered as the possible complications such a scenario would cause.

A song came on, and Sky recognized it as one her mother had loved. It had been Heather Shaw's favorite song in the world, in fact, which was why the first gospel-like strains of "Do You Really Want to Hurt Me" plunged Skylar into an even darker mood. Her mother used to sing this to herself while brushing her hair, looking into the mirror in their tiny log cabin bathroom.

The lyrics were so sad. Had her mom been thinking about Skylar's dad as she sang? Skylar had never asked, and she fought back tears when she realized that she would never ever get the chance to ask her mother anything again.

*Fuck. I am a mess tonight.*

She turned to the group and pretended to be interested in the conversation. Nodding and emitting *mmm-hmm* at appropriate times made her feel a bit more normal, like she was getting back to real life.

"Dude, you want a fireball shot? You're getting a fireball shot. You look like shit," Emily yelled.

Skylar winced then laughed. She had told Emily about her fight with Luca.

Older couples packed the dance floor. Matt tilted his head at them and looked at her with hopeful puppy-dog eyes. "Dance?"

Skylar shook her head and took a big swallow of her drink, pretending to inspect her napkin.

Mercifully, the song ended. Skylar looked up, and Emily plopped the fireball in front of her. She grabbed it, closed her eyes and tossed it back. She grimaced as the candy-spicy liquid slid down her throat, then opened her eyes and saw…Luca?

He stood on the other side of the room, staring at her across the dance floor, leaning against a post. He wore charcoal gray pants, like a businessman. Black shoes. A white, button-down shirt, also very businesslike. His stubble was longer, practically a beard. Everything on him looked dark and brooding. His eyebrows, his hair, his gaze. He was even smoking a cigarette, which should have turned her off. But it didn't. Not even a little. The way he raised the cigarette to his lips and squinted at her then exhaled was thrilling. Bad in every good way possible. The intensity in his eyes left her breathless.

Emily jabbed her in the ribs. "Matt's going for more shots!"

Sky didn't respond, just quietly touched her friend's arm with her fingers and stared as Luca moved toward her, languidly, dangerously. Her mouth felt wet, and as he got closer she saw that his eyes almost seemed colorless.

"Oh. Oh!" Emily's hand gripped her forearm. "Is that Luca?"

He walked up to their table, and every woman within a ten-foot radius, including Skylar, was speechless. He stood nearby and with a glance looked down at an ashtray, casually crushed the cigarette into it. He lifted his gaze to her, and the corner of his mouth turned into a half-smile.

Was it apologetic? Commanding? Regretful? She had no idea.

Skylar swallowed. Anything she could say in that moment—introductions to her friends, a reprimand for being mean, a simple hello—seemed inadequate. Stupid. So she grinned nervously.

Bonnie Tyler's "Total Eclipse of the Heart" came on, and Luca held out his hand.

"Dance?"

Skylar looked around at her friends, who were all either swooning or gaping. Even Matt, who was passing out shots, was grinning. They were of no help now. She tried to laugh away the drama of the moment and shrugged.

Luca leaned close to her ear. "I'm sorry, Skylar. I'm here to apologize."

Her heart racing, she stood up and slipped her hand into his. He pulled her to him, and the heat of his body was magnetic. She couldn't detach herself if she tried.

"This is like a cheesy Eighties video," she whispered as the lights dimmed and colored disco lights bubbled around the room. The song playing was all power chords and theatrical lyrics. How people spent a decade listening to this was beyond her. But, shit. It seemed to capture everything she was feeling.

Smiling and flashing those half-lidded, sensual eyes, Luca led her onto the dance floor. Right to the middle. Memories of eighth-grade dances and awkward moves with boys in a cold gym in Vermont popped into her mind and Skylar giggled. The vodka made her a little dizzy and floaty, and the idea that she was slow-dancing with this dark, delicious man at a place called the Sloppy Iguana on a hot Florida night made her laugh harder.

She wrapped her arms around his neck, and he pulled her close, pressing his lips near her ear and his hands spanning the small of her back. His nose grazed the side of her temple, and she noticed that he smelled faintly of tobacco and spicy limes.

"*Bellissima*," he whispered. "You look gorgeous tonight."

"How did you know I was here?" she murmured.

"Uh, you told the world on Twitter."

She smiled into his neck. So, he *had* been reading her Twitter feed. Moth, meet flame.

"Why are you all dressed up like that?" She pulled back to look at him and traced his jaw with her finger. His almost-beard was soft, and she wanted to bury her nose in his face. So she did.

"You said you wanted to see me in something other than shorts and a T-shirt. Do you approve?"

Her fingers stroked his neck under his collar. "I do. A lot."

They held each other and swayed.

"I didn't know you smoked."

He sighed. "I don't. I quit a year ago, but I was particularly stressed out today. I'm sorry I stink."

She pulled back to look at him and wondered what had made him anxious; they'd had their fight days ago. "Are you here to yell at me more? You were a jerk last weekend, you know that, right? I shouldn't even be talking to you."

His lips were close to her ear, and she shivered, feeling herself get wet from his voice. That was so unfair.

"No. I'm not here to yell at you. And yes, I'm aware I was a jerk. I'm sorry."

"Hmm. Are you here to tell me I've had too much to drink? Because I have."

"No."

"Are you here to tell me to stop snooping into your past?"

"Not at all."

She stroked the back of his head, running her fingers through his hair. God, how she had craved him. Missed him. Those stupid song lyrics matched her feelings. Big, dramatic, messy.

"Then…why are you here?"

"To dance with you." He kissed her forehead as they moved in a slow circle. "To kiss your gorgeous mouth."

They stopped swaying to the music and he cradled her face in his hands and kissed her deep as the older couples danced around them. He didn't hold back with his lips, or with his tongue, and Skylar had never before been kissed in such a wicked, sex-could-happen-at-any-moment way in public. He tasted like cigarettes and smelled like coffee, and it was shocking that she wasn't turned off by his smoking. His big hand grasped the back of her head, and she felt like she was falling.

Falling in love.

Exactly what she didn't want. But couldn't help.

"And again, I came to apologize to you. I'm sorry I was such an asshole. You were just doing what comes naturally to you as a reporter. I shouldn't have been so harsh. You were right to look me up. Florida's a messed-up place. You need to be careful and protect yourself."

She nodded, and he kissed her again then hugged her nice and tight, spinning her around and lifting her off the ground. She had so many questions but let them all slide because his hand went into the hair at her nape, his other pressed on her lower back and her body flooded with arousal. He drew her against him, and they swayed together.

"I'm also here to take you home with me. Is that okay? We need to talk."

"Yes," Skylar murmured. "But can we finish this dance?"

"Absolutely."

"What do you want to talk about?" she asked after a moment.

He shook his head and frowned, stroking her back. "Not here. Not now. Later, okay?"

Squeezing her eyes shut, she clung to him as they moved, concentrated on how it felt to be in his arms. She was whole. Complete. Loved.

It was time she stopped denying herself what she really wanted. Tonight would be the night that she gave herself to him.

# CHAPTER THIRTY-ONE

There was no doubt that Luca loved the reporter.

Annalisa stood in the shadows of the Sloppy Iguana, watching the two dance. It was too crowded for her to be detected, and she wore no makeup, a baseball cap and a ridiculous Tampa Bay Buccaneers jersey that she had picked up at a gas station. Her hair was in a ponytail and she wore her glasses instead of contacts and unflattering khaki shorts. And, horror of all horrors, sneakers. With socks.

She looked like an American. A caricature of an American. Plain, unstylish and fat. She couldn't wait to strip off these unflattering, scratchy clothes that she had bought at a giant warehouse store. Buying those clothes, some disgusting microwaveable food and bottles of water—it was the only time she'd left her hotel room since the murder. Although she had wanted to stalk Luca at his house, she didn't dare leave. Not for several days. But then her curiosity about Skylar had gotten the better of her, and by Friday afternoon she'd followed the American girl from the newspaper to her house to the Iguana. Annalisa noted that Skylar had gotten a ride to the bar with a man, and she wondered if Luca was no longer in the picture. Had hoped.

Now, seeing Luca and Skylar practically devouring each other in public, Annalisa knew otherwise. He'd never publicly displayed this kind of affection for her.

Lifting a gigantic glass of iced tea to her mouth—why were all beverages in America bladder-busting sizes?—she watched as Luca smoothed Skylar's long hair from her face with gentle hands. He kissed her nose then hugged her, squeezing his eyes shut.

She'd considered going over and standing there, waiting until they both noticed her. Telling Skylar that Luca was hers and hers alone. She would watch as Skylar's placid, blissed-out face exploded with hurt… But as she watched the two of them nuzzle and whisper to each other, it was Annalisa whose heart was pulverized. Luca had never kissed her nose. Never danced with her. His eyes had never flickered up and down her face intently like they were doing with Skylar.

No. She would not let him replace her in his life. He couldn't just erase her like a few words from his work-in-progress.

Especially not since she'd killed her cousin's hit man for him.

# CHAPTER THIRTY-TWO

"Why did you let Matt drive you to the bar?"

They were in Luca's Mercedes, and he gripped the steering wheel with one hand. The other reached for Skylar's, and her touch warmed him, made him feel safe. It was exactly what he craved after not seeing her for a week.

She shrugged and turned her head to look out the window then rummaged in her purse and took out a tin of mints. She fed him one, and he was grateful after that cigarette. "He lives near me. I felt like drinking, and he offered. Why?"

Why, indeed? Why was he even here? Why, when he was hours, possibly minutes, away from telling her that he was leaving Florida soon? He wasn't being fair to her, and he knew it. And yet, the idea of her being with another man sent a violent anger through him that he had never before experienced.

"Just curious."

His mouth felt tight, tense. As he pulled into his uncle's gated community, he braced himself for the inevitable talk once they got inside the house. Over the past few days alone he'd brooded and drank and smoked. Then he'd prepared a speech about how he simply couldn't handle everything that had been thrown at him in the past few weeks, between his uncle's crazy revelation and his own, equally insane feelings for her. He was getting too close and that scared the shit out of him.

Really, he should have just texted a goodbye. But there was no way he'd be that cruel to her. And he also shouldn't have gotten dressed up. At the very least he could have simply driven Skylar to her house and ended it there. Selfishly, though, he wanted her for this one last night. It wasn't even about sex, because they hadn't had it and he wasn't about to make a final plea. No, he just wanted to sleep next to her. To hold her in his arms for eight hours straight. Which was probably more damaging and dangerous than making love to her then vanishing. For both him and her.

Maybe he would wait until the morning to tell her. That would be better. She was tipsy and he didn't know what her reaction would be. Better to tell her everything when she had a clear head.

A wave of guilt splashed over him. Saying goodbye was exactly what he didn't want to do, but he saw no other way to avoid the inevitable pain, or worse, that would follow for both of them if he stayed. Maybe he could come back when times changed and he could be a normal person again. If he ever felt like that could happen. If she would take him back.

He opened the garage, drove inside and then killed the ignition. As the door shut behind them, he paused, staring at the glove compartment where he had put his gun before going into the Iguana. Should he take it out in front of Skylar? Reveal that little bit of his life so she could witness the insanity firsthand?

"Did you forget something?" she asked in a soft voice, putting her hand on his forearm and rubbing gently.

He turned and looked into her eyes. A little smile crept onto her face, and he leaned forward for a kiss. Her insistent lips made everything that he intended to say and do vanish from his mind.

"No. Let's get inside," he whispered, and he left the gun in the glove box.

###

The second he locked the house and flicked on the lights, Skylar pressed her body against Luca, pinning him to the door. She stood on her tiptoes to reach his mouth and ran her hands over his chest. She wanted him and would have him tonight.

Now.

"I missed you," she said. She unbuttoned his shirt and purred when she felt his hands cup her ass, gripping her, hard.

"I missed you, too. I'm sorry for everything."

She grabbed his wrist. "No apologies. Upstairs. Now."

They practically ran up the staircase, and when they got in his bedroom she kicked off her strappy sandals and climbed into the middle of the bed. He followed, and she unbuttoned his shirt, stripping it off him. She dove for his pants, unbuckling his belt. He finished the rest, unzipping and sliding his trousers off.

"Is this what you want?" he asked.

"Yes." His voice had been gruff, but hers was firm and clear.

He pulled her dress over her head then groaned when he saw her matching black lace bra and panties. Unhooking her brassiere, he groaned when she guided his hands to her breasts, which filled his palms. Then she and Luca kissed and touched and maneuvered each others' bodies until she was sitting on top of him with her legs around his waist.

They still had their underwear on, and he embraced her while sitting up, his hands fanning her skin, leaning her slightly back so he could kiss and suck her nipples into stiff peaks. He was rock-hard as she ground into him. Already, little noises of excitement escaped her mouth, and she couldn't wait to feel him inside of her. She'd wanted this for far too long.

"Luca," she whispered, sitting up and tilting his head so that he looked at her. He was breathing hard, and his eyes flashed with need. "*Tonight.* I want you. I want you to make love to me tonight."

To her surprise, he shut his eyes and pressed his lips together then rested his forehead on her chest. This wasn't the reaction she'd expected, and panic crept into her chest.

"What? You don't want to? You don't want me? After all this…?"

Humiliating flashbacks of James telling her how inept she was at taking charge in bed ran through her mind, but she reminded herself to be calm. To listen.

"No," he said. "I mean, yes. I do. More than anything. But, Sky, oh God. I can't. Not with a good conscience."

She slipped off of him, and it was as if a bucket of ice had been dumped over her head. "What? Tell me."

His eyes were still closed, as if for some reason he couldn't bear to see her.

"Open your eyes. Look at me. What's wrong?"

A look of pure fear in that green-gray gaze greeted her when he opened his lids. He whispered, "It's not right. I might fall in love with you if we do."

Her eyes watered slightly, and she shook her head, not understanding. He might fall in love with her? That was a good thing, right? But why did he look so miserable? Was she missing something? She had only drunk two vodkas and one shot. She was buzzed but not hammered.

"What are you trying to say? I don't get it. Why—?"

He interrupted. "Skylar. I can't make love to you. I'm leaving."

Her eyes got big, and she sank against the headboard. "What? Why? Does it have something to do with your parents? With me finding out about your parents? Is this why you wanted to talk to me?"

Kneeling before her, he bent his head. He spoke in a slow, strained voice. "Things have gotten really complicated for me in the past few weeks. Much more complicated than I anticipated. Last week, my uncle told me that…I can't even say it."

"What? What did he tell you?" Why was Luca being so damned dramatic and cryptic?

"That he's really my father. That's why I kind of flipped out on you. I felt like everyone was hiding something from me. They have been."

"Holy shit," Skylar whispered, floored and instantly sober. "I don't even know what to say."

"I know. I don't, either."

"So, that's why you want to leave? Because of your uncle?"

He sighed. "Sort of, but that's not all. There's also you."

"Me?" She had the feeling she wasn't getting the entire story, but she furrowed her brow and tried not to act too skeptical or angry, since by the way he was breathing he was so obviously upset. And yet, anger rose inside of her. She felt like screaming at him.

"Yeah, you. I care for you. And I wasn't looking for a relationship when I came here. Like I told you, I'm not boyfriend material. I can't give you anything good right now. Maybe not ever. I don't want to ruin your life."

Skylar let out a long exhale. "Why would you ruin my life if you care about me? I don't get it. You're being too complicated. Stop being complicated."

He finally raised his head and looked at her. "I don't want you to understand. I don't want you in my world. It's too fucked up. It's better if I go and leave you with only good memories."

Skylar sat on the bed, staring into his eyes. After several seconds, she spoke in a soft voice. "Luca, *are* you in the Mafia? Are you involved in something illegal? Just be honest. I won't judge."

He licked his lips, shook his head and gave a wicked, bitter laugh. "No. I'm not. And you can't help me."

"Then what? What is it? You can trust me."

She reached out to stroke his face, and he took her hand and pressed his lips against her palm. The gesture was so intimate, so sweet, that Skylar's eyes started to water. She wanted to leave, wanted to beg him to take her home. But she also wanted to soak him up, spend as much time as possible with him before he vanished from her life forever. And she had to discover his secret.

Coolly studying his hunched posture, she let out a sigh. "Luca, let's get into bed. Go brush your teeth. Let's talk more tomorrow. We're both too emotionally strung out now."

He nodded and leaned in to kiss her before leaving. "I'm sorry. I haven't slept well since my uncle's. I'm pretty destroyed."

While he was in the bathroom, Skylar spun to sit on the edge of the bed and shoved the gauze curtain along the rail, away from her skin. She pulled her dress on because there was no way she would sleep naked with Luca now that he'd rejected her, now that he was leaving. She felt a headache approaching and wished she hadn't drunk so much. Two drinks was her limit, and the fireball shot had been a shitty idea.

Her eyes went to the nightstand. A stack of books rested atop the little table. They weren't there the last time she was in his bedroom, and she also noticed a yellow legal pad. She picked up the pad and read the words, which were mostly Italian. She noticed a phrase underlined, though. It said, *Uomo di Sangue.*

Her eyes went back to the table and landed on the first book in the stack as she set the notepad down. *Uomo di Sangue*, the title read.

Hmm. An interesting coincidence. Or was it? Maybe it was research for his master's thesis, nothing special.

Why was he leaving? She sank back into bed, feeling wide awake and strung tight with a crushing feeling of disappointment in her core. She felt like she was so close to cracking the code of Luca, of figuring out why he was so mysterious. Why he was holding back from her. Then again, it wasn't like she'd given herself totally to him. She had held back, too. Not much, but some. She hadn't told him that her feelings were changing. And she'd denied herself pleasure. All because of her stupid ex and the insecurities he'd planted inside of her, and now it was too late.

She swallowed a lump of tears. No way would she let Luca see her cry.

He came back into the room, looking defeated. After he clicked the light off, they snuggled close, as if their conversation hadn't happened. Skylar was happy to let it stay that way. For now.

His voice was thick with sleepiness. "Thank you for not asking too many questions tonight. I'm just not in any shape right now for anything. You're so sweet and so good, Skylar. Too sweet and too good for me."

She wasn't so sure of that. Especially not when she remembered something he'd said.

He was lying on his back, and Skylar wrapped an arm and a leg around him. "Luca?"

"Mmhmm?"

"Why did you say you were close to falling in love with me?"

"Because I am. You're the first woman I've felt anything for in a very long time."

"So, why me and not the others? What's so special about me?"

He didn't answer. Skylar hugged him tight but said no more. It didn't seem like there was a point.

He began breathing deeply, puffing out little exhales, and she knew he was asleep. She wasn't ready to drift off, though. Her mind was wound tight and the muscles in her legs felt twitchy. Probably because of the Red Bull and their baffling conversation.

Anger bubbled up inside of her, and she considered leaving and walking home. She flipped onto her back. Eyes open, she stared into the dark. What were his secrets? How would she convince Luca to stay? Should she try to get him to stay, despite his shadowy life? Or should she just move on and chalk their encounters up as a hot, strange fling?

She flopped back to her side, facing away from Luca. With a snore, he rolled over so they were back-to-back. In all the nights they had stayed together, he had never snored this deeply.

Where was her phone? Oh, right. Her bag was near the nightstand. Gingerly, she got out of bed and went for her purse, fishing the phone out and quickly checking her email. Sighing softly out of her nose, she decided to take her phone into the bathroom and check her social media accounts, too. Maybe she'd run a bath to try and calm down. Surely that wouldn't wake Luca; the bathroom and bedroom were so huge that they were practically in different ZIP codes.

She flicked on the flashlight of her smartphone so she could see in the dark bedroom. Glancing at the nightstand, she shone the light toward it, and... *Uomo di Sangue*. The image of the underlined words and the book title popped into her head, and on an impulse, she grabbed the book.

Luca didn't stir. She tucked the book under her arm and tiptoed across the room, using her cell phone to light the way. Once inside the bathroom, she locked the door and ran the hot water for the big Jacuzzi tub. She doubted if Luca would wake from his slumber anytime soon.

Setting the book on the sink, she lowered the lid on the toilet seat and plopped down. First she checked her social media accounts and liked a few posts, then she re-tweeted a few news stories. She was numbing her hurt, complicated emotions with the safety and security of her phone, and it felt like shit.

Reaching over, she picked up the book from its place on the sink and flipped through, wondering if there were any pictures inside or if she would understand any Italian. Turning the hardback over in her hands, she ran her palm down the smooth front. It was thick and about four hundred pages. The cover had a photo of an Italian-language newspaper splattered in blood.

Of course none of the book was in English, but Skylar figured out a few things instantly. The words "Mafia" and "Camorra" featured prominently on the book's summary. She pondered whether it was a fiction or a nonfiction book, but something told her it was a true story. It looked interesting, too. Maybe there was an English language version she could order online.

In place of the author's name it had a single word, *Anonimo*. She suspected that meant Anonymous, and she pulled up an Italian-to-English translation website on her phone that confirmed her assumption.

Her eyes scanned the foreign words as she opened the front cover. She flipped to the inside of the black flap. All in Italian.

Tapping the name of the book into Google, Skylar found a bunch of Italian entries and one English-language review in *The Guardian* from London. It was from a year ago.

"*Uomo di Sangue*—which means *Man of Blood* in English—is a frightening and true story of a Mafia boss in Naples, Italy."

Oh, interesting. Maybe Luca was in the book. Or maybe his family was in the book. Or, if he was really a graduate student, maybe his research was in the book, though that would just be about fictional Mafia types, wouldn't it? Curious to see what she'd find, she flipped to see if there was a table of contents or index. There was, but the Rossi name wasn't listed. She returned to her smartphone and scrolled with her thumb to read:

*It's rare that a work of narrative non-fiction would have such an impact on one country. This extraordinary book would be a sure winner for many journalism awards in the United States, but the anonymous Italian journalist who wrote this stunning and heartbreaking true story of a Mafia boss's impact on a city and country probably won't get an award for his work. He will be lucky if he doesn't get a bullet to the head. This is a frightening and detailed account of how the Mafia has influenced every facet of Italian life.*

Wow. It sounded like an amazing piece of reporting.

Skylar rose and checked her bathwater, wiping her wet finger on her bare leg. She sank to the crisp marble floor of the bathroom, her back resting against the side of the tub.

*It's rumored that the anonymous author who wrote this book had previously worked for* Il Mattino, *Naples's largest newspaper, and later ran a popular Italian news blog,* Politica Italiana. *English-speaking audiences wouldn't likely know of the site's popularity, but think of Wikileaks, Edward Snowden, Woodward and Bernstein, and you get a taste of what was accomplished. The wunderkind behind the blog and the book was rumored to be a young man from a wealthy Naples family.*

The journalist sounded brilliant. Why had Skylar never heard of him, or at least of his work if he remained anonymous? She was so ignorant. She needed to read more about Italy—and the rest of the world. Her frown became even more severe as she continued to devour the article. It said the book's author went deep in his reporting to find out little known details of one Mafia boss, going undercover, becoming friends with underworld criminals and hanging out with Mafia members. He'd even witnessed a Mafia massacre. Impressive work, tough work, the kind of stuff Skylar could only dream of.

Thinking about whether it would be feasible or safe for a female journalist to report like that, she reached back and checked the water again. The tub was almost full and the water scalding. She shut off the tap and scanned more of the review, wanting to read until the water cooled. The faucet dripped and steam rose into the air.

*Following the release of this book, the author suffered a great personal tragedy, allegedly retribution from the Camorra for revealing so many details about the crime boss. It's also rumored that the author had to flee Italy and is on the run. It's even possible that he's not alive.*

Heart racing, she flipped to the book's publication date then did a quick calculation. The book was published two months before Luca's parents were killed.

"Oh my God," Skylar whispered out loud. She closed her eyes and breathed in rapid, shallow breaths. Her heartbeat whooshed in her ears, and her stomach flip-flopped. She sat like that for countless moments, wondering what the hell to do. What to think. What to feel. Luca was the journalist. What other solution could there be?

*No. Don't let your imagination run wild. Okay, the author is from Naples. So what if Luca reads a lot about the Camorra? And what about his travels in the past year? What does that prove, really?*

She put her phone on the floor, but the book still rested in her lap. Shaking, she picked it up and thumbed through the pages again, this time stopping at the first chapter. There was a quote at the beginning.

*Chi più sa, meno crede.*
*The more one knows, the less one believes.*

Luca's tattoo.

Skylar let the book fall to her lap, and she set her palms on the cool marble floor, hoping to stop her shaking. It didn't. She forced herself to take deep, yogic breaths to calm down. Everything—from his reluctance to talk about himself to the way he'd reacted to her during their fight—seemed clear now. It all made sense. His evasiveness, his sadness, his interest in politics, it all came into sharp focus. This was why he refused to talk about his past or promise her a future. Why he wanted to leave.

She zoned out while trying to figure out what to do. There was the drip-drip-drip of the bathtub faucet, and then a gentle knock on the door.

"*Amore mio.* Are you bathing?"

Skylar gasped. "Yes! Luca!" she said, crawling over and flushing the toilet. She slipped her phone and the book into her bag and stuffed a towel over the book. With shaking hands, she opened the linen closet and set the bag on a shelf, trying to close the door without a sound. Then she wriggled out of her dress and underwear. "One second!"

She took a deep breath and unlocked the door. A naked Luca walked into the bathroom. It wasn't as though it was the first time she'd seen him without clothes, but looking at his body made her heart flutter faster now that she knew his real identity. Skylar bent over the tub to check the water, hoping that her bare ass would be enough of a distraction from her quaking legs and arms.

"Luca," she said, attempting a bright voice. "You're awake."

She mustered a seductive look and glanced over her shoulder to find him leaning against the sink, staring at her. His eyes traveled down her body. Why did he have to look so handsome when he was sleepy and his hair was rumpled and she had just discovered that he was a crusading journalist wanted by criminals?

"I woke up and you weren't next to me, *amore mio.* I…wanted to see if you were okay."

Skylar stood up straight then slowly eased herself into the tub, shivering a little from the feeling of the near-scalding water on her legs and the cool air-conditioned room on her nipples, which were now taut. "Sorry. Couldn't sleep. Too many thoughts going through my head."

"Why did you lock the door? Were you afraid I was going to interrupt you doing naughty things?"

His accent was thicker than usual, and he sounded a little groggy from sleep, but her eyes drifted down his chest and lower to find he had a giant hard-on.

"Oh, um, I always lock the bathroom door." She leaned back, gently splashing water onto her breasts as he watched, grazing her nipples with the heel of her hand. It made his cock twitch. "I was waiting for the water to cool."

"Can...can I join you?"

She smiled and nodded. Of course he could. Now that she knew his true identity, she knew exactly what she had to do.

# CHAPTER THIRTY-THREE

It wasn't hard to break into Skylar's condo, which was on the second-floor and had a window at shoulder height. The American had left it cracked open a couple of inches, and Annalisa easily slid the glass open, hopped up and launched herself inside.

Careless girl. Stupid girl. Dead girl.

Annalisa would wait until she came home. She knew Skylar wouldn't be back that evening, since she'd driven away from the Iguana with Luca; she'd spend the night with him, fucking. But surely he'd drive her home in the middle of the night. Luca didn't like to sleep next to women—which would of course change once Annalisa was back in his life.

She wandered around Skylar's house, inspecting everything. Had Skylar discovered that Luca liked blowjobs in the morning before he opened his eyes?

Skylar had so many books about The Buddha. Incense. Photos of a woman who looked like Skylar, only older. Her mother, perhaps? Framed sayings from various Zen masters in every fucking room. So annoyingly twee. Annalisa rolled her eyes. Skylar probably drank coconut water and talked about chakras.

"No Mud, No Lotus," read one framed saying.

Tears came to Annalisa's eyes when she realized what was ahead.

No Blood, No Luca.

# CHAPTER THIRTY-FOUR

Luca flicked off the harsh bathroom light so that the full moonlight streaming through the skylight in the roof illuminated the bathroom.

"Too dark?" he asked.

"No, it's perfect."

*She* was perfect. Since he'd walked into the bathroom, he couldn't tear his gaze off her body, or her eyes, which were pure and shining. He hadn't felt right about making love to her earlier, when he knew that he was leaving and she didn't, but now that she was aware of his half-made plans, now that he had all but bared his soul to her—as much as he could in his situation—maybe she wanted one final night of pleasure. If that was the case...well, he would take anything she would give.

Regardless, he needed her touch. Her kisses. Her nearness.

Luca eased into the hot water and she smiled at him beatifically. Her sweetness made his heart ache. How could he let her go? His hand caressed the smooth skin of her calf. The tub was so big that they could face each other and stretch out their legs.

"Come closer," he said.

Moving slowly, she sat in between his legs, her back to him. She swept her long, half-wet hair up, tying it into a messy knot at her nape. Just the tender motion of her doing that sent a current through his body.

*I adore her. I want her. If we make love, I might never leave her.*

He gently washed the curve of her back and shoulders and kissed her damp neck, pausing to softly lick and bite. His hands slid over her breasts, stomach and legs, slippery from the soap that smelled like lime and basil. She moaned and sighed then turned around and knelt in the water to wash him slowly from his neck to his feet.

When she was finished, he kissed the palms of her wet hands.

They didn't speak.

### 

She climbed into Luca's lap and embraced him with her arms and legs.

"Sky, this is dangerous," he whispered.

She pulled back to look at him and saw a look of near-agony on his face. "Why?"

"Because I want to be inside of you."

He sounded desperate, and that made her smile grow. Was she evil for smiling? She didn't care. "And *I* want *you*. I want you inside of me. So what's the danger?" She leaned forward to kiss him, and for the first time she was the one to slip her tongue to his instead of the other way around.

"Are you sure? Even after what I told you?"

She rested her hands on his chest and nodded. "This is my choice. I choose you, and us. I know it might be just for tonight, that this is all we'll ever have. But I'm okay with that."

She didn't get into how she wanted to live in the now, forget her past and her feelings of inadequacy and shame. She didn't get into how she thought she understood and respected him more now. This thing that she and Luca shared, that they were about to share…well, it was more of a gift to herself than to him. Tonight was about her needs, her wants, her desires. Oddly enough, knowing what she knew didn't change that this was the first time in her life that she was choosing her pleasure over a man's.

Ever so slightly, she shifted her hips. She rubbed herself slowly on the smooth underside of his cock, feeling need build within her. Putting just the tip at her entrance, she exhaled…then lowered herself down, inch by inch.

"Oh," she whispered, stunned at how united they felt like this. She didn't move. All she wanted was to feel full of him, his heat finally inside her.

His hands went to her face, gently cupping her jaw. She shifted back and forth, and a groan escaped his lips.

"Sky, we need a condom."

"I'm on the pill," she said, pressing her mouth to his, recalling how he had earlier mentioned he was tested and was clean. She raised herself and slid back down him, slow, and whispered, "I want all of you before you leave."

He touched her face as though she were a fragile, ethereal creature. She stopped moving, and they sat, intertwined and fused. Their faces were near and they kissed, their lips dragging against one another's, scorching and slow.

They paused, foreheads touching, chests heaving, breath blending. She should have been afraid because the Mafia wanted him. Should have been upset that he'd withheld the truth from her so long. Should have gotten up, left and walked out of his life. But she didn't and she couldn't. Now she not only wanted him but admired him. What he was, all that he represented, turned her on. His situation was dangerous. She was stupid for that, she suspected, but other women wanted cops and firemen and soldiers. She wanted Luca.

The room was darker now because the moon had passed beyond the skylight, but the air seemed clearer and she was more hyper-attuned to everything. She moved her hips in a slow, circular motion and he responded with low, guttural moans.

"Sky, I don't know how much longer I can last like this. Let's continue in bed, please?" he rasped, kissing her.

She whispered a yes and slid up and off him, immediately missing the feeling of him inside of her.

When they climbed out of the tub, he grabbed a towel and dried her body with long, soft strokes as he himself stood dripping. They made their way to the bed, and he turned on the light. Instead of feeling exposed or self-conscious, the idea that he could see her as she truly was, naked and needy, excited Skylar.

"You said you wanted me to take charge of us, so I will. Totally. I want you on top of me," she said as he undid the messy, makeshift bun at her nape. She shook her hair free and added, "I don't want you to hold back. I don't want you to be tender. I want you to be primal."

Nodding, he licked his lips. "You got it."

He pressed her against the mattress, kissing her hard. She opened her legs wide, ready for him.

"Touch me," she whispered. "Feel how wet I am because of you."

His lips remained on hers, a feather-light kiss, as his hand roamed into the groomed curls between her legs. Luca muttered in Italian, but when his finger reached her clitoris he switched to English.

"I love how responsive you are to me," he said in a gravelly whisper.

She could only shudder in a breath. Words weren't possible.

He pushed two fingers inside of her, then withdrew and rubbed her clit slowly as she cried out.

"This? Is this what you want?"

"Yes…no." Why was his touch so unhurried, so slow? She fluttered her eyelids shut, overwhelmed by the erotic threads he sent through her body.

"No?"

He rubbed her slower, and that was when she realized he was teasing her. Bringing her to the edge of orgasm. Pulling her toward bliss. She said, "I want you inside of me again."

"Patience, Skylar. We'll get there. Open your eyes. Look at me. Watch me make love to you."

She did, and her breath grew heavy as he licked and tongued and sucked at her breasts. As he dragged his fingers through her wet core, she was unable to hold back how she really felt. "I missed you. I could barely sleep, and when I did, I had nightmares."

He kissed her in response and murmured, "I missed you, too."

"There wasn't a single waking hour that I didn't think about you touching me or kissing me."

His teeth grazed her neck and the rhythm of his fingers made her body bloom with pleasure.

"Every night before I went to bed I thought about you and your body and your mouth."

"And what else did you think of, Skylar?" he asked, staring into her eyes, making her melt.

"This. Your hands in my hair. You inside of me. Loving me."

"Loving you," he whispered, staring into her eyes.

"You know what else I thought of, Luca?"

He rubbed the swollen nub of her clit between his thumb and forefinger, and she whimpered in response. Tears welled up in her eyes, and she said, "How I feel complete when I'm with you and lost when we're apart." *Dammit.* This was getting messy. It was more difficult than she'd thought, trying to separate emotion from sex, which had sort of been her plan. She didn't want to cry, not now, not in front of him, but... "And I cried every night when I realized I might never see you again."

"I'm sorry," he whispered. "I never wanted to hurt you."

She sniffled and looked him in the eyes. Pure sexual craving overtook her tangled emotions. He knew exactly where to touch to make her come, and it didn't take long for her to be even more slippery and creamy and crying out from satisfaction. The orgasm sent long, throbbing contractions through her body, and for the first time in her life she felt completely out of control as the crashing waves of perfection and light passed through her.

"*Si. Si. Si.* Exactly like that, *amore mio*," Luca whispered, trailing his nose and lips over her cheek as she came, and her entire body released all of the need and tension she had built up throughout the night. She held Luca tight, quivering, gasping and nearly in tears from the intensity.

"I have never seen anything or anyone more beautiful than you just now," he said, positioning his cock at her entrance. Teasing her more.

"Now. I need you inside me now," she demanded. "Don't deny me that."

Slowly, slowly, slowly he pushed into her while whispering in her ear. "How could I ever deny you? How could I ever say no to you?"

She gripped his biceps. During their week apart she had ached from his absence; now her heart could explode with joy and pure lusty adrenaline. His cock was bigger than any she'd ever experienced, and it stretched her deliciously like it had in the tub. She rode a faint wave of intensity until her muscles fully relaxed around him.

"You feel so, so good. I know you said primal, but is it okay if I go faster?" he asked, breathless. "I'm not hurting you, am I? You feel really tight." He panted a little.

"Yes. No. Not hurting me. Faster. Just do...anything you want. I'm yours. Devour me."

He laughed, a wicked and sexy laugh. "You're mine. I like that. You're mine, Skylar Shaw. All. Mine."

Luca stopped moving then, leaving her full of his hardness. He stared into her eyes with such a devastating gaze that she imagined she could shatter like a fallen vase. She was with a man who turned her on more than anyone on the planet, and who'd tried to tell the truth against all odds. To her, there was no bigger aphrodisiac.

He moved again, wracking her with furious strokes while pinning her arms above her head with his hands and squeezing her wrists tight. Just as she had fantasized. Their bodies were still hot-damp from the tub and slightly perspiring from the friction, slick with each others' juices. He was more primitive than she'd ever seen him. Feral, like an animal.

"More," she whispered. "Harder and faster and more."

Luca responded, something fierce and Italian, and her entire body shimmered. She didn't bother asking him to translate.

"Skylar," he said, his voice cracking almost imperceptibly, letting go of her arms and pressing even closer. She slid her arms around him, and his energy enveloped her. That's when she knew for sure that this was just as intense for him as it was for her. He was afraid to tell her how he felt, afraid to stay with her, afraid of being hurt. Just as he'd said.

"You are so perfect, *amore mio*," he whispered.

In that moment, Skylar had an epiphany. He needed her, although he probably didn't realize it. No man had ever needed her. Wanted her, yes. Not needed her.

And she needed him. Luca was what made her happy. She would try to protect him. Exactly how, she wasn't sure. But she needed to try. So she could nurture him. Please him.

Love him.

If he didn't leave, she could do all of that.

She pulled his body toward hers and held on as if he would float away if she lost connection with his flesh. Skylar knew he was close to orgasm by the way his body took on a sudden, sweaty sheen, and she said, "Luca, I love the way you feel when you're inside me. It's like nothing else in the world matters. Only you matter," she whispered softly in his ear.

Out of the corner of her eye she saw the thick fingers of his hand gripping the sheet. He buried his face into her neck. With a loud, drawn out groan, he released inside of her, his cock pulsing quickly and then slower. She fluttered tender kisses on his neck as he tried to catch his breath, his body heavy and boneless on top of hers.

He propped himself up on his forearms. "*Amore mio*, are you crying?"

She hadn't noticed there were tears streaming out of the corners of her eyes. Shaking her head, all she could do was draw him tight.

### ###

Skylar awoke at dawn to Luca's kisses on the back of her neck. Maybe they hadn't even slept, because it seemed like they'd spent the entirety of the dark hours touching, kissing, loving.

She was greedy for him and drunk with lust, and she suspected he was as well. It only took a caress of his chest and a soft sigh near his ear for him to spring to attention. His hands went everywhere on her body, her hair wild as he pushed her flat, gripping her wrists. Their mouths were fierce and demanding, and she could only focus on the rough, carnal power of his body as he thrust again inside of her. She cried out, loud. She didn't care that she hadn't brushed her hair or her teeth, or that they were both in a sex stupor.

"More," she said. By this point, she was beyond whispering. "I need more of you."

He sat up, pulling her into his lap so she straddled him. When she sank onto his erection, time slowed and so did their urgency. His kisses turned gentle and she feathered her fingers across his face. Mouths hovered over skin and eyelashes trailed against lips. She traced his face with her finger then leaned back and put her hands under her breasts, offering them to his mouth. His hands eased her backward, and his mouth sucked her nipples into pink points while she rocked softly on his erection.

"I don't want this to end," he whispered into her skin.

"The sex or us?" she asked.

"Both."

Their hands joined, their fingers intertwined while their eyes met. The look they gave each other seemed more intimate than anything they had done prior. They moved together, slow and sensual, continuing to stare into each other's eyes. The sun peeked through the curtains covering the terrace doors and wafted through the gauzy panels covering the bed, infusing the room in a wan, white light. Everything in that moment seemed about to change, to become brighter, clearer, better.

At one point, she turned around and rode him in reverse, allowing him a full view of her ass and his cock sliding in and out of her. She tossed her hair and it fell down her back. Never had she felt so sexy.

"I wish you could see how beautiful you are right now. I wish I could video this and watch it every day for the rest of my life. You are so gorgeous," he growled.

She half-laughed, half moaned, and he ran his fingers down her spine. She owned this moment. This was the best sex she'd ever had. She reached down and stroked herself into yet another orgasm, not caring that it might also be the last time she was with him. Not caring that she loved him and might lose him. This moment was the only important thing.

"*Che bella ragazza,*" he whispered over and over in her ear afterward.

It wasn't until her heart had resumed a normal cadence that Skylar fully comprehended that she would have to reveal she was aware of his secret. She couldn't let him exit her life without telling him that she knew all about him. Maybe it was a point of pride as a reporter, or maybe she just wanted him to know that she wasn't a stupid young American girl. Amazing sex had nothing to do with her confronting the truth—and tomorrow would take care of itself.

While he caught his breath, she climbed out of bed and opened the curtains of the windows and doors leading to the terrace. Even though it was early morning, it was already so bright outside that the sky was a pale white-blue. She blinked several times into the light.

Skylar used the bathroom, and when she returned, Luca was still in bed, lying on his back. He looked a little too somber for a man who had just had a night of out-of-this-world sex. Then again, he was harboring all of those secrets.

Not for long.

She slid under the sheets, and he rolled over to hug her. "I've never done that with anyone."

"What?" she asked, puzzled.

"Had sex without a condom."

"Oh. Neither have I."

He kissed her. She wondered briefly how many women he had been with but pushed the thought out of her mind. Not only did she not want to know, but there were bigger questions to ask.

"Why are you really leaving, Luca?"

He swallowed, clearly uncomfortable. "I told you, things are getting too complicated here. I don't want to deal with my uncle, and I have to focus on my—" He stopped abruptly.

She searched his eyes, unblinking. "I don't think you should leave."

"Sky. Don't. Please don't make this harder. It's what I worried about when we started making love—"

She interrupted. "No. You're the one making it harder, Luca. I'm not going to play games here. I know who you are," she said in a quiet voice, wrapping herself in the sheet.

"Who am I, Skylar?"

Luca's voice was composed, but his eyes looked wide, the same as when they'd first kissed, like he was surprised and a little relieved.

"Let's see." She ticked off each point with her fingers. "You're a journalist. You wrote a book about the Camorra. You had a blog. You worked at a newspaper in Naples. Your parents were killed in a suspicious fire. You went on the run because you thought the Mafia was going to kill you," she added, trying unsuccessfully to keep her voice steady.

Luca went pale.

"When you fell asleep last night, I looked at a book on your nightstand. *Uomo di Sangue*, is that how you pronounce it? I found a review of it in *The Guardian*. It pretty much described everything about you except for your name. Also, the article about your parents in *Il Mattino*. Oh, and the fact that your tattoo matches the quote in the first chapter of your book."

Luca sat up against the headboard and sighed deep, closing his eyes.

She glanced at him, her heart pounding despite herself. "You can't be mad at me. We're both reporters. We're both curious. What did you expect? You chose exactly the wrong woman. Neither one of us will let go until we've found out the truth."

He chewed on his cheek, and the silence was excruciating. "I'm not mad. Maybe I'm relieved? I don't know. I don't know anything anymore."

She sat up and knelt, staring at him with intensity, not caring that she was naked. "You need to explain everything. You might be leaving soon—hell, today even—but you owe me an explanation. I'm not going to tell anyone. But I think we've become friends, right? You can trust me."

"We are friends," he said softly. "You might be the best friend I've had in years, actually."

He looked so sad in that moment that Skylar's heart broke for him.

"Just stop staring at me like that. Come here." He pulled her close, so that she was sitting next to him and her legs were in his lap, and asked, "Do you want to hear the long version or the short version? This won't be easy for me. I've been wrestling for weeks with whether to tell you any of this."

"It's okay. I want to hear it all. We've got all day."

He nodded wearily. "I grew up watching my father prosecute organized crime figures. You know that he was a lawyer. You read that in the article you found. Everyone was always surprised that he took that route because our family is pretty well off, going back generations. My father could have just worked doing wills or real estate and lived an easy life. But my father had a sense of justice."

Skylar hesitated to bring it up but said, "I thought you said that your Uncle Federico is really your father."

Luca grimaced. "Yeah. There's that. But let's not talk about that right now. I didn't even know Federico until I came here. I don't even know what to call him now."

"Why did you come here?" she asked.

"Let me get to that part. When I was at boarding school in Massachusetts, my family assumed I would be a lawyer. But I wasn't a great student and couldn't get into a law program in Italy, much less a prestigious program in America or the U.K. But I did admire my father's bravery, so I decided to be a journalist. I wanted to be like him. Wanted to make life in Italy better. You have no idea how screwed up it is there. When I got out of university, I worked at my hometown newspaper, *Il Mattino*. My first year in Naples was a lot like what you are doing now."

Skylar rolled her eyes. "You probably didn't have to cover golf cart parades and pet-of-the-week from the local animal shelter."

Luca chuckled. "Oh, Sky, I did. I did. I wrote about all sorts of stupid things. And most of the time, I didn't even get bylines. Young reporters at papers in Italy generally don't."

She inhaled, excited. "Oh! That's why—"

He interrupted. "Why what?"

"Why I didn't find any of your articles online. Well, that and your old paper has a subscription firewall. I wasn't *so* obsessed with you that I was going to pay four Euros a month to get access to the newspaper archive."

He kissed her cheek. "You did your homework. Anyway, I eventually wrote about Mafia murders, lots of them. Even those were so routine that I didn't get credit for writing the stories. But recognition or fame wasn't what I was after—I wanted to concentrate on the evil side of my city, so I decided to start my own blog. It was easier and safer to do it anonymously. I started out writing about murders and politics there. And political gossip. That led into writing about the Camorra and the Mafia in a similar way— they're all intertwined there, anyway—and readers loved it."

Now Skylar was even more curious. "I'll bet. How did you conceal your identity? Did you do it while working at the paper?"

"I eventually quit the paper. I had a lot of police sources. A lot of my stories were from public records and tips people sent me. I allowed whistleblowers to email documents, to send information and photos and videos into an online drop-box. My father also helped leak some information out of the courthouse."

"And so that information led to the book? You were so young." Really, he was so smart.

"Yes. I was twenty-four when I started working on it, twenty-six when it was published. A lot of tips came in about Bruno Castiglione. He was one of the most powerful Camorra bosses in Naples. A publisher actually contacted me—well, contacted the blog—about writing an exposé."

"But weren't you worried about your safety when you wrote it? Or the safety of your family?"

Luca groaned. "I didn't think it through. I was reckless. I was a lot younger then. My father encouraged me because he thought I had a great platform for telling the truth. I tried to be just like him, fearless."

"So, no one knew that you were writing the book other than your parents? What about that girl you dated, Annalisa? Did she know?"

Luca was quiet for a moment, and Skylar worried that he still had feelings for her. The thought made her nauseated—and then guilty. Here he was telling her his darkest secret, and she was being jealous and petty.

"No. I never told her. She was a features writer at the paper, and she wasn't really my girlfriend, we just sort of hung out. I ended it with her before my book came out. But, after the book was released, she disappeared."

"What?" Skylar wasn't sure why this shocked her after the news about his parents' deaths. "What do you mean?"

"She abruptly left the paper and never returned. No one I knew ever saw her again. And I received a scary, anonymous email about her that said she ended up in the same place as my parents. It was right around that time that I left Italy."

She sighed. "Wow. That's horrible. I can't even imagine."

Luca said nothing.

There was a long pause while Skylar gathered her thoughts, but finally she asked, "Do you regret writing the book?"

"Of course. In many ways I do. My parents…" His voice trailed off, and from his tone she thought he was about to cry. He drew a long, shuddering breath before continuing, "My parents, they were aware of the risks. My father, or the man who I thought was my father, lived with risk most of his career, and my mom supported him in whatever he did career-wise. But I have enormous guilt over everything. I was away the night of the fire, doing an interview with the widow of a man who was killed by the Castiglione family. I got a call during the interview from a colleague of my father's. I lost everything in that moment, Sky. I miss them every minute of every day. My father was my best friend, and now he's gone."

"Oh, Luca, baby, I am so sorry," Sky whispered. Everything she could possibly say seemed inadequate. She knew what he was going through. Her mom had been her best friend. She stroked his face and hair and just wanted to somehow take away his pain.

They held each other for a long while. Then he spoke.

"My parents are my biggest regret. I also feel guilty about Annalisa."

She interrupted him and pulled back from his embrace. "Annalisa. Were you in love with her?" She hated herself for asking, but she needed to know and trusted him to be honest.

"No, Sky. Not even a little. I've never…well, I would have ended it with her even if I'd never written the book. I'm ashamed to admit this, but it was really only sex. And it wasn't even great sex. It was fun at first, but she was, um, kind of obsessed with me. It was like she idealized everything I did. It got kind of creepy. When I broke up with her, she climbed in my window to try to convince me to take her back."

Skylar grimaced. "Wow. Weird. How long were you together, again?"

"Only a month. And, well, I've come to realize that I've kind of used a lot of women that way. For sex. It's not a good feeling."

She stared at him. "Do you think you're using me? You can be honest. I can handle it."

"No. Not at all. Not even a little. I don't even know if I was using Annalisa, exactly, because I liked her and enjoyed her company at first. And she seemed like she wanted the same thing, something casual. But it was never easy, or comfortable, not even in the beginning. She was really combative. It wasn't normal. Or fun. Or mature, like…like this. Like us."

This made Skylar grin like crazy, which made him laugh a little before turning serious. She did, too.

"You need to know this. I've spent the last ten years avoiding relationships, even before the book. My parents had a really screwed up marriage—though now I think I know why. Because of Federico…" He trailed off.

"Your real father."

Luca nodded weakly. "It explains why my parents were hostile and cold to each other. They stayed together for me. Regardless, I didn't want that in my life. So I settled for sex. I'm not an angel, Skylar, you need to know that."

She shrugged. "I can't change your past. Or mine."

"After the book…I didn't sleep around quite as much. I hated lying to people, but I sometimes did. Before, I hadn't. I didn't like it."

"You lied to me, about working on your graduate degree."

He stroked her hair. "I'm sorry. I told you more of the truth than any other woman. I didn't want to get involved. I didn't want to put anyone at risk. I didn't want to get close. Didn't want to befriend anyone and open myself up."

"You weren't friends with the other women? You didn't get to know them?"

"Friends? I have no friends. Everyone who was my friend before, they're gone. They heard rumors about me and the book, and my parents, and now I represent danger. Although, Sky, it's weird. In many ways I feel proud of everything. Every time I read that my book has sold more copies, or I find another good review, I remember I'm blessed. I feel lucky. I've made a difference. Especially now that Bruno Castiglione is awaiting trial, people in Italy know I stand for the truth. They know I've tried to make things better. What did George Orwell say? 'In a time of universal deceit, telling the truth is a revolutionary act.'"

Upon hearing that, Skylar pressed her face into his neck. She wanted to cry. She was so stupid for asking him about his sex life when he was talking about telling the truth, about writing books, about being brave. More brave than she'd ever be. Her heart broke for him, and she wanted to make his hurt and pain go away. The frustrating thing was, she didn't know how. Or if he even wanted that from her. All of the warm fantasies she'd had while making love now seemed girlish and naïve.

She lifted her head and asked, "Where did you go when you left Italy?"

"I backpacked through Southeast Asia. That's when I stayed at the Buddhist yoga ashram in India. Then I went to Argentina."

"Ah. It makes sense now. How did you avoid the Mafia while traveling?"

"Luck, I guess. Disguises. I grew a beard. I went to remote, sometimes dangerous places. There were a couple of close calls, I think. People seemed to follow me in Prague and in Warsaw. It was really stressful, and that's why I went to Asia. It was more remote."

"You grew a beard." Sky tried to imagine that. "How long?"

Luca laughed. "Long. You wouldn't have recognized me."

"But how did you pay for everything?" She was suddenly ravenously curious about all the details.

"My agent's in London. He doesn't know me personally, but he makes sure my checks get deposited to a Swiss bank account that's not traceable. He also arranged to have the inheritance from my parents' estate transferred to that account."

Skylar nodded slowly. "So, why did you come to Palmira? Just because you were sick of traveling?"

"Yeah. And because of my, er, uncle. He promised I'd be safe. I thought I'd come here and write my next book, but I haven't been able to focus. I have it all reported, but I don't even know if I want to write anymore."

Skylar frowned. "Why?"

"I'm afraid, honestly. Afraid that if I write about another Mafia boss more people will die. I hate violence, Skylar. I hate what violence has done to my country. I hate what it did to my family. I hate what it could do to anyone I ever care about again."

"So, what's next?" Skylar wasn't sure she wanted the answer.

"I don't know, Sky. Because of the reporting in my book Bruno Castiglione was arrested and—"

A smile spread across Skylar's face. "Luca! That's amazing. It also means you're safer, right?"

He shrugged. "That's what my uncle says. I have no idea. I've lost all perspective. Castiglione's on house arrest, and his trial is scheduled for next month. I'll feel better if he's convicted."

Skylar shifted so that she was sitting in his lap, her legs wrapped around him. "So, let me ask you again. If Castiglione's in jail, why are you leaving?"

He rubbed his hands over her arms. "Because I'm still afraid, Sky. I'm still afraid the Mafia might find me here, and it's just become too much with my uncle, uh, Federico. And with you."

She said nothing, just regarded him stonily.

"What?" he asked.

"So you'll spend your whole life on the run?" She put her hand over his heart. "Look here. You have an entire second book reported, no reason to think anyone's found you, and all the luxury in the world on this island. It's a perfect place to write. You obviously were—are—a great journalist. Why would you want to fade away and not help people, your country, with your writing?"

Luca shrugged, clearly miserable.

Skylar sighed. "Even if you don't want to write the book you thought, you could write something else. A memoir. About your parents. About how you went on the run and feared for your life. That would be a huge bestseller," she said. "Especially in America. People would love that. You've got it all. Intrigue. Corruption. Sex."

He shrugged again, and Skylar eyed him skeptically. "You have this amazing platform. You have things to say. You have an entire country—hell, all of Europe, it sounds like from that *Guardian* review—reading your work, and yet you're choosing to stay silent, and you're also choosing to run. You once believed in helping people. If you're going to keep running, you need to find the courage inside of you again to write."

Luca glanced sideways at her. "What's the phrase in English? 'Man up'? Are you telling me to man up?"

She nodded, aiming to look sympathetic but realizing that she'd come off as cold and a bit harsh. "Maybe a little. Sorry. It's just that you have your uncle, or father, or whatever he is, wanting to get to know you. He's still alive. That's a blessing."

Luca huffed out a sigh.

"And you have me. I care about you. I...I could love you."

His expression was full of disbelief. "Really? You could? After everything I just said?"

She nodded and pressed her hand to his chest. "Yeah. I could. You're afraid, Luca, but that's natural. What you shouldn't be is afraid of opening your heart, because living without doing that is like being dead. That's what I think."

He squeezed her upper arms with both hands and raised his voice. "Of course I'm afraid of opening my heart. Why wouldn't I be? My parents were murdered and my mom lied to me. Don't forget, I just found that out."

"Understandable," Skylar said. "But she probably did it to spare you and your father. And regardless, at some point you have to live."

With her finger she tapped the skin over his heart, and he snorted bitterly. "When will I ever be able to really live? How? With all this guilt and fear? How can I trust anyone when I'll probably lose them? Especially if I write another book."

Skylar slid off him, annoyed. "I get that you've been in danger, and I don't know what that feels like. But I do know what it means to grieve and lose someone you love. We all eventually lose people we love, whether it's from cancer or murder or old age. We all suffer. It's just up to us how we live in between the suffering. How we love in those moments between the pain."

They stared at each other, unblinking, not speaking. Luca climbed out of bed and walked to the door.

"I'm going downstairs," he said.

Skylar bowed her head and exhaled as he closed the door. She'd thought they had a deep emotional connection, a mental attachment to each other. Now, she wasn't so sure. It was as if he hadn't heard her at all.

# CHAPTER THIRTY-FIVE

Luca jabbed at the buttons of the fancy coffeemaker. What did Skylar know about life and death and grief? She was so young.

It was a stupid question, though. She had lost her mother when she was a teenager, never had a father, put herself through school. When he thought about it, she was actually much more resilient and tougher than he was. He'd been raised with privilege and wealth, and while his situation was maybe precarious with Bruno Castiglione, he had enough money to hide for the rest of his life. In luxury. Skylar would always have to fight. Unless...

Luca stopped himself. The idea of caring for her had been a constant fantasy in recent days. He was old-fashioned in many ways, and thought that if he was in a relationship with a woman it was his responsibility to care for her. Not just financially, but in every way. Everything about Skylar made him want to protect her. It was one of the reasons he wanted to run far away. What if they were together and something happened to her? What if he was unable to protect her? He couldn't bear the thought of *that* failure.

He was downstairs for an hour and grew surprised that she didn't follow him and press him into talking more. For most of the hour, though, he stared off into space, thinking about what she'd said.

*Love in between the moments of suffering.*

Taking two coffees upstairs, he found her lying on a chaise on the terrace. Her hair was wet and her body was swathed in a white towel, her eyes closed to the bright sun. Her phone rested on her stomach.

"Sky," he said.

She opened her eyes and he handed her a glass. "What's this?"

"I figured out how to make an iced coffee with that machine."

Her mouth turned up in a smile. She sat up and sipped then said, "Very nice. Thank you."

He reached down and stroked her cheek with the back of his fingers. The ringing of her phone broke the silence.

"Hey, Jimmy," she said, answering immediately, her voice crisp and businesslike. "Oh! Wow. Really? Whoa, shit. Where? Thanks for telling me. I'll be there as soon as I can. 'Kay, bye."

"Who's Jimmy?" Luca asked as she looked up at him.

She stood up. "Why do you care?"

"For someone who talks about peace and love and Zen, you're awfully sarcastic sometimes."

"And for someone who's going to leave, you're awfully curious about who I talk to."

"I am curious, and I do care," he said softly.

Her gaze faltered. "That was my police source. The cops found a body in the Palmira Preserve. Murder. I need to go. Can you drive me to my house? I need my car. I want to get to the preserve before the TV reporters."

"Why don't you just take my car?"

She shot him a baffled look. "Aren't you leaving?"

He shook his head. "No. I'm not."

"Well…what if you need your car today?"

"I won't. I'm not going anywhere. I have writing to do. It's not like you're going to steal my uncle's Mercedes. How long will you be gone? Six hours? Eight hours? I want you to come back here when you're done. I have a lot to think about, Skylar. We have more to talk about. Maybe we can go out to dinner tonight. Since it's Saturday, I'll try to make reservations somewhere."

She grinned and hugged him.

"You left some clothes here last weekend. Let me get them for you."

She followed him inside, and he handed her a folded stack. "I washed them."

Skylar kissed him and whipped the towel off herself, tossing it on a bureau. She spoke excitedly as she put on her lingerie and a long, cotton dress. "Apparently a kayaker found the body. And guess what? Half his body was eaten by an alligator."

Luca looked startled then cocked his head.

"Florida," they both said at the same time.

Skylar had covered a few murders in Boston during her internship, but they were always cold and sterile stories, with her on one end of the yellow police tape and the body and the cops far on the other side. Today at the Palmira Preserve she would reap the benefits of being a small-town crime reporter.

"What a way to start the weekend. Come on," Jimmy said, holding up the police tape so she could duck under. "I'll show you the corpse. Or what's left of it."

Her heart went into overdrive. She'd been at her mother's bedside when she passed, and had been so devastated that all she could think was that her mother looked so relieved and so peaceful in death. But a murder victim in a swamp? She wasn't sure she wanted to see the body. But she also couldn't turn Jimmy down. This was a rite of passage for reporters. She needed to ace this test.

The morning's coffee sloshed around uncomfortably in her stomach as she followed Jimmy down a boardwalk. It was so hot and bright out that the sun was almost colorless, pure light beating down on the wooden walkway and the Technicolor green swamp surrounding the path. In the distance, a cluster of cops stood peering over the boardwalk railing, and as she approached Skylar saw men in hip-waders in the water, in the narrow river that flowed between the boardwalk and a thicket of mangroves.

"Who are they?" she hissed at Jimmy.

"Medical Examiner's office. And some of our techs, looking for evidence."

Skylar nodded and held her breath.

Jimmy addressed two of the cops looking down into the water. "Guys, let the reporter have a look."

The men stepped aside, and Skylar felt her entire body trembling uncontrollably.

"Right there," Jimmy said, pointing down.

She stepped forward, mouth open. There, in the shallow water, tangled in the mangroves, was a human body. Or what had been. He—for Skylar assumed it was a man—was bloated, puffed up like a sick, yellow-gray balloon. Pulpy red flesh twisted around what appeared to be arm bones, and Skylar thought she spotted a single eye, half-open in a sickening, horrific gaze. The other eye, the entire left side of his head, actually, was missing.

She quickly turned away and sipped a shallow breath.

"See where the gators got his legs?" one of the cops said, removing a toothpick from his mouth and pointing. "Right below the knees. And when we arrived, a big-ass vulture was snacking away on his face. That guy's probably been in this swamp for several days. Surprised there's anything left of him."

She turned her head, shooting another quick glance to the body as bile rose in her throat.

Indeed, the man's legs were missing. Or underwater. Or shredded, torn and bloodied to the groin. She didn't stare long enough to determine which. If that wasn't horrific enough, Skylar noticed a long cut in a half-circle through flesh. Was that his throat? She wasn't even sure, the body was so putrefied and mangled.

"Holy shit," she whispered, thankful that she still wore her sunglasses and that the cops couldn't see the fear, sadness and revulsion in her eyes. "Was his throat slashed?"

She stepped back, not wanting to see any more. If she lingered, the contents of her stomach might come back up.

Jimmy glanced at her. "You didn't hear it from us, but yeah. The chief's coming to give a news conference soon and he'll tell you all about it."

"Was he killed there?" She swallowed hard. "Weird place for a body."

Jimmy shook his head. "No. We think he was killed further down, at the wooden platform. We found a shitload of blood there on the boardwalk."

Skylar looked into the brown, murky river on the other side of the boardwalk and took several deep breaths but got no relief. She realized the thick, humid air smelled sweet, like rotting meat. "Is that smell...?"

"Dead body? Yep."

Holding her breath for a few seconds, she walked toward the parking lot, trying not to retch.

"Was that your first?" Jimmy asked, catching up.

"Hunh?" She was trying to keep the coffee in her stomach and had zoned out for a few seconds.

"Have you ever seen a dead body before? A floater like that?"

She couldn't help but grin a little at Jimmy's casual yet macabre questions. "That was my first."

"Right on. So, hey, good job on not puking. I had a bet with the guys that you wouldn't, and I won. Thanks."

Skylar rolled her eyes and snorted. She reached up to adjust her sunglasses, which had slipped down her nose from the perspiration on her face. Her hands still shook. "You guys are so bad."

"Yeah, you get kinda jaded as a cop," Jimmy said cheerfully.

They were back at the parking lot, and Skylar slid back under the tape. She quickly pecked out a few sentences in an email to the newsroom so they could update the online story, then tweeted a few details. As she waited for the news conference in the shade of a large tree, she dialed Luca.

"Hey," she breathed, still slightly queasy. "I just saw the body."

"Really?" He sounded genuinely interested. "Was he actually ripped apart by an alligator?"

"Yep. Part of his legs were totally eaten off. So awful."

"Wow. I can't say I've ever seen that."

"Oh, gotta run. The chief's here."

"Be careful, *amore mio*."

Skylar beamed when she heard him say those words, and the unsettled feeling in her was crowded out by a shimmer of adoration for Luca. He was still calling her that after their talk. *Amore mio*. My love.

By the time Chief Judson was ready to address the media, a few other reporters had gathered. They all clustered around the chief, who usually held news conferences about boring things like drunk-driving checkpoints and seatbelt usage. This was only the second homicide on Palmira that year, he said, the first being a man who had bludgeoned his brother with a baseball bat in a fit of rage during a family barbecue on Memorial Day, right when Skylar started at the paper.

She held her phone and notebook in one hand and wrote with the other. Audio recording the chief's remarks was de rigeur, but she liked to take old-fashioned notes, too. That made her feel like more of a journalist somehow.

She scribbled as he talked in a slight New York accent, coupled with a monotone. "So, this is one of those things you usually see on TV or in Hollywood. Shortly after oh-seven-hundred hours—that's seven o'clock—a kayaker in the mangroves called us to report a body. We got out here and found the deceased in the water. We've tentatively identified him as Gianni Innocenti. We got his ID from his wallet, and we have good reason to believe that's his real name. We can tell you that when we arrived on the scene a very large vulture was near the body. We also saw some alligators in the area, but we don't believe that's how the man died because we found other evidence. He's the victim of a homicide, but at this time we're not releasing the manner of death. We think he's been in the swamp for several days, if the condition of the body's any indication."

Gianni Innocenti. The name sounded so Italian. Maybe she was just hypersensitive because of Luca and his situation. Skylar scowled in the direction of the chief and tried to read his sweaty face, but his sunglasses obscured any expression. She raised her hand.

The chief pointed at her. "Yes, Skylar?"

"Where's Mr. Innocenti from?"

The chief sucked in a breath. "Well, that's interesting. He had an Italian passport that said he was from Naples. Naples, Italy, not Naples, Florida. And we've run him in criminal databases and someone with that name is wanted by Interpol on murder charges in Serbia and in Italy."

Skylar felt sick to her stomach again. She wanted to call Luca, but the TV reporters were asking questions about the alligator, about Interpol, and about whether the man's body was badly decomposed. She stopped writing in her notebook, grateful for her smartphone's recording capability. Could the homicide victim have been on Palmira for Luca, or was this all just a coincidence? Should she say something to the chief or Jimmy in private?

The news conference ended, and she approached the chief as he walked to his car. She'd talked with him a few times for stories, and he'd been friendly in the past. Hopefully he'd be accommodating today, when she really needed information.

"Sir? Can I ask you a few things on background? I won't quote you."

"Sure, Skylar."

"I heard the guy's throat was slit."

The chief nodded. "Yep. It was. We think that's how he died. But I'm asking you not to put that in the paper just yet. Only us and the killer know that detail. And you, now."

"No problem. But is the public in any danger?"

The chief's eyes got squinty, and he tilted his head back and forth. "It's hard to say. I don't think so. I have a feeling this guy was here on vacation and maybe one of his Mafia frenemies happened to catch up with him. You like that word, frenemy? I just learned it from my teenage son." The chief chuckled then continued, "This guy was kind of a scumbag according to his criminal record. Wanted for a bunch of stuff in Europe, like I said. The Florida Department of Law Enforcement is taking over this investigation, in fact, and the FBI is coming in, too."

Skylar swallowed hard. "Can you give me any other details for my story? Was he staying here on Palmira? Where's his car?"

"You didn't hear it from me, but he was staying at the Palm Inn. If you go there now, you should be able to get photos of the FDLE techs processing the scene. And his rental car was found near your newsroom, parked in front of the coffee shop, but we towed that to our impound lot behind headquarters. The FDLE and the Feds are taking over this investigation soon. We're just securing the scene here."

"Thanks, Chief."

Skylar walked quickly back to Luca's car. She cranked the air-conditioning and called the editor on duty in the newsroom to dictate all the details. After she hung up, she considered whether to call Luca but decided against it. Gianni was dead. She didn't want to worry Luca if it was nothing—and what if his phone was tapped? No, she should just finish up then get back to his house as fast as possible.

The editor on duty asked Sky to update the story on Twitter—things like the victim's name, in what ways he was eaten by the alligator, a photo of the chief at the news conference—but once she had, she drove fast to the hotel where the dead guy had been staying. A state crime-lab van was parked in the lot, and Skylar pulled up near the hotel's registration office. Her face was slick with perspiration after the thirty-second journey from the car to indoors.

An older woman sat behind the desk, and Skylar introduced herself. Then she asked, "Can you tell me anything about Gianni Innocenti?" She tried to sound casual and not like she was freaking out. Which she was.

"He didn't speak much English. He was only here one night before he, well, disappeared. We thought it was weird that he was never around after he checked in, but we don't ask questions. He said he was meeting his girlfriend here."

Skylar exhaled. Girlfriend? Maybe this guy had nothing to do with Luca, he was just an unlucky tourist. Or maybe his girlfriend killed him.

"Did he seem shady to you? Weird?"

"No. Not at all. He was a quiet man, seemed to keep to himself. Waved at us. Friendly enough."

"Did you ever meet his girlfriend? Did she show up?"

The woman shook her head.

Skylar thanked her. At least she'd gotten a quote for the story. Picking up her phone, she tapped out Luca's number, but a sick feeling soon went through her, similar to when she'd seen the body earlier. Luca's phone rang and rang and never went to voicemail.

### 

Luca swam laps in the pool. The cool water refreshed him, washed away the tension of the morning.

Skylar was right, he knew that. He was running from his own fears. How was it that a woman he'd met a month ago had cut through all the bullshit and diagnosed what was in his heart? He smiled when he thought of Skylar's phone call about seeing the body. She was so funny. He also remembered his excitement and panic when he'd seen his own first homicide scene.

The thought of having Skylar call him with her reporting tales every day made him grin wider. And what if they shared their workdays over dinner and then woke up next to each other every morning? Wouldn't that be something?

He dove underwater, a fantasy flashing through his mind: A wedding, maybe on a beach somewhere. Skylar, pregnant with his child. A house, filled with love. Maybe a normal life was within his reach.

What had changed in him? Why was he now open to love when he had resisted it before? It was baffling that he was so willing to let Skylar into his heart when he had rejected so many other women. It must be the incredible sexual and mental connection between them, an incalculable mixture of need, chemistry and karma. Or maybe it was because Skylar also inspired him to be a better man.

Climbing out of the pool and toweling off, he had the urge to call his uncle and apologize. Yes, that's what he'd do. It's what Skylar would want. Luca hadn't been fair to Federico.

He picked up his smartphone and saw that Skylar had called, and that he had a few alerts from Twitter because he was following Skylar's feed. He swiped to the tweets. She was so quick in posting information.

*Palmira Chief says large alligator was near body when officers arrived.*

Luca smiled.

*Murder victim was likely in swamp for days, officials said.*

He tapped on her next tweet.

*Palmira Chief identifies man as 30-year-old Gianni Innocenti of Naples, Italy.*

Luca's fingers fumbled and nearly dropped the phone in disbelief. Innocenti was one of Bruno Castiglione's men. A low-level thug. A low-profile one, too. A rush of sheer panic gripped him so hard that he felt a tightening in his chest.

Looking around, Luca suddenly felt too exposed in the bright sunlight of the pool deck. Head bent, he walked inside and made sure every door was locked and every window was darkened.

*Oh fuck.* His gun was in the glove box of the Mercedes. With Skylar.

*Skylar.* Was she safe?

He dialed her number and exhaled when she answered.

"Luca. Are you okay?"

"I'm fine. *Amore mio*, you need to come back to my house now. I can't talk about it, but trust me. Please?" He didn't want to reveal more for fear that someone was tapping one of their phones. Was that possible?

"Luca, I'm on deadline. I'll be done in about a half hour." She paused, and he heard urgency in her voice. "I need to ask you a few things, but I don't want to do it over the phone. I'll be there soon."

"Skylar. Now."

"I know," she said. "But I have to go. I'll be there as soon as I can. Stay safe."

Her voice had an edge, and she hung up. *Stay safe?* Was she aware of the danger? He shook his head, thinking about how Skylar had a stubborn streak. There she was in her newsroom, filing her story.

He drank a beer, hoping to calm his nerves, and wished he hadn't smoked all of the Marlboros he'd bought after his big fight with Skylar. He paced the dark house for thirty minutes and was making another loop around his bedroom, about to call her again, when the doorbell rang and the phone in his hands vibrated almost simultaneously. His heart sped up even more when he picked up.

"I'm at the door," Skylar said.

"Be right down."

He flung the door open and pulled her inside. "Give me the keys," he demanded.

She did, and he ran to the car. Thank God the gun was still there. He moved the Mercedes into the garage.

He walked back inside, not even trying to conceal the weapon.

"Luca, oh my God. What is that?"

He locked the door and turned to her. "Uh, it's a gun. And we need to talk."

Her bottom lip quivered and she gulped in air. She hiccupped a few breaths then tears slid down her cheeks. Oh, shit. She had seen a dead body in the swamp and now this. He hadn't meant to scare her.

He rested the gun on a table near the door and took her in his arms. "*Amore mio*, please don't be scared. I'd never hurt you. Ever. Quite the opposite. Please stop crying."

She shuddered in a breath. "This is about Gianni, isn't it?"

"Yes."

She swore and shook her head. "The motel manager said he was waiting to meet his girlfriend. That he was a nice guy. A tourist."

"Skylar, he works for Bruno Castiglione."

### ###

She knew she was rambling, recounting what the chief told her about Gianni, as Luca pulled her into the den and flipped on a light. "Why is it so dark in here? Why are the curtains drawn?"

He looked at her, incredulous.

"Oh. Right. You don't want anyone to be able to see in. Duh."

Luca's shoulders tensed toward his ears. His hand squeezed her arm tight.

"Luca, you're hurting me. Please stop squeezing like that," Skylar said.

"*Amore mio*, I'm sorry. I'm worried."

Luca moved her to the leather sofa and he sat down, pulling her onto his lap and hugging her tight. He was breathing fast and she could feel his quick heartbeat. She felt self-conscious because she was sweaty and stinky, but he didn't seem to mind because he buried his nose in the hollow of her neck.

"Sky, this is not good. At all. We might have to leave Palmira."

She wriggled to look at him. "Hold on. What? *We?*"

Luca's voice was firm. "Yeah. I need to think about this. It might be safer if we leave. Maybe my uncle can help put us up somewhere. But yeah. We."

Was he crazy? What was he talking about? If she left Palmira, she wouldn't have a job. If she didn't have a job, she wouldn't be a journalist. She couldn't do that.

"Luca, I can't just leave Palmira. I've got the paper, remember? Can't we just call your uncle?"

"Skylar, our lives are in danger. Your life is in danger because of me. My uncle's life is in danger. If Gianni was here, he was looking for me. If he was parked by your office, he must know who you are." His voice was cold and harsh, and Skylar felt a familiar sense of panic, almost as if James had suddenly appeared in the room to berate her.

"But, how do you know that?" she asked. "What if it's just a coincidence? What if he really was here with his girlfriend? And anyway, who killed him and why? And could there be more, um, hit men?" She felt odd just saying the words *hit men*, like she was an extra in some bad TV crime show. What was this, *CSI: Palmira*?

"That's the big question," Luca sighed.

"I seriously doubt if anyone knows we've been spending time together. And would they want to kill an American journalist?" She reminded herself that Luca wasn't trying to sound like a jerk, that he was legitimately scared for them both. His parents had been killed in retribution, right? But—

"I wouldn't put it past them just to torture me. The other alternative is that I leave Palmira. Alone."

"What? But I don't want you to leave. We're... I..." Her voice trailed off. She had almost just told him that she loved him.

Luca didn't seem to notice. "Would you rather go somewhere with me and have me alive, or be here with you and die?"

When he put it that way, everything seemed so bleak. She blinked several times. "But your uncle..."

"I've tried calling him. I got his assistant. He's out on his yacht."

Skylar let out a long breath.

"Money isn't an issue. I can support you," Luca said.

She bristled. What kind of a statement was that? Did he think that's what she wanted? His money?

"What? No. I can't leave my job. I can't have you support me. I don't think you get it. I don't want to be supported by you. I wasn't raised that way. What would I do? I've worked for years to do this one thing. Do you know how hard it is to get a job at a newspaper these days?"

"Sky. *Sky.* I know what you're feeling," he said as she sniffled.

She couldn't help the anger. "How do you know what I'm feeling? How *could* you know what I'm feeling? You barely know me at all. You never wanted to."

Luca's mouth dropped open.

"Oh God, I'm sorry. I'm so sorry. I didn't mean to be harsh." Fat tears slid down her cheeks, and she tried to keep the hysteria out of her voice. "I'm not handling this stress all that well."

He kissed the top of her head. "It's totally understandable."

"I know this is stupid of me. It makes me think of my mother."

"What about her?"

Skylar exhaled, pushing out her lips. "It was when my mother was in the hospital, about six weeks before she died. She was trying another round of radiation. My mom was really angry that the treatment wasn't working, and she told me not to end up like her."

Luca shook his head. "Wasn't your mom a yoga teacher?"

"Yeah, she was. She also worked at a health food store. We were pretty poor when I was growing up. My grandmother put all of her retirement savings into her condo and couldn't help."

"I'm sorry."

"Don't be. But my mom made me promise I'd do something with my life. She made me promise that I wouldn't get married young or have babies until I was older. That I would try to make a difference in this world first. That I wouldn't screw up my life like she did when she was young."

"Ahh. Now I get it," Luca said.

"You get what?" Skylar asked.

"Why you want me to keep writing. Why you don't want to leave with me. Why your career is so important."

She grimaced. "I...I can't just run away with you and have you support me. There are other reasons, too."

"And those other reasons? Want to talk about those, *amore mio*?"

"I love the paper. I love being a journalist. And...well, if I leave the paper and everything I love here, you could eventually leave me. Then I'll be alone and poor and aimless, just like my mother. I'll have to be a yoga teacher or a waitress, and I'll never use my mind for anything."

Luca was silent for several seconds. Then he said, "That won't happen. You're too smart and ambitious. And you're a fighter."

"I don't know, Luca. I feel like a failure a lot. I worked so hard in school, and all I was able to get is this job at a small paper. I want more from myself. I feel like I'm not living up to my mom's expectation of me, and that just fills me with guilt, you know?"

Luca paused. "Skylar, have you thought about what will happen when you start living the life that's right for you instead of the one you promised to live for someone else?"

She looked at him with raised eyebrows. "I think I could ask you the same thing."

He nodded and drew her close. "*Calmati*. Calm. We need time think about this, no? How we'll handle what's going on. Okay? I want to talk to my uncle. For now, let's just stay here. We're as safe here as anywhere, I guess. The cops said Gianni was dead for days, no? If he had a partner you would think he'd have made a move by now, right?"

Skylar chewed on her lip. "Can we just go to my house for a few minutes? I need some things."

Luca shook his head vigorously. "No. Why risk it before I talk to Federico? We have all we need here. We're a little trapped, but we have a fridge full of organic food and a full wine cellar."

He tried to kiss her but she wriggled away. "I need to go home. I need my birth control. I don't want to get off my cycle. Please? We'll only be a few minutes. It's two miles away."

"No."

"I'm sorry. We have to. Please? I can go alone. That might be safer."

He sighed. "Out of the question. I'll go with you."

"It'll be fine. Like you said, Gianni's been dead for days, and I'm sure that whoever killed him won't do anything to us while cops and the FDLE and the FBI are crawling around the island. So, let me take a shower and then we'll go. I feel gross and dirty after today."

They walked upstairs, and Luca followed her into the bathroom. He set his gun on the marble sink counter and locked the door.

"Um. What are you doing?" Skylar stood in the middle of the large bathroom, looking from the gun, to him, back to the gun.

Luca took off his shirt. "I'm keeping you safe, *streghetta mia*. And I'm going to help you bathe."

"What did you just call me?"

He grinned. "My little witch. It's a term of affection in Italian. Really."

Skylar playfully swatted him, and he caught her wrist and kissed the palm.

"Witch? You think I'm a witch?" she joked.

"A little bit, because you've cast a spell on me."

That elicited a laugh, breaking the tension that had built up. "That is so cheesy."

She watched as he stripped naked and turned on the shower, then walked to her and lifted her dress over her head. He unhooked her bra then slid her panties over her hips and down her legs. Even now, even after their tense talk, after the weird and sick day, after all the fear, the sight of his body made her ache with lust.

They stepped under the spray and Luca soaped up his hands, caressing and cleaning every part of her body. She closed her eyes and reveled in the pleasure of his touch, unraveling every time he stopped to kiss her. He poured shampoo into his palm and scrubbed her hair and massaged her scalp, an act so kind and intimate that Skylar wanted to weep.

"That feels incredible," she sighed.

"I want to take care of you. Protect you," he murmured.

Then he turned her around, facing the tile, and spread her arms high above her head. He rubbed his naked body against hers, raking his hands over her breasts. Pulling her hips back so she was bent over, he entered her as he slid one hand around to part her labia. She cried out as he simultaneously stroked her clitoris and drove into her, and she saw his other hand covering hers on the wall. Together, their fingers tangled together in a primal clench.

He withdrew and slowly spun her around. "I can't do it like that. I need to be able to look at you while I make love to you."

They kissed long and deep, under the rain-like showerhead.

"Sit," she commanded, pointing to the teak bench that was out of the water's reach, something she'd been fantasizing about for some time. He did, and she climbed atop him, her legs on either side of his, inhaling sharply as she sank onto his erection.

"We were made for each other, you know that?" he murmured. "Please, please, let me take care of you. Will you?"

"Yes, Luca," she said. "I will. But I'm still going to be me."

"That's exactly who I want you to be."

She rotated her hips and made him moan with long, slow strokes. Their bodies molded together, silent but for the water falling from the shower above, their deep breathing, and their primal cries. There were no more words, no more questions, because each found the answers they had both been seeking.

# CHAPTER THIRTY-SIX

"Do you have to put your hand on that gun like we're in the Wild West?" she hissed at Luca as they climbed out of his Mercedes and walked up the stairs of her condo.

"Stay close to me. I don't feel safe anywhere."

As she scanned the corridor of her sleepy, retiree-laden condo, she didn't know what to think. Was Luca overreacting? Was she underreacting? It seemed that her whole life had suddenly taken a turn for the surreal, between the revelation of who Luca really was, the mind-blowing sex, and seeing her first murder victim—who'd turned out to be a Mafia hit man. Who was probably on the island to kill her boyfriend.

Wait. Was Luca her boyfriend?

Skylar opened her mouth to ask him then closed it when she saw his eyes flit around in fear. No, this definitely wasn't the time for that question. She suspected she knew the answer, anyway. She was just being needy because she was tense.

They reached her door. "Give me the keys," he said.

She did, and he unlocked her top and bottom lock.

"I'm going inside first."

"Oh, please. Come on." Skylar brushed past him, impatient to just grab some things and get back to his house so he would stop making her nervous, stop being so paranoid, stop making her afraid.

He reached out to take hold of her arm but she powered past. "Let me just grab my pills and a few things and we'll be good."

She heard him lock the door as she buzzed into the bathroom for her birth control. She rested her purse on the counter then flicked on the light.

She screamed.

It was a woman. Holding a knife.

She backed up, but the woman was too fast, like a little lethal hummingbird. She grabbed Skylar's arm and— Holy shit. It was the woman from the café. The woman she'd spilled coffee on.

Skylar writhed and twisted, not wanting to get cut by the crazy woman's knife, which looked sharp and steely.

"*Amore mio*, wha—?" Luca came to the doorway and stopped. His expression morphed from one of concern to a look of pure confusion. He lifted his gun and pointed it.

The three stared at each other. Skylar looked at Luca, who looked at the intruder. The woman, who had huge, tawny eyes, gazed at Luca. Skylar had never seen a woman look so intently at another person. Almost worshipful.

*What the fuck?* was all she could think.

The woman's nails dug into her upper arm and yanked her closer, and Skylar let out a whimper. With a slow rhythm, the woman feathered the blade down Skylar's upper arm as if she was sharpening it on her skin, not quite cutting her.

"Annalisa," Luca said softly, lowering his gun.

"What?" Skylar whispered. "Do you know her?"

The woman said something in Italian. Skylar noticed that she smelled good, almost too good, like an expensive department store. Her knife blade was practically exfoliating Skylar's arm now, making a soft scraping noise like a shave. Skylar's eyes flashed down in horror.

Luca responded, also in Italian. Skylar just gaped, terrified by the cold blade of the knife on her arm.

"What is going on?" she demanded in a louder voice.

"I'm his girlfriend," the woman said in accented English, tightening her grip on the underside of Skylar's bicep. Surely those nails would draw blood. "He didn't tell you?"

Luca's voice was velvety soft, and he now spoke in English. "Annalisa. Please stop. Don't hurt Skylar. Let her go and we can talk. I haven't seen you in so long."

Annalisa rested the flat part of her knife blade on Skylar's neck.

Fear. Skylar had never known such fear.

"I could do to this girl what I did to Gianni."

Skylar gasped, and Luca blanched. Annalisa had killed Gianni?

"Please tell me what's going on," Skylar whispered. She glanced in the mirror and saw the underside of one of Annalisa's arms in the reflection. They were covered in dozens of neat red lines. As if someone had intentionally cut her.

Annalisa turned her head toward Skylar and grinned. "I see you looking at the stories on my arm. Yep, I'm a cutter. They're my marks. Each represents a story. You're such an observant reporter, and asking questions until the end. Good job. For you I'll explain everything. I mean, we're all journalists here, right?"

"Annalisa," Luca said, his voice stern. "Let her go. Whatever you have to say, you can say it to me in private. This is between us."

"Sorry. You need to hear this too, Luca. After all, I'm the reason why you're in this situation. I'm the reason why your parents are dead."

"What?" His fingers holding the gun twitched. Some words in Italian followed, and Skylar hadn't though Luca could sound so menacing.

"Don't do it, Luca. Don't pull the trigger. In the time it takes for you to shoot me, I can slice your friend's neck nice and deep."

Skylar whimpered again, and she felt a trickle of sweat from her armpit running down her arm and probably onto Annalisa's fingers. Or was that blood from her captor's nails? How were her fingers so cold?

"Skylar." Annalisa's voice was shaky. "Do you speak Italian?"

"No."

"I didn't think so. Americans don't speak other languages, do they? In that case, I'll talk in English so you both understand. Luca, you did a great job on your book. Bravo. Very well-written, but I wouldn't expect anything less. You were always the star at the newspaper. The only thing you didn't uncover was that Bruno Castiglione is my second cousin. You trusted me and didn't do your homework."

Luca swore in Italian, his face getting red. He inhaled and took a step toward Annalisa.

"I told you. Don't do it, Luca. I'll cut her. Anyway, after you broke my heart, I hacked into your computer. You thought I was stupid." Annalisa turned her head to address Skylar. "Luca thinks women are stupid. I don't know if you've discovered that. Anyway, Luca. I found all the notes on your book. Then, when you published, I told my cousin that you were the author. I didn't think he would take it out on your parents, though. I'm truly sorry about that."

Skylar watched as Luca's expression turned from anguish to rage. "I'm going to fucking kill you," he whispered.

"Wait. There's more. Because of my issues, you know, my cutting, my self-destructive behavior as the doctors call it, my cousin sent me away to a very nice luxurious institution for a year. They thought I was all cured, and when I went to thank Bruno for his help, he told me that you were in Florida. Apparently they got into your Skype or something."

"You're lying. You're fucking insane. I got a letter from the Camorra that said you disappeared."

Annalisa sniffled. "That must have been Bruno, playing with your head. I've never lied to you, Luca."

He gulped in a few breaths, and Skylar wondered if he was about to shoot Annalisa. She squeezed her eyes shut, but then Luca spoke.

"Did Bruno send you here?"

Annalisa shook her head. "No. He's under house arrest, as you're probably aware. He's trying to find you, though. I kind of screwed up, I guess. He knew that if he told me where you were, that I would be obsessed enough to find you. So I did. I want to be with you. I love you. But some things got in the way. Gianni got in the way."

Skylar raised her eyebrows. This was like some bad soap opera. "What the fuck?" she said. She couldn't help herself.

Annalisa started to cry. "It does sound insane when it's told aloud, doesn't it?" She shook Skylar's arm, as if to demand a response. Skylar nodded weakly.

"Gianni wanted to force Luca back to Italy to testify in court that his book was a lie. But I knew that Gianni and Bruno would kill Luca afterward. So, I eliminated Gianni. Luca, do you see how much I love you? I killed for you. I murdered a hit man for you. For us."

This woman was obsessed with Luca, and Skylar gasped. For a half-second she wondered if she would ever love Luca as much as this woman did; then she realized the thought was almost as insane as the situation they were all in.

"You slit his throat. With this knife," Skylar said, incredulous. And Annalisa was about to do the same thing to her. She took a deep breath and tried to conjure the mental calm and clarity she allegedly possessed in spades, but, nope. That Zen-like aura was nowhere to be found, and tears rolled down her cheeks.

"Correct, Skylar. I did slit his throat. Don't cry, *bambina*. I saw your story online about Gianni. Very nice, and on deadline, too. I used to be a journalist, so I know a good story. Yours is a perfect final article. I'm sure the paper will write a nice obit about you. I've been at your house all night and all day waiting, so I had lots of time to read your Twitter feed and look through your books and your photos."

Skylar's mind went blank, unable to process that this awful person had poked around her condo. Probably looked at the photos of her mother. She was crying so hard now that her nose was snotty and clogged. Annalisa was crying, too, and shaking. The knife tickled Skylar's throat.

Again, Luca spoke in a soothing tone. "Annalisa. Let Skylar go and we'll go away together. I promise."

"Please. I'm not that stupid, Luca. Skylar upset me by spilling coffee on me. Did she tell you that? No? I don't want her around. She's going to call the cops if we let her go, so we're going to have to kill her."

"Okay, Annalisa. Just hand her over to me. I'll do what you want. I'll take you anywhere you want. Tell me. Tell me what you want to hear so you trust me."

His voice was seductive, and a sob wrenched from Annalisa's mouth. "Tell me what you remember about the last time we made love. Or do you even remember?"

Skylar watched Luca swallow hard then say something in Italian. She squeezed her eyes shut, not able to look at him. What was he going to reveal?

"No, in English," Annalisa said. "So your friend understands. Open your eyes, *bambina*, and look at your boyfriend. Tell her, Luca."

"We were at my parents' house," he said in a low voice.

"And?" Annalisa demanded. "What did you have me do?"

"You got on your knees and sucked me. And then I fucked you from behind."

"Then he texted me a week later to break up. Skylar, can you believe that? He broke up with me by text."

Skylar whimpered and shook her head. Luca hadn't taken his eyes off Annalisa, and Skylar wondered for a brief moment if he was going to go along with this crazy witch. She *was* gorgeous and alluring, Skylar had to admit, and the confidence and coolness with which she laid out her plan was terrifying.

The entire room took on a hyper-real state, the fluorescents of the bathroom suddenly harsh. Skylar stopped weeping, and her eyes went to the bathroom mirror to study the twisted scene. What the fuck was going on? Was she disassociating because of the insanity and trauma of it all?

As Luca and Annalisa stared at each other, Skylar realized that she was bigger than Annalisa. Probably stronger. Definitely more muscular. The Italian woman was tiny and frail-looking.

Still, she had killed Gianni.

"Fine," Luca said. "I'll kill her. Just give her to me."

Skylar's eyes went to Luca, wide and incredulous.

Annalisa shook her head. "No. Not going to fall for that. We'll have to kill her together, I suppose. I want to see her blood. She's a sacrifice. She represents all of the women you've screwed, Luca, when you should have been with me. How many were there?"

He shook his head, so Annalisa pressed the flat side of her knife blade harder into Skylar's neck.

"How many? Tell us both. Let your little American whore know the truth about you."

Luca said something in Italian, and Annalisa laughed. "I'll translate. Skylar, he's fucked about ten or so women since me. What, in two years? But he's probably lost track of a few. How many of those women have you loved, Luca? I want you to include me and Skylar. Tell us."

He swallowed hard. Skylar bowed her head and sobbed. This was too much.

"One," he whispered, his eyes terrified.

Annalisa shook Skylar's arm. "Sorry, *bambina*. You're just one of many. This is who you're going to die for. How does that feel?"

Searing rivulets of sweat streaked down the backs of Skylar's legs, and her chest felt heavy, as if she couldn't get enough air in her lungs. Trying to calm herself with breathing and the memory of her mother chanting "OM," she inhaled long and pleaded silently for her heart to stop beating so fast. This woman was seriously going to kill her.

*Do something, or else you'll die.*

"*Amore mio,*" Luca said in a buttery voice, and both Skylar and Annalisa looked to him. "Annalisa. Come here. *Per favore. Vieni qui, amore mio.*" Luca said more words in Italian, softer than Skylar had ever heard him speak. He stretched out his free arm, looking at Annalisa with the biggest, kindest, most puppy-dog loving eyes.

Annalisa faltered in that moment, sniffling loudly, and Skylar felt the woman's petite body melt a little. The knife shifted downward, hovering just above her left breast.

Skylar clamped down on Annalisa's forearm. Wrenching with all of her strength, she twisted her body, launching herself both from her captor and the knife. Panted for air. Writhed as Annalisa tried to recapture her. Skylar had never screamed so loud, but she did so then, a primitive sound that surprised something in her soul. She pushed Annalisa back toward the toilet, putting the full weight of her body into the shove.

Annalisa staggered and reached for her. A searing heat blossomed on Skylar's chest, but she ignored the sensation. All she wanted was to *get the fuck out.* Annalisa's knife, covered in someone's blood, hit the tile.

Skylar felt Luca grab her from behind. The next few seconds went by in a blur. His arm wrapped around her chest and pulled her toward him as he simultaneously stepped forward. Skylar steeled herself for the shot. It didn't come, but she was equally horrified to hear the sound of metal crunching against Annalisa's head. The woman crumpled to the floor.

Luca released her, and Skylar, gasping, caught her reflection in the bathroom mirror. There was blood. Everywhere. Staining her white cotton dress. All over Luca's bare arm and grey T-shirt. Dripping onto the floor. Coming from her skin. From her chest. Somewhere.

A dull throb surfaced, and it quickly grew intense.

"Luca," she whispered. Her fingers went to her collarbone, which felt aflame. That's where the cut was. Just above the right collarbone, stretching from almost her windpipe to her shoulder. It was big. Deep. Hot.

Bloody.

"I'm going to fucking kill her," Luca shouted, releasing Skylar and standing over the unconscious Annalisa. He pointed his gun at her head, which lay near the base of the toilet. His eyes were crazy, and Skylar shook uncontrollably. She pawed in her purse, which she had left on the bathroom counter when Annalisa first ambushed her.

There. Her phone.

She stood in the doorway and quaked. She barely remembered the password to unlock her phone and tried twice, unsuccessfully, hitting the wrong numbers each time and leaving streaks of blood on the screen. She pawed for a towel on a nearby rack, pressing it to her throbbing, gushing wound. Then she remembered the phone. She let the towel fall, and on a third try she unlocked it.

Luca screamed something in Italian, and she looked up.

"Luca," she said sharply, watching him tremble and glare at Annalisa. "I'm calling the police."

"Do what you want."

"Luca," she screamed. "Stop. Look at me. Don't. Don't kill her."

Luca's back was to Skylar, and despite wincing in pain she could see his hard profile in the mirror. He shook as he aimed the gun over and over again. "Why? She's the reason my parents are dead. She's turned you against me with my own words. She ruined my life."

Tears welled in Skylar's eyes. Her voice took on a pleading tone, and she felt a little floaty, as if she were watching everything unfold from the corner of the bathroom, somewhere near the ceiling. "Luca, no. You'll have so many problems if you shoot her. Please don't. Let the police deal with her. Please? You'll be in a world of shit if you kill her. You want justice for your parents. Not death. Choose life."

"I have no life, Skylar."

He moved a half step back but didn't lower the gun, so she continued to plead. "She didn't turn me against you. Choose the future, Luca. Choose me. Choose *us*."

She was shaking now, and an odd, cool feeling washed over her. Why was her mind foggy? She shook her head as if to clear it, and for the first time in many long seconds, Luca looked up, glancing into the mirror. Upon seeing Skylar, he gasped.

"Oh fuck," he whispered.

He quickly stepped away from Annalisa and fumbled for the lock, letting them out. Closing the door, he guided Skylar away from the bathroom. She felt faint. Wobbly.

"It hurts," she whispered.

"I'm here, *amore mio*. Just hang on for me, okay?"

Luca put the gun in his waistband and took the phone from Skylar, tapping on the screen then wiping it on his shorts. He tapped again and put the phone between his ear and shoulder and held the towel to her torso. He let out a long string of Italian words.

"Hello," he said a moment later. "My name is Luca Rossi and I need help right now. Now. Someone broke into my girlfriend's home and attacked her with a knife. She's really hurt and bleeding bad. Address? Skylar? What's the address?"

She leaned against the wall and recited the words robotically. As she slid downward, Luca followed her to the floor, kneeling in front of her as she sat. He kissed her forehead.

"Skylar. Stay with me, okay? Please, *amore*? Please? I love you." He kissed her forehead again, talked into the phone, pressed the towel into her shoulder. She saw the bottom lids of his eyes well with moisture as he continued, "Please, we need an ambulance right away. As fast as you can. Now. She's in shock, I think. She's bleeding badly. Yes, we need police, too."

Luca stammered more words loudly into the phone, and Skylar saw tears streaming down his cheeks. An image of her mother, looking blissful in a meditation pose, soared into her mind.

"Did you just say, 'I love you'?" she asked Luca. She looked into his beautiful eyes, and they were the last thing she remembered.

# CHAPTER THIRTY-SEVEN

He sat in the too-small room, elbows propped on the table, head in his hands. If Skylar lived, if she still wanted him after this whole fucking mess, he would stay with her until his last breath. Just thinking about her alone and in the hospital made him almost hyperventilate with regret. She knew everything. About his book, his parents, and his morally questionable past with women. She'd never want him now.

It was bad enough that the paramedics and cops wouldn't let him go to the ER with her, but now he felt like a criminal here in the police station. And helpless, because he couldn't just leave and be at her side. He had to wait until Federico arrived, and then God knew how long it would take to spring him. Would he have to spend the night in jail?

Was Skylar okay? She'd been unconscious when the paramedics took her away, and no one at the police station would tell him how she was, regardless of how many times he demanded and pleaded. Instead, a detective had endless questions about why he'd struck Annalisa with the gun. How he knew her. Whose gun it was.

*She deserved to die,* is what he wanted to say. But he didn't. Instead he insisted on calling his uncle. Or father. Or whatever Federico was.

Luca rolled his eyes and sighed into the empty room. He wasn't about to tell the cops that Federico Rossi, the well-known attorney on the TV commercials, was his father and the person who had given him the gun. Probably illegally, he realized now. Thankfully, Federico had returned from his afternoon on the yacht and answered Luca's call.

"Don't say a word to that detective," he'd growled, hours ago, and Luca had stayed silent since. But being alone with his thoughts and his guilt in a sparse interview room at a police station was his personal hell.

The door swung open. Federico stepped in, looking fresh and jaunty in a white polo shirt, khaki pants and tan boat shoes, followed by a man in a police uniform. Federico had a hand on the cop's back.

"Luca, I want you to meet someone. This is Chief Judson. We just had a nice talk, and you're free to go. Come on."

Luca stood, incredulous. He shook the chief's hand.

"It turns out that girl you knocked unconscious with your gun was our suspect in that Palmira Preserve homicide," the chief said. "We found the victim's prints in her rental car, and we have video surveillance of them in the parking lot of the preserve. The two of them went into the preserve, but she was the only one who came out. Perfectly matches his time of death, too."

Luca swallowed. It was still difficult to believe that little Annalisa would slash the throat of a Mafia hit man. "She's crazier than I thought," he said sadly.

"That's for damned sure," the chief said. "Anyway, you're free to go. We're not going to charge you. You hit her in self-defense. Hell, you would have been justified in shooting her. Stand Your Ground and all that."

Luca thanked him and shook his hand again. He wasn't about to ask why he wasn't being charged for possession of the weapon, or why he wasn't being questioned about his potential ties to Gianni. Florida was such a strange place. And although part of him wanted Annalisa dead, he knew that Skylar was right. Retribution, violence, vigilante justice—they were all things that he abhorred. In his darkest moment, poised to kill another human being, Skylar had forced him to be a better man again. To stay true to what was in his heart.

He loved her for that. And for a million other reasons. He needed to tell her. If she was well enough to listen. If she even wanted him anymore. All he could think of was the hurt in Skylar's eyes when Annalisa forced him to reveal what a dick he'd been.

Zombie-like, he followed Federico out of the police station and into the parking lot. Federico smiled grimly and clapped him on the back.

"Did I ever mention that I donated bulletproof vests to the Palmira Police Department? I even donated vests for their police dogs."

Luca snorted a laugh as he opened the passenger door of his uncle's Mercedes. While he had before suspected that his uncle's business and political dealings danced on the razor-thin edge of unethical behavior, in that moment he was grateful for Federico's savvy.

His uncle climbed into the driver's seat.

"Federico, I owe you an apology. And a thank-you."

Luca's eyes searched the older man's face, looking for anger or annoyance. He didn't find anything but kindness. Maybe Skylar was right. He should get to know this man. His father.

"No, Luca, you don't owe me anything. You've been through too much. It's a fucked up situation, our family. As is this episode with the girl from Italy. We'll talk about it later. Let's just try to move forward, okay? Unless you're going to leave, and then we can part as friends."

Luca shook his head. "If it's okay with you, I'd like to stay here on Palmira. At least until Bruno's trial is over. Maybe longer. And I need to go to the hospital now."

### 

Skylar felt his kisses on her hand and arm before she opened her eyes. She stretched, hoping to wrap her arms around Luca, then felt stiff, achy and... *Ow.* Pain. In her shoulder and down her arm.

"*Amore mio,*" Luca whispered, kissing the back of her unhurt hand, then her palm, then her wrist. "*Amore mio.*"

She didn't say anything, just looked groggily around the hospital room. It was half-dark, and a machine behind her beeped.

Luca's face registered concern. "Can you speak? Are you okay? Do you need anything?"

"I'm...in pain. But yeah. I can speak. What...? Where...?"

"Shhh, Sky. You're safe. We're safe."

"I'm really tired," she whispered.

"It's the drugs. Just go back to sleep."

"But," she said, struggling to keep her eyes open. "Are you leaving?"

Luca moved forward and brushed his lips over hers. "No. I'm not. I'm yours. I love you. As long as you want me, I'm yours."

"What if that's forever?" Had she thought that or said it aloud? Her brain was so foggy.

He kissed her again. "That's what I'm hoping."

She smiled and closed her eyes. Then opened them again to see Luca staring at her, concerned.

"Luca?"

"Yes, *amore mio*?"

"You're everything I once thought I didn't want. Or didn't need. But now you're everything I need and the only thing I want."

She slipped back into a deep sleep.

### 

Skylar's mind was clearer the next time she woke up. Emily sat in a nearby chair, reading a magazine, and her eyes got wide when Skylar stirred.

"Dude, you're awake!" She moved to the edge of the bed, breathless. "How do you feel? You were stabbed!"

Skylar grimaced. "How do I...? Wait. Help me sit up."

"Don't move. Here." Emily pressed a button on the side of the bed and shifted Skylar into a sitting position.

"Thanks. That's better. I feel okay, actually. How long have I been here? Been asleep?" She glanced down at her injured shoulder. A thick bandage covered the skin, and she couldn't move her right arm much at all. How was she going to type and work? Her shoulder felt itchy under the dressing.

"Let's see. Everything happened Saturday afternoon, and it's now Sunday afternoon. You had surgery to repair the tendon in your shoulder and then they stitched you up. Fed you some good drugs. Oh, and I gave you blood."

"Hunh?" Skylar shook her head, bewildered. It seemed as if every time someone spoke to her, a new weird detail was revealed. Luca had said something surprising at some point overnight, although she couldn't remember exactly what.

"You and I have type O negative blood. That means we can give our blood to anyone, but we can only receive our own kind. They were low here at the hospital, so I donated a pint to you."

Skylar felt tears well in her eyes. "Thanks, Em," she whispered, reaching out to grasp her friend's hand. It might have been the kindest thing anyone had ever done for her.

"No problem, dude." Emily squeezed her good hand. "We're blood sisters now."

A wave of fear surged through her body as Skylar looked around, panicked and stiff. "Where's Luca?"

"He's out harassing the nurses. They brought you eggs and toast but you were asleep. He wanted you to have fresh fruit and oatmeal, because he knows that's what you like. He's a little bossy, did you know that? But God, so sexy. Protective, too. He hasn't left your side since the cops let him go."

"Oh, God." *The cops.* Skylar groaned. "Luca wasn't charged with anything, was he?" She recalled the horrible sound of the gun hitting Annalisa's skull and shivered.

Emily shook her head. "Nope."

"And Annalisa?" Skylar shuddered as she said the woman's name. "Is she alive?"

"Yeah, Jimmy said that Annalisa was checked out by a doctor. Luca didn't hurt her too bad, just knocked her out, apparently. She's being charged with murder, home invasion and attempted murder. She's in the hospital ward at the jail over in Fort Myers."

Skylar let out a long, thin breath. "I feel a little sorry for her."

Emily scowled. "Why? She tried to kill you."

"I know. I mean, I don't want to be friends with her or anything. I hope she's locked up forever. But she needs help. She just seemed so pathetic."

At that moment Luca entered carrying a tray. "Who's pathetic?" he asked.

"Look who's awake," Emily said quickly.

Luca set the tray of food on a table near the bed then kissed Skylar's forehead and sat. His gaze was fearful, concerned. He put his hand on her forehead as if he was monitoring her temperature then brushed her hair away from her face. "*Amore mio,*" he sighed.

She reached to hold his hand, and their fingers tangled together.

Emily rose from the bed, grinning. "Okay, I'm gonna let you lovebirds have sexytime here in the hospital. I need to get back to the paper. I'll tell everyone you said hi."

"Wait. Em?" Skylar tried to reach her arm toward her friend, but she was stopped by the IV, which poked uncomfortably into the crook of her arm. "What's going on at the paper? What does Jill think about all of this? Did we write a story?"

Emily nodded. "We did. Front page. But we didn't put your names in it. They said you both were victims of a domestic stalking and that's why they left it out. The article focused on Annalisa's murder charge, anyway. That's much sexier. You know, if it bleeds, it leads." Emily winked. "Oh, and guess what? Jill and Federico were spotted at breakfast together this morning."

"What?" Skylar yelped, and she struggled again to sit up. Luca shushed her, settling her back against the pillows.

"Luca will fill you in," Emily said. "I gotta go."

"Bye, Em."

Her friend waved and left.

Luca pulled the table on wheels close to the bed and fiddled with poking a straw through a foil-covered juice container. "*Amore mio*, you need to get something in your stomach."

When he held the container and straw up to her mouth, she let out an exasperated sigh. "Luca, I can feed myself. My shoulder was sliced open. My arms weren't cut off. Tell me about Federico and Jill."

"In a minute. Open your beautiful mouth."

She smiled and did, her eyes meeting his. She put her lips around the straw and sucked in the juice. Somehow, even though it wasn't fresh-squeezed or organic, it tasted delicious.

"Jill and Federico did go to breakfast this morning. I can't tell if it was just a business thing or what. I sensed something between them. They came to the hospital together. Jill's happy you're not dead. She joked about how she's glad she doesn't have to hire another reporter."

Skylar laughed and noticed that he only had mustered a small smile. "What?" she asked, in a whisper, handing him the cup.

He leaned forward to brush her lips with his. She closed her eyes and shivered a little from the feeling, but when she opened them, he was frowning.

"Sky. I'm...I'm so sorry. I feel so much guilt about not telling you my secret earlier. Maybe if I had, you would have wisely stayed away from me and we wouldn't be here now."

"No." She shook her head and tried to sit up straighter, fumbling for the pillow that had wedged uncomfortably in the small of her back. She leaned forward, and without her asking Luca adjusted it. "I wouldn't have stayed away from you. Don't you understand? I couldn't stay away from you."

He sighed. "And I couldn't stay away from you. But it would have been better if I did."

Reaching with her good arm, she grabbed his hand and slipped her fingers in between his. "You don't have to apologize," she said in a quiet voice.

"I don't think I'll ever stop apologizing. I'm sorry that you had to hear all of that between me and Annalisa. I told you that I wasn't an angel." He drew in a breath and opened a fruit cup. "Can I persuade you to eat a little?"

She shrugged then opened her mouth, wanting to please him because he seemed so concerned. He fed her two apple slices, then grapes, and she chewed in silence. Finally, he spoke.

"Federico, Jill and I have talked about increasing security for you at the paper, and for us at home. But we'll discuss that later, when you're better."

"Wait. Us? 'At home'?" She reached for the fruit cup.

Luca took it from her hand. He speared a banana slice with a fork and fed her. "The doctors said you'll be getting out soon, maybe tomorrow morning. They just want to make sure there's no infection in the cut. I'm bringing you back to our house to recover. Federico's hiring bodyguards and drivers for us. It's going to be a little delicate when you go cover stories, but we'll figure it out."

"Bodyguards?" She looked at him, alarmed. "Why?"

Luca sighed. "We all agreed that it's for the best, at least until Bruno Castiglione's trial is over. Who knows if he'll try to send someone else here. Until we can talk to the Italian consulate and international authorities, we're not taking chances. There's someone"—he pointed with the fork—"outside the door of this hospital room right now."

"But, but," she stammered, reeling at the idea of a bodyguard just steps away. "We? Us? Why are you making all of these plans? Are you definitely not leaving Palmira?"

Luca shook his head and brushed a kiss onto her lips. "No. I told you in the middle of the night, but you were half asleep. I'm not leaving. I'm staying to write my book. And most of all, I'm staying for you. For us. I'm with you for as long as you want me. I hope that's forever. I hope you can forgive me for everything."

He kissed her again, and she stared at him, her mouth open.

"You need to eat." He popped another banana slice between her lips and she chewed. She began to cry, unable to contain all of the feelings. She swallowed and cried harder. It was as if all of the emotions inside of her—about her mother, about how James treated her, Luca, the attack—poured out all at once. She'd never felt such a massive rush of sadness. Or relief. Not after her mother died, not after she broke up with James, not ever.

Luca set the fork down then hugged her gingerly. She didn't move much because of all the tubes. He leaned to kiss her further, and eventually her crying stopped.

"It's all going to be okay, *amore mio*. We've got no more secrets."

Through her tears, she eyed him. She couldn't help saying, "Why would you want me when you've had all of those other women? You could just keep traveling and screwing—"

"No." He wiped her tears away with his fingers then found a napkin and blotted her cheeks. "No. I'm sick of traveling. I'm sick of empty, meaningless flings. Being with you makes me happier than I've ever been in my life. Being with you makes me a better man, Skylar. It's you. Don't you see? I found you when I needed you the most. We found each other."

She shuddered in a breath. "When we were at my house with Annalisa, for a second I thought you were still in love with her. I thought that you were going to choose her over me. I thought—"

"Please don't ever think that," he interrupted. "I can't believe you had to go through that because of me. I'll never forgive myself for what she did to you, or for putting you in that situation. For saying all those things in front of you. Will you let me prove to you how much I love you? Will you let me protect you? Please trust me when I say that I'm a different man than I was in Italy."

She sniffled and nodded. "Yes. I do trust you. I love you," she whispered.

He stroked her hair. "You're my only choice, Skylar. You're my now, and my future. I love you, too."

# EPILOGUE

*Three years later*

"*Amore...e hora di cenare*! Time for dinner!"

Luca stood on the balcony of the log cabin in the mountains of western North Carolina and called out to Skylar. It was the first real long vacation they had taken in their two years together, and both agreed they wanted to get away from the beach and palm trees and immerse themselves in cold weather and mountains for New Year's Eve.

Skylar waved at him as she ran toward the cabin, followed by Pucci, their shaggy rescue mutt. Luca laughed when Pucci jumped like a rabbit through the ankle-deep snow. He loved watching the two of them play while the snow fell in big, fat flakes.

Luca poured two glasses of champagne as Skylar and Pucci bounded inside and up the cabin stairs. He flipped the knob on the stove to the off position and covered the simmering tomato sauce. "Baby, it feels so amazing here. The air is crisp, not swampy and humid like in Florida."

Skylar's pink cheeks practically matched the hue of the fuzzy earmuffs that she pulled off her head. Standing near the top of the stairs, she unzipped her fleece jacket. Luca's eyes went to her breasts, which looked full and sexy in her tight, white sweater, and she turned and bent over to undo the laces on her boots, giving him a full view of her delicious rear in tight jeans, reminding him that even after three years of living together, he still got a charge every time he thought about running his hands over her curvy body.

For months she had been self-conscious of her shoulder, largely because of the scar near her collarbone. But they had found a good plastic surgeon and now it was barely visible.

The dog shook the snow off his tawny fur and settled with a sigh near the crackling flames in the hearth.

"Sky, come over by the fireplace," Luca called. *"Vieni qui."* He tried to speak in Italian more because she was trying to learn his language. Sitting on the carpet near the dog, he smiled as Skylar joined him, kneeling down while finger-brushing her long, snow-dampened hair.

"Brrr," she said. "I'm not used to cold weather anymore. Every part of me is cold. But I love it. I just need you to warm me up."

Handing her a glass of champagne, Luca kissed her then rubbed his warm nose against hers. "Warming you up is my job."

She giggled and kissed him again. *"Cento anni,"* she said. They clinked glasses and sipped.

"Maybe we should think about buying something here. The book is doing so well, we could take the money from that...," he suggested.

She grinned and raised her glass. "To the *New York Times* bestseller list."

"To beautiful reporters with great ideas."

Luca had followed Skylar's suggestion to go public with his story. Instead of the book about the second Mafia boss, he'd written an autobiography about his parents' deaths and the years afterward. Just like she'd predicted, Americans loved a good secret. His story had not only garnered support from press freedom organizations around the world but had sold like crazy. He touched his glass lightly to hers again and leaned in for another kiss.

He also no longer felt like a hunted animal. Because of the worldwide support, he was more confident about living a safe and normal life. Bruno Castiglione was convicted of all ten counts of murder and twenty of racketeering in Italy and sent to prison for life, in part because Annalisa testified against him and had surreptitiously recorded their conversations in Italy with her phone. She had testified against her cousin, she said in court, because she still loved Luca. Fortunately she was also behind bars, though in a Florida prison, having pled guilty to Gianni's murder.

Those outcomes had emboldened Luca to be hopeful for the future. Sure, he still wanted security for a while longer, maybe for the foreseeable future. Federico insisted on it, anyway. Even now, as they vacationed in luxury in a gated Smoky Mountain enclave, an armed bodyguard sat in the driveway.

He'd forged a tentative, solid relationship with Federico—although he hadn't quite gotten to the point where he called the man Papa or Dad. Federico didn't seem to mind, though. He seemed happy just to have Luca and Skylar in his life. They socialized regularly, and were relieved when he decided not to run for governor. They mostly saw him in Palmira, because he and Jill were dating. At first Skylar had felt odd about having such a personal connection to her boss, but Jill had slowly become something of a mother figure, even encouraging her to apply for jobs at bigger newspapers.

Skylar leaned close to kiss Luca deep. She had become wonderfully assertive during their time together, and she no longer hesitated to take what she wanted from him sexually—if she ever had. It drove him wild when she was on top, and recently they had experimented with her tying him to the bedposts. It seemed that his once-meek kitten had a dominant streak, which was more than okay with him.

She pulled away and said, "I'm glad we could take these two weeks before I start at *The Herald*. We really needed this, baby. We still have so much so do, though, with the move to Miami I feel a little guilty for taking such a long vacation."

Luca shook his head. She was such a workaholic sometimes, but he loved her drive because it inspired him to want to do more, work harder, be a better man. "No, *amore*, you needed a break. I want you to be completely rested when you get to the Miami paper."

He leaned forward to kiss her again, and their tongues collided. Although he wanted to make love to her, he had something more important to ask. "*Amore mio*, close your eyes. I have a surprise."

She grinned and did what he asked. He took her champagne glass and set it on the table alongside his. He tried to be silent as he reached into his pocket. Sitting on his knees, he opened the box that contained a two-carat diamond flanked by two sapphires in a platinum setting. His hands shook.

"*Apri gli occhi.* Open your eyes."

Her gasp was followed by tears. Luca swallowed a lump in his throat and spoke in a hoarse voice.

"Skylar, I love you. *Ti amo.* Will you marry me?"

He took the ring from the box. Skylar trembled as Luca took her hand and slipped the ring over her finger, and she whispered, "Yes," holding out her hand to admire the diamond's sparkling beauty. She crawled into his lap, tears running down her cheeks. "Yes. I love you, too."

She nestled her face in the hollow of his neck, and he could feel her shaking. Luca hugged her tight as she softly sniffled and laughed.

"Amore, we don't have to get married anytime soon, so don't feel any pressure to plan a wedding. We can do it anytime and any way you want. You just focus on your new job and I'll focus on taking care of you."

She pulled back to look at him, cradling his face in her hands. Her eyes went from him to the ring, then back to him. She kissed him sweetly.

"Is this our fairytale ending?"

"*Amore mio*, I love you. This is our fairytale beginning."

As the diamond sparkled in the firelight and Skylar covered his face with kisses, Luca knew that risking everything for love was the best story of all.

# ABOUT THE AUTHOR

Tamara Lush is an award-winning journalist with The Associated Press. She first started writing in grade school, penning elaborate stories involving heroes inspired by Indiana Jones. After completing her undergraduate degree at Emerson College in Boston, she began her reporting career at a small, weekly newspaper in Massachusetts. Her work has appeared in *The Village Voice, People* magazine, *The Boston Globe* and *USA Today*.

When Tamara isn't writing or reading, she's doing yoga, experimenting in the kitchen or chasing her dogs on a beach. She loves connecting with people on social media. She lives on Florida's Gulf Coast with her husband, two dogs and a kitty.

# Boroughs
Publishing Group

Did you enjoy this book? Drop us a line and say so! We love to hear from readers, and so do our authors. To connect, visit www.boroughspublishinggroup.com online, send comments directly to info@boroughspublishinggroup.com, or friend us on Facebook and Twitter. And be sure to check back regularly for contests and new releases in your favorite subgenres of romance!

Are you an aspiring writer? Check out www.boroughspublishinggroup.com/submit and see if we can help you make your dreams come true.